Sheryn George is a journalist and lives in Sydney.

Also by Sheryn George

Miss Lonelyhearts

My First Divorce

Sheryn George

HarperCollins*Publishers*

HarperCollins*Publishers*

First published in Australia in 2008
by HarperCollins*Publishers* Australia Pty Limited
ABN 36 009 913 517
www.harpercollins.com.au

HarperCollins*Publishers*
25 Ryde Road, Pymble, Sydney, NSW 2073, Australia
31 View Road, Glenfield, Auckland 10, New Zealand
1–A, Hamilton House, Connaught Place, New Delhi – 110 001, India
77–85 Fulham Palace Road, London, W6 8JB, United Kingdom
2 Bloor Street East, 20th floor, Toronto, Ontario M4W 1A8, Canada
10 East 53rd Street, New York NY 10022, USA

National Library of Australia Cataloguing-in-Publication data:

George, Sheryn.
   My first divorce / author, Sheryn George.
   Pymble, N.S.W. : HarperCollins Publishers, 2008.
   ISBN: 978 0 7322 8416 9 (pbk.)
   Women television producers and directors – Fiction.
   Spouses – Fiction.
   Marital conflict – Fiction.
   Divorce – Fiction.
A823.4

Cover design and illustration by Darren Holt, HarperCollins Design Studio
Typeset in 10.5 on 14.5 Sabon by Kirby Jones

for my mother, and for my daughter

ONE

Caitlin Cooper usually hated parties, but as this one was for her, she was trying to act like a professional TV producer and not run screaming into the night all the way back to her office. At least then I could get this stupid dress off, she thought, struggling to breathe through the Gucci corset that had cost most of a junior TV producer's yearly salary. Which meant she could afford it, because she was a very *senior* TV *executive* producer, even if she had yet to turn forty.

'Not breathing, not good,' she panted to herself, trying to get enough oxygen to face the heaving crowd of beautiful folk. The chic harbourside venue sparkled with fairylights, and all the cool young things who'd contributed to the new program they were there to celebrate, and the jewels on the advertising executives who'd decide how many of its thirty-second slots they'd sign up for.

They looked like they were having something very close to a good time — unheard of at an uptight industry do where everyone has an agenda. Maybe, Caitlin thought, gazing out over the manicured A-listers, none of whom appeared to be wearing corsets, they were all breathing properly.

(The fact was, Cait looked amazing. The other fact was that looking amazing didn't count for all that much with her. Not that she was ready for comfortable shoes and a nice grey cardigan. She loved looking glamorous — she'd just prefer oxygen to be part of the look. She needed to be able to do her job and, somehow, part of doing her job was wearing clothes that made her wonder about fashion designers' knowledge of female anatomy.)

Caitlin's life was peppered with these sorts of contradictions. She missed her kids, but she loved the job that stole her away from them. She was always, always stressed, and somehow she thrived on the adrenaline of deadlines. Her husband was fed up with her never being home, but there he was, standing next to her, stroking her back. And the biggest contradiction of all: she was terrified no one would want to watch the show she'd just poured millions of the station's dollars and six months of her life into, but she was just as certain it would be a hit. Not a doubt in the world.

Caitlin's hunch that the show would be a hit was not without foundation. *Date Squad* had enjoyed the sexiest run-up to any launch she'd ever experienced. Channel Five's new flagship program had advertisers, sponsors and television executives betting very scary amounts of money on massive success for the sexy but family-friendly reality show.

Caitlin loved her work. The actual working part of it, that is. Casting, combing over scripts, finding and approving locations, knowing how to hold the audience's attention, making decisions in a second that would have implications for years. And cost a lot of other people's money. That was completely intoxicating.

It was intense, exhausting and demanding. She always had so many things to do, all at the same time, that it seemed impossible to achieve what she set out to achieve. *Seemed* impossible; she always pulled it off.

Just to be sure *Date Squad* would be a hit, she had the lucky pebble in her bra that Molly had given her while she'd been dressing. (Okay, *squeezing*.) She could feel its warmth just below her heart, as reassuring as her six-year-old's sticky kisses, while she chatted and nodded and said completely benign things to all the conspicuously important people in the room. No politics. No philosophy. Nothing personal. Lots of nods and smiles and compliments grounded in reality. And while she smiled and nodded, Caitlin simultaneously ran through the checklist that had taken up residence in her head for the last six months. She knew it off by heart, but its repetition had become a kind of mantra by now — it had a soothing effect on her gathering nerves, giving her the impression that everything couldn't help but be okay.

Masses of sexy pre-publicity, a hot young cast and a great twist on a reality show. Tick.

Party smoothly chugging along. People drinking, laughing, flirting, dressed up and excited. Press in attendance. Photographers snapping. Tick.

Kids. Happy, eccentric, adorable. Tick.

Husband. Still sexy, funny and hot. Still charming everyone she worked with — men and women. Tick, tick, tick.

Now all that needed to happen was for the show to rake in the numbers … and they'd know that in about two hours.

'Don't breathe,' whispered her assistant, Kennedy King, sneaking up behind her and giving her a hug. 'Your boobs will escape.'

'I couldn't breathe if I tried,' Caitlin muttered, hugging her back. 'Can I pass out?'

'No. You can drink this instead.' Kennedy flashed her killer grin and handed her a mad-looking cocktail.

'Oooh,' Caitlin cried, taking the bright green cocktail and giving Kennedy a smile.

'Where's yours?' she asked. It wasn't like Kennedy to refuse a cocktail. Or two. Maybe Kennedy was nervous, just like she was, Caitlin reasoned. *We can celebrate later,* she thought. *Once the madness is over. Tonight's not about fun yet!*

Working with Kennedy was like working with your perfect teenager-best-friend. She was professional, witty and fun, and, because the two of them made such a great team, they could spend time high-fiving, giving secret hand signals and confiding in each other. Kennedy was a very cool girl to work with. Not like some of the monsters in TV, Caitlin thought, wincing at a random flashback. She didn't have to *worry* about Kennedy — she'd been at Channel Five for nine months and had consistently backed Caitlin up. She came up with great contacts who she networked with ease, and had even pulled off a killer sponsorship deal. Occasionally, Kennedy had stepped in and saved Caitlin's personal life from meltdown by volunteering to collect the kids from school when Caitlin had a meeting that just wouldn't finish. All of which was why Caitlin had just sorted a pay rise for her perfect 2IC. She'd worked hard enough for it.

Meanwhile, she could feel the hours of breathlessness starting to make her faint. She'd lied to herself and Kennedy when she'd blamed the corset. Caitlin looked extroverted and confident, but inside she often fought a fierce battle with her own nerves. And she could feel them sparking now, urging her to run and hide … She froze, feeling slightly unsteady on her feet. Or was it the six-inch Jimmy Choo black velvet ankle-strap stilettos? she wondered, light-headed and feeling more nervous by the moment.

'Haven't you got Important People to talk to?' Max said in her ear. She turned to face him. He was looking a little dishevelled and ever-so-slightly sexier than usual.

'Are you trying to get rid of me?' she said teasingly.

He looked at her, eyebrows raised, and nodded his head toward the people quietly clamouring, she knew, for her attention.

'Oh come on, Max. I've done the room,' she said, knowing she hadn't. Not completely. 'Can't I go and hide in the toilets now?'

He grinned. 'Come on, one more circuit. It'll ease the nerves.'

'I'm not nervous,' she protested, half laughing, half arcing-up.

'Sure,' he said with his trademark crooked grin.

She took a step back, red head tilting to one side, and checked out her husband. He was gorgeous, dark-haired and long and not too lean. He was smart and just a little bit cocky, which was okay, because there'd never been any question about his being anyone's but hers. He was, as he reminded her often enough, crazy about her. (Not crazy about her not being there, though.)

Her mobile bleeped at her, and she wrestled it out of her evening bag. Sean and Molly.

'How's it going, Mum? We're waiting for it to come on,' Sean demanded as soon as Cait pressed ANSWER. She sounded excited — amazingly excited, considering she was fourteen and put so much effort into acting like everything her parents did was faintly ridiculous.

Cait snuck behind Max to chat happily to Sean. It was one thing to have great kids. But it was another to have great kids who actually thought what she did was cool, even if they acted like it wasn't most of the time.

'Make sure Molly only has half an hour online after the show finishes, okay?' she said eventually. 'It's a school night. And we'll be home soon as we can. Hang on.' Max was gesturing with one hand for the phone. 'Dad wants to have a word, sweetie.'

'Hi, honey — how are my girls going? Yes, I miss you. No, I'm not drunk. Now don't forget to tape it, okay.' He turned to wink at Cait. 'Yes. She's very nervous. Bye now.'

He hung up and squeezed the phone back into Caitlin's bag, taking it off her for safekeeping. 'Come on, you've got a speech to give.'

She grabbed and held his free hand for just a second longer than she needed to.

'I hate this part of it. I want to go home …'

He squeezed her hand, and looked at her with love and faith. 'You know what to do. Come on, you know you can knock them out.'

And she knew he was right. She could. Every Caitlin Cooper show so far had been a ratings winner. She crossed her fingers behind her back, which was turned to the wall. This one needs to be a hit too, she thought a little wildly, so that everyone here can go on to the next stage. And although she knew she'd gotten *Date Squad* exactly right, as much as she could know anything, as much as she knew that Max was her husband and that Molly and Sean were her girls, it was just that this part — the in-front-of-the-scenes stuff — still had the power to make her shiver. She'd done this so many times, and yet she still felt like she'd raided the wardrobe department's Professional Working Woman dress-up box.

That she was, in truth, a fraud.

Oh, come on, she told herself impatiently. Just step aside from the scaredy-cat, and act like you're a confident professional who knows what she's doing. Channel Barbara Walters. Mind-meld with Oprah.

'Okay,' she said quietly, nodding to Kennedy, and getting ready to walk forward to the front of the crowded room. 'Show time.'

TWO

CAITLIN WALKED TOWARD the podium, glancing about to ensure everything was in place. Out of the corner of her eye she saw Kennedy keeping the press happy, cocktails and glossy programs at the ready. Within minutes, Kennedy had somehow managed to help over-excited staffers Gus and Carol shepherd two hundred media executives, gossip columnists and news crews to their lounge-style seats at the front of the warehouse. *Now all I have to do is make this speech, deliver a hit program,* Caitlin frowned at her watch, *and our job here will be done.*

Kennedy signalled to the lighting crew to dim the spots trained on the hovering crowd. That doubled as the deejay's cue to play the upbeat remix of the middle eight of *Date Squad*'s theme track. The room hushed just enough for her to hear feet start tapping to the dance-inspired sound sequence. They'd pulled it and a mini light show together late the night before, Max bringing them cups of tea while they edited the music at Caitlin's home. Neither Caitlin or Kennedy had run this by the station, but they'd known it would give everyone's adrenaline a kick-start. Caitlin smiled at the delighted faces around her. Her choice. Right choice. A nice way to build into hearing the theme itself when the show started. She nodded at another member of the crew; the light show and soundtrack faded; and a thick red velvet curtain swung back to reveal a massive plasma screen.

She peered through the violet haze at Kennedy, who was due to give her the cue to step forward and deliver the speech they'd stayed up writing last night, when even the music was done.

Their eyes met through the misty light — Caitlin's green, Kennedy's pale blue — and both smiled. Suddenly, Caitlin felt different. Come on, she urged herself. You only have to do this bit. Kennedy's taken care of all the hard stuff. She looked over to where Kennedy stood, about to signal her.

Right on cue, Kennedy raised her left hand and gave Caitlin a little, definite, nod. Everything was ready to go.

'Ladies and gentlemen,' Caitlin began, stepping forward into the light that washed over the stage. She smiled; suddenly all traces of fear had gone. She was a warm, funny, gorgeous woman who held the intimidating crowd's attention lightly, effortlessly.

'We are very grateful that you have all sacrificed an evening,' she paused, raising one arched brow, 'at home watching television to join us here — to watch television.' She grinned infectiously.

Everyone was excited now; Caitlin could see it on their faces. Advertisers' chequebooks were practically open before the show had even started!

'A new show is always an event — an investment of creativity, ideas and of course money … much of it yours,' Caitlin said with a cheeky smile. An appreciative laugh rippled across the warehouse.

That's it, Caitlin coached herself. Be a little bit rude, but never offensive.

'It may seem to be a voyeuristic mishmash of reality styles … in fact I think that's what you said to me, Kevin, when I first pitched this show. Yes, and he was right,' Caitlin laughed, as everyone turned to see how the chief executive was taking his public ribbing. 'He made a few good points, and after we went a few rounds, we all won. We've got a very, very hot show for you all.'

Up on the stage, she took a deep breath, and changed gear: sincerity time.

'It's not all hot bods and beautiful faces though: it's really about seeing other people's fragilities; seeing the impact of putting your heart on the line; feeling for them; fearing for their rejection; wanting them to be loved. It made me wonder about love and relationships. Why the hell do we put ourselves through it?'

Most of the audience laughed. Some winced. Caitlin noticed one of the gossip columnists at the top-selling Sunday paper nodding in wry agreement as she took notes. She glanced over at Max, who smiled at her, eyes shining, urging her on, as caught up as everyone else.

'Well, why do we date? And fall in love? And take those risks with our hearts? We all yearn for a mate; it's the human condition. And with the help of our panel and of our very courageous stars, we're going to help everyone out there understand his or her drives ... the science behind the social scene ... and we'll entertain you while we're doing it.'

The screen behind Caitlin pulsed into life, the audience began to applaud, and she left the stage to the show. Perfect, she thought. They might be applauding their own ads, she laughed to herself, but still, the energy in the room felt great. It buzzed with expectancy, exactly the right way for *Date Squad* to start up ...

Caitlin joined Kennedy, and they gently high-fived each other, grinning.

'How did I do?' Cait whispered.

Kennedy kept smiling, rolled her eyes and said, 'You did great.' Max came to Caitlin's side and drew her away and still Kennedy smiled. The smile never left her face, even when Caitlin and Max had found front-row seats, leaving her alone in the wings, watching another success story unfold.

THREE

Approximately thirty-nine minutes and thirty-two
seconds later (the exact length of the premiere, minus
commercials featuring a talking tampon, miracle de-
frizzing products, cool cars and home-delivered pizzas)
Date Squad was declared a smash. Well, it was by the
audience thronging the warehouse, Caitlin observed,
pretending to enjoy a drink and dulling the keen thrill of
her returning nerves by chatting to staffers. One test
down. One more to go, she thought, frowning. The
tension couldn't even begin to dissipate until the
preliminary ratings came in.

She checked her watch, wondering how much
longer they'd have to wait, and looked around for
Kennedy so they could muse about the possibilities.
Soon she'd know. She crossed her fingers and continued
talking to the man who'd drawn the dancing tampons.
Her mouth smiled, her head nodded, and inside she
counted down the minutes till she'd know. She kept one
corner of an eye out for Kennedy, but she was, Caitlin
reasoned, probably caught in the whirlwind of
schmoozing. They'd talk soon enough. So she charmed

advertising executives, congratulated her staff, and was introduced to a dissipated director whose name she immediately forgot, a jaded but brilliant freelance producer called Larry Allen, two hungry young soapie starlets both named Bec, and a group of hairdressers who wanted to tell her who they'd loved and hated on the show — a very auspicious sign, she knew.

And about sixty-eight minutes and plenty of celebratory drinks after that, the figures came through.

Kevin Casey, CEO of the most successful television station in the land, at least according to the share market, strode to the front of the room and slowly raised his large meaty hands to call for quiet. Of course, everyone hushed on cue. You didn't disobey a Kevin Casey directive, no matter how important you thought yourself.

'I think we all understand that even though we enjoyed *Date Squad* — immensely,' he began, 'it isn't ever really clear whether we've been successful until the public votes.' He was using his man-of-the-people voice, noted Caitlin, trying to assess whether that meant good news or bad. She knew Kevin better than most of his colleagues did, and she still couldn't tell. Scattered applause broke out, but he made another small gesture with those great pink hands and the crowd settled back down. Kevin Casey, mused Caitlin, light-headed with nerves, looks exactly like a butcher. (Which was funny, because that's exactly what his family had wanted him to be. Which, of course, only they knew. Caitlin *was* very good at casting.) She stifled a giggle at the thought of him in a striped apron behind the meat counter. He frowned in her direction, and she immediately adopted her taking-Kevin-seriously face.

'Thank you, Caitlin and co-conspirators,' Kevin Casey continued wryly. 'But ...' he went on, sounding very stern.

Oh, he's using the make-the-slaves-tremble voice, Caitlin observed. The one that used to make me stay awake at night. Did it mean good news or bad?

'... the real test is in here.' Kevin took a deep, gusty breath and waved the envelope at the audience. 'I have the figures. Let's,' he said quietly, 'open the envelope.'

The crowd hushed.

Cait felt dizzy. Even though she knew Kevin too well to imagine he'd do anything like this without having been delivered all the information first, she felt her heart rate go up ...

'Bastard,' she muttered to herself. 'He could have told me first ... I shouldn't have to worry that I'll faint and my boobs will burst out in front of everyone I work with.'

Kevin's face gave nothing away. Not a thought was etched there.

'Come on!' the gossip columnist from the *Daily Telegraph* pleaded, 'I have a deadline, Mr Casey!'

An advertiser who'd committed five million to the series' first season mopped his forehead, nodding.

'Gah,' muttered Caitlin to Max, who'd just turned up next to her. 'Where did you get to? Kevin needs to put me out of my misery! Please!'

Max grinned, and put an arm about her waist.

Kevin Casey cleared his throat. Which made his

throat wobble. He looked meaningfully at his assistant, Linda, who reverently handed him his reading glasses.

'Yeah, Kev, you freaking bastard,' Max whispered. 'Like he needs those glasses.'

'It's all about the dramatic pause,' she giggled somewhere near his ear. She loved that she had to stand on tippy toes to actually reach it, even in heels.

His arm drew her closer. She squeezed his hand, pushing the side of her head into his shoulder and grimacing. 'Come on, Kev. What are the numbers?'

'One point two million viewers, people! Aged —' He paused as the room broke into excited applause, talk and cheers. '— aged between eighteen and thirty-five. Predominantly women and, I think I can safely say, horny young men. Lots of couples. Lots of families, too.

'Ladies and gentleman, we have a hit,' bellowed Kevin, face going even pinker as his thick arms punched the air with triumph.

The crowd burst into applause. One half — the young staffers — surged forward to congratulate Caitlin and Kennedy, who had shown up and was now standing just in front of Caitlin's right shoulder. The other half — the older powerbrokers — surrounded Kevin and took turns pumping his hand. Max stepped back graciously to let the inevitable team love-up happen, and leaned back against the wall to watch, a wolfish grin on his face. It wouldn't take long. After she and Kennedy had kissed lots of cheeks and squeezed lots of hands and generally agreed that it was incredible, great, fantastic, give it at least three seasons, the entire crowd descended on the bar, and they were free.

'God, I'm so glad that's over,' Caitlin burst out, exulting in the relief, bounding over to Max and leaping at him, holding him close.

'Now I can't breathe either,' he protested, unwrapping her arms gently.

'Better my arms than this crazy dress,' she parried, struggling to take a breath in.

'Crazy dress is sexy,' said Max, eyes changing colour as his pupils grew larger.

'Still can't breathe.'

'Want some mouth to mouth?'

'Max!' she said, moving closer. A thought flashed into her mind. 'Hang on,' she said, pulling back and reclaiming her handbag so she could once again prise her mobile from its grip, 'we have to ring the kids.' She dialled Home. 'They'll be *so* waiting for us to call.'

Sean answered, which meant Molly was online.

'Mum!' Sean exploded. *'Finally!'*

Caitlin's wide mouth stretched into a grin, and she reached over to Max and held onto his arm, tightly.

'So. Tell me. What did you think?' Caitlin asked in a rush.

'It was hil*arious*,' gasped Sean. Teenaged and hyperbolic, she was at once super-proud and super-sensitive about her mother's career choices. If she hadn't liked it, there would have been hell for Caitlin to pay. If she'd loved it, and it sounded like she had, Cait would be in cool-Mum-who-can-do-no-wrong heaven for about two weeks.

'The figures are really, really good, too,' Caitlin

confided, excited and proud. Sean was an old hand at this kind of industry chat and didn't miss a beat.

'Duh. Course they are, Mum,' Sean shot back. 'They'll be *crushingly* good numbers.'

'Still have to wait for the calls, though,' Caitlin said, fretting out loud. Stations did still pay attention to letters and calls — especially when religious or community groups were involved.

'Taken care of. Molly already rang everyone and told them to contact the station to say they've watched *Date Squad* to get the ratings stats up. She's online now and all the chat rooms are talking about it.'

Caitlin held the phone tight. Her kids were amazing. Sean was still too excited to finish up.

'Fingers crossed for a massive hit, Mum. All the girls at school have texted stuff like *It's fully sick.*'

You don't work in television without knowing what *fully sick* meant. 'Wow, that's *great*, sweetie.' Maybe she'd get to spend three weeks in cool-Mum heaven. 'Now, Daddy and I will be a little while longer ... you can handle that, right?'

'Yeah, but Molly —'

'Just make sure she's in bed with a book and some warm milk by nine-thirty, okay? It's usually eight-thirty, so she knows she's getting a good deal. Take my laptop and the phone if you have to; she knows the rules.' Molly was addicted to technology, and the best way to get her to comply with anything was to take away her Nintendo DS for a day. Molly may have been six, but she'd been reading laptops over her mother's shoulder since she was four. She was a true child of the digital age.

'Dad left a new book with you about ...' She looked at Max, questioning. He made flapping motions with his arms, and gestured toward his forehead. She smiled at him, then returned to the call. 'It's flying unicorns or something — that'll get her into bed.' Molly might have been technologically sophisticated, but she still liked wearing pink, dressing up as a fairy and reading about unicorns. When she wasn't playing soccer or earnestly studying how to be a hacker, that is.

'And, Sean, you get into bed before ten. You've got school tomorrow. Dad and I will be home a bit after that.'

'Ergh. Are you guys going to stay up pashing on the couch?'

'Possibly. So if you don't want to catch us, get to sleep as soon as possible.'

'Sick, Mum. Going to go and sort her out.'

'Bye, teen-angel,' Caitlin said, but Sean had already hung up. Just as well. She *hated* it when Caitlin got 'sooky' over her or Molly. 'Yeah, Mum — we *know*,' was the usual response when she told them how much she loved them.

As long as they know, she thought. I don't mind being a dag.

Caitlin rang off, still holding Max's hand. 'They're great,' she told him, putting her phone back in her bag. 'I told them we'd be home soon-ish. And you're brilliant, getting Molly that book.'

'They'd better be fast asleep when we get home. Because as soon as we do ...' he said, moving in to kiss her neck.

'What is this strange feeling?' she said, faux-wonderingly. 'Why! I do believe it is my husband's lips upon me! What a rare pleasure this is!'

'That's your fault, Caitlin. Very, very bad wife. No conjugal activity at all for … Hmmm. Let's see now, let me check my diary …'

'Oh, come on,' she protested, laughing up at him. 'It's been a week! And you know I've been pretty distracted. This has been the most demanding launch I have ever worked on.'

He nodded. 'I know. But I'm glad it's over,' he said seriously.

'Me too,' she said. 'And it's not all bad. We can play catch-up.' She reached out and took his hand and rubbed it against her cheek.

'Pussycat,' he smiled.

'Can we go home now?' she asked, eyes twinkling.

'No, you can't,' interrupted an impatient voice.

Max and Cait pulled apart. Something about the way Kennedy was standing, arms crossed, somehow just felt … *weird*, thought Caitlin. 'Kevin wants to talk to you,' Kennedy said, sounding stressed. 'About the talking tampons commercial,' she said meaningfully, raising delicate, vertiginous brows.

'Really? Surely it can wait till tomorrow?' said Caitlin, thinking of all the catching up she had to do with Max.

'He's over there looking for you,' Kennedy insisted, gesturing vaguely at the far side of the room, which was rapidly emptying.

Caitlin suddenly felt a little off-balance — as though she'd been caught doing something wrong. Nah, she reasoned with herself. Kennedy's just tired. And she's had a couple of drinks. And she's been a bit sick lately. No wonder she sounds shitty, Caitlin thought, making a mental note to tell Kennedy to take a week off once the launch debrief was done. 'Sorry. I won't be long,' Cait said to Max, letting go of his hand.

Kennedy smiled and the warmth returned to her voice. 'You'd better hurry up, Cait. He seemed a bit … in a mood. Go on. I'll keep Max out of trouble for a few minutes.'

'Okay, okay,' Caitlin said, laughing. 'I'll go talk to Big Kev Kahuna. See what's up.'

Max looked worriedly at her. 'I won't be long,' she said reassuringly. 'Thanks, Kennedy.'

Kennedy grabbed Max's arm in a resistance-is-futile kind of way and hustled him to the outdoor balcony.

'Come on. There's a producer out here who's casting for a commercial,' she said, voice carrying over the dwindling crowd.

'Right then,' thought Caitlin, smirking as she saw how annoyed Max looked as he was led away. 'Where's my fearless leader?'

She trawled the room for Kevin, almost tripping over a few tangled and barely dressed soap stars who had started pashing openly — obviously the show had been a *big* hit. 'Hi,' she smiled at one young guy she'd cast a few years ago who'd since joined a prime-time soap and was currently white-hot with Sean. They had the obligatory five-minute catch-up, and she got him to write *Sean, you're the coolest* on an abandoned but reasonably clean serviette they found on the floor, before she continued the Quest for Kevin the Missing Media Mogul. Caitlin combed the bar area and peered into the dimness of the starless green room behind the stage area, but she couldn't see any sign of her boss. And he was sort of hard to miss, she thought to herself. Standing six-foot-three and weighing in at some scary amount, he wasn't the kind of man you'd have trouble finding in a room so close to empty. She sighed, pulled her mobile out of her bag, threw herself into one of the plush abandoned couches that ringed the room, and called him.

He answered right away.

'Caitlin!' he boomed. He certainly sounded happy enough, Caitlin thought. But you never knew with Kevin.

'Kevin, hi. How's things?' she said noncommittally.

'On my way home after shaking off the wankers, so I'm fantastic — couldn't be better. You've done a brilliant job. Congratulations again, Caitlin.'

'Um. Thanks,' she replied vaguely. This is weird, she thought. 'Anyway. Talking tampons?'

'Pardon?'

'Didn't you want to speak to me about the talking tampons?'

'There's a problem with the talking tampons?' he repeated, a dangerous edge in his deep voice.

'Not that I know of,' she said, giving her phone a quizzical look. Maybe he'd had a lot more to drink than she'd thought. 'Um. Sounds like a crossed wire,' she said. Whatever it had been, he'd forgotten, and she wasn't about to remind him. Time to get home and have some fun. 'Anyway, I won't keep you. Great night. Thanks for everything, Kev,' she said sincerely.

''Night, Caitlin. See you tomorrow. Don't come in till nine or ten, okay?'

'Sure. See you then.' She smiled, relieved. Good on you, Kev, she thought to herself. He might look like a butcher and scare everyone half to death, but he'd supported her all the way.

She wondered what he'd said to Kennedy to make her think something was up with the tampon deal. Oh well. She shrugged, dismissed the feeling that something wasn't quite right and, inspired by the thought of getting home, pulled herself out of the couch, checked that her boobs hadn't staged an escape, and said one last goodbye to the stragglers filing out the door.

Everything became very quiet and rather ugly as the music faded out and the lights went up, giving the venue an abandoned feeling that did nothing to steer Caitlin's instincts away from the sense that something was not quite right. Being a person who prided herself on being practical, she shrugged that off too and went looking for Max.

She went outside, pushing aside the heavy glass and wood sliding door with some effort.

Which is the point when one very angry voice floated up to where she was from below. And one very gentle and concerned-sounding voice followed it.

They were down there? She peered into the lush gardens. How weird, she thought, heading down the stairs. Taking it outside indeed. Her husband and her assistant were outside and ... were they *fighting*? She shook her head. Ridiculous. She looked over the balcony into the darkness of the garden.

It took a moment for her eyes to adjust, and then she saw them. Max, arms folded, face white and cold. Kennedy, arms flailing, face red, hot with fury.

Caitlin's stomach lurched. This looked wrong, she thought, at exactly the same time that she started to control her breathing — as much as her dress would allow her to. It's nothing, she told herself. Get real, pointed out her inner realist. No one else was out here. Down the stairs. In the garden. Obviously not wanting to be seen. She slowed her breathing down further, deepening it as she reached them. Maybe they were just having a passionate fight about commercial television standards, she soothed herself, trying to find that same quiet place she'd found hours earlier, just before her speech. But it wasn't there any more.

'Busted!' she called out jokingly, hesitatingly, with a crooked smile. Just in case she was wrong, thought her inner optimist. Who was about to get a very big shock.

Max turned to her in slow motion, his face stricken. Shit, Caitlin thought. Something's going on. Simultaneously Kennedy turned away, her hair whipping behind her. But not before Caitlin had caught the look — angry, tears streaming down her face. Caitlin drew in a ragged breath, feeling slightly dizzy. What happened, she thought, in shows when this sort of thing happened? Where was her script?

'Um ... am I interrupting something?' she managed, clearing her throat.

Max went to move forward, and she held up a hand, taking a step back.

'Because it looks like I *am* interrupting. You see, the room's deserted up there, and Kevin didn't want to see me at all, Kennedy, and here you two are …'

Kennedy made a choking sound. It could have been a sob, a laugh, a growl. It sounded ferocious and bitter.

'God, Kennedy. Are you okay?'

'No, clearly I'm not okay, Caitlin,' she spat, her voice caustic. She turned around, glaring at Caitlin, her thin arms across her chest, her lovely face wretched and furious and miserable.

Max was silent. Before he lowered his head, Caitlin noticed he looked horrified. And ashamed. And *scared*. And that frightened her to death.

'Max? Want to tell me why Kennedy's so upset? With *me*, apparently? Why Kennedy's having a meltdown?'

She and Kennedy stood in silence, waiting for Max to say something.

'I'll go get the car,' he muttered, abruptly striding off. 'You two wait here,' he called back, somehow managing to sound authoritative.

Once Max had disappeared, Kennedy started crying in earnest, dashing tears away, head lowered, and refusing to look at Caitlin, who knew better than to try to speak to her right now. Besides, she was too numb herself to really care how Kennedy was, let alone what she should do about it. So, instead of demanding an explanation, Caitlin pulled open her handbag, rummaged till she found a tissue and silently passed it to her assistant. She didn't think she wanted to know what was wrong. Some instinct, some notion of self-preservation made her hesitate to push this scene any further, just in case it played out the way it seemed doomed to. And just as she felt the scream inside her begin to build, Max pulled up in the car. She opened the back door and gently prodded Kennedy inside. She opened the front door and slid in, keeping her body as far away from Max as possible.

There, she thought to herself, is an explanation for this. A simple, sensible one. So, I am going to keep it together. And wait, she said to the scream inside her.

They drove in silence, streets with thin traffic making their journey fast.

'I'm so sorry about this, Caitlin,' he whispered, glancing at his wife, who looked as anguished as he felt. He turned away when she looked at him, unable to bear it. So Caitlin stared at his profile, tense and hard, and wondered what he had to be sorry for. She knew, of course, but another part of her said no. No. No. They reverted to silence, which was broken only by Kennedy's muffled sobs. She couldn't seem to stop crying, Caitlin noticed, even up to the moment Max pulled up, opened the car door, helped her out and walked her to her apartment block's door. He disappeared inside for a minute, and she heard voices raised in anger again. A few moments later, he came back, sliding in next to Caitlin, looking grim.

They made it home quickly. Caitlin snapped her seatbelt off and practically bolted for the door, fumbling in her bag for the keys. I have to get inside, she thought.

I can't let him near me. She stumbled through the door and closed it behind her. She knew it was childish, and that he'd just let himself in after her. But it seemed important, somehow, to not be nice about this. To lock him out, he who had been able to go everywhere, anywhere with her. Forever and ever.

She sat down on the couch and looked at the blinking light on the answering machine. Probably Mum, she thought. Or Sarah. Or Myra or Nadia. The thought of friends didn't make her happy. It filled her with dread. I'll have to tell them about this, she thought, her head beginning to pound. Whatever *this* is. Or maybe not. Maybe it's just something really stupid. And we'll be okay. Eventually. She got up and got a glass of water. Max let himself in.

'I'm so sorry,' he whispered, going to her and folding her in his arms.

Wow, she thought, letting him hold her, not able to look at him. She moved away, though every part of her wanted to stay within the circle of his arms, took a sip of her water, and went to the bathroom to get a painkiller. She swallowed it, and looked at herself in the mirror.

She reached around to the back of her corset, desperate to be free, but equally fierce about not being found by Max in a state of undress. Feeling a fresh surge of resentment, she realised that she couldn't get herself out of Gucci's prison alone, so she welcomed the pain, seeing it somehow as a way of staying right there in the sick shock of betrayal.

Sorry. How completely, pathetically inadequate. She wondered what his justification would be. Because she'd worked a lot? Because she'd been distracted and tired? Because they'd been together for so long that their need for each other had cooled? Because Kennedy was young and hot? Because, somehow, being his wife's assistant had made having her just that little bit naughtier?

'Caitlin, there's something I need to tell you.' Max was standing behind her, sounding as sick as she felt. She turned and walked past him. She couldn't be near him, so she headed out into the backyard. Jasmine was just beginning to bud, and its sweet smell took the edge off her anger. Just breathe, she instructed herself. The kids are here. Remember that. Don't give them this memory. It isn't worth it. It isn't fair to them.

She sat down on the garden seat, and told herself to look up at Max, to reply, to take some control back. 'I think I see, Max.'

'I'm so sorry, Cait. I've really …' He choked, stopped, and wiped his eyes with the backs of his hands. 'I'm just so furious with myself, Cait. So stupid,' he muttered, stumbling into remorse.

She just shook her head, willing him not to come near her.

'I've never been unfaithful to you before.' She'd never been unfaithful to him, either. Strangely, he wasn't checking on that right now.

'It was just one of those colossal fuck-ups. Those stupid things people do.'

'When?' she forced herself to ask. Her voice sounded rough.

'It started a while back. It wasn't serious.'

She laughed harshly. 'For you. It looked serious for Kennedy.'

'It was meant to be over,' he said.

She turned to him. 'It isn't over?' she asked, tears starting. Was he in love with her?

'It *was* over, Cait. I finished it. I tried to stop this from happening.'

'Tried?' she repeated, feeling stupid.

'It's complicated, Cait,' he said, sounding tense and angry.

Well fuck you, Caitlin thought, unclenching her hands and looking away. I'll never look at you again, she vowed.

'It's complicated,' he said, more calmly. 'That's why she wanted to talk to me. And she had every right to. I didn't answer her calls, once it was done. I didn't see the point in talking. And so she cornered me tonight.'

Caitlin braced herself. Maybe this is the bit where my husband tells me he's in love with another person, she thought, preparing herself for the blow. (But there was no preparing for this particular blow.)

'Cait,' Max said, his voice dark and sad and scared. 'I'm really sorry. But it's bad. Kennedy's pregnant.'

FOUR

At first, Caitlin heard the words like they were just words, instead of what they were — tiny knives carving deeply into her love and her heart, separating the life of her family into small, painful pieces. Then she *felt* the words, like sharp, poisoned darts, and as she did, she gagged, rushing a shaking hand to her mouth to stop herself from being sick. (Her body knew exactly what was going on, even if her mind couldn't grasp it immediately.) At exactly the same time, she had a stunningly vivid visual fantasy playing out on the screen of her mind: suddenly an action star, she had somehow managed to punch him so hard he crumpled over and simultaneously jam her other hand over his mouth so the kids wouldn't be woken up by his bellow of pain.

I'm multi-tasking my marriage breakdown, she thought to herself, swallowing back hysteria. And I've gone nuts.

She glanced over. Instead of lying crumpled and moaning on the paving, her husband was still standing there, looking all tall and handsome, staring intensely at his feet, his whole demeanour attractively repentant and visibly awash with heart-rending pain.

Jerk, she thought, feeling cold and stupid for trying to use such a silly word to ease the pain. Then he looked up at her, and she saw his face. Twisted with regret. Possibly even genuine, she thought bitterly. She felt sorry for him, and the instant she did, a fresh flood of warm rage poured through her veins, rushing around her body, lending her strength.

You see, it's hard when someone we love is in pain. So, when Cait saw her husband's, her *beloved*'s, sorrow, and then felt her own empathy for him, she felt like another massive punch had been landed in her stomach. Except that this time, she'd been the person delivering the blow. You feel *sorry* for him? her insides shrieked. *He's* created this, and *you* want to comfort him? Take *that*! If she'd had time to think about it, which she certainly hadn't had, not yet, she would have realised it was entirely natural to want to make everything all right. After all, whenever he'd used that wounded expression over the last however many years it had been, she had immediately held him, comforted him, and made it better. Helping, nurturing, the whole damn thing. Now she *still* wanted to make it all right for him, even though she also wanted to kill him.

'Fucking genetic triggers,' she muttered, beginning to understand she was reacting out of long-established habit — something the very first episode of *Date Squad* had covered that very evening. This time, she needed urgently to remind herself of just *why* he was in pain. Think, Caitlin, she ordered herself. Kennedy, baby, husband, sleeping with. Did all that slip your mind? She smirked bitterly to herself. Somehow, dark humour helped. But not much, she realised, as she began to feel sick and scared instead. What am I supposed to do?

He stood very, very still, watching her be so very quietly at war with herself. Max was betting, hoping, praying that the nurturing Cait, the kind Cait, the understanding Cait would somehow win out over the killer, caustic, betrayed Cait that he'd forced into being. He'd seen her killer side before — she'd fiercely defended him, or the children, or friends all their lives together — but he'd never felt her terrible power turned onto him. He just had to keep being sorry, looking sorry, feeling sorry, saying sorry, and she'd help him fix it. Meanwhile, he wished she'd hurry up. He was exhausted, shattered, shocked and relieved that it was all out. Now she knew, there was nothing to do except sort it. And his body was complaining. His leg was going to sleep; he tried to give it a subtle shake. He gave her a look, his wistful-longing-plus-regret look, and waited for Cait's love to win over Cait's hurt.

Caitlin barely noticed Max's effort. I hate drama, she thought to herself. I hate it, she repeated, frantically running through what seemed to be her options. Right then, none seemed at all attractive. What could she do? Vomit everywhere? She wasn't far away from that. Run around the yard tearing at her hair like a madwoman? Punch him ineffectaully in the chest till he held her and kissed her, like some daft heroine from a fifties flick? It's all so *Streetcar*, she thought contemptuously, wondering if he had the commitment to rip his shirt off and bellow her name. Should she crumple in a flurry of skirts like Scarlett O'Hara?

She took a deep breath. No. She'd do better than that. No fainting.

Meanwhile, Max was feeling like some words might hasten the forgiveness he was sure he'd receive. 'Cait, I'm so sorry. I'm so sorry she's pregnant. It's such a mess. And it's all my fault.'

No being sick. Or violence. Or wailing.

Max had never seen her so still, and pale, and silent. He felt worried, more worried than he'd ever really felt before, in his whole happy and comfortable life. 'Cait … please. Just talk to me, sweetheart.'

Cait suddenly knew what she'd do. 'I already knew,' she heard herself lie smoothly. Somehow, lying made it all feel faintly unreal, she noticed. And that, under the circumstances, was a very good thing.

His face fell apart with shock. 'You knew?' he said. 'Why didn't you —'

That's better, she thought. Not feeling sorry for him now. 'I knew she was pregnant, of course,' she specified, wondering at how a person who was so annoyingly proud of never lying could just start like this. And be good at it. And feel faintly triumphant. 'Suspected it for weeks, of course,' she continued, hitting her stride. 'I know Kennedy pretty well. Not as well as you, *of course*.' She paused and looked up at him under her raspberry lashes, and felt a stab of gratification as he flinched. 'She's been sick nearly every morning. And getting a bit, well, bloated,' she added nastily.

He nodded, looking pale. And a bit angry. He

quickly rearranged his face into bewilderment and admiration and a little more wistful-longing-plus-regret.

'Didn't *you* realise?'

He shook his head. Then nodded. 'Well. I wasn't planning on this. On any of it ...' He spread his beautiful hands toward her in a vague gesture of repentant pleading.

Caitlin stared at his hands. 'Did you think I was going to fix this for you?'

Nothing. (And if ever silence was confirmation, it was now.)

'I hadn't thought about anything, Cait. Unfortunately,' he said wryly.

'So. You're caught with Kennedy, Kennedy's been sick every morning, she's having your baby and *voila*! Instant soap opera. I'm in the wrong genre. My life has now turned into a scripted drama.'

'I'm ... *so* sorry, Cait.' Even his breathing sounded sad. She fought back the urge to break into mocking applause. But she couldn't stop the sarcasm pouring forth.

'I mean, this ... this is big, isn't it? You score a total babe, years, no *dimensions* younger than you, and you get to knock her up. You're hot, Max,' she said, knowing how bitchy she sounded, somehow exhilarated by every drop of venom in her voice.

'Don't be like this, Cait. You're my best fri—'

'Don't you *dare* call me your friend,' she said, her voice cracking. She moved away and folded her arms, in a gesture that looked exactly like the one Sean made when she was hurt or sad or defensive. 'You get your ego stroked, she gets to feel great because she's worked over her boss, I'm the one you both cheated on, and you consider yourself my friend? You were more than my friend; you were my husband. Now you're neither!'

He sat down next to her, shoulders slumped.

'I always thought we could handle anything like this … I thought we were solid. I guess I was wrong.'

'Oh, this tactic? I know this one. Make me prove you wrong. I hate being labelled a quitter — and you know that. You're an arsehole, Max,' she said.

'I made a mistake, yes. A huge mistake. But can't we —'

'You're joking, surely? You think we can … what? Work through this?'

'Cait. I'm prepared to do … whatever it takes for us to get through this —'

'It'll take none of it ever happening. And it has happened. No. That makes it sound like an accident. You chose it. Now you have to live with it. I didn't choose it, and I get to live with it too.'

'I love you,' he said quietly. 'But if you're going to be so negative, I'll …'

'You'll what? Leave me? Fuck my staff?' Cait's voice had hardened a notch, but she was struggling to keep the volume under control. She was, quite literally, in shock, but as the situation began to actually seem more like reality, rather than a particularly lucid and paranoid nightmare, she could feel the numbness of shock abating — and her hysteria waiting in the wings, ready to make an entrance at any moment.

It would be quite nice to go completely nuts, one part of herself thought whimsically. I could just be a blithering mental mess, and wake up in a few weeks in a nice white room. Then she remembered Molly and Sean. Damn, she thought. I can't go completely mad. They'll … well, I can't. So calm down, she ordered herself harshly. Breathe.

She had to really, really concentrate on not going crazy; now that the thought had occurred, it was very tempting indeed. No responsibility, and the possibility of a nice soft room and meals. It might just happen, she thought. She felt that if she let herself, she might hit him. And Cait knew that if she hit Max, if she let one surge of anger have its day right now, the rampage would truly start. There'd be no end to it. There'd be the traditional scissoring of suits, the prawns in his new curtain rods, the newspaper ads speculating on the state of Kennedy's sexual health … the greatest hits of revenge; all the classics played out. She felt the rage build, and willed herself to stay in control.

He had no answer to the look on her face. He wondered if he would be able to remember exactly how her eyes did that, look so enraged and so terribly shocked and sad … how her mouth looked pretty even turned down … the way she bit her lip and shook slightly. That she was so fragile had never occurred to him.

'You might just need time,' he said, feeling for a lifeline.

'No. I don't,' she said definitely.

'If you won't forgive me then … I wonder what we thought we had …'

'Don't you dare judge me, Max,' she said in a desperate whisper. 'Guess what? You're in the wrong.

And no amount of psychobabble or reverse bullshit psychology is going to absolve you.'

Some time later, she thought to herself, I'll kill him. Or her. And it will be enormously good fun. But right now, he has to get out.

'We have to stop this *now*. Sean and Molly.'

He nodded miserably, his body sagging.

'Anyway,' she said, feeling ice-cold but calm again. She stood up and headed for the back door. 'Better get a bag.'

She stole through the house, Max at her heels. In their room, the door firmly shut, she went to the wardrobe, the smooth, sleek built-ins that she'd had installed seven years before. His stuff had crept through to her side.

She pulled out the internal stepladder, climbed it and stretched to the top shelf.

'Let me,' he protested, trying to help. He couldn't have done anything to make her angrier.

'I've got it.' She let the suitcase fall down past his head. It landed on the bed with a muffled thump. He cringed.

'Scaredy-cat,' she mocked, climbing down. 'Guess it's time to start packing.'

'Look, you don't have to go, Cait,' he said softly.

'I know *that*,' she said, stunned. 'This,' she said, turning around and pointing at the bag, 'is for you.'

Max looked shocked, and fumbled for time. 'Do I get to say goodbye to the kids?'

'Not now. We'll talk some other time.' Caitlin could feel her temper growing ... any second now it was going to refuse to behave any longer … and once her temper gained control, Max was in serious danger of a killer kick in the balls. At the very least. And that wasn't a memory she wanted to give Molly and Sean.

'Hurry up,' she snapped, struggling to keep her voice down. 'I don't give a shit about losing it at you. But I don't want the girls to hear the kind of things I'm trying not to say.'

He sat down on the bed, grey-faced. She noticed how sections of his hair were silver under the light, how the lines around his eyes and mouth were deep and harsh. She looked at him, the man she'd been with since they met at uni. And felt cold. And sick. And angry. So angry it hurt.

She turned and walked out.

Ten minutes later she was waiting at the front door. He came out, suitcase in hand, looking uncomfortable and near tears. He stopped, walked over to her, and put the bag down deliberately.

'I know you don't want to hear it, but I didn't want this to happen. It was a mistake. And we *don't* have to do this …'

And he meant it. He truly did. So he couldn't really see why she went right on to tell him to go.

'Bye, Max. We'll talk later this week. The kids need to be told by both of us.'

Afterwards, it felt the way people always said those significant moments in your life would feel, Caitlin thought. Like when Max proposed. Blurry, but with frozen scenes of a ring being slid onto her finger; his smile; his smell as they held each other close. The kids being born. A rush of images and sensations.

First she went to the kitchen, took out her sharpest pair of scissors and ruthlessly sheared through the layers of leather constricting her chest. She struggled out of the skirt, tore off the tights and kicked the shoes from her feet. Free finally, she fell in slow motion onto the bed. Starting to cry truly hard, truly painfully, in jagged dry sobs, wasn't supposed to turn into one of the memories that would flash before Cait's eyes when she died. But somehow, along with the image of her husband closing their front door softly behind him that night, she knew already that this was definitely one of those unforgettable moments.

FIVE

Caitlin didn't wake up till 9.30 a.m. That might not sound particularly late if you're someone who lies in till 11 a.m. Every day. Of your life. But for Caitlin, this kind of hour was unheard of, outside of the few times she'd succumbed to a post-launch hangover. And on those mornings Max had risen, blearily organised the kids and driven them slowly and carefully to school. Even when she'd pulled an all-nighter, she struggled up and went to work. (Which, by the way, is not a good thing.) So the complete lack of any parental movement whatsoever well after the time they were meant to be at school had Sean and Molly's alarm bells ringing. Loudly.

By 9.32, both children were standing by their parents' bed, wondering why their mother's mobile was off. And where their father was. And why their mother appeared to be comatose.

Sean wandered over to the stereo. 'This is weird,' she said to Molly. 'She's taken my Kelly Clarkson CD.'

'That's crying music,' Molly said, scowling. (Remarkably astute, Molly is.)

They would have stared at Caitlin's face, except it was hidden by a tangled thicket of red hair. So they both sat down on the edge of the bed, staring at their mother's hair.

'Do you think she's dead?' asked Molly, looking curious.

'Don't think so,' Sean answered, sounding casual.

'She *looks* dead,' Molly whispered, feeling excited. She was in the phase where deadness was still an intriguing concept. She spent weeks at a time wondering if things were dead — flies, fruit (*Fruit doesn't die, darling*, Cait had explained), lizards, and now her mother.

'She's not,' Caitlin heard Sean explaining in a normal voice. 'Look, you can see her breathing.'

'Where's Dad?' Molly asked, sounding nervous.

Caitlin groaned. Consciousness was not a place she wanted to visit right now.

'Oh, she made a sound,' Molly breathed, relieved, a faint scent of Weet-Bix and understanding reaching Caitlin. A small hand on her chest made her smile, and somehow, though she felt drugged, she tentatively opened her swollen eyes. (Sobbing herself to sleep had seemed the only reasonable thing to do after Max had left.) Molly's sweet round face swam into view, pale and pudgy, mellow brown eyes and sticky-out hair. She patted her mother's face with soft, fat little hands.

'Mum. *Mum* — can we get in?' she asked, smiling.

Caitlin couldn't help but smile back, even if the change in her face was barely perceptible. 'You can.'

'Oooooh, come on, Sean,' urged Molly, creeping in and peering into her mother's sleep-smudged face.

'You've got junk in your eyes,' she observed earnestly. 'And you smell yucky.'

'Conjunctivitis, sweetie. Probably,' Caitlin agreed, wondering how she looked.

'Oooh. Maybe I'll get it. No school!' Molly started sucking her thumb and rubbing her head closer to Cait's. 'Maybe you have nits, too! Then we can stay home and —'

'What time is it?' Caitlin demanded faintly, suddenly feeling panicked. 'Can someone look for me?'

'It's just *there*, Mum,' Sean pointed out the clock. 'It hasn't moved.'

'Have you hurt your neck?' Molly asked her mother, puzzled.

'No. Can you look for me, sweetie?' she asked. She knew she sounded pathetic. She knew she should be getting the kids to school, rushing to work, doing the postmortem on the show, bitch-slapping Kennedy into the ground …

But no. Even the idea of pulling Kennedy's hair didn't inspire her. Wondering if she was in fact dead, Cait tried wiggling a finger. Nope. Exhausting. That decided it. She couldn't move. She officially didn't care.

Molly snuggled under the sheets, strong arms and legs pushing into her. 'Mum,' she breathed into her face, in Weet-Bix-y little pants. 'It's nearly ten o'clock. We're late, so it seems sort of silly rushing. We don't want to stress ourselves. So …'

'So …' Caitlin repeated, feeling all sorts of love rush through her.

'Can we watch TV all day?'

Sean, who'd been watching all of this, wondering just what was going on and where her father was, snorted.

Damn. A tiny bit of caring began to sneak its way in. I'm alive. Goddamnit, Caitlin thought blearily. Now I'm supposed to get on with things. If I can't die and be done with the whole mess, can't I at least have a breakdown? And if I can't have that, can't I at least play dead for the day? I'll be both sensible and responsible tomorrow. Right now I want to not care!

'Mmmm,' Molly said, burrowing deeper into the bed. 'Cosy. Mum, you haven't said anything. Aren't we going to school today?'

'I don't know, Molly,' she heard herself saying in a soothing voice. She even sounded all right. How utterly unfair. 'I don't know,' she repeated, sitting up before she noticed she'd just ruined her plans for a breakdown. 'It's late, huh? I guess we could take a day off.'

'Are you insane?' Sean asked, astonished. 'You launched a show last night!'

'I know,' replied Cait, leaning over and pulling back some of the quilt Molly had stolen. 'And Kev said to have a slow morning.'

'And you think he meant it?' Sean asked, in a voice that clearly implied she didn't.

'Probably not. But it's not a normal morning,' Cait said. Not at all normal, she thought to herself, flinging an arm back over her face to hide the tears that had sprung into her eyes.

Normally, Caitlin would have marched everyone out of there, leaving Max to clean up after breakfast and get on with his day.

Normally, the kids would go to school.

Normally, she and Kennedy would work on schedules and casting.

Normally, she didn't get to feel the pain of a headache brought on by three hours and twenty minutes' sleep.

No, there was nothing at all normal about this morning. And there probably wouldn't be any more normal mornings, not ever. Max was usually here, and he wouldn't ever be — not ever again, she told herself, feeling slightly bewildered.

She had no idea how or why she was so utterly sure that she couldn't take him back. But she felt sure that her love was now a broken thing. The idea of 'working on it', while occurring to her, made her feel sick.

Max had been able to stay home. Once a promising theatre-type person, he'd easily picked up jobs when they were first together. Cait worked full-time while he manned the house between castings. He'd had handsomely paid acting gigs regularly enough to cover some bills, put quite a lot of money in his bank account and give him a huge amount of charisma at the local shops. The ladies at the fresh fruit section couldn't believe their luck.

'It's him — the one from the chocolate ad — go ask,' said one sweet, not-so-very-old but not-so-very-young woman, nudging a fellow shopper in the ribs.

'Oooh, I can't,' replied the slightly younger nudgee, one hand to her matte red lips in wonderment at the mirage before them. A celebrity — in Safeway!

'I will then,' said the rib-nudger's glamorous daughter, who'd been appraising Max through very black, very permed eyelash extensions. And while he'd often been subjected to this sort of attention all through their marriage, he'd never actually slept with any of the women paying it. Till Kennedy.

Max was truly talented. He was certainly extremely good-looking. He'd been in *Gallipoli* with Mel Gibson, in whose class he'd been at NIDA, and whose fame he envied in a charming, bittersweet kind of way. He loved to hold forth about Mel's 'lack of real talent'. He loved discussing the anti-Semitism in *The Passion of the Christ*, and he adored lacerating what he said was Mel's lack of historical accuracy in *Braveheart* and *The Patriot*.

What he didn't ever mention was that they'd been close friends. Until he'd slept with Mel's girlfriend. He told lots of friends — all the male ones. 'Unsurprising, really, having a girl's name and all,' he'd laugh, in his deeper-than-Russell's voice.

Caitlin hadn't known that her husband had slept with Mel Gibson's girlfriend. But she did know about Kennedy. Kennedy — who'd be at work on her show today. Who had to be faced, sooner or later. Who, she admitted, she really wanted to talk to. Who she also wanted to squeeze till her eyes popped out. Therefore, lying in bed and waiting till it all went away just wasn't an option.

'Okay. Molly, come on, sweetie, let's get up. I don't think you guys should miss school today.'

'Phew,' Sean breathed. She hadn't wanted to say, but missing school on the day after her mother's new hit program had been on was not a good outlook. She didn't often have this sort of social capital. Within days, her scary frenemies would discount *Date Squad* altogether, returning Sean to weird-outsider status. Molly beamed. She loved school anyway, but being there *and* being the centre of attention was too good an opportunity to pass up.

'Um, Mum?'

'Mmmph,' said Caitlin, careful to keep her back to Sean who, she could tell, was starting to wonder what was going on. And she wasn't ready to answer any questions. Not yet.

'Is Dad out running?'

'Er. Yeah. Something. He had some stuff to do.' She turned around, shooing Sean and Molly out. 'Come on. You guys go get dressed and ready, and I'll get it together.'

She lurched about the kitchen, pulling together breakfast and wondering how to get through the day. If she was a smoker, or a drinker, or an eater, she would have opened a cask of cheap wine and started smoking her way through a carton of cigarettes while cramming chocolate cake into her mouth to dam the pain. But instead, she found herself crying in the depths of the pantry because she couldn't find any Weet-Bix (Molly had eaten them all). She stayed there for as long as she dared, letting the tears trickle down, then wiped her face with her hands and backed out into the kitchen. She stood up, rubbed her hair and glared at her phone, sitting innocently on the counter. She'd switched it off last night after she'd spoken to Kevin, but she felt the time had come to turn it back on. She pushed the button, winced and held it like a hand grenade, ready to throw it if it went off. Which of course it did, the moment she turned it back on. (She didn't throw it.)

It beeped out for at least a minute, message after message. She didn't bother to check them, but scrolled through the phone book and hit Sarah's name, unnecessarily firmly.

'Finally!' Sarah said. 'I've been trying to get a hold of you —'

'For hours.' Caitlin finished for her, sounding disgustingly hungover.

'Oooh, you had a late one.'

Caitlin interrupted. 'Look, I need a huge favour. Badly. And you can't say no.'

'I can't?'

'No.'

'Why can't I say no?' Sarah asked, curious.

And Caitlin started to cry.

'Can you *please* just come over?'

And so Caitlin left her children in the capable hands of Sarah, who had sensibly left her whole business with her overjoyed assistant for the day. 'The yoga centre can run without me,' she declared staunchly when she arrived at Cait's, secretly thrilled to be able to come to the rescue.

'Why am I here?' she asked. 'Why were you sniffling?'

'I'll tell you everything,' she promised, cringing at the thought. 'Can you take the kids in to school first? They're really late and if I start telling you ... well. It might take a while.'

So Sarah, being the friend she was, and even though she wanted nothing more than to get everything out of Caitlin immediately, made lunches (wholegrain, with sprouts) and forged Caitlin's signature on notes explaining why the kids were so very late to school. She then drove through eight red lights in her old red Datsun to get Sean and Molly to their respective schools by recess.

Then she came back as fast as she could, and found Caitlin dressing for the office.

'Do people have serious car status at your school?' she demanded, looking offended.

'What?'

'Everyone was driving Beemers, and they gave me funny looks. Maybe that means only rich people are ever late for school.' Caitlin said nothing, so Sarah cleared her throat and gave her oldest friend a look. 'Um, were you trying to escape before I got back?' she asked, hands on hips.

'Er. Yes,' Caitlin said, going slightly red.

'Want to tell me what's happening?'

'No, not really.'

'Cait! You're being weird.'

'I'm too embarrassed to tell you,' she muttered. 'If I tell you I won't stay angry. If I get sad, I'll crumple. If I crumple, I can't go in and find out what's going on.'

'*What?*'

Caitlin sat, crossed arms and crossed legs, and stared at the wall.

'Max has left.'

'He's left? Have you guys had your first fight or something?' Sarah's eyes were starting from her pretty face. Cait and Max did not fight. Cait had always been adamant about that.

'Well, we might start now,' Cait said.

'Hmph,' Sarah said disbelievingly. 'So … he's left.' A pause. 'Why?'

'I made him go.'

Another pause. 'Why?' asked Sarah, patience wearing just a little threadbare.

'Because he has been having sex with Kennedy, and she's having his baby.'

Quite a long pause this time.

'Well,' said Sarah. 'Has he really left, or is his body in the back of your car?'

Caitlin smirked. Sarah sounded faintly hysterical.

'Don't think I haven't thought about it.'

'It seems entirely reasonable.'

'And so I need to go to work.'

'Why? Shouldn't you be crying, or something?'

'I already did that,' Caitlin replied, strapping on her watch.

'Wow, you've already written a divorce to-do list,' Sarah said sarcastically. 'I would have thought we were going to do something broken-hearted, like get really drunk?' Sarah was actually disappointed that she wasn't at least having to talk her friend down from a ledge. Would nothing crack Caitlin? Probably not, she thought, looking at her storming about. 'You're too angry to go to work,' she pointed out. 'You might do something really stupid.'

'No, Sarah, I need to go in to work. She's there, and I'm not, and that makes me look weak. And fuck her,'

Caitlin said, wrangling in a fairly comical fashion with a plain white shirt.

'Stop fighting with your clothes, Caitlin,' warned Sarah.

'Gah! I can't decide what to wear. My clothes don't want to get put on. I can't even get my clothes onto my body. I'm rooted.'

Sarah moved behind her and looked at her oldest, truest and very best friend. She took her by the shoulders and sat her down on the bed.

'In the foetal position,' she commanded. 'Now. Five minutes! Do nothing but breathe.' She pushed Caitlin gently onto her side and held her down with one hand.

'Let me up!'

'No! Stay there for a moment,' Sarah insisted, pushing her back down.

'I'll cry!' threatened Cait.

'Oh, scary,' said Sarah, rolling her eyes, but taking her hand off her friend and walking over to the wardrobe.

'Now, what's in here ... oh.' She ran her hands over Max's clothes, screwing up her perfect nose. 'No wonder you feel so confused — all his stuff's here.'

'Well, he only told me he's having a baby with my assistant about five minutes ago. Sorry I'm not more ... more ... organised ...' Caitlin's voice began to sound dangerously close to a wail.

His stuff. Not their stuff.

Caitlin looked at his side of the wardrobe, which Sarah was staring into critically.

'What an arsehole — look at all this stuff you got him.' Her pretty brow wrinkled. 'You know what? Let's smudge your clothes.'

Caitlin felt slightly ridiculous burning sage and gingerly wafting the sweet-smelling smoke through her clothes. 'This is why I love you, Sar — you're smudging my clothes. It's also why I'm embarrassed to let anyone outside of this room know you're my best friend. You totally blow my image.'

'When you're out of here — I'm driving, by the way — I'll do more than that.'

Cait grinned faintly. 'You have permission to do whatever you want. God, I wish I *was* a drinker, or something. It's so frustrating being normal and responsible!'

'I'll bring something home. Wine. Or maybe something like ... vodka.' Sarah flushed with excitement. 'Should I try and score some pot or something?'

'Come on, Sarah. I can't tonight.'

'Maybe tomorrow then. I'm staying for at least a few days, Cait.'

Cait looked up, her green eyes wide. No argument, Sarah noticed. Bad sign.

'I ... I'll need to talk to the kids tonight. About what's happening. Max will come. He and I should do it alone.'

'It's okay, I'll vanish for a while. I'll sort dinner, then get out of here, then come back. It'll be fine.'

'It'll be disgusting and they'll hate me.'

'No. It'll be whatever it is, and the most important thing is for me to get his stuff ready so it can go with him when he leaves tonight.'

'I don't know if I'm ready to let go of how pissed off I am. It happened *last night*!'

'Come on.'

Caitlin turned and looked in the mirror. She looked — well, just the same. Except for the boxer's eyes, she thought, squinting to make out whether the puffy mess that was her reflection really was as bad as it seemed. That'd fade soon enough, of course. 'I feel like Harry Potter had it easy: when his parents died, he had a lightning bolt on his forehead to remember it by.'

'No one's dead, Cait. Unless you really have got him in the boot.'

Cait smirked, then her face sort of crumpled, collapsing inward from the hurt.

'Do you think he's been doing this for a while? Do you think, oh God, should I get tested for HIV or something?'

'No! I mean, maybe; I don't know. But I can't *believe* he's been doing this for ages, Cait. He loved you. Loves you, probably. I'm sure he's cursing himself, and that this was all a stupid mistake that's got out of control. He'll be utterly,' she paused, searching for the right word. 'He'll be wretched.'

'That's what *he* said. And that makes the cheating worse. So I suppose you think I'm being melodramatic or something.'

'God, no! Proud, maybe. But come on, take a breath. We'll talk later. Today's mission is to go to work, be brave for a few hours and get home, and then you can curl back into the foetal position and drool for days.'

'Now you *want* me to go to work,' Caitlin said.

Sarah looked at her appraisingly. 'Stop being so narky. Maybe you need a *doula*.'

'A *doula*?'

'Yes! I'm brilliant! You know, those fabulous Greek women who move in after you've given birth.'

'Maybe *Kennedy* needs a *doula*,' Caitlin replied, looking a bit sick. 'God, why am I even being sarcastic? It's not funny. It's just revolting.'

'Leave the whole day with me,' Sarah replied.

An hour later, she walked into her office. Sarah had driven her, weaving through traffic and making her laugh. She'd made Caitlin drink a lot of water — tears are dehydrating, she'd explained — and dropped her off here. Back on her stomping ground. Only instead of it having the comforting feeling of familiar territory, it felt like a hostile landscape.

Usually Caitlin felt at home when she went into the station, but today she felt like she was walking into a room of mirrors — ones that made her look and feel fat, wide, thin, weird and painfully stretched and distorted. Behind every one was a potential enemy with an assassin's weapon, eager to dart out and stab her, over and over. She felt unsafe, out of her depth, and very, very angry. Which was about the only thing keeping her together. The truth was, she thought, nothing was at all how it seemed.

First mission, she thought: Suss out Kevin. See what he knows. She bypassed her own office, not at all eager to encounter any looks that indicated that her staff had known all along. That just made her feel sick. She went straight to a thankfully empty lift, and went straight up, up, up to the executive floor. It opened onto quiet, neutral tones: The Home of the Station Gods. She walked out to where Kevin lived, guarded by Linda but tantalisingly visible if he was in his main room, screened only by Perspex.

'I need to see Kevin,' she said politely-but-firmly to Linda, who was parked in a forbidding position, the guardian of the gates.

'When would you like your appointment to be, Caitlin?' Linda smiled bossily.

'Now, thank you, Linda. It's an emergency.'

Linda's lips pursed disapprovingly.

'Oh look! I can see he's in there,' Cait bluffed. She waved and smiled.

Kevin turned and looked at her, understood that he was trapped, and waved her in. She walked in, closed the door on Linda and sat down.

He high-fived her, picked some fluff off her shoulder and said, 'Well, how do we follow up a night like that?'

She crossed her legs, looked at him. Hard. 'In my case, Kevin, by finding out my husband's been shagging my assistant.'

He glanced away.

'Did you know, Kevin?'

'Well ... yes, I thought they were on.'

'Kevin, I've got a show to pull together. It's just rated —'

'— its tits off,' the Big Kahuna interrupted. 'Look, while I don't mind jelly-wrestling, bitch-fighting or hair-pulling on TV, in the office it's another matter.'

Cait grinned an entirely fake grin. 'Kevin, there won't be any problems. Kennedy's got to go.'

'Weeeeell …'

'And she's got to go today.'

'You know, Caitlin, a few things have happened this morning … and now, because you got in so late, I can't just get rid of her. I would like to, but I can't.'

'What do you mean *you can't*? Kevin, she's been fucking my soon-to-be-former husband.'

'Cait, she's not stupid. She *knew* you'd do this. She went to HR this morning and put in a complaint about bullying and discrimination. Our hands are tied till you're investigated.'

'Till. I'm. What?'

'You'll have to see HR. Go through the motions.' He shook his head, regretful. 'She's very clever.' He sounded, Cait noticed, half admiring. Which, knowing Kevin and his penchant for ruthlessness, he probably was.

'*What?!*'

'Shit happens, Cait.'

'*She's* pregnant. *I'm* going to HR?'

'The fact she's pregnant makes it far, far worse. Now we have to be really careful. Pregnant women are the worst. This shit happens all the time now; bloody HR people. People used to just go to the pub, slug it out, then come back and get on with it.'

'Mate,' she said, harried enough to use his own language against him, 'sorry to interrupt your lament for the good old days, but this girl is pregnant. *To Max!* I have to go home tonight and tell my kids why their dad's not home. And right now I have to walk into my office and that girl's going to be there. I'm telling you, I haven't even *started* to bully her!'

'You're a professional, Cait. And clever enough to outsmart her.'

'She hasn't been *professional*, Kevin. And this situation will only be resolved by one or the other of us not being here.'

'And I'm telling you how to stay! Cait, do you really think this is the first time something like this has happened? This place is like that. It's television. People are always going off the rails and doing stupid things.'

Caitlin felt defensive. How was any of this even her doing? '*I* didn't do anything stupid, Kevin,' she pointed out. 'I haven't bullied her, either. My only mistake was never thinking my husband would get off with my closest colleague. I really don't get it — we were so busy! How did she even have *time* to kidnap my life?'

Kevin cleared his throat loudly. 'So busy you asked her to hold the fort? At home?' he asked, slightly accusingly.

'Well. Yes. Your point is?'

'Mate, next time, get an ugly girl to look after your family. Now, I have work to do. See Geoffrey in HR. He'll know the next step to sorting this out. And I need to see the rough cuts of the next three shows. ASAP, okay?' And with that, the meeting was over. Caitlin gave up and left.

'Bugger this,' she thought as she walked through the hall of mirrors formerly known as her office. She was walking as calmly as she could, but her hips felt weird. Her eyes felt wide and dry. Her mouth felt stuck on, ends twitching in something like a smile when she walked past people she vaguely recognised.

'Where's Kennedy?' she asked briskly, walking into the production room.

'She's, um …'

Kennedy walked in and saw Caitlin. And stared.

Everyone froze for a split second, and, feeling the atmosphere quicken with tension, bolted like the scared little rabbits they had every right to be.

'Right.' Caitlin looked at her nemesis. This was a new one. Where was the guidebook?

'Caitlin,' replied Kennedy, appraising Caitlin ruthlessly. She's gutless, deep down, Kennedy thought. I've won.

Caitlin said nothing, looking at her for a long, slow moment. And then pulled out the live file, and started to go through the ratings with Kennedy.

SIX

'WHAT HAPPENED THEN?' asked Sarah eagerly, approximately three meetings, including one painfully embarrassing 'chat' with HR, later.

'I don't know. I just felt frozen. I went through the ratings, went through what needed to be done, set up meetings for next week, and I didn't say ... anything.'

'Wow. That must have freaked her out.'

'It freaked *me* out. Why didn't I eat her?'

'Fucking Kevin. He's a dickhead, but he's right. You can't cave. How are you meant to work with that girl?'

'Apparently by being professional. And by being driven mad and going to HR ...'

Sarah grimaced.

'Are you going to be professional?'

'I thought I might get a professional to kill her.'

Sarah snorted briefly, before giving her a stare.

'Seriously, though.'

'Seriously, now there are other priorities. I've taken two weeks' leave. They can sort things out without me for that amount of time. I need to think about the kids. I've been thinking. I'm telling them tonight. It can't wait.'

She checked her phone. She'd switched it off. There were nine messages from Max, one text from Kennedy and one from Sarah. She dialled Max's number and announced her intention.

'I'm having The Talk. With the kids. Tonight,' she said, trying not to think, not to feel, just to relay the information coolly.

'You can't tell them tonight,' he replied. 'Not if I'm not there.'

'Well, that's why I need to tell them, because that's what I need to explain to them, Max. They need to know why you're missing, they need to know what's happening.'

'But *we* haven't even discussed things. I don't think you're handling this well. Give yourself some time, at least, to —' But she cut him off, cold and angry.

'Well, I didn't get a chance to discuss whether shagging Kennedy was a good idea, did I? *Discussion* packed its bags and left town a while ago. But the kids don't know that. We need to tell them what to expect from here — at least an outline, so they can begin to get their heads around it. Shit, Max, Molly's only six!'

'Six and a half,' he said forcefully. 'And you threw *me* out. I love you!'

She relented. Sort of. Then she rallied.

'Come round at five,' she told him. 'We'll tell them together.'

'You're not letting him in!' Sarah blurted, looking angry.

'Well, I'll need to if we're going to talk to the kids.'

'Well, then he can't enter the bedroom. It's smudged. It's off limits,' Sarah stated in a take-no-prisoners fashion.

'He has to get his stuff,' Caitlin pointed out.

'Already done! I packed it today,' said Sarah, glancing at her watch. 'It's twenty to four. I'll go get the kids, bring them back, and get out of here.'

'Thanks for everything, Sar.'

'I have a price. It's called Full Disclosure.'

By five, Sean and Molly were perched awkwardly on the couch. Sean looked tense and suspicious; Molly looked curious — she even kept scratching her head like a cartoon scientist.

Caitlin felt she would scream any second. She had to wait near the door for Max so the kids wouldn't see her jump when he knocked.

'Ah, here's your dad.'

'Why,' asked Molly, 'is Mum telling us Dad's here?'

'And since when did Dad ever knock?' Sean observed, dryly. 'This is weird.'

Caitlin opened the door, and Max went to hug her. She took a step back, shaking her head.

'Max, we're here to tell the kids,' she said quietly, refusing to make eye contact.

'Tell them what, Cait?' he replied tersely. 'We have to know what we're saying before we're saying it. At least I do.' He looked confused, and sniffed the air. 'God! What's that smell? Have you been smoking pot?' he asked, looking horrified and running a hand through his thick dark hair. One clump stuck up waywardly, and she fought the urge to smooth it back down.

'It's smudge stick.'

'It's what?'

'Never mind. What do you think we should say?'

He tried. He asked the kids to give them five minutes. They went and stood on the verandah, and he told her how sorry he was. She let him do most of the talking, and said very little. It wasn't so much that she was still furious. It was that she couldn't even muster the energy or willpower to discuss anything with him. She listened, but none of it sank in. He reached out his hand, and she pulled away like it was poison. Finally, he pleaded to come home.

She felt cold, and hard, and slightly crazy. She stared at him, and her eyes were full of pain and her voice was neutral and dull.

'Do you want some money?'

'Cait. I know you think I'm hopeless, but I just got paid —'

'The chocolate commercial?'

'Yep. It'll keep me going for a while.'

Cait didn't feel better. If anything, Max's financial bounty made her feel more and more redundant.

'Oh. So. You're staying where?

'I've found somewhere. It's temporary, unless this is how you want it.'

'You make it sound like I have a choice,' she laughed, hearing the bitterness in her voice.

He did make it sound like she had a choice. Like he hadn't already chosen what was happening. Like he hadn't done plenty wrong. Like she was mean and petty for being shattered by his betrayal. How did he do that, she wondered.

'How can the girls contact you in the meantime?'

He sighed. 'On the mobile.'

'Max. Are you at Kennedy's?'

He sighed again. 'No.'

'But you've been there, right?'

'No.'

'That won't last long,' she said, sounding bitter.

'I've got one of those serviced apartments. The building's full of separated men.'

'You know the kids are not going anywhere near you if you're with her.'

'I can't even believe we're talking like this,' he thundered.

'I can't believe this has happened, and she's sabotaging me at work, and you're standing here like I'm being unreasonable and this is some kind of thing that's just going to blow over. I won't have the kids near her. Not now.'

'Okay. The apartment is for the kids and me. Only. But I want them with me three nights a week, and part of the weekend.'

She thought.

'Why? What are you going to do? You'll have a new family to think of.'

'Look, let's not get ahead of ourselves,' he said, somehow managing to intimate that this might all blow over. 'Let's just tell them we're having a break for now. You come and look at the serviced place with me, and then we show them.'

(You may think that Max is hopelessly avoiding an issue he is destined to collide with. And you would be correct. But the truth is that Max has now found himself in circumstances even he is surprised by. And he is the kind of actor who prefers a script. Improvisation scares him.)

'Max, no. You have to wear this. I'm not lying to them.'

'And I don't want any of this, but I know you're angry and you don't trust me and you need to make this … this gesture. Punish me. That's okay.'

'Please! Do you know I have to work with her, Max?'

'Yes, of course I know you do.'

'I can't even do what other people apparently do when their hearts are broken, which is called losing yourself in your work,' she whisper-yelled at him. 'Because when I go to work, I am supposed to behave professionally to a woman who got more than professional with *my husband*. Not to mention my career!'

'Oh yes,' Max replied. 'Your career. You care more about your job than you do about me!'

Caitlin was about to let fly but the unsubtle sound of a teenage throat being cleared stopped her. Sean and Molly stood awkwardly at the door. Sean was holding Molly's hand. Their five minutes were up. She tried to put her face into an expression that conveyed calm, soothing motherliness, but she knew it was a bit of a stretch to think she could fool Sean. Molly might just think she had a tummy-ache, but Sean was able to spot a fake emotion all the way from another room.

'Okay,' said their teenage daughter in a very un-teenage way. 'You wanted to talk?'

Molly looked nervous.

The four of them drifted into the lounge room and the girls returned to their spot on the couch.

'Sit down, darlings.'

Max went over and hugged them both tightly. Caitlin tried hard to keep herself from howling. He might be a bastard, but he was definitely still their father.

He looked at Caitlin, moved over next to her, and nodded. 'Your call,' he said, his voice miserable.

'Um. We have something to tell both of you.' She cleared her throat.

'Daddy and I are going to be living in different houses from now on. We still care very much about each other, but we need to be apart.'

'For now,' said Max, managing to give the impression that everything would be back to normal soon. Caitlin frowned.

'Are you going to get unmarried?' Molly asked softly.

'Well, we'll see,' said Cait gently, her heart overflowing with love for her children, and already missing her past awfully.

Max gave her a look, and shook his head, frustrated. 'Mummy and I may take some time to work things out. But we both love you very much,' he said looking like he was going to cry.

Molly's face brightened, a huge grin broke across her little face and she jumped to her feet. 'Does this mean I'm going to have two houses?' she demanded, looking excitedly from one parent to the other.

Sean rolled her eyes and gave her parents a disgusted-teenager look, before burying her face in her hands and pulling her long legs up onto the couch.

'Yes, it does, darling,' Caitlin replied at the exact same time Max said, 'Well, we need some time …'

'YES!' Molly's chubby arms sped skywards, and she triumphantly turned and marched in the direction of her room. Sean sat there, peeking out through her fingers, glaring at Max and Cait.

Caitlin was perplexed. She'd been all ready for the burst of concern. She was aching to hold her youngest child and indulge in some wailing. Instead there was Molly, striding off, six years old and so lovely and funny her mother's heart was breaking up with pride.

Sean, however, cross-legged, crossed-armed and very, very hostile, was still glaring at Max. 'What have you done?' she hissed, wild like only a fourteen-year-old, blonde, adolescent, premenstrual female can be. 'Are you having issues? Who cares?'

Max and Caitlin looked at each other, sudden allies against the onslaught of teen fury.

'This is the time when I need everything to be kind of normal. I have school. I have music. I have homework. I have … stuff going on! And I have a concert coming up and you both promised to help. But this stupid break-up is going to be the star of the family now, right? *Fuck!*'

She slumped in a teenage heap on the couch.

Max looked stern. 'Don't talk to your mother like that,' he said.

'I'm not. I'm talking to you,' she snarled at Max.

'You've obviously done something much worse than be a smart-arse. Haven't you?' she snapped.

'Sean,' Cait said hurriedly, moving over to the couch and sitting with her. 'Honey, it's going to be okay. I'm going to help you with the show. It'll be really good. I'm not breaking that promise. And neither's your father,' she said, glancing at Max.

'Is this something you did?' Sean demanded of Max, her green eyes glaring.

She never cries any more, thought Caitlin. When did she get so tough?

'I can't talk about those things. But you won't be rude,' he said softly, giving his head a shake. 'Caitlin, I should go. I'll talk to you later,' he said, getting up and putting on his jacket.

'You idiot,' Sean replied contemptuously under her breath. She unfolded her long legs from the couch, and rubbed her face against her mother's for a moment. They looked so alike sometimes, except for the long, so pale it had no colour at all, straight-as-rain hair that fell down Sean's delicate back.

Max watched, his pale face unreadable. Cait caught his eye and shook her head, signalling there was no need to say any more.

'Your dad's right, though,' she said to Sean. 'We're not going to talk to each other like that. No matter what's happened, that's not okay. Okay, Sean?'

'I thought you said it wasn't okay.'

At that point Molly marched back in, carrying a pink suitcase stuffed with soft toys, sunglasses and one set of dress-up clothes. 'Okay, I'm all packed.

When do I go?' she announced, looking around for her transport.

Caitlin grinned despite herself; Sean just raised her eyebrows.

'It won't be too long to wait, sweetie. Back to your room for now, honey — but very good packing: well done. You keep your special bag for Daddy's place — you'll be able to use it very soon.'

'Awwww,' Molly complained gently, trailing back out of the lounge room.

Caitlin felt her heart shatter into little pieces, but was distracted by Max's voice. He was using his special gentle-and-masculine tone, she noticed.

'That was unexpected,' he grinned (slightly) at her. He knew using the usual full-power grin combined with the gentle-but-oh-so-deep tone wouldn't go down too well at this moment.

Apart from the careful monitoring of his every facial movement, Max wasn't sure exactly what he was going to do. He had been lonely, and stupid, and just a little more angry at Caitlin's success than he could ever admit, and even angrier at Caitlin herself for being away so often. He had been ready for a distraction: for something to excite him, and to make him feel important, attractive and necessary again. He hadn't known or planned that that something would be Kennedy. She was very pretty though, and had fallen attractively, suddenly, and quite hopelessly in love with him, and had been prepared to work very, very hard to keep him.

But he had never wanted to end his marriage. That,

and the possibility of becoming a father again, had never even crossed his mind.

'Can I go and get my stuff, then?' he asked quietly, with the great respect he knew would be his most powerful weapon against Caitlin's armour of self-righteous indignation.

'Sure,' Caitlin said, walking to the door and opening it for him. 'It's in the garage.'

SEVEN

'CAN YOU TELL me why I'm going out two weeks after my life collapsed?' hissed Caitlin. She was pulling away, stubbornly leaning back into the heels of her stilettos, while Sarah pulled her forward relentlessly toward a queue of devastatingly fashionable young people. 'If we could have gone anywhere better designed to make me feel like my life is over,' she said, glancing around at tiny skirts and perfect legs, 'and I have only HRT and a prolapsed vagina to look forward to, I don't know where …'

'I know where — we could have gone to Fashion Week. So don't worry. You're not going there. And besides, your vagina isn't going to prolapse. You've only had two children. You have to stop Googling weird things.'

'Google may soon be my only friend,' Cait said, grinning.

Sarah gave her a look. 'And I'm …?'

'You're my true friend.'

'Anyway, you're here because you said before that staying home and crying tonight was not an option,' Sarah said sternly.

'But when I said it to you, I thought I'd be on leave — for real. I've been so busy talking Gus and Carol through how to cope with Kennedy that I haven't had time to think up an excuse not to come. I need *more* time to sob!' Caitlin protested.

You see, *this* was a dinner that had actually been arranged for some time — Cait had a monthly get-together arranged with some of the women she knew (loosely) from television. Its purpose was said to be *mutual support* and *getting to know each other better*. Its true agenda was *networking* and *gossip*.

'This was organised before your life fell apart — remember?' Sarah reminded her, and not particularly gently, either. 'Besides, you said you'd rather get it over and done with in one night than answer forty text messages about it over the next week. It's heroic, what you're doing. Anyway, we don't have to stay long. You just had to get some fresh air.

'And you told me before we left that it was fine and you wanted to come,' Sarah continued. 'Remember? After *I* said I'd sooner just not show up.' Because Sarah might not have admitted it, but she had never felt at home with Cait's work friends. They were all very, she thought privately, unevolved.

'Is this the introduction to speed dating — speed get-back-on-the-horse-and-ride? You'll have me married off by the end of the week,' said Cait, who was now out the front of the venue she'd been pulling back from for the last five minutes. Sarah was small, but she was strong.

'Ooooh.' Sarah took Cait's hand and led her past the queue of people waiting to get into the club next door to the (allegedly) classier lounge bar nominated for their own gathering. Even Cait knew that said club had everyone in town fighting to get in — and that was literally. A brawl had just broken out behind the velvet rope …

'Have you been in there?' Cait asked, pausing to look back.

'Are you serious — does that look like somewhere I'd go?' Sarah demanded.

'There are children here,' said Caitlin, bathed in wonderment at her reintroduction to youth culture. 'I keep thinking I'm about to see Sean.'

'I hope she's not under that girl there,' said Sarah, distracted by a mohawked girl wrestling with a frail-looking boho blonde on the cigarette-butt-covered pavement. 'Hey! Get off the road, you two — there're cars coming,' she ordered. But the fight rolled on, with the blonde now pulling what was left of the mohawked girl's hair out.

'Wow — they look just like Pink and Ashley … or Mary-Kate. Whichever one doesn't eat,' said Cait.

'It's not them, but they're Sydney's versions.'

'You know, Sean despises those girls.' Another tussle broke out behind them. 'Is it really that hard to get in there?'

'Oh yeah,' replied Sarah, eyes widening at the sky-high legs of a transsexual hailing a cab. 'But anyway, yes, it's *trés* exclusive. Especially if all you have is a look. That girl probably did that to her hair just to get in tonight. And that girl underneath her probably pushed in. It's very competitive.'

'But they're babies,' Cait protested, thinking of Sean

at home. Was she at home? She fought back the first urge of the night to chew her nails.

'No, they're not. They're AAs ... Alternative Adults,' explained Sarah in response to Cait's bewildered expression. 'I can't believe you work in television and you don't know this stuff. If you don't get *them* watching TV, your medium's dead. Lost to X-Box and clubs you have to fight your way into.'

'Tell.'

'They're over eighteen and under-paid, under-fed and under-loved. Many of them call themselves Indigo Children; they're a brand-new generation of gifted kids with a spiritual mission. Haven't you heard about this?' (Cait shook her head.) 'You really have to come down to the yoga centre. They've been brought up by narcissistic parents who may or may not be hippy-ish new-agers who told their children they're not disruptive and borderline evil, they're special and have psychic powers. Getting into that club might mean they feel all right about themselves for a day. Or an hour. Anyway, they are not children, they are just a teeny bit younger than you and me and *we* are going to have dinner *here*,' she said, striding up to a red velvet entrance, a fountain of light playing over their features. They were nearly at the door now.

'Oooh, look, I'm an Indigo,' she intoned as her hands turned blue under the light.

Cait giggled.

'I know as an Indigo I have special powers, but I still don't know who's coming,' laughed Sarah, looking around.

'Ladies,' announced a bouncer wearing a reptilian smile and the world's tightest T-shirt. 'Enjoy your evening.' Sarah and Caitlin stepped through the doors, and squinted, not particularly glamorously.

'So where did they say they'd be?' Sarah asked.

'They didn't.'

'Hang on, I'm getting a feeling. Lots of money ... never have sex ... accessorised children ...' she intoned pseudo-psychically.

'They're not that bad,' Caitlin scoffed. 'I hope. We'll probably just talk about our jobs. Oh. Not that I'll want to talk about mine tonight.'

'Remember when I tried to talk about mine?'

Cait grinned. 'Yes, you rocked their world.'

Between the affluent citizens of Cait's stylish industry, fast friendships had formed. Some were true friendships between people who really did like and rely on each other. Others formed friendships mainly defined by who was no longer acceptable to the inner sanctum, a core of taste-Nazis who ruled the entrance into their company.

(Call it just like high school. You'd be right.)

'I feel sort of like I'm being tested to see if I get into a club,' said Cait, peering around myopically. 'And not this one! I can't see anything!'

'Why don't you get your eyes done?' The eyes in question gave Sarah a scary look. 'Not plastic surgery, silly; you know, the laser thing. Anyway, why can't you pick them out? You're not that blind.'

'I don't know that I'll recognise them all out of their corporate-wear. I kept saying I couldn't make it to these things. They were just interested in my work and the gossip about telly people *and* they all fancied Max —'

'The bastard,' they both said automatically.

'— and sometimes … sometimes they'd say nasty things about people who weren't there.'

'Ooooh! Nasty things!' Sarah mocked gently.

'And there are different people every time I come. Which was twice.'

'But Myra and Nadia are coming, aren't they? And anyway, Cait, of course the others said nasty things. What do you expect?'

'I expect that we'll be good to one another.'

Sarah gave her a pitying look. 'I run a yoga and healing centre, right?' Cait nodded impatiently, still searching for her associates. 'I run a place where spiritual healers work, right?'

'I *know*, Sarah.'

'Do you want to hear how much bitching and backstabbing goes on? How I practically have to separate the healers?'

'Oh. I thought they'd all be really Zen,' Cait said, disappointed.

'You just wait — hours of entertainment for you, my love. Not everyone's like you and me. We're lucky.'

A glimmer of an idea wriggled into Cait's mind.

'What? What's that funny look on your face? You just had an idea,' Sarah said accusingly.

'Nothing. Anyway. You're telling me what — we're all human or something?'

'We're not saints, Cait — and neither are you. Even though you're so … good.'

'I'm not good! I was late getting the kids to school *again* this morning —'

'Ssh! This has to be your gang.'

At least ten women was seated around a long, low table, perched on cushions and smoking cigarettes like it was desperately fashionable. (Which it was, again, seeing it had practically been given outlaw status.)

A flurry of *hello*s and surreptitious assessments of outfits took place. There was nothing at all wrong with this group of women, despite Cait's instinctive avoidance of them ... was there? Perhaps, she thought, I'm actually paranoid. They might be okay, she reassured herself. (Not very successfully.)

Within five minutes, she realised she *wasn't* paranoid. And catching up with the group was even worse, now that she was Cuckold, Exhibit A, and about to become the test case for everyone's divorce fantasy.

'We heard, Cait. Don't worry,' said one honey blonde, waving a cigarette at her. 'How is it, is it fabulous?'

'Great material for a show,' drawled a woman with long dark hair and unnaturally arched brows.

'Grist for the mill, darling,' shouted another.

Cait winced, and struggled to smile, and pretended not to see that nearly everyone was waving her over. 'Don't leave me,' she muttered to Sarah, who was sticking close by.

'Don't worry. I'm here,' she replied reassuringly.

'Is it great?!' shrieked a segment producer she recognised from the drama department of a rival station (who'd clearly had more than one glass of wine).

'Oh, yeah. Fabulous,' she said hollowly. Am I faking divorce joy? she thought. And if I am, *why?*

'Are you fucking loads of boys? What about that one in the coffee shop?'

'Are you all right?' said Nadia, looking up from the quiet end of the table, worry on her sweet face.

'I'm okay,' Cait said, feeling little pinpricks of heat break out on her face. She sat down next to Nadia, and Sarah parked herself on her other side.

'What happened?' asked a designer she'd worked with on a few programs.

'Look. He was … there was someone else. I found out. He's moved out. And it's still really new, so if …'

'Bastard!' cried Myra, a well-known PR executive who was sitting next to Nadia. The two women were the only TV-types to make it past the acquaintance category for Sarah and Cait. Nadia was a cheerful, hard-working stylist whose soft heart made her pretty rare in entertainment. They'd all seen Myra struggling to give up smoking ('It's not a good look to push a pram and suck a fag — I can't bear the disapproval.') and survive her own divorce. She'd never had the baby she wanted so badly, but she had given up cigarettes. And, after finally succeeding, she looked stricken with the level of temptation around her.

'I'm going outside for a joint,' Sarah announced. 'Come on, Caitlin (breathe, breathe … consider it good training),' she muttered to her friend as they escaped back to the footpath.

'This is hideous,' Cait protested. 'They all want to —'

'They're just fantasising about greener grass, no pun intended,' Sarah interrupted, rolling a joint.

Caitlin grinned. 'I can't believe you still smoke pot.'

'I can't believe you still think I'm going to stop anytime soon.'

Myra and Nadia escaped the club and joined them, flocking around the joint like seagulls at a chip.

'How fun!' hooted Myra.

'May I have some?' Nadia asked politely.

'You know, you'd get executed in some countries just for having that in your handbag,' Cait said darkly. 'And you travel all the time.'

'Oh, shut up, Cait, and have a bit.'

She grabbed it. 'Okay then. I will.'

She took a deep, strong drag, held back the gag reflex and the desire to cough, and passed it round. After everyone had a puff, they went back in, giggling and stumbling slightly.

It was kind of fun to be out, she admitted to herself, even if arriving to Twenty Questions had actually been awful. The kids were fine — Sean had insisted on her going out, and Molly was still busy separating her belongings into old house/new house categories.

She wondered about the supreme self-confidence and satisfaction of the women back at the table. So very, very hard and cynical and couldn't-care-less. Had she been like that? How is it, she thought unsteadily, that I could have been one of them two weeks ago, and now I'm someone else entirely?

She trooped back to the table with Sarah and Myra and Nadia, feeling slightly drifty and suddenly fourteen again, and looked around with stoned-red eyes. There was wallpaper, crimson, flocked and French on the walls, which were painted silver from the picture rail up. All over the room were enormous oil paintings featuring naked women with rolls of flesh unseen on any of the patrons. If *she* lined up to get in here, Cait thought to herself wryly, staring at a demurely smiling chubby nude, she'd be told to go back to the *Biggest Loser* auditions.

She stared at the menu, which was written entirely by hand, and chose something with goat. I'm not likely to get goat at the butcher's, she thought. She then thought about biting her nails at the table, but decided to go to the toilet and do it there instead.

(Here's the thing about Cait. While everyone else saw a slightly dazed, tall, beautiful woman with long red hair, slightly vintage-style clothing, green eyes with long crimson lashes, a full red mouth, long limbs and a small waist, she didn't. She occasionally felt she looked pleasant, but the truth was she hadn't really thought that much about her appearance — or *herself* — for ages. She was always tired, and generally figuring out how to get from work to school to home, and everything had just sort of been *running* for ages. [Or running her.] How had Max found the time to have an affair? How does anyone have the time to have an affair, she thought? And while she could do glamour and gossip for work purposes, she didn't really feel at home with these women.)

Back at the table, she concentrated on eating, and distracted herself with wondering what on earth those things were on everyone else's plates. The gossip and the wine were flowing equally freely. Bored waiters hovered, and Cait felt suddenly hot, and horrible.

'Don't do it, Cait,' she heard Sarah mumble.

'I think it's the goat,' she said, pretending she had no idea what Sarah was talking about.

'You can't fake it with me, Cait. I can feel it — you're about to do your Fleeing Doe impersonation. Don't.'

'I don't like being here. It feels all wrong.' Suddenly she wanted to weep. 'I want to be home. I want … oh shit.'

'I know. You know. But eat. Look — here's some more goat.' She pushed a steaming white dish with something very small on it over to her. 'Mmmm,' Sarah gestured to a woman opposite them, with long dark hair (perfectly smooth) and very pink lips. 'How are your shanks?' she asked cheekily. The woman glared back at Sarah. She'd had lipo that week and her thighs were killing her.

'This is awful, Sar. It's like I'm a tragic extra in *Desperate Housewives*.'

'*You're* not. *You're* wonderful.'

'So why are we here again?'

'Because there're some women here who are gorgeous. Like Myra and Nadia, for instance. They're lovely. You're going to need support, Cait. Friends. Not work friends, like most of us make.'

'Why, where are *you* going? I was never any good at this. I'm surprised if someone likes me, you know that.'

Sarah gave her a burning glare. 'Don't start with that.'

Caitlin grinned weakly, not wanting to cop a speech, and turned her attention to a conversation happening at the end of the table, between three women she hadn't met.

The lipo woman looked at her with knowing eyes.

'You know what you need?'

'No. What do I need?'

'You need to come out more. Shopping!'

'I can't come out more. Not really. I work.' Caitlin sounded stubborn, even to herself. Maybe it would have been fun.

Around the table, shoulders visibly slumped in disapproval. She wasn't playing the game at all! No, she thought. Not fun. Not honest. A sudden desire to tell them how it really was surged through her. Why not? she thought recklessly. Let's be honest. Let's be radically honest.

'The hardest thing right now is just getting up ...' Some nodded their heads sympathetically. Like they knew. But others looked slightly puzzled. Was Caitlin actually going to embarrass herself and everybody else at the table by saying how tough her life was? That was what therapy was for!

'Really?' asked the honey-blonde brightly, warning her to stop now, before they actually heard something true about her life. 'I would have thought it would be a relief,' she smirked at her colleagues, who nodded, relieved that the possibility of someone displaying raw emotion in public had been damped down.

Caitlin realised what was happening. She knew that was her cue to make a joke about it all or join them for shoe-shopping and ask for their therapists' cards. But she just wasn't in the mood. 'Well, it's hard ... the kids won't be with me for a few days each week.'

'You lucky bitch!' an older woman brayed. 'Maybe I can get *my* husband to have an affair,' she added, smiling.

Caitlin stared at her, stunned. But if she insisted on her version, she risked being labelled a victim. She didn't want that either. Too late, she realised. 'The truth is, you see, that it's hell,' Caitlin answered. 'And it hurts. And it's not easy, or a relief. It's really, really horrible. And if I were a nicer person I wouldn't wish it on you. Not ever. But maybe one day you will find out. Then you can say sorry to me.'

The table went silent, except for one woman with stiff platinum hair, who had been ignoring Caitlin's over-share. She held three others enraptured with her delighted mutterings.

'*She's* been working her butt off, and *he's* been fucking her assistant.'

Cait stood up and folded her arms across her chest. Everyone suddenly became very quiet, except the gossip.

'And the assistant's *pregnant*!' she finished triumphantly.

'Ssshh,' someone hissed pointlessly.

Caitlin, preferring private to public disintegration, made a dash for the door.

'Goodnight, ladies,' Sarah said, following Cait outside.

Myra and Nadia came out with them. 'Honestly,' explained Nadia, giving Caitlin a hug, 'she had no idea it

was you. It was just that she was filling the others in —
it's the latest story doing the rounds, only you've turned
into a magazine editor and he's a voice-over specialist ...'

'But the story has been doing the rounds,' said
Myra, mouth twisted sympathetically.

'How do they know?' asked Caitlin, frustrated. 'I
haven't told anyone Kennedy's pregnant. What did she
do — ring *Mediaweek*? Send out a press release?'

'Stories have a life of their own,' shrugged Myra,
'especially when the people telling the story haven't.
Look, let me take you both home, okay?'

'No, I need a drink. But I should go back and give
them some money for dinner,' protested Cait, scrabbling
around in her handbag for her wallet.

'Let them pay,' said Sarah. 'We're outta here.'

An hour later, Cait, Nadia and Sarah were in a bar,
laughing, this time at Nadia's tragic break-up stories.
Myra had already revisited the highlights of hers, and
Sarah's were (and still are) unprintable.

Seriously.

'I had to split up with him — he wanted me to
douche!' Nadia said, eyes wide open at the memory.

'Yes — he was American!' Myra pointed out, wiping
her eyes.

'But he wanted it to be strawberry shortcake
douche!' Nadia said, horrified.

They collapsed over their drinks, convulsing with
mirth. Cait wanted to laugh some more, but couldn't
quite summon up the energy. Instead, she sat back and
enjoyed the warm wash of bonhomie.

'I've never been divorced,' said Nadia sadly. 'It sounds so much better than breaking up.'

'It's a lot uglier than breaking up,' said Myra. She knew.

'But it gets so much more respect,' complained Nadia.

'Do you think?' Cait asked, wondering if there was an upside that had been seriously camouflaged until now.

Myra's brow started to wrinkle. 'Well, it *did*, didn't it? I mean, first it was a curse, and you were no longer an acceptable member of society. You were a social … pariah.'

'Yes,' said Nadia, 'but no, back then it was more like a disease … a social infection … carrying an invisible virus no one else wanted to get … like you were cursed. Shunned. A leper! Like my Aunt Rita. She scandalised everyone by *initiating* a divorce — unheard of — then she went and made it worse by living with a man!'

Caitlin winced. Was she in danger of being a social leper? Times didn't change *that* fast.

'Hang on, my mum didn't go through that,' interjected Sarah.

'No … But when was that?' Myra demanded.

'The seventies …'

'Well,' Myra started. (She was sharp as a tack and she loved a rant, did Myra.) 'By *then* it was *I Am Woman* and "you have the right to sex" and the Pill and marches and flopping your boobs out in public and going to Woodstock and having threesomes and orgies and things … you know! Songs like *D.I.V.O.R.C.E* and *Love the One You're With* and big weepy films like

Kramer vs Kramer with Meryl Streep looking attractive while she was getting divorced and all that ... And now, well, thanks a lot, bloody Britney.'

'Britney? Spears?' Nadia asked, perplexed.

'Celebrities and their stupid, farcical divorces have completely ruined the whole institution for the rest of us. Women in the US were having divorce parties, and melting down their wedding rings and turning them into symbols of freedom and newfound sexuality ... It was about to become the biggest, coolest rite of passage — you know, the first time you get a divorce. A big life lesson. Rebirth.'

'Wow,' said Cait. If she hadn't been so depressed she would have punched the air triumphantly.

'But *noooo*!' Myra continued passionately. 'Now we have idiot celebrities and their twenty-seven-minute marriages! They're so irritating. Not only do they *not* have to worry about the cost of a lawyer, they can afford to hire people to get them back into shape. To put their lives back together. To go out with them.' She paused for breath. Caitlin hoped she wasn't finished. This was very entertaining. 'Then they win Academy Awards for putting all their misery on screen. It's not fair! We just get to eat, get fat, and get even poorer.'

'Shit,' said Cait. 'That was fun till the fat and poor bit.'

'Sorry. But it's true,' Myra apologised. 'My sister, my mum *and* me. Except, as you know, I lost the weight,' she added smugly.

Caitlin felt a wave of fatigue, and knew the time had come to be sensible. Again. 'I need to get home.'

'You do,' Myra said. 'But listen, let's do this again. And before everyone makes *mmm*ing noises, agreeing but secretly thinking *it's a load of shit and we'll see each other next year some time*, let's make it this night, every week. Okay? At least until your divorce comes through. We can be your support group!'

'And we can keep each other filled in on what's happening,' said Sarah. 'You know what we've done, don't you? We've formed a breakaway splinter group. Every Wednesday night. We're on. And until you sign whatever horrible piece of shit papers you'll have to sign, Cait, the club endures.'

Cait started grinning. It didn't quite reach her mouth, but her eyes started to glow. Everyone noticed. Especially the man in the corner, who winked at her. Which, finally, was the moment when the smile truly broke through, and the bar suddenly seemed flooded with light.

EIGHT

'I suppose Madeleine's already on her way down,' Sarah remarked casually from the open-plan kitchen the next evening.

'Um,' said Caitlin shiftily, slumped back in a corner of the couch. 'I haven't spoken to her, actually.'

'What?' Sarah stopped putting dishes away long enough to turn and glare at her. 'You haven't even spoken with her?'

Sean looked over from her table under the lounge-room window, where she was doing her homework. 'You haven't told your own *mother* what's happening?' she demanded, sounding outraged.

'Ouch! No need to yell, Sean — I know. I'm *going* to tell her. I just don't know what to say,' Caitlin said in an aside to Sarah, who'd come and sat next to her, looking concerned.

'Just tell her you and Dad have split up. Then she'll burst in the door with presents,' smirked Sean.

'Yeah. Hurry up and tell her. Then I can talk to her about it,' said Sarah, who, besides being Caitlin's best friend, was probably her mother's closest friend, too — a situation Caitlin was painfully aware of.

'I kind of thought you might have already talked her through it,' Caitlin said, slightly sheepish.

'Is that what you were hoping for? Most things — definitely. This thing — no way,' Sarah said, shaking her pretty head. 'Divorce is definitely *your* domain.'

'Yeah, Mum,' said Sean, a slight edge to her voice.

Caitlin looked over at her eldest daughter. She was behaving very, very much like they were all characters in a TV show, and she was the smart-mouthed teenager who could handle anything the world threw at her. Caitlin didn't like it. Not at all.

'Okay, then,' said Caitlin, getting up and rinsing her tea-cup in the sink. 'I'm going to do it now.'

'Can we listen in?' Sean asked cheekily. 'Then I'll know what to say to the kids at school.'

'Sean!' Sarah warned.

'You know that's a no. And if Molly comes home from Allie's, just distract her, okay? Keep her busy till I'm done,' Caitlin said, giving Sean a serious look before leaving the lounge to head to the relative privacy of the office.

Calling your mother to tell her you've split up with your husband shouldn't be like this, thought Caitlin as she quietly closed the office door behind her and sank into the camouflage of a huge, overstuffed chair. She knew there was no more escaping the dreaded deed (Informing the Parents), but she really, really didn't like admitting failure to Madeleine and her father, who had always been so supportive and pleased that she'd been happy. Her marriage being a success felt like a present she'd given them, at least as much as a sort of achievement for herself. Caitlin, who was suffering one of her first experiences of failure, couldn't help but feel she was letting them down, and that their pain would be just another burden at the moment.

And while Caitlin hadn't said a thing to Sarah or Sean, telling her parents had been on her mind — constantly — and she'd been finding the build-up excruciating. In just over two weeks she'd endured the discovery of Max's infidelity and Kennedy's accusations of bullying; she was contemplating new arrangements that involved kissing her kids goodbye for three days every week; she'd fronted up to a social event as a newly single person; and now she had to do the grown-up thing and Tell Significant Others.

She felt her panic surge as she pushed each digit of her parents' number, thinking over how her mum and dad would, well, take this. Her parents had been together since the sixties, and while they were probably slightly bored from time to time (or so Cait assumed), their relationship seemed completely easy, if unconventional. It was bound, Caitlin thought as the phone rang, to last till the end of their natural lives. She hated being forced into a position whereby she had to admit to what was, in her eyes, a colossal failure.

She waited as the phone rang, a little bubble of hope that they weren't home beginning to rise. Maybe, she thought, she could just leave a vague message, buy herself a few more days.

But no. Her mother picked up just as she was considering easing the phone back down. Damn! she thought, adrenaline surging.

'Hi, Mum,' she said.

'Caitlin!' her mother sang out. Madeleine had a very loud voice. 'Hang on a moment, darling. Allan,' she bellowed, forcing Caitlin to hold the phone away from her ear. 'Caitlin's on the phone! Caitlin,' her mother said, turning her voice down a notch, 'can't you ring me back on the mobile thing with the pictures? You know I love to see who I'm talking to.'

Caitlin did not want her mother to see her face — it still bore the telltale signs of sleepless nights punctuated by sobbing. And raging. And resentment. And ... (Oh, never mind. You get the picture.) At least I haven't chewed a hole in my pillow and woken up with feathers in my mouth — *yet,* thought Caitlin bleakly.

And although she was about to tell her mother that something had gone very wrong, in fact her entire marriage, she didn't want her mother to see her distressed. So no silly phones with pictures.

'No, Mum. I need to talk to you,' she said, feeling awkward.

'Oooh, have I done something naughty? It sounds like it. Was it that toy I sent to Molly? Because frankly I do feel that your no-shopping policy is beyond ridiculous. And if it's about talking to Sean about contraception ...'

What?! thought Caitlin.

'No, Mum,' she said. You'll keep, she thought. She shook her head to clear the shock of the thought of Sean actually contemplating having sex. Who with?! she wondered. And when?! She made a mental note to thoroughly search Sean's room at the first opportunity, then carried on.

'It's not about whatever you bought Molly. Or Sean's contraceptives ... It's not about anything you've said or done to or with the girls. Without mentioning it to me. This is important. Really important.'

'Come on, then — get the picture phone. If it's that important I have to see your face,' her mother said, wheedling, with volume.

'I can't,' Cait said sharply, temper fraying. 'It was stolen,' she lied. 'I live in Sydney. People steal phones.'

She felt her mother freeze. Uh-oh. I've put her on daughter-breaking-down alert, thought Caitlin anxiously. Now she'll get some crazy idea about helping.

'Anyway. A couple of weeks ago the new show launched ...'

'I know that, darling. I've been ringing and ringing ...'

'Mum, it's not about the show. Just hold on.'

She breathed, feeling slightly sick. Oh, this sucks, she thought. I'll only get one chance to tell her this, and tell it the right way.

'Mum, am I on speaker? Never mind, of course I am. Hi, Dad.'

'Hi!' he replied cheerily. She could almost see him waving at her from the couch. 'What's the news?' he bellowed delightedly. He adored Caitlin. He adored his wife. He adored waistcoats and Scotch. And tennis. And food. And guessing the good news behind every phone call. (He was relentlessly positive.)

'Don't tell me,' he continued before she could speak. 'Two weeks ago the show started. It's a huge success. And they're about to give you an all-expenses-paid holiday to —'

'No, Dad,' she sighed, 'it's —'

'No, no, don't tell me. Let me get it —'

'Dad!'

'They've transferred you to Los Angeles to head up —'

'*Dad!*' Caitlin exploded.

There was a brief struggle, and Caitlin heard her mother's triumphant yelp. No doubt she'd launched an attempt to wrestle the phone back off her father. (They may have been on speakerphone, but whoever held the actual phone held the twenty-first-century talking stick.) Cait paused, annoyed the moment of her announcement wasn't being given the serious platform she thought it warranted. She waited.

There was a longer struggle than expected. She could hear her father losing his battle to hold onto the phone.

'Ha! Got it back. Well, come on then, darling, what's the news?'

'The news is that,' Caitlin began, clearing her throat. She choked up, coughed and cleared it again. 'The news is that Max and I have separated.'

Silence. Cait worried for a moment that one or even both of them had been struck dead by the shock of her news. But then she heard her mother breathing.

'He moved out a couple of weeks ago,' she continued. 'The kids are okay, here for the moment. Nothing's really been worked out. I just wanted —'

'Hang on, darling ... just take a breath ... now, can you hear me?'

'Yes, I can hear you.' Of course she could hear her mother. Everybody in the entire street could probably hear her mother. Now that she'd said it, and everyone still seemed to be alive, she felt suddenly dazed. It still didn't feel quite real.

'Mum,' she said, finding her mother uncharacteristically silent. Was she really just *gutted*? Caitlin wondered, ears pricking at the strange noises making their way through the phone.

Footsteps; female, as they were light — pit-pat on the wooden floor. They were followed by a sucky noise and a creak.

'Mum, did you hear me? Max and I have separated.'

'I did, Caitlin. Can *you* hear this? This is the sound of me opening the fridge,' her mother said, sounding slightly unhinged — excited, even.

'Right.' Caitlin couldn't be bothered being annoyed: she was intrigued. Maybe Mum has lost it, she thought.

More sound effects followed. Glass tinkling, scrunchy noises.

'This is the sound of me getting something out of the fridge ...'

'Ah-huh ...'

'This is the sound of me opening ... ooh, Allan, can you get it out? I'm struggling a bit, darling!'

BLAM!

'Mum, did you just shoot Dad?' Caitlin asked, feeling like giggling. She didn't know what this phone call had in store, but this was definitely not what she'd been expecting.

'That, my darling child, is the sound of the bottle of champagne I've had in the fridge for the last fifteen years, waiting for this day to come!'

Caitlin started laughing for real now; little ripples of humour worked their way up through her body, pushing some of the heartbreak aside for a moment. 'Are you mad? Sorry, of course you are.'

'Your dad and I are just pouring ourselves a glass to celebrate. Congratulations, darling!' her mum trilled, sounding genuinely happy.

'What? Are you serious?' Caitlin was still laughing. Was divorce meant to be this funny? And was fifteen-year-old champagne all right to drink?

'Yes, of course we are. And we replaced it every year, darling, drinking to this moment in advance. So don't worry, we're not getting alcohol poisoning — that'll come after the next bottle!'

'Hoorah,' came a masculine bellow from the background ... 'Hoorah again.' And clapping. *Enthused* handclapping. 'I gave it five years at your wedding — and you hung in there for sixteen! Sixteen! You're a saint!' said her father, sounding teary. (Champagne always went straight to his head.)

'Um, I knew you weren't his greatest fans, but I didn't realise you didn't like him that much.'

Her mother snorted. Snorted! 'Well, we never *liked* him, darling, but you were absolutely cross-eyed about him. And we never really knew if we were being reasonable or not … but we always thought he was, well, sort of awful.'

'Oh. Well. Anyone else you don't like that I should know about? Sarah? Me? The kids? How do you feel about them?'

'See, this is why we never said anything, because you're so loyal. Even now you're defending the silly old thing.'

Her mother calling Cait's soon-to-be-former husband old was a bit rich, but she let it slip by.

'But this is pretty strong stuff — cheating, I imagine. So we can say whatever we like! Hoorah, free at last,' shouted her father in the background.

'So, you never liked my husband,' Caitlin said, mock-sternly, holding back tears and laughter. It was sad and funny that they'd felt this way — especially as she'd been worried that her perfect and oh-so-modern marriage breaking up would hurt them. Would let them down. Would mean she was a failure in their eyes.

She'd been wrong, wrong, wrong. She tuned back in to the conversation, where, it seemed, her mother and father were unleashing years of repressed … dislike!

'We *hated* him, darling! Oh, such a wonderful relief to say it. Hated him. Smug, arrogant poser who never did a thing except mooch about and —'

'Hang on, Mum. You *hated* him?'

'Oh, he was *horrible*,' she said with relish.

'Okay, I get that. Don't you want to know why we've split up — or about the kids — or —'

'He's a filthy cheater!' yelled her father from, she guessed, somewhere behind the bar, fumbling about for more champagne. 'This is the best thing that could have happened to you. You were never going to leave him. Here's to the Other Woman! She finally came along!'

Caitlin felt a little cross. 'How come you're so all-seeing? And given that you are, why didn't you give me warning?' she said, half cranky, half delighted.

'Of *course* he had an affair. He's very good-looking, darling, and he's very, very susceptible to flattery. He's growing older and you were too busy to pay him quite so much adoring attention. So I'm sure he feels justified. Let's see. She has to be someone younger than him — and you — because he's so horribly vain and frightened of getting old.'

'Always thinking he looked like Harrison Ford! Pah!' shouted her father.

'That's right, he did. And it's your father who *truly* resembles Harrison Ford,' said her mother smugly.

'That's what I said! He always thought he was so —' her father said, eagerly picking up the thread.

'Hot!' finished her mother. Caitlin felt horrified. Caitlin always cringed when her mother used words like *hot*. Caitlin cringed a lot when talking to her mother. But this was a very, very unusual situation. And even Caitlin, after all these years of knowing her parents, couldn't believe their reaction. And how very much she hadn't known.

(A little background may be in order. Caitlin's mother Madeleine was a very beautiful woman who considered herself free-spirited and bohemian. Which she was. To the point where people often wondered if someone famous had just wandered past them while they were doing the shopping. She wore drifty silks and claimed she'd never allowed a man-made fabric near her skin. She wore vivid colours that reflected and 'held' the energy she was working with that day. She'd done a lot of healing, and would have spent most of her life at Sarah's yoga centre if she'd lived in Sydney. Which Caitlin was glad she didn't, because Sarah and her mother got along almost too famously.

She didn't have many clients, because usually when people asked her what she did, she would say, 'Why don't you ask me who I am?' The questioners would usually assume she was someone famous, and not the amazing healer they had thought for a semi-second they were in contact with. So she had many confused fans and hardly any paying customers.

Madeleine, who hated being called *Mum*, was one of those people who saw very little difference between her opinions and The Truth. She didn't in fact believe in objective truths, which made it very easy for her to always persuade her husband why her point of view was the one that should prevail. She was not a bully; in fact she was a delightful person, entertaining and very funny. But she certainly liked things done a certain way. And the demise of her daughter's marriage was an opportunity to boast, with the benefit of hindsight, of her psychic skills.)

'I knew it when we were last down ... I looked at him sitting there and I could see it.'

'In his eyes?' Caitlin wondered aloud. She wasn't sure about her mother's skills — but Madeleine *had* immediately known the one and only time she and

Sarah had ever wagged school. And she certainly looked a bit spooky.

'Anyway, so he's probably been having it off with some bit of fluff ... and now you'll have to do a revolting property settlement ...'

Cait's stomach lurched alarmingly. 'What? Oh, Mum. That's a horrible thing to say. Besides, it's all just happened. I don't even want to go there.'

'Mark my words. Your Nan left you that house, but he feels like it's his. I've known for years this was coming,' she said, sounding doom-like.

'What are you, the oracle of Delphi? Mum, no, he's honourable. Well. About this. And I said I don't want to talk about it. I've got enough to handle right now.'

'He's not honourable, darling! He thinks he looks like Harrison Ford! Going on about Mel Gibson —'

'Well, oh wise one, there's not really any point telling you anything,' said Caitlin, changing the subject, the only possible way to stop her mother's rant. 'Like the fact that the kids are probably going to have a little brother or sister?'

'NO! You're *not*!' Her mother sounded horrified.

'No, I'm not. But *she* is.'

'*Oh*!' Both her parents sounded satisfyingly gobsmacked.

'*That bastard*!' they shouted in unison. No wonder they were still together, Caitlin thought.

The phone was dropped, and a mini-conference was obviously held. Cait waited, slightly exasperated, but full of affection, as well as a sick feeling that her mother had a point that she just wasn't willing to even contemplate right at that moment. Maybe she wouldn't have to do this alone, she thought. Her parents were annoying, but they were absolutely on her side. In a world full of weirdness, their affection and loyalty was one rock she could cling to. There was a clatter in her ear as someone picked the receiver up.

'Well, you can tell me all about it in person!' her mother stated in a take-no-prisoners manner.

'What?' Oh, bugger, Cait thought. Here she comes.

'Now, obviously I will be down soon … oh, how fun! We can go into therapy!'

Caitlin's mother had always wanted to 'be in therapy'.

'If I do, Mum, you won't be there,' Caitlin said, her head whirling at how fast this was all moving.

'Psssht. You'll need support! Which means I'll be moving in for a while.'

In Madeleine's mind, that's what mothers did. In Caitlin's mind, it was what happened when God decided to take the joke a little too far. Caitlin supposed her mother thought that moving in was a lovely, supportive thing to do. Which it was. Except it meant her mum was actually going to be moving in.

Caitlin immediately plastered a fake smile onto her face and prepared to protest. She wasn't sure why she was fake-smiling … it wasn't as though Madeleine could actually see her. Perhaps she would *hear* the smile.

'Mum, I —'

'Shush,' her mother lowered her voice, suddenly a co-conspirator. 'To be honest, darling, I could do with a little break from your father,' Madeleine whispered in the manner of a trusted friend discussing a boyfriend's sexual shortcomings. Then she hung up, eager for some more champagne and a postmortem around the bar.

Caitlin stared at the phone, shocked. She hadn't even talked to her dad. Well, not really, apart from shouts and bellows. He was probably happily drinking champagne, equally filled with glee and relieved at her mother's escape plan, planning tennis outings and antique shopping.

Meanwhile, her mother was on the march. *Groan.*

NINE

'I HAVE,' CAITLIN was saying in morose tones, 'about five days to get my life together. If I don't, my mother is going to walk right in and sort it out for me.'

Sarah smiled, linking her arm through her friend's. It hadn't been the easiest of mornings.

It was Saturday. The day families reacquainted themselves with the people they barely spoke to during the week, when women who worked wheeled babies for the first time in days, only to notice they'd grown while they weren't looking, the day when teenagers fought off the ravages of Friday night parties and thought about how they might be able to fool their parents into letting them out for another night of fiercely joyful self-destruction. In a kinder, better place she called the Land of Happy Married People, Caitlin imagined devoted husbands driving children to sports while beloved wives slept in before waking up to eat pastries in bed. Their sheets were snowy-white, 1000-thread-count Egyptian cotton, their kids won their soccer games and their husbands never even thought of other women.

There had to be such a place, she thought. For every action there is an opposite and equal reaction. So, if this is my world, the opposite exists, she reasoned.

In her world, called the Land of the Recently Cast Asunder, she got to have Sarah wake her up, practically force her to smile at the kids, then wave goodbye apathetically as Sarah drove Sean (scowling) and Molly (beaming) over to Max's In-Between Serviced Apartment. (He was pretending to look for a house, though everyone seemed to assume he'd give up the struggle at some stage soon and just move into Kennedy's. It had been very strange to hear from Carol that she had been having phone conversations about 'renovations' to help her 'partner' settle in.) Sarah had returned to find Caitlin preparing to cry for the day, and had made her friend eat an omelet before insisting she come down to the beach to perve at young men for 'fun'.

They'd driven down, Caitlin feeling herself a bleak, black cloud amongst sunshiny happy people. The tops of cars were down, people's clothing was entirely Sydney — barely-there — and smiles were non-negotiable. Meanwhile, Caitlin pulled her sunglasses on tighter, feeling conspicuously miserable. 'I'm an emotional leper,' she muttered to herself, as she stared at people holding hands in the sunshine. She'd cried enough to be fairly certain there were no more tears to be squeezed out from behind her reddened eyes, and more than enough to know she looked, well, terrible. 'Like shit,' she told herself, glancing in the rear-vision mirror. She felt like she'd swallowed a rock, as if walking about hunched over was natural, and her body took an emotional punch to the solar plexus every time she thought of Max and Kennedy, which was, on average, more than the normal male teenager thinks about sex. But, she thought wanly, there's hope. There's the part where my heart freezes over to look forward to. The defrosted version still burned. Anger, Rage and their old friend Pain were running relays through her arteries, and she felt blistered on the inside with frustration and fury. It wasn't at all pleasant.

'Now, I know it's okay to let you be upset and miserable, but I need an ice-cream,' chirped Sarah. 'Can I leave you alone, with this cliff, and all this sunshine, and this sparkly water for a moment? Or will you fling yourself off?'

'I love you,' Cait said in a monotone. 'You don't try and cheer me up.'

'Hell no. This is great fun,' she scoffed. 'I feel like I have a mission,' she said semi-seriously. Sarah liked having a rescue to conduct. But confectionery called. 'Be back soon.'

Caitlin waved her off, then clambered over the rocks, sat down on a ledge, and stared glumly out to the vast and impersonal sea. Go on, she thought, staring at the twinkling sea and perfect clean green waves. Cheer me up. I dare you.

A happy laughing couple jogged by on the path behind her. Stupid people in love, she scowled, staring at the super-fit lovers, their muscles locked and loaded. You'll get yours.

Someone smiled at her. You'll have to try harder than that, world, she thought. She stifled a giggle. She was enjoying being bleak and nasty too much to ruin it with some good humour.

Two dogs started sniffing each other, before one leaped upon the other, commencing standard reproductive activity. Stupid dogs mating, she thought meanly. You're a poodle, he's a German shepherd. How can it ever work?

Pigeons coo-cooed nearby. 'Stupid pigeons, cooing. It's just biology at work. You could be any girl,' she said out loud to the pigeon being courted.

Couples, human, dog and pigeon, all ignored her. (Except for one nice elderly lady nearby who noticed the sad young woman talking to pigeons, and squeezed her handsome elderly gentleman partner's hand. She'd been sad like that too, once, when she'd thought her life had been squashed. Thank God for internet dating, she thought, smiling into her man's face.)

Love was everywhere, but Caitlin, ever so naturally, hated every single bit of evidence that beauty hadn't died at the same time as her marriage. Why did *her* life get to be so vastly inequitable? Life's justice stops for me, she thought, quite unfairly as it happens, and it goes on for other people. At work, *Date Squad* had taken off, and she'd heard all about the schmoozy lunches with advertisers braying about the delights of feel-good programming. All her smiles and self-control had been used up, drained away by the daily phone calls from the HR department, who were desperate to debrief her on the next stage of the bullying charge. So far, they'd suggested that everything would calm down if she apologised to Kennedy and did an anger management course. No questions asked.

She'd said no, and Kevin was furious.

'You don't have to *be* sincere about it,' he'd bellowed down the line at her. 'She'll have nowhere to go if you do that.'

'I'm not,' she said stubbornly, 'saying sorry to Kennedy. She's stolen my husband, and I'm about to lose my kids for three days a week. She can get stuffed, Kevin.'

'You know what we all have to do to be successful?' he'd roared. 'To survive?'

'No,' she'd replied, bracing herself for the answer.

'You have to eat the occasional shit sandwich. I've eaten plenty. Your pride won't get you through this.'

So Kevin's answer to everything was a diet of turds. It just did not feel right.

It wasn't going to stop there, though. She had a meeting scheduled with Kennedy and Geoffrey from HR on her first day back next week. That was something that even sparkly water and perfect autumn temperatures couldn't stop. And she felt sick at the thought.

The greatest joke was that everyone at work already knew what had really happened. Everyone tacitly agreed the whole thing was ludicrous, a waste of time and energy. But Kennedy had made a killer pre-emptive strike. She should have been a hitwoman, an assassin, thought Caitlin. It's not about justice. It's about strategy. She's so clever, Caitlin thought, admiring her begrudgingly. I can't even be properly mean because she's pregnant.

But none of this, she reminded herself firmly, would have happened, could even have had the remotest possibility of happening, without Max. Her soon-to-be-former husband.

Bastard, she thought, her head aching, looking at her ring sparkling on her finger, matching the sparkling of the deep blue water way below. The diamond-like glitter of the water gave Cait a brilliant idea: make a grand gesture. Finish things off.

Caitlin stared angrily at her wedding ring, all shiny and innocently sparkling. Why shouldn't she? She thought to herself. There it was, wrapped around her finger, *lying* about the state of things. No taint. No tarnish. 'Liar,' she growled at the ring, half laughing at herself.

She'd officially lost it. I'm like Gollum, she thought. Talking to a ring. Muttering at pigeons. It's just a few fluffy-slipper steps down to hanging out with the woman who sells the *Big Issue* at the bus shelter.

She smirked at her own bitterness, and gave her ring a semi-serious glare. It was just a ring. It hadn't *done* anything. Still. It didn't seem fair. It was the same now as when he'd put it on her finger, but her life was absolutely different.

She closed her fist around it and squeezed, daring herself to ease it off for the first and last time. She realised that she was squeezing the ring tight. Just the way she wanted to squeeze her soon-to-be-ex-husband's throat. Way too tight. As if the (unlucky!) $13 000 diamond- and sapphire-studded platinum band with its rosie-ring promise of love neverending engraved on the inside was responsible for everything, instead of her lying, cheating … (She struggled to come up with more insults. *Lying* and *cheating* kept doing the rotations at the moment.)

She slid it off and held it in her hand. She drew her arm back and readied her throw. There, she thought, with satisfaction, staring into a rock pool metres and metres below. That's where it would go down. Right near the rocks over there.

It wasn't as if Caitlin's busy schedule wasn't already spilling over without her spending a morning wondering what to do about the symbol of her marriage. She had a lot to think about, and more than that to do. There was, oh, the future, her kids, and her financial situation, her mother's impending visit, whether she had to move, or leave her job, or maybe even the country, just to avoid killing Kennedy. But every time she tried to sit down and form some kind of plan of action, she found herself staring at her ring, wondering what on earth she was supposed to *do* with it.

She was still technically married, so taking it off didn't exactly solve anything. Keeping it on was just painful. She had toyed with the idea of keeping it on to annoy Kennedy, but that wasn't going to be worth it.

Like Myra had said, in America women were apparently transforming their rings into necklaces or other pieces of jewellery. There were so many options, she thought. Should she melt it down, sell it off, or pull some kind of clever and elaborate insurance scam? Or, when that seemed too exhausting, she fantasised about giving it away to the homeless *Big Issue* woman, even though she never showered.

However: she didn't know how to melt anything down; selling it was too confronting, and she'd probably never get the true value; she hated filling in forms so that meant the scam was out. And the homeless lady would probably stick it up her bum, or eat it, or jam it in her garbage bag full of belongings, or make one of her cats wear it, thought Caitlin. So now that she was finally allowed to be alone, she was thinking that she should maybe just fling it into the ocean that was laid out like a carpet of blue and green before her, shot with light. The perfect place, she thought grimly, to send the ring. Then it'll end up on the hands of a mermaid, or in her treasure chest. After all, that's just what this relationship is. Sunken.

She gave it another glare. The ring was antique in style, though it wasn't actually an old ring. They'd bought it from her favourite jewellers, Briar Rose, where she'd always thought she'd get her wedding ring.

Except she hadn't thought about the after part. So, she thought, here I go!

'Excuse me, crazy lady,' interrupted Sarah, sounding annoyingly normal. 'What do you think you're doing?' Sarah was very sharp, eyeing her best friend's twiddling with curiosity. 'Have I told you you're very entertaining when you're having a breakdown? I don't mean to be heartless, but I should be taking notes. You could use them some time.'

'Ha. Do you really want to know what I'm thinking of doing with this?'

'Your ring? Putting it on eBay? You're not!'

'Nope. I'm thinking of chucking it in there.'

'Nah,' retorted Sarah confidently. 'That's just how you feel right now.'

'Oh really?' Caitlin dared, glaring. 'Watch me.' She drew her arm back and screwed her eyes shut. She went to thrust her arm forward, but she was blocked, her wrist caught in Sarah's iron grip.

'Yoga gives you hand muscles? Ow!'

'Ow yourself. You're being silly.'

'*My* ring.'

'Stop. Right now.' Sarah's hand held her arm.

Caitlin shook her arm free and turned around, grinning despite her fury. 'That really hurt.'

'Give it to me. For now. If you still feel like chucking it in three weeks, it's all yours.'

'The moment is now!'

'No, it's not a smart idea at all.'

'Who made you the boss of me?' Caitlin demanded.

'You did. Since you lost it.' Cait poked her tongue out, feeling ridiculous and loved at exactly the same time. 'Oooh, you look a bit chirpier. I thought if we could just get some of that rage out you'd be feeling better. Were you really about to chuck this beauty in there?'

'I think I was, you know,' Caitlin said, pushing hair out of her eyes and grinning.

'You're crazy,' Sarah said tartly.

'It just feels so embarrassing. The whole thing.'

'Come on. Hand it over,' demanded Sarah sternly, or as stern as her baby whisper voice could get. (Most people who knew her never really got just how tough she was.) Caitlin giggled suddenly at Sarah's Goldilocks hair whipping around her face, tangling in the ice-cream she held out to Caitlin. She de-haired the cone with assumed dignity and a smirk, and did a little curtsey.

'It's pistachio, mad lady who flings rings off cliffs in heartbroken despair. Your favourite.'

'Thanks. Sarah, doesn't anything get to be sad any more? Is everything ironic? Can't I just be miserable without having to see the funny side of it, all the angles?'

'You're a TV producer. You're trained to see the possibilities of the story. You know everything's a tragedy *and* a comedy. You know however sad it gets, there'll be great moments. And you know however great something is, there'll be shit ones.'

'It's too involved. I'd like to be more detached.'

'From your own divorce?! There's medication for that.'

'Maybe I'll just have an ice-cream,' she said, grinning. Caitlin plunged her tongue into the icy-cold scoop. 'Mmmmmm.'

'Give it to me. Come on — hand it over.'

'What?' mumbled Caitlin through a mouthful of delicious cold fatty stuff. 'My ice-cream?'

'The ring. Come on. Hand it over.'

Caitlin scowled, and grudgingly put it into Sarah's dainty, outstretched hand.

'Thank you, mental case.' Sarah stared at the ring, sliding it onto her finger.

'God, Caity,' she said softly. 'You just can't chuck this away. It's beautiful.' She turned her hand from left to right, admiring the silvery flashes the ring gave off as it caught the sunlight. Cait held her hand up, tentatively feeling its new lightness.

'Oooh, look at the mark it's left on your finger,' Sarah pointed out helpfully. Caitlin grimaced, rubbing her left hand. It felt naked, and very weird. One very exposed, telltale sliver of pale flesh *shouldn't* make her whole hand, her whole being, feel so very different. So very raw. So very vulnerable. Should it? Wonderingly, Caitlin stared at the magical third finger on her left hand with its distinct pale ring.

'Oh look. I'm still married,' she grimaced.

'Well, you are, technically …'

They both laughed. 'It's a ghost ring. A ghost marriage,' Caitlin said sadly. 'So … I wonder how exactly I go about getting a divorce?'

'Oh, right. You haven't done this before.'

'Neither have you, smartypants spiritual and oh-so-together person.'

'Well. It's an important thing, then. It's your first divorce.'

'My first divorce. So …' she said, smiling slightly and blinking back tears. 'There could be a second. Even a third?'

'Sweetheart,' Sarah said softly. 'Some people do this every two years. Clearly they're crazy, or numb, but you could go on and do this all again. It's a new world. The choice is yours …'

Cait smiled, feeling the sizzle of heartburn ease off ever so slightly. 'Have I told you about my parallel-universe theory?'

'No,' Sarah said, threading her arm through Caitlin's. 'Fill me in.'

TEN

But the discussion didn't last long. Because just a half
an hour later, Caitlin's parallel universe invaded her
present time. In waves. That wouldn't stop.

'No, Max,' Caitlin was shouting into the wind,
which was giving her a good excuse to shout. 'I don't
think it's okay for the girls to be packed up in the
morning, and sent off to be with you for days, for the
very first time, then find out that you want them back
here,' Caitlin continued down the phone as she walked
along the sandy track that led from one city beach to
another. She paused momentarily, face pale. 'Yes, I do
want them with me.' She moved forward again, faster,
fuelled by aggravation. 'It's unfair to say I don't, and
you know it. I just don't want them to get unsettled any
more than they have to. And they were prepared to go
to you for three days, now you're saying they should
come back to me instead.'

Sarah mouthed *are you okay?*, but Caitlin hardly
noticed, focussed as she was on moving forward and
making it through the conversation without breaking
down. Sarah shook her head and strode along in Cait's

wake, letting the movement carry away the intense wave of resentment that flashed through her at the thought of what Max must be saying. Just as all her efforts had helped Cait feel less like death and more like there was some hope after all, Max made one call and ruined everything. Bastard, she thought (not for the first time).

'I understand it's while you work things out,' Caitlin was saying, sounding strained. It could have been the hill they were climbing — or that she was fighting back tears. 'And truth is, I'd rather they were with me. Till you get settled, then.' She paused, listening. 'Right. Pick them up at five o'clock? And we'll sort permanent arrangements out later.'

Sarah noticed when Cait looked at her that it hadn't been the hill — it had been tears.

'I'll be there then. Bye.' She snapped shut her phone and pushed it into her beach bag. 'We need to go around and get the kids at five. Max needs to look at a house.'

'You okay?' Sarah asked, concerned.

Caitlin nodded, looking faintly deranged. 'It's all good.'

Sarah looked at her friend. 'It's all good? How exactly is it all good, Caitlin?

'It kind of has to be, Sarah. God, I thought you were the Queen of Positive Thinking. Now I'm in trouble for affirming it's all right.'

'Don't get snappy. You're not in trouble with me,' said Sarah firmly. 'He is, and the truth matters more. So tell the truth. It's not okay, is it?'

'Of course it's not. It's just ... just *manure*,' spluttered Caitlin. 'But the other truth, the bigger truth is that it's not about me, or Max. It's about the *girls* today. I thought it'd be okay: that I'd hate handing them over, and that I'd come down and feel sick about it with you, then they could have a chance to get used to it. But this ... to-ing and fro-ing is just vile,' she said. 'They already feel angry, Sean especially. He's risking his relationship with them, for what?'

'I guess, if he needs to see a place ...' faltered Sarah.

Cait couldn't say no. It seemed she couldn't escape. Not really. In the last half-hour, she had fended off two phone calls from Max, one from Kevin (who said he was just 'checking in'), two from Sean complaining about how her father's new place was way too small, and one from Molly, who was wondering if it would be okay if she made a bid on a new laptop on eBay. (The answer had been no.)

Sarah had watched Cait's heart breaking that morning as she (re)packed Molly's bag, and helped Sean select what clothes to take over. 'How's this supposed to work with homework and stuff?' Sean had huffed, clearly not loving her lot.

Caitlin had just got on with it, and kept it together, and Sarah had hustled her out of the house and down to the beach immediately after taking the girls to Max's, hoping to distract her. Well, she thought, at least we're outside. And at least she's moving. No one can be totally depressed as long as they keep moving. They reached the tip of the next beach and without consultation turned back to retrace their steps. Caitlin's jog slowed to a walk.

'And then as soon as he had them there, he said he needs to go house-hunting, because the serviced apartment thing is too small and they're not happy. He said he'd rather they be happy with me, even though he said he wants them there,' she explained, puffing slightly. 'Wow. I haven't exercised for ages.'

'Just pretend with every step that you're stomping on Max's face,' Sarah said encouragingly.

Cait ran a hand through her hair, forcing one mad spiral to stand on end like a corkscrew antenna. 'I don't hate him like that,' she said, grimacing. 'And if I start with imaginary violence, it'll end badly. I can feel it.'

The phone rang again. 'Darn,' Cait said, slowing down and fishing it back out of the bag.

'Hi, Sean.'

'I'm not doing this, Mum,' Sean's panicked voice rang out, even against the wind. 'I'm not going back and forth like ... some parcel or something.'

'We'll talk when you get home,' Caitlin attempted to shout soothingly.

'Good,' Sean snapped. 'Because this sucks. And it's not my fault. So I should get some say.'

'Talk to you later,' Caitlin shouted, and rang off. 'Let's hurry up or we won't get this run in,' she said to Sarah.

'We're not running, we're walking. And talking,' Sarah pointed out.

Sarah had her eye on the clock. She was noting just how long Caitlin could keep the long face up for. And her other eye was on the lookout for fine pieces of distraction. Caitlin wasn't noticing her friend's truly heroic efforts. She barely even noticed her mood lifting as she walked, despite the blow from Max.

'When your mum's here we can all do this together,' Sarah said, hoping to distract Cait.

It didn't work. Caitlin just rolled her eyes, and sped up again.

'Why are you doing that?' Sarah demanded, catching up as they rounded the headland sheltering the original beach.

'What?' Cait asked innocently, knowing full well how much it annoyed Sarah when she failed to appreciate the blessing that being born her mother's daughter obviously was.

'That thing with your eyes. Stop it. The wind might change,' she said. 'Anyway, surely it'll be great to have the support. She can help take the edge off with the kids.'

Cait hesitated, but then decided to go ahead and indulge in another eye-roll anyway. 'She's not *your* mother. She's your *friend*. She's not *my* friend. She's my *mother*. And don't you know why it's going to be awful?'

'Nah,' panted Sarah, guiding Cait onto the sand for some last-minute exertion. 'Still don't get it.'

(Caitlin never failed to exaggerate her fear of her mother to Sarah. Because her best friend defended her mother so valiantly, she just couldn't resist stirring, and was now particularly enjoying regaling Sarah with improbable explanations about why her mother's visit would be awful.)

'I kid you not,' she said, hands waving around with the kind of enthusiasm that looks a lot like panic. 'My mother is coming down, and I can *feel* her on her way. It's like I have an early warning system.'

'Not listening,' Sarah said, pointedly staring at a surfer emerging from the water just metres to their left. 'Besides, you know I love your mother. She'll help you next week. So will I. Plus we all get to watch.'

'You like to watch,' noted Caitlin. 'Sorry, that was cheesy. But how do you manage to get away with looking? At men. Not my mother. I'm confused.'

Sarah had always been unselfconscious when it came to ogling. She'd been straightforward about staring when she was at school, and had enjoyed plenty of visually stunning moments as a result. She hadn't grown out of it. At that moment, she was simultaneously listening to Caitlin wonder aloud whether Max had found a place, or was just faking it and planning on staying at Kennedy's after all, and very unsubtly checking out a gorgeous man, who just happened to be standing under a shower on the nearby boardwalk. Water streaked down the hard curves of his pectorals, glossing his flat, taut stomach and dripping off strong thighs and calves, washing away sand and salt. He stepped away from the flow of fresh water and shook himself, almost exactly like a puppy. Sarah and Cait ducked the spray.

'Hey!' Sarah called out playfully, grinning shamelessly at him. 'If I'd wanted to shower with you, I'd have got in.'

He winked, beckoning her in, but she smirked, waved and continued walking. 'My friend's single,' she sing-songed flirtatiously at him as they passed, just a little too quietly to be heard.

'How can you do that?' Caitlin protested, deeply embarrassed. 'You're —'

'*I'm* not interested … really, I'm not,' Sarah said quite seriously. 'I'm trying to give you some pointers. Hey!' She yelled again, turning her smile up to full strength after catching another guy's eye. 'My friend is pretty and single.' He laughed and slowed down his run to a jog, then sped up once again after Cait gave him the glare of a thousand deaths, before turning away and glaring at Sarah. It was a super-grade death glare. The one she usually reserved for Kevin. 'Look, stop that,' she said.

'What for? Why don't you ask him out?' dared Sarah cheekily.

'Well, I don't know,' replied Caitlin sarcastically. 'Because my marriage unexpectedly ended a few weeks ago, my children are traumatised and due back home soon and I guess I'm just a bit old-fashioned. I take at least a month to get over my husband dumping me.'

Sarah frowned at her friend. 'He didn't actually dump you, you know,' she corrected her.

'Oh. What would you call it?' Cait muttered, fighting to keep the bitter edge out of her voice.

'Sarcasm is very low vibration, you know,' Sarah said reprovingly.

'Oh, low vibration is my natural state right now, Sarah. Add it up. My mother's moving in, too … and she and my best friend will have loads of fun watching me mope about Max and the Great Betrayal. Oh, the bitterness … now *that's* low vibration … oh God. I don't want to be a bitter old woman.'

'You're an angry young-ish woman. It's okay,' said Sarah, steering her back up the steep hill away from the beach and toward the car. 'What did you think you were going to do — move on like *that*?' she clicked her fingers. 'Anyway, you've only been horrible for two hours today. It was four last night. You're losing your touch.'

'Oh, I'm just faking it,' Caitlin protested, puffing as she forced herself faster up the hill. 'I *miss* him …' *puff*, 'and I hate him …' *puff*, 'at exactly the same time.' They reached the car and she stopped and leaned against it, exhausted. 'I want to rip his head off and eat it, and at the same time I want to have him home and, maybe, maybe see if I can forget any of this ever happened.' She pointed her keys at the car and they heard the *beep* that meant it was open.

'You can't,' said Sarah as they climbed in and strapped on their belts. 'You work with Kennedy, remember? She's having his baby.'

Caitlin indulged in a strong glare at her irritating friend, who giggled.

'Nobody else giggles when I give them that look,' she said, smiling. 'And of course I remember. It sucks. It's so embarrassingly soap-operatic. Everyone else *loves* it. I see her every day, and I have to be professional. I have to have another meeting with HR about my "bullying", which Kennedy will attend; all the kids on *Date Squad* are falling in love; my assistant, not content with bagging my husband, has stolen my show; and somehow my entire life has conspired to make me feel pathetic. Bitter seems a less *wimpy* option than pathetic. Every time I stop feeling furious I feel sick. At least I can stand up straight when I'm angry. I used to be happy. I feel like an alien who's taken over a perfectly good life and ruined it.'

'Er, last time I checked you were human. Unlike some of my clients. Seriously. Some really are from another planet.'

'Are you talking about Indigos or whatever they are again?' asked Caitlin, remembering their conversation at the bar. She'd been thinking about that sort of thing a lot — usually between two and four o'clock every morning. Questions like 'what did this all mean?' and 'if everything was meant to happen, what on earth was the cosmic plan behind being cheated on and bullied at work?' were also on high rotation in the wee small hours.

'Oh, noooo,' replied Sarah. 'Nothing as mainstream as Indigos. That would be too simple for my folk. Mine call themselves starpeople, aliens, illuminati ... all that.'

'Oh. I feel momentarily distracted from my heartbreak. Aliens?'

'Anyway,' said Sarah, repressing a laugh at the look on Caitlin's face, 'you're not an alien, or a starperson, you're a *person* person, and therefore this situation sucks, and it hurts. Cuts bleed, then they heal. You're still bleeding.'

'Oh. Again, I'm momentarily distracted. Thank you.'

'Pleasure,' smirked Sarah. 'Anyway. I won't let you get all mean and awful — but you are allowed supervised rants. You've got, oooh,' she paused, checking out the clock on the dashboard, 'five minutes more today —'

'Where are we going?' Cait asked herself, dismissing Sarah's Rant Rules out of hand. She pushed an address into her Sat-Nav, and backed her Beetle out of the carpark. 'We should be there just on five,' she said, with a glance at her watch.

'Yep,' said Sarah. 'It's not too far away. Not too far away from you, either — that will be good for the girls.' (Cait glared at her.) 'Well, you don't want them travelling ridiculous distances. It's best to make things simple, easy for now. For Sean, especially.'

'God, thanks for reminding me,' Cait said, turning down a crowded street, thick with slow-moving Saturday afternoon traffic. 'Oh no, I forgot. Bondi. Oh well, we'll just have to be a couple of minutes late.'

Ten minutes and plenty of traffic later, Cait turned the car into the garage of an apartment block in the kind of street that belonged anywhere sad and defeated people were looking to live.

'Oh God,' groaned Caitlin, taking in the dingy surrounds as they emerged from the Beetle. 'No trees. Stains. Concrete. No wonder they don't want to stay. No wonder he wants to come home.'

'Yeah,' said Sarah, looking at a flickering light on the dim stairs. 'It's sort of sad, isn't it?'

'It feels sort of unsafe, too,' Cait said, noticing broken windows and double-locked doors. They climbed up three flights of concrete steps, stopping on Max's floor. 'This is it, I think,' Cait said. 'Number twelve. Or it was before the "2" decided to fall off,' she said, nudging the brass numeral with her foot. She took a deep breath and knocked gingerly on the flimsy door.

Which opened.

'Mum!' Molly sang out, throwing herself out of the darkness into Cait's arms. Caitlin peered in. 'Hi, baby,' she said, hugging her tight. 'How are you?' She felt as though she hadn't held her little girl for a much longer time than the hours it had been.

'Mum?' said Molly. 'Can the baby have my old toys? I've started writing a list. I don't want the baby to think I don't love it just because it's only half.'

Cait flinched, eyes widening, searching. Who had told Molly? She forced her voice to be calm.

'Honey, sure you can get some toys for the baby,' she soothed, her eyes full of love. 'Sure you can. And of *course* you'll love the baby ... but we can talk about this in a minute. Let me get Sean.'

Where's Sean? And where's Max, she asked herself as she looked around, wondering if he'd left them there alone. She could hear the sound of low voices from down the corridor. 'Sean,' she called, edging her way further into the tiny apartment.

The voices grew louder.

She opened the next door, and saw Kennedy and Sean, locked in what seemed like a stand-off. Sean's eyes were flashing, Kennedy's arms were crossed, and both of their faces were flushed. Cait felt herself swallow, her shock followed by a white-hot surge of adrenaline. *What the fuck was Kennedy doing alone with her kids?*

'Hi, Mum,' said Sean, not taking her eyes off Kennedy. 'I'll get my bags.'

Cait nodded, and turned to face Kennedy, who was looking a little nervous. (As well she should.) Kennedy looked away; Cait stared, dumbfounded.

'What are you doing here?' Caitlin asked, her voice quiet. (She didn't want the children to hear its psychotic edge. Nor did she wish to remove the edge. Kennedy was with her kids. Game on.)

'Look, you're late. Max had to go, so —'

'He asked *you* to mind the kids,' Cait finished for her. She felt herself start to tremble. 'Did you just tell them you're having a baby?' she said dangerously.

'They had to find out. I thought they'd already know. It's a good thing, really, so I wanted to tell them in a way so they could be happy about it.'

'Come on, kids,' Cait said, a little louder, glaring at Kennedy. 'We're going. Are you out of your head?' she added in a whisper, disbelieving. 'What are you even doing here, Kennedy? Max said he wants it to be over. I don't think the kids want to see you. Why are you forcing yourself onto them, telling them about your good news, while their lives are in chaos? It's not up to you, to tell them that. How do you know you'll even have this baby?'

'I am having this baby, Caitlin. It's not a business decision — you get no say. And Max asked me to come here. To help with the kids. You're late, he needed to look at an apartment, and we —'

'We? What *we*? Are you thinking it's okay for you to be here with my kids? To tell them stuff that they shouldn't have to hear, or face ... to not even run it by me?'

'Run it by you? This isn't work! It's *my* baby. I don't have to get an embargo lifted by you! I already have a relationship with your kids. *And* Max and I talked about it!' Kennedy said, her voice ringing out through the empty apartment.

Cait backed away, fearful of her own anger. 'Tell Max, when he gets back from looking for apartments, that the kids won't be coming back. The kids are not to be with you. Not with you at all. Not alone, not with him. Not with you. Don't you dare talk to them again. You hear me?'

Without waiting for a response, she turned and left the room. So Max had asked Kennedy here. What else had he asked her? What else wasn't she aware of?

'You were fine with them being with me before,' Kennedy said, following her out of the dingy room.

'That was before I knew you were shagging my husband. God. What's with you? He doesn't want you! You're a mistake, Kennedy!'

'He does want me,' she said. 'He's out now, looking at a place big enough for all of us. And you're going to have to learn to live with it. He does care about me, Cait. He's spent enough time getting to know me,' she said, a note of triumph in her voice.

'You were supposed to be —'

'Your assistant? I know. There for you. I know it! Well, I'm not letting you push me out of my job, my relationship and being a mum just because it's not what an assistant of Caitlin Cooper does. I'm done being your Girl Friday. I've spent ages making sure your life works, Cait. Shopping. Meetings. Babysitting. And now you're pissed off that you asked me to get involved and I crossed the line. That's what happened. I was sorry. But you have no respect for me. Or for what I've done. For you, or for the show. Or for the kids. I think I can make this work with Max. And I'm not going to back off just so you stay happy.'

'You're supposed to be my friend.'

'On your terms, Cait. Doing everything for you. Well, I'm not any more. I'm out for me, and her, and Max, and for the kids now.'

'Her?' Cait said, feeling dazed. Had she really been such an enormous bitch? Such a selfish monster?

'Her,' Kenedy said. 'I'm having a little girl.'

'Oh. Max does seem to produce girls,' Caitlin said, faltering, feeling punch-drunk, shock replacing anger.

'The kids are in the car,' Sarah's gentle voice came up from behind her. 'Do you want to go?

'Yes,' she said, regaining some of her composure, and putting steel into her voice. 'Tell Max the kids won't be back here till where he lives, and who he's living with, is settled. With me.' Without another word, she turned, and walked out with Sarah.

'Tell him yourself. I'm not your assistant any more, remember?' Kennedy roared down the stairs after them. Neither turned, so it seemed right to slam the door so hard that its one remaining number swung free from its mooring and fell to the floor.

ELEVEN

By Monday morning, an idea that had been fermenting somewhere in the right frontal lobe of Caitlin's brain had decided to nudge its way into the left side of her brain, resulting in action. Rather than waking up at 3 a.m., and lying blankly for hours, as had been her new routine, she woke at 5 a.m., and reached for her laptop. Propped up in bed with toast and tea, she hammered out an outline with her strange two-fingered typing style, getting it all down. By 6 a.m. she had spoken with Gus about cameras, studio time and effects; by 7 a.m. Carol was looking into wardrobe; and by 8 a.m., she was still working, and feeling like her concept really had legs. She only stopped when a small, strawberry-coloured head appeared around her door.

'What are you doing, Mum?'

Caitlin moved over in bed, and propped up some pillows and cushions to make room for Molly, who clambered into bed with her, snuggled in close, then stuck her thumb in her mouth and started sucking noisily.

'Just some writing, baby,' Cait replied, ruffling Molly's drifty hair. 'You're up early.'

'Um, not really,' she murmured, sliding her sticky thumb way over to one corner of her mouth to squeeze the word out. 'I've been doing some work, too.'

Cait smiled. Molly was always one step ahead of her. 'So, how's your stuff going?'

'Good,' replied Molly, sitting up and leaning her head on her mum's shoulder. Caitlin adjusted her laptop, leaned into her daughter's warmth, and kept tapping.

'Mum?'

'Uh-hmm?'

'Can I have Weet-Bix?'

'Yes, honey. Do you want me to make it?'

'No, I'll make it,' she said, stretching her body up and out, fingertips reaching toward the ceiling. 'I think it's time to learn to be independent.'

'Oh.' Caitlin was listening, but she'd mastered the mother's art of paying attention and continuing with what she was doing. Molly was adorable, she thought. She always had a fresh thing to say. You couldn't script that stuff. Maybe, she thought to herself, there should be a kid in this program? Someone smart and innocent.

'Mum?'

'Yep?' She stopped tapping, and gave Molly all her attention.

'Are you writing another television show?'

'I think I might be …'

'Do you think I could? Why can't I write a television show?'

'Yeah, I think you can, honey.' She smiled, and not at all indulgently. Molly would. And why not?

'But ... would anyone take me seriously? 'Cos I'm only little.'

'You're not that little. But you are busy at school, and with being you. Maybe just be you for a while, then start working.'

'I am pretty busy,' Molly conceded. 'For example, I make my own Weet-Bix.'

Caitlin hugged her, and kissed the top of her head. Molly usually hated that, but she didn't want to stop her mum kissing her at the moment, even if it was annoying. Caitlin noticed and kissed her again, knowing that someday soon she'd be sick of it again. 'You're an amazing girl, Molly. You're a philosopher. You're very young, but you are insightful and honest and imaginative and creative. Plus you're hard working.'

'So, I can write a television show? Like you?'

'You can, only like *you*.'

'Oh.'

That's what Caitlin loved about her youngest daughter. She got it. Immediately. She trotted off to make her breakfast, then returned, scrambling into the bed, handing Caitlin the Weet-Bix to hold while she did so.

'Don't spill this on the laptop, honey. Sit up and eat it. And this is a one-off, okay?'

'So, what's this?' asked Molly, nodding at her mother's instructions. (She knew better than to spill anything on laptops. They had them at school.) She stared at the luminous screen of her mother's computer. '*Freak Squad*? What's *that* about?'

'It's just a working title, something to call it till it gets a proper name. Like a nickname.'

'Is this new? Or are you just being mean about *Date Squad*?'

'Yes, it is new — and it's really different from *Date Squad*. It's just an idea at this stage. I want to get it down while it's still fresh in my head. I almost can't talk about it till it's down. It's like the screen ... holds my thoughts for me. But this is how they all start,' she explained, hitting Spellcheck and letting the laptop do some work for a moment while she rubbed her temples.

'Oooh. Does the computer give you a headache? They do for me, at school. And here.' Molly's face looked serious, her eyes screwed up against the glare of the screen.

'That's because you don't have enough breaks. Your eyes need them. But I love doing this. It makes me so happy when I have ideas,' Caitlin said, smiling. 'I like this bit, 'cos I don't have to do much work — I just say yes or no.'

'Yeah. Spellcheck is cool,' Molly agreed companionably. 'Well. I might do that now too. Start my TV show, I mean. It has a working title, too.' Molly grabbed her Weet-Bix, sloshing it around, and backed out of the blanket cave she'd made for herself. 'See you soon,' she said over her shoulder, nearly bumping into a wall.

'Okay, honey,' Caitlin said, forcing herself not to warn her not to spill anything, or fall over. It was hard letting her go sometimes. Molly was like the ultimate antidepressant. Speaking of which, Caitlin said to herself. Time to make an appointment at the doctor's. She needed some help to get through this — she'd make an appointment later that day. Sort things out. Make sure she was all right.

Caitlin snuggled back into her pillows, and spent more time honing her outline. She'd had the laptop for over a year, but it had only just migrated from the office to the home office. She'd never had it in her bed before. I'm not sleeping alone, she thought. I have a friend.

This, she thought, reading over what she'd written since waking, was shaping up to be … really good. No one's done this yet. Supersleuths. Superspooks. *Backyard Blitz* with dead people. *Supernanny* for the supernatural …

She kept working, and although she did hear the clatter of the house in the morning, and Sarah laughing at Sean's mock-metal song, and she felt Sean come in and kiss her, and could have recalled, if pressed, that they had talked about band practice and a song, and that she'd promised to read the lyrics and work on them with her later that day, a whole lot more noise and clatter and dishes and laughter went by before the house grew silent, and Caitlin vaguely realised she was alone.

Caitlin came back from the otherworld of writing with a start. She'd been so completely into her work, she'd lost track of time. Her work trance. She felt a drizzle of guilt and a spurt of worry over the kids getting to school, but then a surge of wellbeing completely deluged those foes of feel-good. The work trance took her to another world, which was far more intriguing than the work that was checking ratings and having meetings and making sure she held her place on the tipsy ladder of success; the work that meant her attention span had to be narrowed down into three-second grabs to deal with the constant questions, adjustments, arrangements, budget worries and personal dramas.

This was what she loved. Hello you, she whispered to herself. You're back. I missed you. She gave herself a little hug.

She pushed her consciousness around the interior of her body, probing for pockets of pain. Tired? No. Headache? No. Sad beyond belief? Sad, yes, but somehow not desperately so. She felt her chest ... no pain. Touched her solar plexus. No rock. She swallowed. Her throat didn't feel like it wasn't worth the effort to make it past the pain of swallowing. She felt ... *better.*

She was still very sad, and kind of angry. But better. Definitely better.

She looked at her bedside clock. 9.30 a.m. She had the HR meeting at 10.30 a.m. She'd been writing since five. Time to go.

'Don't worry,' Sarah called out, hearing movement. 'I've taken them in.'

Cait again felt momentarily guilty. What was happening to her? 'They'll forget who I am, Sarah,' she said, mildly irritated. (She was actually annoyed at herself, but it came out sounding like she thought it was Sarah who was doing something wrong. And she's not, she affirmed to herself. She's been an angel.)

'Nope. They won't.' Caitlin looked at her friend, who'd appeared in the doorway. She didn't look upset. Actually, Sarah was looking very pretty at the moment.

Flushed and happy. Falling-in-love pretty. It's a certain kind of look that no tube of space-technology cream could ever even get close to replicating. The look women get when they're feeling their heart come alive again. When they're having lots of sex. Except she wasn't at home. And she clearly wasn't having sex here, thought Caitlin. So why's she so happy? Maybe it's not a why. Maybe there's a *who*, she thought to herself. Just because Sarah was so quiet about her love life didn't mean she didn't have one. She knew that. But this seemed a little more … intense than usual. She shook her head, uprooted the distraction, and brought her wayward mind back to the present.

'You look terrible,' Sarah said.

'Ouch,' replied Caitlin faintly, heading to the shower, and continuing to talk to Sarah over the sound of running water. (They had, after all, known each other since they were seven.)

'You need to rest,' Sarah murmured to herself, waiting for her friend to come out.

Caitlin, long disciplined at the speed-shower, came out of the bathroom already in her underwear, looking refreshed, and finished drying off.

'And those have seen way better days,' commented Sarah, looking at Caitlin's knickers.

'What? Oh, the underwear. I thought you meant me, for a horrible moment!'

'No, I meant those,' said Sarah, reaching over and twanging the elastic of Cait's knickers. 'Eew. They're almost a disgrace. We should definitely take you shopping,' she said thoughtfully.

'Not now, Sarah. I have a meeting to go to. Besides, who's going to see them?'

'Well, I will, for one. And your children. What sort of mentor are you for your daughters if you wander about in awful knickers, just because you're sleeping on your own for the moment?' Sarah said, being deliberately provocative. She knew Cait needed to fire up. This meeting needed a certain level of energy. And her friend flopping about in grey knickers with seen-better-days elastic just wasn't going to cut it.

'Here,' she said, passing Cait some boots. 'Wear these. You need the energy and sass of red.'

Caitlin grinned, loving her friend's attention, and obeyed, pulling on her crimson suede boots, while Sarah reached into her closet and pulled out a scarlet lightweight pullover and a pair of red velvet pants, and handed them to Caitlin, who, despite feeling loved-up by Sarah, was still anxious about her meeting.

'Hey,' continued Sarah, 'you're dressed from the shoes up. And you look hot. Except for those underpants. Interesting. Red suits you — funny how it doesn't clash with your hair if you have the right tone. You need cherry lipstick now.'

'Thank you,' said Caitlin, turning to the mirror and running her fingers through her hair. 'What about the kids — what did they say?'

'Oh. Anyway, Sean hated the apartment. Molly's more ambivalent. Sean's way more upset — Cait, you know Kennedy had kind of befriended her. Older sister thing, so now she feels doubly betrayed.'

Caitlin gaped at Sarah. 'What did she say?'

Sarah sighed. 'Sean told me some kids had asked her about her new sister. I just didn't know what to say.'

'I really need to talk to Sean. Myself,' Cait said pointedly, and stalked out of the room. She grabbed her notes from the printer in the office, shoved them into a folder and into her handbag. She returned to the bedroom, where Sarah was sitting, looking a little forlorn.

'I really wish I'd asked you to help me out when things got tough here. But Kennedy offered and ...' she paused, groping for the right words. 'And it's done,' she finished with a heartbreakingly indifferent shrug.

Sarah leaned forward, catching her eye. 'You did kind of ask me, Cait, and I kind of felt too busy. As I remember it, I kind of made excuses. And I feel really bad about that now, because if I had been there for you then, instead of overcompensating now, maybe none of this would have happened.'

'At least you never worked so hard your marriage broke up,' Cait said mournfully.

'Oh! I've only worked so hard I've neglected *any* relationships. Nope. Just like you wonder if you're being a bad mother, I feel bad because if I'd been a better friend then, this wouldn't have happened.'

'Well, if we're really honest, none of this would have happened if my husband had remembered he was my husband, and if Kennedy had remembered he was off limits. Anyway. It's done, like you said. And now I don't have any idea what's going on in my own family because I've got you doing most of the work.'

Sarah winced, and Cait turned to her, catching her

up in a huge hug. 'Sarah, I'm sorry. That just sounded bitchy. I'm grateful, so grateful you're here. I'm just … tired of being grateful. I wish I could do this for myself. I'm supposed to be able to do this for myself, goddamnit! You're telling me about how my kids are, and how they're feeling, and I *knew* they were feeling that way, but I wasn't paying attention, and I have this meeting, and now I just feel guilty.'

'Come on. Let's get going. Besides, you should know all about Superwoman syndrome. Perfect mother, perfect friend, perfect executive, blah blah blah. Most people mess up in at least one category, so they try to overcompensate in other areas — you know, they give up sex and start working on their career, way harder, getting off on it.'

'I didn't give up sex, though. I was still having sex with my husband, apparently while he was having sex with someone else, because I was substituting even more sex with work. That's just so wrong!'

'I know. But now you get to think about balance, just a little bit. I'm here. Your mother will be here. The kids will be here. We'll work it out together. Don't even worry about it. You get to slack off for a bit. Besides, I like being here.'

'I do feel guilty, though. Maybe I need therapy. God, don't tell my mother I said that.'

'There're books about this at the centre …'

'Look, speaking of your work … Can you do me a favour?' Sarah raised an eyebrow in response. 'Okay. Another one?' Caitlin amended, her lush lips twisted ever so slightly in apology.

Sarah giggled. 'I'm not counting, really. So it's a definite maybe.'

'Okay then. I need five different girls, with different powers — do you know what I mean?'

'Er, I think I know what you mean. Are you researching *Charmed Again* or something? I didn't think you did scripted programming.'

'I don't — it's definitely not fiction … It's an idea for a non-scripted drama, more documentary style than *Date Squad*. But still reality.'

She pulled her over to where the laptop was perched on the bedside table, scrolling through the notes on the screen. Sarah squinted, reading. 'Oh. I see. You're still substituting work for sex,' she grinned.

'No, because there is no sex now. So I'm being productive. But what do you think?'

'I think you want to do a show because your marriage has broken up.'

'Maybe. But it's definitely a new show. Reality TV about … unreality. Or, the other reality. Maybe we could call it alternative reality TV.'

'Hang on, hold that thought. I need to worship the Goddess Caffeinea — want to offer a libation to her?'

When Sarah came back to the bedroom with two steaming *cafés au lait* in huge mugs, Caitlin had her lipstick on, her notes open and references on screen.

'Look, I need — I think — a witch, a ghost hunter, a medium, someone who does something else and someone who does something else. Real people. No, you know, loopers or woo-woos.'

'Well. Can they be woo-woo and sane? If so, I can definitely get some candidates together.'

'They exist? You're not making it up? There are woos who don't just talk drivel?'

'No, they do exist,' explained Sarah patiently, despite feeling slightly offended. (She was a woo herself.) 'There are a lot of people out there who are having a fun fantasy time of it. But there are good people in this industry who are serious, and smart — and who are funny too. It's not the easiest gift for people to live with. It takes someone pretty stable to be able to handle it well. I try to employ those people, and those people only. Satisfied?'

Caitlin nodded. 'What do you think I need? I have a witch down as a must, a medium person, and the ghost hunter, then I got stuck. What else is there?'

Sarah thought quickly, a tiny frown on her face. 'You need a ... how about an animal communicator? Or an oracle. You know, someone who can see into the future. Maybe someone who can orb — you know: shapeshift and visit other places, come back and report on them.'

At the mention of orbs, an image of giant breasts streaming light pushed into Caitlin's mind. She moved the fake breasts along, grinning to herself. 'And what's an animal communicator — someone who talks to dead pets? And a time-traveller? There are actual humans who do this stuff? Or who *think* they do?'

'Look, rather than me talking you through a crash course in metaphysics, why don't you just come in — like you've been promising to do for the last five years?'

'I got busy! Anyway, can I can bring a camera ... do a reccie? This could be exciting. Oooh,' she cried, sliding a scarlet sleeve up her slim arm and holding out her wrist to Sarah. 'Feel this,' she ordered.

'What's *this*?' asked Sarah, puzzled.

'It's my *pulse*,' Caitlin replied, delighted. Sarah still looked puzzled. 'It's beating again,' she explained, triumphant.

Sarah giggled, then stopped short. 'I have a better idea. There's a weekend retreat thing taking place soon. Wild Women's Weekend. There's going to be lots of things to shoot — it's at the full moon, and the location is gorgeous.'

Cait's eyes widened with excitement. 'That sounds perfect.'

'Now, I don't want to be a buzz-kill, but you remember you have your HR meeting today, don't you? Have you prepared?'

'Oh yes. Kennedy, today's the day the teddy bears have their picnic.'

Caitlin ran off to the car before Sarah could attempt to escort her in to the station, asking her instead to get busy with background into *Freak Squad*. She knew that Sarah would want to drive her in, but it was time to be strong, she decided. Sitting there being helpless had been nice. It was too easy, though, to stay in shock if she didn't have to make herself actually *do* anything.

Starting with driving her own car to work.

She backed the yellow VW out of the garage, and headed to the office, ready for war, armed with the caffeine singing through her veins and the confidence a new idea always gave her.

Twenty minutes later she pulled into her car-space, and made her way straight to HR after a quick stop in the Ladies to make sure her lipstick was on her actual mouth. I will not, she thought, face Kennedy with lipstick on my teeth. I already have egg on my face.

'Come in, er, Caitlin,' panted Geoffrey of HR, who was hovering outside his office. 'Kennedy is already here, inside,' he said by way of explanation. Caitlin looked over at her nemesis coolly.

'Good morning,' she said to Kennedy.

'Caitlin,' nodded Kennedy.

Geoffrey looked like he'd rather be mauled by a shark than enter the room with the creatrices of their spicy station's most infamous scandal to date. He was scared. And that took some doing. He'd mediated many a bust-up, but to date none of them had erupted from Caitlin's department. That era, he thought sadly to himself, is over.

Caitlin was late. And he was puffing. And he was sweating. And he'd been instructed to make this work out. By Kevin, no less. Their boss wanted both women to stay. Personally, he didn't know why they just didn't send him in to single-handedly bring about world peace, at least. Apart from being the talk of the station, this situation was untenable, defunct, impossible and any other number of adjectives meaning *completely dead in the water*. Within minutes, there'd be a stolen-husband-induced rage and he'd be mediating what was destined to be a Channel Five HR classic.

But here he was. Such, he'd said to his wife that morning, is life at the station. She'd hugged him, pinched his puffy bottom and waved him farewell. To her, Geoffrey was a white knight, a diplomat of the corporate peace corps.

Kennedy swivelled impatiently to and fro in her chair, avoiding Cait's green eyes directly, but stealing little glances sharp as daggers at her former friend. What's that look? Caitlin wondered, catching a hint of a frosty blue glare. She took a deep breath in and held it a second before letting it out. This wasn't going to be easy.

Get ready, Caitlin thought, coaching herself like a prize-fighter about to slug out a title bout. Look at that hatred pouring out of her. First punch flying soon. Let her wear herself out. Then go in. Hard.

Cait's mouth made no smile-like movements. Her eyes were steady. If she'd had guns at her hip, her hands would have been itching to draw.

'So,' stammered Geoffrey, flinching at the shards of fury in the air, and mopping his prematurely steaming forehead. 'We're here to resolve, or to work at resolving, the issues that have arisen between the two of you of late. It's my job to let you know that the company would prefer to have this matter worked out and for both of you to know how valued you are. There is a process here that we adhere to that respects all participants. Take a moment to read this over,' he said, handing both women a form outlining the regulations regarding disputes. Both glanced over it, and then their eyes went back to him.

'Right. As you know, the company has a duty of care, and as such, must investigate all matters such as these in order to protect the staff's wellbeing. This dispute,' he said, a little primly, 'has ramifications for all the staff, particularly those people you both work directly with.'

Caitlin looked at Kennedy. Kennedy looked at Geoffrey. Neither said a thing.

'Er. Well. Kennedy King, as you brought the matter to our attention, perhaps you'd like to outline your complaint?'

Geoffrey, he instructed himself, seeing Caitlin bristle at the word *complaint*, get ready to duck and weave.

'Well,' Kennedy began with a gusty breath. 'Caitlin has been very erratic and most unprofessional — wanting me to do everything concerned with the launch of *Date Squad*, from taking care of her children to running meetings for her — neither of which is in my job description.

'The casting process for this show was very difficult,' Kennedy continued, her voice hinting at unimaginable horrors. 'She wasn't sure what she wanted. Day in, day out, changes ...' she looked at both Caitlin and Geoffrey, half expecting someone to stop her.

Caitlin said nothing, just tilted her head slightly to show she was still listening. 'Unfair and deliberately obstructive ...' continued Kennedy.

La la la, thought Caitlin.

'On a whim ... no planning ...'

Blah blah blah, thought Caitlin, beginning to feel her temper being tweaked.

'Dangerously close to deadline ...'

Now that is a load of shit, Caitlin objected to herself, reddening. She watched Kennedy talk and talk and wondered why she hadn't just come to her, said, 'I love your husband' and quit?

'And then she disappeared for two weeks after the show launched!'

Geoffrey was desperately finding the right point to interject and wind Kennedy up, but an appropriate gap in her tirade just wasn't appearing. So Caitlin gave him a prod with her foot under the table.

'Ow!' Geoffrey exclaimed, glancing at Caitlin.

'Yes, Geoffrey,' said Kennedy, taking his yelp as some kind of agreement. 'Now, *I* can be professional. But my concern is that Caitlin will let the team down, badly, and then I will be the one who is … held responsible. No credit for the show's great success, but all responsibility if it fails.'

Kennedy's monologue finally faltered, and she looked at Caitlin. She *was* on edge, observed Cait, she's not faking that. She *does* resent me. Not faking that either. Caitlin pondered their history. Secret signs. Laughter. Teamwork. And she knew she hadn't made any mistake other than to work too hard, neglect her family, and trust Kennedy King way too much.

Caitlin tuned back in to find Geoffrey noisily fiddling with some paperwork. 'In your original, er, complaint, you mention, um, bullying. Could you clarify what you mean by that, please, Kennedy?'

'Taking credit for jobs I've done. Telling me how to do things. Stopping me on one job before I start on another. Assuming authority.'

Caitlin shot Geoffrey a look.

'Thank you, er, Kennedy. Caitlin? What would you like to say?'

Caitlin bit back her panic, and waded in. 'Well. I think I need to outline the facts from my perspective in order for Geoffrey to have a balanced view.' She took a deep breath, avoiding the death glare issuing from Kennedy's eyes.

'So. Kennedy and I worked together on this project from the beginning. And projects take shape over time — it's an organic process. Experience has shown me that you can't force a show, though you can be organised and meet deadlines. We did all that. I regularly told you that you'd done a superb job, Kennedy, and I recognised that publicly by seeking a pay rise for you. My e-mails will show the praise you received from me. It's true that I assumed authority as, being executive producer, I am in authority. And we did a very good job together. Kennedy regularly said that she was happy to pick up my children and take them home. She volunteered for such extraneous tasks, in fact.'

She paused. Kennedy was gathering herself up, ready to launch her defence. 'And *that's*,' Caitlin said, raising her hand to stop Kennedy's take-off, 'where I really did make a huge error. Because you started sleeping with my husband, and you're now pregnant to him.'

Kennedy sprang up like she'd been stung by an especially large wasp. 'I don't have to listen to this,' she cried, arms out to Geoffrey, who looked mortified at the inevitable turn of events. 'This is *personal*,' Kennedy said, appealing to Geoffrey.

'She's right, Caitlin,' Geoffrey said in a voice squeaky with anxiety.

'Well, obviously it's *personal*,' Caitlin snapped impatiently. 'This whole business is obviously a tactical move by Kennedy, and a clever one too, to negate any complaints arising as a result of *her* unprofessional behaviour.' She nodded her head at Kennedy. 'Very smart, too.' Kennedy almost smiled for a second, then stopped herself.

'Caitlin, five minutes. Outside,' Geoffrey pleaded.

'Please,' he said to her in the hall, running his hands through what remained of his hair and going very pink. 'I know you're in the right. Just let her have her say, ramble on, let me listen, you just need to look like you're listening, you agree to hold more meetings, and then the symbolic gesture is over.' He moved closer, and his voice dropped to a desperate whisper. 'Look. Just apologise for bullying. Everyone does it. Then the whole thing will blow over.'

Caitlin knew what Geoffrey really wanted was Kevin back onside — rumour had it he was furious at the matter having gone this far already. Well, tough, thought Caitlin, lifting her chin just a little. This was no jelly-wrestle over wages and entitlements. She sighed, wondering what her next move should be, and decided to play along. For the moment. For a very brief moment.

'No worries, Geoffrey. I get it,' she said, conciliatory. They re-entered the room, and she sat down. Geoffrey, meanwhile, hovered.

Kennedy went to open her mouth, but Caitlin stepped in first.

'I can't apologise,' she said quietly. 'We both know I've done nothing wrong. So, I'll need to get further advice. For now, Kennedy, we work together. We keep running the show. But I won't admit to bullying. And I won't say sorry. And I know one day, *you'll* apologise to *me*.'

Kennedy looked like pleasure and suspicion were staging an internal war, both emotions struggling to win. Her face morphed between the two options, before settling on suspicion.

'You say you'll work properly with me, but you won't be able to.'

'Maybe you're right,' Caitlin said. 'Geoffrey?'

'She doesn't mean a word of it,' Kennedy said.

'As a sign of good faith, I'll start with handing over meetings to you. From now.'

'Now?' Kennedy hesitated, suspicion still evident on her face.

Geoffrey, sensing a collapse into chaos, leaped into the breach.

'Let's wrap this up for today. I'll be in contact.'

'We'll need to have another meeting. This isn't finished,' Kennedy said.

They packed up, Geoffrey looking like he couldn't wait for them to leave so he could slump over the desk. He needed a holiday. Badly. Shame he'd just had one.

Caitlin and Kennedy walked out together. Caitlin headed straight for the stairs, but was stopped by a firm tap on her shoulder. She turned to see Kennedy looking at her strangely. She suppressed the urge to tell her to never, ever touch her again.

'Caitlin. About Max … I never meant for it to …'

Caitlin went pale, and looked away. 'Not now,' she warned, moving away.

'Okay. But let me tell you this. I'm not going to lose everything,' Kennedy said defensively, her resentment staging a comeback on her face. 'My job. I need to protect myself,' she said, her hand moving unconsciously to her belly.

'Well, you've done very well. Nice work,' Caitlin said coldly, before walking away.

TWELVE

Twenty minutes later, Linda was perched, purse-lipped, right on the edge (if there is such a thing) of her steel-grey exercise ball. Each and every one of her shoulder-length and carefully frosted Nordic blonde hairs was bristling — Caitlin hadn't even made an appointment. Now she (Caitlin) was just marching up and down, practically harassing her, until, she supposed, she (Linda) broke down and gave in to her request to see their boss — instantly. It was like she just *expected* to be able to see the CEO. Just. Like. That. Well, she'd make this more difficult than Caitlin expected — even if she was the executive producer of the station's latest hit program. She knew there was talk of bullying going on — no wonder she was having marital problems, Linda thought smugly, continuing her satisfying little bitch to herself.

(Satisfying little bitches are the thing that keeps many a corporation from collapse. They provide a much-needed safety release valve, reducing pressure and making work actually viable, even when personal relationships have reached levels of hostility that would see nations declare war. Forget the office gym. Install a bitching room with a confessor and absolution in every corporate building, and productivity would really start to climb.)

However, right then, Linda's self-bitching wasn't changing the fact that Caitlin was striding up and down the deskfront, looking very determined. What's more, she didn't seem to be taking the hint to make an appointment, go away and come back later — when her boss decided *he'd* see *her*. ('He is a very busy man, Caitlin. He doesn't just have meetings because *you* want them,' she'd sniped. Linda's hints were rarely subtle.)

This, she thought primly, watching Caitlin pace back and forth in front of her, was too much for an executive personal assistant to take.

Finally, the suspense broke. Linda's phone rang, and in the time she was distracted by answering, Caitlin slipped by and casually sauntered into Kevin's office. She had business to wrap up. She'd face Linda's wrath later. (Linda almost put the phone down on a Very Important Politician, so great was said wrath.)

Meanwhile, the object of Linda's wrath was already inside Kevin's office, giving a distracted and faintly bored Kevin the PG-rated rundown of the HR meeting.

'So, it's all sorted out, then?' Kevin asked, assuming that her smile meant she'd backed down and apologised. He felt a surge of wellbeing flood his large body. He'd known, he told himself smugly, that it would just take an apology to calm this whole bitchfight down. He smiled to himself. He'd have to take that Geoffrey out to lunch. One day. Next year, he thought, feeling like a true Man of the People.

She nodded, and sat down on one of his designer chairs that no one ever actually sat down on. 'Just a few loose ends to sort out, then it's done,' she said easily.

Kevin relaxed, feeling secure that his show was back on track.

What I didn't get, Caitlin thought, seeing his eyes glaze over at the thought of details to iron out, is that I didn't do anything. And yet it's still a giant cock-up. Think, Caitlin, think. How can this start to work for me. How?

'You may have noticed I've been ...' Caitlin struggled to come up with the right words. My life's been nuked, she thought. But I have to sound professional about it.

'Down for the count?' offered Kevin sympathetically, leaning forward and grasping his meaty hands together.

She nodded, ever so slightly, her mind preoccupied with the desperate search for the right strategy under the circumstances. She kept wavering between options. Stall, and sabotage Kennedy? Swallow her pride, apologise for being a bully and keep working? Take legal action, and never work at this or any other station again? Get Kevin so angry he fired her? Think, she told herself, knowing there had to be a better option. Sabotage, lie, or give up her career? There has to be a way for this to work for me. I have an idea for a new show. I have a track record. He needs me to run *Date Squad* ... And just like that, the sequence of thoughts suddenly lit a match under the fire that was Caitlin's solution. Astounded at its simplicity, she moved deeper into her chair, and in perfect clarity, the approach unfolded. She sat back, a little stunned, ready to talk it out with Kevin.

Who was still inappropriately musing on her misfortune. 'Yes, I'd say you've let the team down ... word has it you've been missing in action!' he added jovially.

She raised an eyebrow and tilted her head. Kevin didn't notice that she'd gone ever-so-slightly icy on him.

'But you and I both know you've been hit and nearly hospitalised,' he went on, trying not to laugh out loud at his own joke.

Finished yet? Caitlin wondered, beginning to feel twitchy.

But he wasn't.

'Skinned and left out to dry — Lord knows I'—'

Caitlin noisily cleared her throat, cutting Kevin off, causing him to send a warning glance her way. Nah, he thought. She's not interrupting me. She wouldn't. She's probably, he thought, feeling alarmed, getting a cold. He promptly sat back up in his chair, pulling away. Don't want to get sick, he thought, leaning away. Playing golf.

All right, you can shut up now, she thought, knowing she was beginning to look pissed off. Max had always said everyone knew exactly what she was thinking. Her features were too mobile, flickering and shifting with every thought, each emotion. No secrets in her eyes, no lies on her lips. Stop thinking about Max, and anything he might have said, she ordered herself, trying to arrange her features into something more neutral — she couldn't rely on Kevin not paying attention forever. He's a bastard. Keep your mind on the job.

But Kevin hadn't started paying attention to Cait's face, or any expressions on it, yet. He had not yet reached the finale of his speech, so was still very much in the moment. He was at the part of his talk where he dispensed wise advice in an avuncular style. (He loved that bit. It made him realise all over again what a wonderful human being he was. And you know, he wasn't that bad. It's just that he was not actually paying much attention to the person he was saying these things to. He never did.)

'Look, I —' started Caitlin, knowing he was getting the wrong idea and wanting to interrupt him. She wasn't about to apologise, not even if he did give her his famous great forgiveness speech.

'Mate,' he said, leaning forward again (but not too far, in case he got sick) and giving her his compassionate, warm, caring look, the one he used on all staff who'd taken their eyes off the company ball, but who he wanted to keep in the empire. Oh no, thought Caitlin, feeling the approach of the inevitable, and actually beginning to feel embarrassed for Kevin. He's going to do it. Not the speech! He's thinks he's going to forgive me. For going *on leave*!

'I *know* that it won't happen again,' he said, somehow simultaneously implying that it had better bloody not happen again, and that he was a prince of a guy for understanding exactly what she'd been going through.

'We all have our … moments; times when we go off the rails. But you're a pro,' he added, sitting back, pleased with himself. 'You're back on track. And I'm glad to have you back.'

Works every time, he thought. They love you when you've shown them kindness. Especially after they've been such fuck-ups. He glanced at Caitlin, awaiting her thanks, apologies, gratitude and departure. He had a golf game to get on with. He looked, a little pointedly, at his watch. Tee-off in half an hour.

He looked expectantly at Cait. No response. A pause, by the looks of it. Nothing. Bit of an embarrassed silence, come to think of it. And why did she have that funny expression on her face? He felt slightly annoyed. She wasn't saying anything. She knew this script! Why wasn't she getting out of his office? And why was she actually, well, actually looking a bit … pissed off?

(Because she was.)

Bloody Kev, she thought. He just doesn't get it. Caitlin cleared her throat again, and shifted uneasily. 'Right. Well.'

What now? he thought. Shouldn't she just piss off back to work now? I've taken the meeting, I've forgiven her and she hasn't even said thank you. Shouldn't she just get on with it? Women, he thought, exasperated, always wanted time. And talking. Same thing said twenty different ways, when he could have been getting on with —

'Actually, I was going to say that I have an idea.'

— golf. Did say she had an idea?

'A great idea. If we get to it now we can launch it at Halloween, last day of October. It's so great. It's everything you've been saying you want. Brilliant TV. Different. Fresh. And cheap as chips.'

He shifted in his seat. Experience had taught him not to ignore Caitlin's ideas, but he was more than a bit over her at the present moment. Plus, his clubs were calling. 'Mate,' he said slowly, carefully, a little like he was talking to a criminally insane person wearing a vestful of live explosives, 'we've just launched a program — it's exhausting. Ha! I'm exhausted. You're exhausted! Surely we should see how *Date Squad* builds, then look at next year for —'

'Kevin, excuse me, but no. It can't wait.' Caitlin was firm. She met his puzzled eyes, hers strong and clear. 'This is the time to be aggressive. To take out the opposition. We have to build those numbers and completely stake our claim to this audience that we've dragged kicking and screaming over from the other stations, and we have to give them reasons to stay, and that means shows that follow up. We can't slack off,' she finished passionately.

He thought for a second, feeling defensive. He hated enthusiastic staff when he was ready to take it easy for at least five minutes and have just one lousy game of golf. And slacking off? Was she saying he was slacking off? After he'd forgiven her? He decided to do the benevolent thing again, see if she'd take the hint and shut up, and really go away this time.

'When our lives go to shit, Caitlin, it's natural to try and keep busy. But surely you should take it easy. Relatively speaking. You've done the right thing, apologised, even though both of us know there's so much more to that story. Just, you know, concentrate on getting through the next six weeks, then we'll talk about it.'

'I didn't say sorry, Kevin. And I won't be saying sorry.'

'What?' He went pale under his beefiness. 'You said everything went well,' he said, suspicion flaring. What was she playing at?

'I didn't actually say what went well — and I mentioned there were details to be ironed out.'

'The first detail is: Say. Sorry.'

'For?'

'For, well, picking on your staff,' he said, feeling nasty.

Caitlin gave him a disbelieving look. 'No. That has never happened,' she said, shaking her head. Stubborn bitch, he thought, almost admiringly, beginning to feel curious. She did always have fantastic ideas. Station-savers, he'd called them once in a meeting. Boy, did he regret letting her know that. Now she thought she could run the whole show.

'Saying sorry isn't going to happen. Because I'm not going to lie about my life. And we both know Kennedy and me working together is not going to happen either.'

'Sure you're not just spoiling for a fight?' he smiled, struggling to keep it friendly, get it back on buddy terms. She shook her head, adamant. 'Okay,' he said indulgently. 'So. *No* apology. The fight continues — the show suffers — all because your pride's been hurt,' he said, managing to imply she was being petty, unprofessional and irresponsible. 'I thought,' he actually said, 'you were bigger than that.'

'Not big enough to lie for you, Kevin. My life's been totally skewered, she's taken my reputation to town with this complaint, and you've tried to force my hand into apologising for something I have not done, so as to avoid what is, basically, an annoying interruption to the show's potential success. You've gone along with the idea of me apologising, because you think it's the clever way out.'

'Steady on — I have no idea what's happened between the two of you, but —'

'Yes, you do,' she said, raising her voice. 'The whole thing's a crock, Kevin,' she said, crossing her arms and looking about as disgusted as she could. 'I'm disappointed in you.' Oh my God, she thought, mentally slapping her hands over her mouth. Now I've totally blown it.

He bristled, mouth agape.

'So. Now that I've said my piece, I'd like you to consider a solution. It's a good one,' she said, with enough edge to demand attention — and a smile. She knew how to dangle the bait with Kevin, and was hoping like hell he'd bite.

He sat back, fury fighting it out with curiosity. He looked offended, she noticed, but he hadn't thrown her out. Yet.

'You're going to hire me as a contractor. Then I'm going to sell you a fantastic, brand-new idea that's a television first.' Slight exaggeration, she knew. But she had to hit Kevin hard.

And it appeared she had, if his change from fury to fascination was any indication.

He looked shocked. She grinned, feeling a surge of confidence. This might just work. It wasn't every day that Kevin got a shock.

'Kevin, listen,' she said, leaning forward, sensing she had him. 'I resign. You keep me in charge of *Date Squad* as a freelancer, and you get my new pitches first, every one, every time, and we minimise all the politics.'

'You can't resign,' he said, wishing he had her contract handy so he could wave it in her face. 'You can't resign during the start of a series. Your contract doesn't let you.' He could feel his face reddening, and tried to breathe slowly.

'We can look at my contract if you like. I have it here,' she said, pulling it out.

'Smart-arse,' he said, this time warming to her game. She nodded, accepting the compliment.

(Insults work differently in television. 'Smart-arse' is a television compliment that loosely translates as 'you genius'.)

'If we do it your way, Kevin, the way it says on the contract, I give it five days before Kennedy's back in here with an "I can't work with her" ultimatum — so my contract might as well be ripped up anyway. That will happen if I apologise, *or* if I don't.' She shoved her contract back in her bag. 'You know that if I stay here, I'll spend more time in HR than working. So will Kennedy. Result? The show will suffer and the staff will follow suit and there'll be an explosion of time-wasting and politics and ... bitching ... Advertisers, Kevin, won't want a piece of this show if that happens. Then families will get wind — and there goes the audience.'

Kevin grimaced, feeling somewhat sick. He hated having to confront problems, especially the problems he hired other people, like Caitlin, to solve.

'But if you don't like that option,' added Caitlin, 'I have another suggestion.'

'This had better be good,' he guffawed, feeling slightly relieved, and deciding to pick up his coffee even if it did raise his heartbeat. Screw the doctors!

'Well, I've told you I won't apologise. I think, technically, you can sack me,' she said quietly. 'For refusing to cooperate with the investigation.'

Kevin choked, spluttered coffee, much of which hit his shirt, and started laughing.

'What? I don't *want* to fire you.'

'But that's the *beauty* of it, Kevin. You can sack me, and hire me back as a contractor. If there's a big enough payout I may not even sue,' she said, half joking.

'Caitlin, that's — bloody hell,' he said, looking at his shirt. 'Look what you've done. I've got meetings this afternoon. And you know if you sue, TV's off limits for you for the rest of this lifetime.'

'Get Linda to bring you in another shirt,' she said soothingly. 'Kevin, listen. It's brilliant. I can resign, or you can sack me. And I'll set up a satellite office. This way, you have me working for you — you've got me, *and* you keep Kennedy, for now,' she said, unable to resist reminding him. She knew how much paid maternity leave grated on Kevin. 'I have input on *Date Squad* by feeding suggestions direct to you, and you instruct Kennedy. Problem solved.'

'You're dreaming if you think I'll sack you —'

Caitlin hadn't actually thought he'd go for that option at all. For starters, there'd be fallout in the form of publicity. Plus he'd have to pay her a whole lot more to go, and even more than that to go quietly.

'So, you accept my resignation?'

He hesitated, shaking his head. 'Why can't you just apol—'

'Because I just won't,' Caitlin interrupted, losing patience. 'Because it's not a solution. This way works for everyone. Especially you. Come on, mate,' she said, holding her breath.

'Give it to me,' he said, frustrated, holding out a hand for the resignation letter he knew she'd have ready. Women! She reached into her handbag and extracted a small, neat envelope, which she handed to him. 'I'll let Linda know she's to set up a meeting this time next week for the pitch. But not here. Best to keep it all under wraps.'

'Okay,' he said, getting up to see her out, rubbing his head, slightly dazed. 'Don't try and outsmart yourself.'

'I won't. I'll make this *so* worth your while,' she said.

'Linda,' he bellowed, his voice so full of rage that his assistant's carefully balanced behind nearly rocketed off the surface of the fitness ball. 'Get in here.'

Caitlin went to HR, revisited Geoffrey (who didn't look at all thrilled to see her), did the paperwork, and went to brief Kennedy.

'I'll make the announcement,' she said to her reassuringly, after Kennedy's face had slackened with disbelief. 'I can see you're a bit shocked.'

She went right to the centre of the *Date Squad* office, where producers were manning phones, watching tapes of prospective talent, researching and having massive bitch sessions about other staff members.

About twenty people gathered around her. She propped herself on a desk, and called out to the rest of the show's staff, all of whom were on calls, or gathered around whiteboards, plotting logistics of shoots and castings. They abandoned their tasks and joined the producers.

'Kennedy?' she shouted over her shoulder. 'A minute, please. It's important you're here.'

Everyone looked at her expectantly. She gazed around at the team she'd hand-picked, from Gus, who could sense whether someone was TV-worthy the moment he heard their voice, to Carol, who could sweet-talk talent into doing practically anything on screen, including falling in love.

They were good. Very good. But it was time to go.

Caitlin saw Kennedy approach from the corner of her eye, and took a breath. 'Well. Thanks for your time. I would like to thank you all for your amazing work on getting *Date Squad* up, running and into the top ten. That's a huge feat. We've managed to make the station a lot of money, rate very well, and give Channel Five a fresh new face for their programming, proving we're definitely staging a resurgence. I'm so proud of us all.'

Kennedy leaned back, eyes narrowed, arms crossed, possibly fighting off morning sickness.

'Anyway. As you all know, I like to create programs, set them up, then move on with new ideas.' Caitlin took a deep breath, and let it out slowly.

'I'd like to announce that after thinking very carefully about it over these last two weeks of unexpected leave, that I have decided to leave *Date Squad*, and resign from

Channel Five, effective immediately. I can't — in fact I *won't* — tell you of my plans. But they're very exciting, and I'm thrilled to be leaving. Sorry,' she grinned, as a simultaneous group ripple of laughter and moans of complaint went out round the room. Kennedy frowned even harder, looking viler than even the most truly horrible morning sickness could really account for. 'I do know I'll see many of you again.'

Everyone started clapping. Well, everyone except Kennedy, whose scowl looked painful on her small face, especially as the expression had to make its way around her paralysed brow, which had recently been given a rather large shot of Botox.

'Meanwhile, I'd like to announce that my last act as boss is to appoint Kennedy King as executive producer now in charge of *Date Squad*. She will be reporting directly to Kevin. So, I'll ask you to give Kennedy your full support.'

She smiled, feeling elated, and slid off the desk. Out of here, she thought, heading toward her office to collect her photos and a few files. A very few files. I'm free, she thought, feeling light.

Kennedy followed her into her office, looking ready to combust. Caitlin took a step back. 'Are you thinking I'll have a termination if you do this ... that I'll be too busy at work ... that you'll split Max and me up?' exploded Kennedy.

Caitlin stopped and looked at Kennedy, wondering at the way her mind worked. She was truly shocked.

'Because it's not happening, Caitlin. I *can* do both — have your job, and be a mother — even if you can't.

You can't just show up now and say, look, Max, I've decided to be interested in you, and win him back.'

Caitlin looked at her, remembering her friendship, with her high-fives and the raucous meetings, and the feeling of camaraderie and bonding over the ridiculously late nights. She felt a wave of sympathy for Kennedy, and what she was facing. 'Good luck to you, and the baby,' she said gently, walking away from her, wondering at how she could have said that, and more to the point, why she felt it, sincerely. Where was her desire for revenge?

She didn't stick around to find out, but set a cracking pace for a departure.

Kennedy flung the door open, following her former boss into the corridor (crowded with gossiping staff) to station reception.

'Caitlin, I'm not going to balls this up,' she said, voice raised in defiance. 'And you're not going to end up looking good, if that's what you think.'

Caitlin kept walking, stopping to farewell a couple of people with hugs, before walking toward the office entrance. She left without another word.

Kennedy bit her lips. Was everyone staring? Too right they were. She tried to glare at them but her brows just wouldn't knit together, not like they used to. She went into her new office, and fought back the urge to chase Caitlin down. Instead, she sat behind her new desk, while everyone stared at her from behind their partitions.

Outside, she was already being discussed.

'Abandonment issues,' Carol said to Gus, who nodded wisely.

'Unhinged,' said Gus, as Carol smothered a snort.

Meanwhile, Caitlin left the building, headed for the yellow VW, grateful she'd never felt the urge to accept the offer of a company car, and drove its small brightness toward her home.

She had other issues to think through. Her mother was due to arrive shortly: she really did have to tidy the house.

THIRTEEN

CAITLIN'S MOTHER'S ARRIVAL may have been much dreaded by her daughter, but Sarah, Sean and Molly were straining over the other end of the anticipation scale. Myra and Nadia were desperate to meet her too, having been filled in on Madeleine's blowtorch charisma by Sarah as Caitlin had listened in, distracting herself by contemplating getting a drinking problem. If she was drunk all the time, she reasoned, she wouldn't be held responsible for her behaviour when Madeleine was staying. Hell. If she got drunk enough, she might not even notice she was staying at all.

The night before Madeleine arrived, the house got a makeover in preparation for the great event. Caitlin sat back and twiddled with a drink, watching everyone excitedly move furniture about, clean cupboards, change sheets and empty the fridge of anything less than perfect. It wasn't even like she'd have her own room, Caitlin thought, scowling faintly as she watched the momentum pick up. Things had got momentarily ugly when Sarah had insisted that Madeleine stay with her in the spare room. 'No way, Sarah. You're in there. Madeleine can sleep on the couch.'

'Your mother cannot bunk down on the couch, Cait.'

'Well, if you're here, you have the spare room, and she's on the couch,' Cait said pointedly.

Sarah pouted. 'I don't want to go home. I want to stay here and help you through this.' She folded her arms, looking like a cross cherub.

'Then you need to do it my way,' Caitlin said, imperious. 'You're in the spare room.'

'She won't like that,' grumbled Sarah.

'That's the point,' Caitlin said, chucking a cushion at her friend. 'Here. I'm not going to make it easy for her to stay forever, Sarah,' she said, going to her bedroom and climbing the stepladder in the wardrobe.

'Don't talk about my friend like that,' Sarah said, following her.

'I can talk about my mother however I like,' she said, reaching into the built-ins and pulling out some sheets. 'Nope. Not those.'

'What's wrong with them?' asked Sarah.

'They're the nice ones,' explained Caitlin, sounding reasonable.

Sarah stood back, looking disapproving.

'Are you judging me?' Caitlin teased. 'Look at you, you cranky thing. Listen. Mum doesn't need to be encouraged to stay for long. Not too long, anyway. I'm not saying I don't love her —'

'You're acting like you don't even like her.'

'I *don't* like her sometimes. But you do, and the kids do, and I need her, and it will be good. In some ways.

But in others? No. She's not using this as the opportunity to move in with us that she's always wanted. And if pilly old sheets make the difference,' she said calmly, handing them down to Sarah, 'so be it.'

'I just don't get you. Anyone else would be stoked to have her as their mum.'

'She didn't really do all that much mothering, Sarah,' Cait said, pushing the good sheets to the back of the cupboard. 'Nan did most of it — remember?'

'But still …' Sarah trailed off.

Caitlin pulled a face, climbed down the ladder, and put it away inside the area of the cupboard Max's clothes used to inhabit.

'I know you don't get it,' she said comfortingly, putting an arm around Sarah's shoulders. 'No one does. Even Max thought she was splendid, and it's just not right when your husband carries on about your mother.'

'Are you sure you're not just jealous?'

'I might be,' she answered, shrugging like she didn't really care if she was. Which she was, and she didn't. Much, that is.

'Come on. Let's finish up with the lounge and have a drink.'

As they got dinner together and made the lounge into a bedroom, Caitlin thought about just how differently everyone felt from her. She knew the other residents of the cottage just could not wait till her mad mother burst through the door and turned their lives upside down. Madeleine may have been Caitlin's mother, but to everyone else she was a woman full of surprises: generous, eccentric and so embracing they felt colder when away from the furnace of her warmth. If pushed, they would all have agreed with Caitlin that her mother was endlessly busy, loud, dominating, annoying and bossy, and seemed unable to listen, and was, Caitlin knew, relentlessly competitive — even (perhaps especially) with her daughter. But they loved that she was never boring. Her visit loomed over Caitlin's recently fractured and rather wounded household like an enormous piñata over an orphan's birthday party. She was wanted, needed and just a little bit resented for her relentless aura of irrepressible fabulousness.

Madeleine's extreme generosity didn't hurt, either. (Madeleine tended to be extreme about everything.)

'What should we do with this?' Caitlin asked, feeling a twinge of guilt, holding up an enormous box that had taken up residence in the lounge room. 'I feel a bit rude putting it away.'

'You're worried about being rude to your mother? You just gave her the crappy sheets!' Sarah wasn't really that puzzled — she'd seen all the contradictory aspects of their relationship before. But she had to protest. After all, Madeleine was her second-best friend. And even for Cait, this was getting silly.

'Well, yeah. These were really nice.' Cait looked at the boxes.

Sarah shook her head. 'I really don't get you. This is way too complex for me.'

'Probably,' Cait agreed, smiling. 'Besides, she should suffer for the Roboraptor.'

'So, let's pack the boxes away, so we can actually

move, and keep the pressies out, so Madeleine feels like we appreciated them …'

'Perfect,' Caitlin grinned, feeling the guilty twinge dissolve.

Madeleine, you see, was famous for her presents. Her arrival had already been heralded by the delivery of jewel-bright care boxes, arriving each day since the previous week's revelatory phone call, courtesy of a courier who could contain his curiosity less and less as each day went past. 'Honestly,' he told his wife later. 'They were enormous. Day after day. Must've cost a fortune.' (They weren't that expensive — they were just nicely wrapped.)

And though Caitlin would never openly admit it, every little package had been a lifeline.

Inside each box had been three smaller packages: pink for Molly, red for Sean and green for Sarah. Sarah was the only person who wouldn't reveal what hers had contained, but in the general excitement of unwrapping and show-and-tell, no one ever quite got round to pushing her.

The first package had arrived the day after Caitlin had revealed the truth about her marriage to her parents. Somehow, within hours of getting off the phone to her daughter, and while drinking a lot of champagne, Madeleine had got together a package the size of a television, wrapped in sparkly pink paper.

It hadn't all been for Caitlin, but the section of the package which *was* all about her contained a subscription to a magazine called *Spheres: The Spirit Guide. Food for the soul*, her mother had written in her card. The latest issue, glossy and featuring a very blonde woman with utterly radiant teeth, lay nestled inside like a precious egg in a tissue-paper nest.

'Let me look at that,' Sarah had said, jockeying for prime position behind Caitlin. The house felt crowded and warm. Sean was sitting next to her, Molly was leaning in from her position curled up on the floor, and Sarah was poking her head in from the back of the couch.

'Wow,' Molly said solemnly, pointing at the magazine. 'I can see her aura.'

'Where?' asked Caitlin, giving her youngest what could only be called a funny look. The special ones mothers give daughters when they start seeing auras. 'Shouldn't you be getting ready for bed, honey?' she asked, in the particularly special manner of mothers who knew they'd feel much better once their child was asleep, and not thinking about auras.

'It's there,' Molly said, drawing circles around the cover girl's teeth with one stubby chocolate-coated finger.

'That's not an aura. It's the glare from her chemically whitened teeth,' mocked Sean, turning away to open her package. 'OhmiGod,' she said reverently. 'It's an iPod!'

Caitlin could feel herself getting irritated. She'd tried to keep the kids away from the technology they were flooded with. She'd relented with Nintendo, but held firm on PlayStation and dolls that really did need their nappies changed. Now the floodgates had opened, it would be wii and Play-bloody-Station and Second Life games, she thought, biting her lower lip, watching Molly dragging a huge package out of the box.

Molly scrambled to open this impressive package, which was substantially larger than anyone else's. 'A Roboraptor,' she said, agog, dragging a glistening and enormous silver dinosaur forth from the destruction.

Sarah leaped over to help Molly open the enormous box, dragging from its confines a reptile only slighter smaller than a T-Rex. Sarah quickly snapped in batteries, and Molly went bright red in the face with excitement. 'Listen!' she commanded, and all conversation ceased. She turned a switch on, and the dinosaur began clawing the air and bellowing. *Scraw! Scraw!*

'Turn that down!' Caitlin snapped before she could slap her hands over her mouth.

'She can't turn it down, Mum,' said Sean, 'it's a dinosaur.' The dinosaur roared and glanced about malevolently, before stalking toward Caitlin.

'Molly, how are we going to get you to bed now?' she complained. But that wasn't really the problem. The problem was she couldn't handle how her mother had not even arrived and everyone was already excited. It's my divorce, she thought, meanly, she knew. A surge of shame flooded her; rapidly replaced by that first, mean voice. But how come her mother had to be nice to everyone? It *was* her divorce. Everyone else seemed to think they were just having a holiday from having a father.

That's not true, snapped her conscience, and she flinched, knowing she was throwing the world's greatest pity-party for herself, and was doing the thing that drives most mothers mad with guilt — resenting her own children.

She scowled at Molly playing with her horrible new toy. Molly, face suffused with joy, remained serenely oblivious to her pissed-off mother. It reached out its claws and rent the air. *Scraw! Scraw!* There was no denying it. Conscience or no conscience, the dinosaur's shrill call and threatening moves were stretching her last nerve. I'm going to kill Mum, Caitlin thought, thrilling to the undeniable deliciousness of uninhibited rebellion. I've avoided that bloody Roboraptor for years.

'How about we just leave the room?' Sean snapped, tugging Molly away, simultaneously giving her mother a look. The kind of look daughters give mothers when mothers are being just a bit nasty. The kind of look that got Caitlin's mother-guiltometer operating again.

'Sorry, Molly,' Caitlin called out to their departing backs, feeling horrid. 'I just really hate that noise,' she complained to Sarah, who shrugged.

'I really *do* hate that noise,' Caitlin protested, feeling guiltier and guiltier. 'And why am I repeating myself?'

'I don't blame you,' soothed Sarah. 'It's awful.'

Neither of them said what was really on her mind. Sarah thought about it, but put it to one side in favour of the old tried and true favourite — distraction.

She hopped over the couch, bumping and squeezing herself along till she sat next to Cait, who giggled. She turned herself upright slowly, and started reading over her friend's shoulder.

'Oooh, that sounds good,' she said eagerly, looking at a dolphin reactivation light something-or-other course.

'Sarah?'

'Mmmm?' she answered, distracted by shell essences.

'Why is my mother sending me spooky magazines filled with crazy people?'

'That's a rhetorical question, right?' Sarah grinned. Cait didn't grin back. 'Oh. It's not. Well, I confess. She knows you have an idea.'

'How?' demanded Caitlin. She was joking. But a little serious too. Did Sarah have to talk to her mother so much?

'I mentioned it to Madeleine. I speak to her a lot, you know. I always have. I was just waiting for you to make The Call.'

'Before that, I hadn't spoken to her for ages — and the last time I did she said, "Caitlin, darling, breathe! When was the last time you took a conscious, aware breath?" Silly Mum,' she said fondly, tearing up at her mother's generosity, which mingled strangely with the resentment she felt about the horrible Roboraptor.

'She sent you the magazine because you need to get your mind off ... things,' explained Sarah patiently. As though Caitlin was tipping over the edge and only her steady voice would drag her back from the precipice.

'Oh. Well. It'll come in handy,' Caitlin grouched, layering over her excitement. Caitlin already had her mind on things. Somehow, her new idea had played some kind of magical trick on her brain, her emotions and her stomach. And that meant Max's presence on her brain's centre stage had slipped just a little. And she had work to do.

What her mother had given her was everything she needed for her idea, thought Caitlin, as she'd pored through magazine pages filled with crystal healers, witches and people who apparently interviewed fairies and angels by travelling to other dimensions. She made notes as she read, and copied down a couple of names. (Both of which she had no chance of spelling without careful reference to the magazine.) Sarah had promised to put her in touch with a medium through her work, and an animal communicator, but here, staring at her from the pages of the magazine, was the most wonderful-looking woman, who was writing about her initiation into witchcraft after carving out an amazing career as a lawyer in the music industry, and offering up spells.

'Do you think she's had work?' Caitlin pondered out loud to Sarah, gazing at the forty-something blonde's suspiciously smooth unlined face. 'I mean, she looks my age. Only better.'

Sarah snorted. 'Of *course* she has,' she said, incredulous.

'Maybe it's Photoshop,' butted in Sean, walking in from the hallway, fiddling with her iPod. The faint sounds of the Roboraptor echoed down the hall. 'Everyone at school Photoshops their MySpace pictures,' she added, standing next to the couch and fiddling with her new toy.

Caitlin grimaced, reaching over and pulling Sean down next to her and kissing her hair. 'Thanks for getting Molly off to bed,' she said.

'She's not asleep,' said Sean, implying she hadn't really done a great job.

'You got her to bed. She'll drop off soon. She can't

help it if she's excited. Anyway,' she said, drawing her nearly-adult and heartbreakingly beautiful daughter's attention to the photo they were all staring at. 'What do you think?'

'Is that who you were talking about?' Sean asked.

'Yes, it is,' Sarah said, nodding eagerly.

'Do you think she's had work?' Sarah said to Sean, who moved closer, narrowing her green cat-eyes with teenage contempt.

'Or maybe she just looks good?' Caitlin commented disingenuously, wondering just how much her daughter knew about cosmetic surgery.

Nobody said *bullshit*, but a very long pause and two faces gazing at her, both with one eyebrow sardonically raised, answered her clearly enough.

'Mum,' said Sean with a heavy sigh. 'It's *obvious* this woman has had help. Very good help. But help. Haven't you seen *Extreme Makeover*? I thought you worked in television,' she said disbelievingly, sitting back and shaking her head, before tucking her iPod away and easing into the couch with a smile.

What could Caitlin say? She was right. Silently, she added cosmetic surgery to the list of things she needed to worry about. It was filed somewhere to the back of teen sex, pregnancy, STDs, failing her exams, eating disorders, teen fashion, mood swings, illegal drugs, legal drugs sold illegally and the fallout from having a mother who worked so hard her marriage broke up.

Great, thought Caitlin. It doesn't take a psychic to realise that my destiny includes some very expensive therapy bills.

Sarah, meanwhile, was still scrutinising the picture of the glamorous woman in the magazine. Caitlin stared at it too. They sat there, silently wondering if their time had come, knowing that each of them was wondering exactly the same thing

'Do you think,' Caitlin muttered softly to Sarah, first checking to see if Sean was listening. 'That it might be ... you know ... *time?*'

'And you *can* get good surgeons,' said Sarah, sounding cautious.

Sean gave them both a look. 'If either of you get anything done, it'll be time for me not to bother talking to you any more.'

Caitlin and Sarah started laughing. Caitlin drew Sean close for another hug, and noticed Molly had crept back from her room, a small round shadow at the end of the hall, a lost child holding her only friend — a silver mechanical dinosaur. She waved her in, and Molly sleepily crawled onto her lap, snuggling close.

'Anyway,' she continued to Sarah. 'Should I talk to her about being in the show? Or what about a spell consultant?' she asked, now going through the classifieds, which weren't at all what she'd expected. Sure, some had overdone the crystals, rainbows and dolphins ... but most were, well, surprisingly intelligent and articulate.

'I know I'm onto something with this.'

'Course you are,' muttered Sarah, engrossed.

'The trick is pitching it to Kevin perfectly,' Caitlin mused out loud. 'And that means getting some of these people on tape,' she said, tapping the picture under

Sarah's upturned nose. 'As soon as I can,' she said, feeling equal amounts of stress- and excitement-inspired adrenaline surge through her already overworked system.

'I still can't quite get my head around the fact that you're taking a professional interest in what's usually considered my kooky line of work,' Sarah said, closing up the magazine.

'What do you mean?' Caitlin replied defensively, taking it off her, and frantically flicking through in search of the spiritual facelift story.

'You, Caitlin of television and media, Caitlin of home and shoes and budgets and children, are reading about dimensions,' Sarah chortled.

Ha ha ha, mouthed Caitlin, annoyed. 'Well, I've always been a bit spiritual. Max completely squashed that part of me,' she said, her face all earnest.

Sarah kept a straight face. Just.

'It's not *that* funny!' Caitlin protested hotly. 'Oh, okay, so I've never been spiritual. But it *is* sort of delicious reading this stuff. I feel, oh I don't know … like I'm a fourteen-year-old boy reading porn,' she said, struggling to explain. 'It's fascinating and weird — and forbidden. And there's so much stuff I have no idea about …'

'Really? Like what?' Sean demanded.

'Well, like what do woo-woo people mean when they're talking about dimensions?' Caitlin replied, her face emerging from behind the magazine's pages.

'Dimensions are things like how big something is —'

'Use it in a sentence, Molly,' Sean instructed.

'Sean, what dimension is your love for Matt Damon?' Molly asked innocently.

Sean whacked her. But gently. Molly giggled. 'Use it in a sentence.'

'My hatred for school is beyond dimensional,' Sean said, looking at Cait.

Sarah cleared her throat. 'Well, strictly speaking, there's the scientific view, the theosophical view, and now there's the string theory view which has been adopted by the theosophists. Or there's the quantum view. And the chaos view. And the subatomic particle accelerator view ...'

Everyone looked at Sarah. She'd sounded just like a university lecturer.

'Yes, but what does all that actually mean?' asked Caitlin.

'Oh! Well, that's easy.'

Pause.

'So what is it then?'

'You have to meet someone who can tell you properly. I know this guy who can explain everything,' Sarah fumbled. 'He's like this cowboy shaman, he's brilliant. I'll introduce you. He's very attractive.'

'Why don't you go out with him?' Cait demanded.

A shadow crossed over Sarah's face. 'He's not my type,' she said tightly.

Cait gave Sarah a look, wondering why she seemed so edgy. She mentally shrugged it off. 'Can you explain some more of this spiritual stuff to me?' she asked, and Sarah's face softened as she began to talk again.

Cait let her friend's voice wash over her, still curious, but not caring. Accompanied by the red wine and dark chocolate and warm socks her mother had sent down, talking about dimensions and spiritual facelifts seemed like exactly the right thing to be doing. Later that night, after Sean had put herself to bed, and Molly had been read a story about eagles and fallen asleep, and long after Sarah had crept off to bed, Caitlin had sat propped up in her very large bed with her laptop for over an hour. Miraculously, she went without thinking more than three times of Max, or aching with hate for Kennedy, or feeling the urge to put the Kelly Clarkson CD on.

Back in real time, the night before her mother arrived, Caitlin and Sarah put the finishing touches to the lounge room. A lamp had been moved in to create ambience (Madeleine, like Blanche DuBois, didn't do bright lighting). Cait fiddled with some flowers in a red vase, before standing back and realising that everything was ready.

And because the fuss was over, she began, quietly of course, because you can't tell your friend these things, to notice evidence that she was secretly longing for her mother to arrive. She was longing to be annoyed with her.

And increasingly desperate to pick her brains about the project that was taking shape so quickly in her head.

FOURTEEN

'My daughter's life has been through an apocalypse. An *apocalypse*, I tell you!'

Caitlin heard Madeleine arrive well before she got anywhere near the front door. In fact the whole street probably heard her. And probably several people in the next suburb over heard her, too. Caitlin's mother had the kind of voice that could melt mould off bathrooms, rip roofs off houses, strip scales off dragons. Bright and far-reaching, Madeleine's voice either had you checking to see who was making all the noise, or running for cover with your hands clapped over your head.

Unsurprisingly, Caitlin was considering running for cover, but that had more to do with content than volume. From her office, where she'd been working on her pitch and fending off calls from Kevin, she could hear her mother clearly outlining every intimate detail of Max's affair. To the taxi driver. And if she could hear her, no doubt everyone else could as well. Thankfully, the kids were at school, she thought, feeling hot, cold, excited and furious all at the same time.

Wrestling with her resentment, Caitlin closed her laptop and went to stand just behind the front door. She'd only just managed to persuade Sarah to go into *her* office this morning, so she could greet her mother on her own.

'You know what you two are like,' she'd said. 'I won't get a moment. And I want to read her the riot act without you two ganging up on me.'

Sarah had reluctantly shoved off. 'Just don't blame me,' she intoned dramatically, 'if you miss the buffer.'

'The what?'

'The buffer. *I* am the buffer. Without me, your relationship founders.'

Caitlin looked mystified.

'You'll see,' Sarah muttered darkly, and left, still talking to herself about ingratitude.

Now Caitlin was wondering whether she'd been at all smart to face her mother on her own. Maybe Sarah's right, Caitlin thought. Maybe we do need a buffer. A safety ramp. An impact dampener, like on the sides of Greenpeace vessels. There's no Dad. No Sarah. No kids. Just me ... and *her*. She suppressed a shudder. Stop being so melodramatic, she told herself. She's just your mum. And she's here to help.

Before Madeleine could make it to the front door, Caitlin yanked it open and stuck on a smile. It was only partly insincere. Confusingly, though her mother could be heard, she could hardly be seen under the bags, and bags, and bags that appeared to be exiting the cab.

'Oh!' she roared, catching sight of Caitlin. 'I wanted to surprise you!'

Caitlin smiled, shaking her head. How her mother thought she could ever sneak in anywhere unnoticed was beyond her. 'Thank you! Thank you!' came that enormous voice from somewhere underneath all the packages, addressing the taxi driver, who by now was holding the cab door open for her, a bit like she was the Queen on an official visit. 'And then he's decided he wants to have the baby — with this Kennedy bimbo! Which is ridiculous, for it's not the first time he's fooled around.'

'Oh, he's got to have been doing it for years,' bellowed the driver from beneath a baby Everest of luggage. 'But,' he puffed gallantly as he struggled up the garden path, 'it's better she finds out now. New start, new friends,' he spluttered, staggering past Caitlin, who stood at the open door with burning cheeks, her smile feeling more frozen by the second.

'Hi, I am the child of the apocalypse,' she said wryly, wondering how her mother could make her feel so much in such a short time.

'Thank you again,' Madeleine bellowed as he dumped the bags in the hallway. She handed him a generous tip, and he stood, obviously eager to continue their conversation over cups of tea. 'You must go,' she commanded, giving him a kiss. 'You're a very good man, and passengers need you.' Beaming, he backed out through the open door, another victim of Madeleine's charm. Caitlin closed it behind him, and turned to look at her mother.

'Mum! I love you. So don't take this the wrong way. Who else have you told my marriage is in bits ... the pilot on the plane? Was there an announcement at the airport?'

'I didn't know it was a secret, darling,' said her mother, like she'd seen her five minutes ago, and like she was standing on the other side of the planet. 'Where's Sarah? Why aren't the kids here? Have you been on a date yet? What about counselling?' Caitlin fought back the urge to clap her hands over her ears. It wasn't her mother's fault she was so loud, she reasoned. Led Zeppelin was to blame, she reminded herself sternly. She watched her mother sailing through the kitchen, pulling out cups and saucers, launching random questions at her daughter, unearthing a brown paper bag from her handbag.

'Sarah's at work. The kids are at school,' Caitlin answered nervously. 'Um, Mum? Is that pot?' she winced, feeling grateful the kids were at school.

'At this hour?!' laughed Madeleine. 'It's herbal tea, silly. For your nerves!'

Her every move was like a bloody scene from *My Life as a Fabulous Mother*, Caitlin thought, frowning. You'd think she was putting it on. Except she wasn't that good an actress.

'Madeleine!' Sarah's face hovered at the door for a moment, panting with excitement. She burst in, waving her hands up and down, her mouth an 'o' of wonder, and jumped up and down on the spot before catapulting toward Madeleine. Caitlin almost smiled. So much for Sarah's return to work. They really couldn't help themselves, she thought.

'Sarah,' waved Caitlin's mother, dropping her handbag on the counter and opening her arms wide.

'I got your text,' squealed Sarah, running for her best friend's mother.

Caitlin sighed patiently, like a mum watching two toddlers make friends. *Next comes the little dance they do around each other*, she thought. Right on cue, her mother and her best friend did a little dance around each other.

Now they'll stand back and look at each other, before plunging back into each other's arms. And they did.

And now, finally, they'll remember I'm here, she thought. They turned to beam at her, looking like two naughty children.

Caitlin grinned, joining in with a group hug. She stepped back. 'Mum, your packages have been a huge hit.'

'A bit like you, my darling. Now give me another hug.' Caitlin hugged her back, love, irritation and a feeling like home washing over her.

'My clever girl! My strong girl! In the midst of tragedy, you triumph!'

'Um. Really? Well, Sarah's been amazing and the kids are handling it really —'

'No, silly. How that show's taken off! *Date Squad*.'

Caitlin was shocked — her mother had the name right, and she hardly ever watched TV. She really *was* trying.

'And I hear you've been every clever — you have a wonderful new idea! I think she's so creative — but *why* did she *waste* it on television?' Madeleine asked Sarah. Sarah stifled a giggle. 'And she married an awful man, and now —'

'Mum, shut up,' said Cait, good-naturedly, glowing with the attention.

'Oh no, I'm proud of you. And now I'm here for the good bit — the battle!' She twinkled. 'Oooh, I can't wait! Here. I've more goodies. Tea! Can I put the kettle on?' she asked (pretty unnecessarily, as she already had it under control).

Caitlin pointed at her mother's little pile of herbs on the table. 'Battle? Is this a potion for courage or something?'

'Indeed!' said her mother, smiling at her daughter. Even Caitlin melted. 'Now. How *are* the battle plans going?'

'Battle plans? That's twice you've said *battle*, Mum.'

'Darling! You're going to have to fight this man, you know. Oh, that's right,' she added, when she saw the horrified look on Caitlin's face. 'You and Max never did fights.'

'I had this weird idea that *not* fighting was the sign of a healthy relationship.'

'It's the sign of a repressed relationship ... not a real one, sweetheart. Here, taste this,' she ordered, thrusting a steaming mug at her daughter. 'Sarah, you'll like this,' she beamed, passing another. 'Anyway. Your father and I always fought. Don't you remember?'

'I have some vague memory of a jug flying over my head,' said Caitlin sarcastically. She took a sip, and was surprised at how much she liked the brew.

'It's got damiana — good for energy,' nodded her Mum.

'Oh. Why *did* you fight so much, Mum?'

They had always fought. She'd always hated it. And she felt smug for asking. She may have a stuffed-up marriage that was smashed, lying wounded and dying in the middle of the road, but at least she hadn't *scarred her children*.

'I don't know, darling. We just did. We stopped a few years back when it stopped being fun.'

'It was horrible for me,' Cait said, feeling annoyed and putting her tea down. 'I don't like it that much,' she fibbed. Her mother had never seemed contrite enough about it, somehow. In fact, her mother never seemed contrite about anything, come to think of it.

'You should drink it, darling. So, if you don't fight how are you ever going to have make-up sex?'

Caitlin laughed. 'Make-up sex? Mum, any sex at all is no longer an issue.'

'What? You're never going to have sex again?' her mother said, a little smile twitching at the ends of her mouth.

'I might,' Caitlin said defensively. 'One day, when I'm very old. I might have to pay for it, but I might. If I want to. Just to see what it's like.'

'Max probably fights with Kennedy,' Madeleine muttered, looking thoughtful.

'Everyone fights with Kennedy,' Caitlin replied bitterly. 'Several of the staff have called me already.'

'That's a good thing, Cait,' Sarah said, enthused. 'People are calling you because they're going to need you back on *Date Squad*.'

'I guess so. In the meantime, I've got a pitch to put together. But it's weird, doing it on my own.'

'You're not on your own, darling — what about me? And Sarah? And Nadia and Myra, right?

'Speaking of,' interrupted Sarah tactfully, handing Caitlin a piece of paper with a number scrawled on it, 'Myra called while you were working this morning … she's left a number. It's a mediator-solicitor-type person, the one she used. She said she's really good, and she's left her a message to expect your call.'

Caitlin pulled a face, squaring her shoulders. 'I know I'm going to have to do this at some stage,' she said, 'but surely it can wait another week or two? At least till we get into a routine with the kids?'

'Course it can. Sort of. If you like,' soothed Sarah.

'Well, I don't think we should,' said Madeleine.

We, thought Caitlin, rearing up. 'We?' she repeated, only out loud this time.

'Yes, *we*, darling. I'm not letting him get his hands on your Nan's house. And he'll try. I can see it!'

'Surely we just have to be honourable, and honest. He won't want to …'

She trailed off. Both Sarah and her mother were staring at her.

'What? What? Have I got a gibbon on my shoulder or something?'

'Honourable?' scoffed Sarah gently.

Caitlin felt tears start up, and struggled to hold them back. 'Look, I know he's done the wrong thing. But we're talking about his kids now, and where they live, too. Surely …'

Madeleine looked at her with large eyes, full of compassion and love. She reached over and held her hand. 'Darling,' she said, taking the volume down a notch or two, 'I love how you see the best in people.

But, sweetheart, we have to prepare. He's going to try and take so much more from you.'

Caitlin felt despairing. Her mother looked like she actually felt sorry for her. Why did they all think that she was stupid for thinking better of Max than they did? And why should she have to handle this when she felt least able to? 'Like what?' she demanded, feeling panicky. 'What more than money, Mum? There's not much to take, really.'

'There's your income. The house. He could go for maintenance ... Your self-esteem. Your soul. Your beauty. Your youth!'

'What? No, no way, Mum. I'm not up to all this now. I'm trying to just handle everything, be okay for the kids, keep some kind of work going and bloody hell ... It's only been a couple of weeks. Isn't there some kind of moratorium on this?'

'Well, you can delay if you like. But ... it's always going to be awful. And the longer he has to contemplate his position, well. Perhaps that's an advantage for him. He's sure to have seen a lawyer.'

'Or Kennedy has,' said Sarah.

Caitlin paused, knowing the truth when she heard it. 'How do you know all this?' she demanded of her mother, frowning. 'You've lived in avant-garde shouty bliss with a wine buff for forty-something years ...'

'You think *I* haven't had affairs? You think we haven't had to work things like this out? Do you think you're the only one with an interesting life?' Madeleine blurted, managing to sound both histrionic and completely justified at the same time.

'Look at the time!' Sarah blurted abruptly, standing up suddenly and grabbing her bag. She knew better than to witness this showdown.

'What are you doing?' snapped Caitlin. 'You can't leave me here with this! You're the buffer!'

'Ha! You're funny. I need to get back to the office. It's an emergency!' And just as quickly as she'd arrived, Sarah bolted so fast that her departure left a little breeze behind her.

Leaving Caitlin and Madeleine alone, and having a good long look at each other.

'The kids will be home soon,' Caitlin said, staring her mother down. 'So you'd better start talking now.'

Madeleine looked meek. 'Wouldn't you rather talk about your new TV program?' she said hopefully.

Caitlin moved her chair closer. 'Later. Right now,' she said, in her best TV detective interrogation voice — threatening, soft, full of menace, 'right now, you've got some explaining to do.'

FIFTEEN

'So. Let's find somewhere really sinful,' said Myra, as she and Caitlin walked through the super-shiny halls of a brand-new shopping centre. 'And then you can tell me about your mother's affair with Jimmy Page.'

Caitlin didn't want to talk about her mother, or what else she'd said, to *anyone*, thank you very much. Fortunately, she physically couldn't actually speak at that moment, she was walking so fast in her attempt to keep up with Myra. And while *she* was still technically walking, what *Myra* was doing was striding. Her long legs pushed through the ambling crowds, her large nose leading the way, Caitlin hurrying along in her wake. Thankfully, Myra came to an abrupt halt outside a particularly heavenly smelling bakery.

'Oooh, nice,' she grinned, breathing deeply. An aromatic haze of chocolate and coffee, ginger and vanilla settled deliciously around them. 'Let's indulge!'

Inside, Caitlin sat down gingerly, balancing awkwardly on the tiny canvas stool, watching girls in oversized sunglasses and boys with gravity-defying hairstyles strike poses. She winced as she shifted in her chair — everything had gone back to hurting since her temporary recovery-through-creativity, and she wasn't sure why. 'Did you feel like this?' she asked. 'Like you were a bit ... bruised or something?'

'After the break-up you mean? Bruised was the least of it,' Myra replied, smile lines fanning out around her green eyes. 'Oh, I felt black and blue all right, inside and out, for ages. Don't worry.' Myra tended to look her friends right in the eye, like she was willing them to be strong, feel better. Caitlin could feel her determination. 'It's all normal, and it's going to be fine. Oooh look, ginger *brûlée*-thingies.'

A gorgeous waitress (one of the out-of-work models who make Sydney cafés the eateries with the best-looking staff on the planet) came and moodily took their order. (They're moody because they don't eat enough. But that's another story.) 'It does feel awful,' Caitlin elaborated once their waitress had drifted out of earshot. 'Physically, emotionally. Entirely. Even though I know I'll be fine,' lied Caitlin, trying her best to sound bright, pushing her curls back from her face in a bid to look like she had nothing to hide. (She didn't feel like she'd be fine at all. But saying so just seemed too close to the bone.)

'But look,' said Myra briskly, focussing on Caitlin to the extent that she wondered if she was being hypnotised, 'I thought you might be like I was. You know, bruised all over and wondering what to do. That's why I came and got you this morning.'

Caitlin nodded. 'Yep. That's about it. Add to that Mum arriving,' she said, pulling a face. 'But how did you know how I'd be feeling?'

'That you'd be feeling shit? Well, it's what ... nearly three weeks now? Time for the shock to wear off, the relatives to arrive, and the pain to set in,' she said starkly. 'Everyone feels like that. Sort of. You know, like wine. Regional variations, but essentially the same thing being squeezed out of grapes,' Myra explained.

Caitlin nodded. It was true. She *did* feel squeezed.

'I know I'll have to see a lawyer ... eventually,' Caitlin conceded. 'But I can't face it yet,' she said. 'Yesterday Mum and Sarah started on about the settlement. And I thought I'd just go mad.' She rubbed her forehead, as though trying to banish the mother of all migraines. But if she was hoping for empathy, she wasn't about to get it.

'Okay, it comes down to this,' said Myra, looking around for their order. She knew what she was about to say would go down a whole lot better with a sweetener. 'You were there, and I told you a certain amount of what was going on, but there's stuff you didn't hear then — stuff you really have to hear. You can start mediation now, and you can organise your life now, or you can do it later. If you do it later, it's a bit like pretending there are aren't some serious things that need to be done. And there are.'

'This is too weird, too much, too fast,' protested Caitlin. 'I'm used to being in charge at my workplace. That's completely demolished. I'm used to having a husband. He's gone. I'm used to earning money. Who knows? I'm *not* used to sitting at a café at 11 a.m. talking about settlements. It's just surreal.'

'Anyone who thinks separating is fun, or just a way to have more sex, or easy money or any of the other clichés is just completely full of it. It's nothing less than traumatic. We should get free counselling for it. Especially when there's a third party,' Myra said.

'Yeah. And what about when the third party is growing a fourth party?' Caitlin said with a wry grin.

Myra laughed out loud, looking delighted. That's what she loved about Caitlin. She'd never seen her looking as beaten as she was right then — and she still could make her laugh. She wagged her finger at her playfully. 'I know your game. Distract me with snappy banter till I get off the lecture. Besides, that's why I want to bring this home to you. Because babies are expensive. And he's going to start worrying.'

Caitlin didn't bother denying that one. 'Okay. So. Mediation … it sounds, well, more civilised than court, anyway.'

Myra grinned again, even more broadly this time, a gummy, endearing smile that was part of why practically everyone couldn't help but love her. '*Supposedly* more civilised,' she corrected, a chuckle in her voice. 'It's where the two parties — people — sit down face to face and talk, with mediators present. Now this is where it gets weird. They can be good, and my guy was great, or they can be awful. And some people's are. But the idea is to save you money — and pain. Court hurts more than your hip pocket.'

'So who's on whose side? Do you get one and they get another? Or is there just one person called The Mediator? Like The Terminator,' she said with a smile, unable to resist finding the humour in it.

Myra smiled. 'Nah. That's the weird thing. No one's on anyone's side. They are not there as lawyers, although they might be lawyers. They're sort of there to referee your potential prizefight — I think the technical term is *facilitate*. You know.'

Caitlin thought of Geoffrey and her HR experience. 'Yep, I get it. Does everyone do it? ... you know, the settlement, so soon afterwards?' The gorgeous, moody waitress interrupted for a moment, sliding a hot chocolate for Myra and a skinny latte for Caitlin across the table. A delicious pastry appeared, wafting out-of-this-world aromas toward them both, shivering on its plate. Caitlin neatly sliced it into two pieces, pushed Myra's toward her, and stared at the perfection of her half. Myra, on the other hand, began to eat. And describe every mouthful.

'Mmmm. *Mmmmmm*. Oh, oh, oh my God, *mmmmm* ...' Caitlin watched, fascinated by how unselfconscious Myra was.

'Oh God, that was beyond anything I've experienced, outside of a sexual fantasy. Anyway, back to you. Look, some people leave the settlement thing for ages ... but then, some people never get an actual divorce, either. I'm guessing someone maybe hasn't made up their mind or doesn't want to admit that they're actually not together any more. No matter how deep the denial, they still have to work things out at some stage.'

Caitlin took a bite of her pastry, little bits of *brûlée* crust falling to the table. Myra scooped them up, unabashed. 'Now, my feeling is that leaving it for ages is a bit like having a half-life.'

Caitlin fiddled with her coffee, and pushed some pastry round her plate. The feeling of embarrassment was excruciating. 'How could I have been so stupid?' she said, unable to resist worrying at herself. 'To not know?' she asked, her voice bitter.

Myra noticed. 'It's normal to go through the I-hate-myself-and-I-want-to-die-because-I'm-not-a-tough-bitch phase,' she recalled kindly. 'Don't worry! I'm barely out of mine.'

'Right, then. So far I'm doing okay. Bitterness, self-hatred, profound mortification,' she said, counting on her fingers. 'Ah! You forgot guilt,' she pointed out triumphantly. 'Guilt over my kids! And guilt over working too hard!'

'Oh, I only have remorse for not *having* kids,' said Myra.

'Sorry 'bout that.'

Myra shrugged, as if to say it didn't matter. Which everyone knew was a lie. It mattered. 'But back to the point: you.'

'I *was* sticking to the point. The point is that there's too much going on for me to even think about all this legal stuff.'

'So, when will you be ready? No, don't answer that,' Myra said, waving her hands at Caitlin. She took a deep breath. 'What if what you really want is to give it another go? Get back with him?' Myra pushed, raising an eyebrow. She knew this was tough, but she could sense a breakthrough in the armour Caitlin had built around herself.

Caitlin nearly inhaled her coffee. 'Are you saying I'm still in love with him?'

'Well, clearly you *are*. But what I'm really implying

is that you're possibly hoping you'll get back together. That all this will just go away.'

'No, not at all,' Caitlin protested, spluttering. 'You made coffee come out my eyes,' she said, wincing. She wiped them with a napkin and continued. 'Look. I couldn't. After what's happened, what other way could it be? I just don't feel I really have much of a choice.'

'I think you *do* have a choice. That's the problem. He's given you all the options. So it's *your* fault if you break up. What a prick. How irresponsible.' She checked herself with a bite of *brûlée*. 'Oooh. That's better. You'll notice how much food can help. Just don't —'

'— get fat,' finished Caitlin. 'I know. I was there.'

'It makes you even more angry, Cait! I had to make friends with the gym for eight months, remember? It was boxing class or feeding my face, and I had to nip it before I crossed over into the never-go-back zone.'

She took another bite of her *brûlée*, looking distracted. 'God, that's so good. Now. For what it's worth, I think the length of time between the separation and the settlement also depends on how, well, angry people are. And some people just don't like fighting for themselves … till they have to.' She gave her friend a steady glance. Caitlin was pale, but she was listening.

'Max made any noises yet?' Myra asked.

Caitlin shook her head. Then thought again. 'Well,' she sighed. 'He has asked when we can work things out, you know. Kind of alluding to money. But I thought he meant how we'd do the kids' school fees, you know, that sort of stuff. I'm getting all the bills.'

'But didn't you always handle those?' Myra pointed

out. Caitlin nodded, feeling prised open — and foolish. 'You know,' her friend continued. 'Kennedy still has a job, but she's pregnant and she's probably expecting him to support her. He might have been generous with the presents … and may have slightly misrepresented his contribution, you know, with you … She might be proving to be less generous than you were.'

'Less stupid,' Caitlin said sourly.

Myra laughed. 'Don't be so hard on yourself. We've all done silly things for people we've loved. You should hear what I did.'

Caitlin smiled. 'What did you do?'

'Not now. You need to stay focussed on you.'

'Because …?' She waited. 'Come on. Give me a reason.'

'Be honest with me,' Myra said, her voice very, very firm, her eyes piercing. 'Are you sure you're just not stalling till he's abjectly sorry, grovels sufficiently, and then you'll let yourself take him back?'

A stab of pain went through Caitlin, just underneath her ribcage, somewhere near her heart. 'No,' she said, her voice dry in her throat. 'I can't see how that would work. And I've thought about it. I've fantasised about it. Kelly Clarkson doesn't get played at that volume for nothing,' she said. 'It's not going to happen. I can't believe I'll ever forgive him.'

'Oh, but you will. You'll want to! So, nothing to wait for, right? Oh — you're not …' Myra, head cocked on one side, laughter and compassion in her eyes. 'You're not waiting till you're not insane with anger or crying your heart out every night? Till you've got more of a hold of yourself. Till you're, in the immortal words of Cher, strong enough?' Her tone was lightly mocking, but full of warmth.

How did she know? thought Caitlin, wondering if her eyes were still red from crying despite the layers of concealer she'd plastered around them. Damn under-eye concealer concealed nothing, she thought.

'Well, you won't feel better till you take action. That's what my counsellor said, and I'll tell you that for free. She told me that for $4 000. Here's the bad news about mediation — it's horrible. It'll be hell. You'll see a side of him you never wanted to believe existed, and you'll hate yourself because you knew all along he was capable of this.'

Caitlin winced, but managed a wry smile. 'What's the good news?'

'Ah, there's lots of good news. You can start — wow, I can hardly believe I'm going to say this —' She sucked in a deep, deep breath. '— healing,' and let the breath out in a noisy whoosh. 'My, it feels good to say that word without a trace of sarcasm! Wow!' She shook her head, and continued. 'Anyway, healing … and then forgiving him … and then feeling free. And you get to never repeat it again.'

Caitlin's endlessly mobile face organised itself into disbelief. It sounded not so much too good to be true as wishful thinking.

'Oh, you're thinking, "bullshit, Myra!" But it's true! And you get to have the, well, the really nasty stuff out of the way. And your situation is a bit like mine. Except for a few things.'

'Like Sean and Molly?' She had a slight edge to her

voice. There were other people involved. Kids. Kennedy. A baby.

'Right. Except for them, and that's a big except, I grant you,' she conceded. Myra seemed very certain of herself, and ever so slightly deliberately provocative. And Caitlin was beginning to feel very defensive. For some reason, she was beginning to feel just a little ... miffed that everyone — her mother, Sarah, and now Myra, seemed to know what her heartbreak was all about. She wasn't herself any more; she was a statistic, a social phenomenon. And everyone had been there, done that. But for her it was painful, and dark, and awful. No matter how much everyone insisted she'd be fine. She felt she couldn't be. It'd be almost insulting to her pain to get over it.

And Caitlin didn't know why, but she felt compelled to defend Max. Who she hated. (It had more to do with defending her own choices, as you've probably worked out, but she wasn't quite at the point of realising that yet.) She felt herself getting a bit hot, so cleared her throat and shifted uneasily on her seat. 'He *did* work ... he's an actor, and that's not easy. He found it really hard to go for the big parts, you know, with the kids. He said he didn't want to be away.'

Myra felt like bursting into endless laughter, but she resisted the urge. Caitlin was at that stage, she mused, the one where she could abuse Max, but other people doing it just made her feel stupid. So she resisted. 'Okay. Well, Craig had a job. A *job* job. So I believe,' she smiled warmly, trying to let Caitlin know she wasn't saying she was any better or smarter or savvier than her. 'You see, I had no idea where that money went. I know he got us take-away about twice a week. And he paid a couple of bills. But there's no way of knowing if he had a girlfriend or a secret account, or … well, just spent it. I mean, I could have hired a private detective. But to be honest that didn't occur to me at the time.'

'It seems way too TV … even for me.'

'Agreed. And it's expensive,' Myra said primly, with the air of One Who Knows. (Caitlin was learning that *divorce* and *expensive* were words that spent a lot of quality time together.)

'Anyway, the details that I might have accidentally on purpose left out back when we were having my Divorce D and Ms. He didn't have any assets when we got together. And I worked really hard to pay off the bank so I didn't have to continue to work really hard at a job I didn't love for, well, the length of a mortgage — which in Sydney's about the term of your natural life, right? We were planning on doing fun stuff like travel next, then we would put down a nest egg with an investment property, then we were going to get to work on co-creating a perfect little baby. After the mortgage was paid off, he kept saying. So, I went for it. For years and years and years.'

Caitlin felt for her friend. After twelve years of marriage, and a whole lot of promises, Myra didn't have any kids. At thirty-nine, maybe she wouldn't ever be a mother. So Cait had a bastard soon-to-be-former husband — *but* she also had Sean and Molly.

On the other hand, they'd put their money into renovating the house. And the kids. And schools. And some had gone to wherever it goes — to food and bills and fixing things and dry-cleaning and car upkeep and

… She hadn't minded but now she looked back at it, she felt stupid. She felt a little sick. What have I done? I've trained him into being a selfish bastard, she told herself. Did I think I had to pay to keep him?

Caitlin shook herself, and forced her attention back to Myra.

'Anyway. So, when I'd paid it off —' (The house, Caitlin reminded herself.) '— no mean feat in Sydney — with a lot of freelance work, and not many shoes at all, he …' Myra took a deep breath, which was the only pause she'd taken for a while, Caitlin noted. 'He suddenly thought it would be good to upgrade. You know, a bigger place. For space. For the baby! And I said fine, as long as he carried that mortgage and I could get on with having a baby. I'd waited long enough. Well, that,' she deadpanned wryly, 'didn't really go down that well.'

'Oh, Myra.'

'The weirdest thing was that I found *nothing* when he moved out. So I still have no clue what was going on in his head. And I looked everywhere. The therapist's office. Any number of self-help books. Up the back of the cupboard,' she said, grinning wryly.

'What were you doing up the back of the cupboard?' wondered Caitlin aloud.

'That *was* random, wasn't it?' replied Myra. 'Having the traditional purge and clear-out, of course.'

Caitlin looked puzzled.

'Oh, you haven't done that yet? Fantastic! I'll come over and help you. It's great. You get to cry and shout and rant while you throw anything that's vaguely "his" into a gigantic garbage bag. Then you can burn it or you can bin it or you can be magnanimous and post it to him. Or we can be charitable and take it to St Vinnie's.'

Caitlin cheered up. 'Sarah already did some of that, but there's plenty left. I like that option — the charity one.'

'He deserves it,' smiled Myra.

'Bastard,' agreed Caitlin. It felt delicious. She swooshed the last of her coffee and drained it, feeling the caffeine thrill through her veins. 'So, you didn't tell me what you and Craig agreed on — you know, in mediation.'

'Short story? He didn't get as much as he wanted, and I gave away a whole lot more than I thought was fair.'

Caitlin made a sad face.

'Oh well,' shrugged Myra, philosophically. 'Just another pair of pissed-off and disgruntled love-gone-wrong people working out how to end it all ...'

Caitlin felt numb. 'But how can he, well, take *anything* from me? Us,' she corrected herself. 'I earned everything we had.'

'Well, he won't see it that way. For example, did he take care of the kids?'

'He dropped them off at school and picked them up if that's what you mean.'

'Put a load of washing on?'

Caitlin gave Myra a look. 'Sometimes. Hardly ever. If I asked him to and left instructions.' She crossed her arms, warding off the feeling of being very, very threatened. Where was this going?

'You know, I think he's going to make out that he's the traditional house-carer, homemaker-type nurturing person. Soulful new-age man. Gave up promising career to support career-driven wife. You know the sort of thing.'

Caitlin felt the blood drain out of her face. 'Do you think he'd do that?'

'Honey. Face it. He's going to go for a very generous settlement.'

She put her long-empty cold coffee cup down and felt her hands clench. Her eyes narrowed, and anger kept the tears at bay. For the moment.

'He cheated on me. And lied. And didn't ...' she said, voice cracking, stomach and chest feeling awful. How had she let this happen? 'Idiot,' she said out loud, smacking her forehead, the word stinging. Which somehow felt good.

'No fault in settlement, Caitlin.' Myra said. (She was relentless. They were nearly there, and her work would be done.) 'It doesn't matter, technically, what anyone's done. The property is supposed to be divided up evenly.'

'But we didn't *acquire* the property evenly,' Caitlin protested, hating the way her voice was rising. A few people looked around. She glared back at them. Go on, have a good stare, she thought. You probably know all about it too.

'I know, I know,' soothed Myra. 'It's just how a court sees it. I'm trying to wake you up. Your mum says ...'

'My mum!' exploded Caitlin.

Myra ignored her. 'Don't go on. Your mum had a word with me before she came down. And she thinks you think he'll be all nice about it. Won't take anything. Well, he will. I'd put money on it, if my husband had left me any.'

Caitlin willed herself to calm down. There is no way that's happening. He leaves, takes his stuff, sees the kids when I choose, and gets on with his wonderful new life. She felt better — sort of — immediately. *He knows he's done the wrong thing. There's no way he'd try to take something that belongs to me. No way.*

'Look, Myra, I know he's a prick,' said Caitlin hotly, gesturing for the bill. 'But he's not *that* much of a prick. Just because I'm an idiot doesn't make him a super-prick. And just because my mother says he is doesn't make him one either!'

Myra just looked compassionate.

'Oh. I am stupid,' Caitlin said.

'Ah, don't call yourself names, now,' Myra consoled. 'You were busy, working and taking care of the family.'

'Working,' Caitlin interjected dolefully.

'And being a mother yourself.'

'Working,' Caitlin corrected, more forcefully. 'It took up everything. Most of my life was spent at the station.'

'Was?'

'I know, it was only five minutes ago. It hardly rates the past tense.'

They sat in silence for a moment. (Well, as silent as a huge super-shiny supercentre can get when there're 5 000 shoppers and a huge PA system pumping out some of the world's greatest shopping hits.)

'So, even though it does happen, I know he wouldn't do that. He's decent,' Caitlin said. 'Well, sort of.'

'I bet your mother doesn't say that.'

'Oh, let's not start on her.'

'When do I get to meet her? I reckon she's got to be better than television.'

'You've already met her.'

'Oh, come on, a phone call. Don't hold out on me.'

Caitlin rolled her eyes. 'Next weekend … You know Sarah's planning a getaway. I can get footage for this new concept I have … and you guys get to come and watch.'

'Ah — yep, that's booked in. So your mother's coming too? Awesome,' Myra said, grinning toothily.

'It'll be interesting. And you're right, by the way. Mum thinks Max is the devil incarnate.'

'Really? I thought she was like Sarah — all new age?'

'She is. Or was. She's gone all hellfire on me though. She would believe in a hell only to be able to imagine sending Max there.'

Myra giggled. 'Okay. I hope you're right about him, though. It would be good if that happened.' And I can't blame you for hoping, she thought to herself. Myra knew when to stop — but she did have one card left to play.

'You know, I had a bit of an agenda bringing you here. Apart from the pastries … and nagging you about when I get to meet your mother, and telling you what to do with your life. You know,' she said, shrugging toward a shopfront across the way, 'there are lawyers here … their offices are just there,' she said, turning and pointing across the tiled floor. Caitlin tried to repress a glare, then just went with it. 'I know. But look. Let's just go in and see if there's an appointment available. You should find out what you're up for.'

'Why now?'

'If not now, when?' Myra snapped back. And within moments they'd packed up, paid up and were in the sleek offices of a professional family-law-type person. Somewhere Caitlin was convinced she had no business being. 'Isn't it a bit of a waste of money?' she said to Myra, crossing her arms.

The receptionist let her hair fall over her face to hide her half-smile. One of the hopeful ones.

'Talk to a lawyer first,' the receptionist said, handing her some pamphlets.

'*Separation — keeping it nice,*' Caitlin read out disbelievingly.

'I know,' said the receptionist with a grin. 'It's never nice.'

'Just make the appointment,' Myra said. 'At least you'll get to see the lie of the land.'

'Why would I want to see the lie of anything at all?' she grumped to Myra, brows knotted together. 'It's not going to happen. Max isn't going to take everything from me.'

'Great. So don't trust me. That's fine. I'm the voice of doom. I had a bad experience, I know. Maybe I'm projecting all my stuff onto you. But see a lawyer. Get independent legal advice. That's all.'

Caitlin sighed. 'How much is all this going to be?' she asked the receptionist.

'Heaps,' she said cheerfully. She handed her a card. 'Here's your time. You wanted an evening appointment, night? Tuesday, 7 p.m. We'll ring to confirm.'

And I can cancel, thought Caitlin. Just as soon as Myra pisses off. Nosey, confrontational —

'And don't even think about cancelling,' Myra interrupted Caitlin's rather critical stream of thought, exactly as if she knew what she was thinking. 'I know what you're thinking,' she said spookily.

Caitlin's eyes widened in surprise, then she shrugged, resigned to being easy to read. 'Why are you doing all this? It's going to be okay. I'm going to be okay.'

'Because I know what it's like. And nobody showed me the ropes,' Myra said. 'Humour me. Just to be on the safe side.'

(What she didn't say was that *she'd* thought her husband would never, ever, not in this or any other lifetime or incarnation together, not even if he was broke and driven insane, try to steal her home, her wage, her super and her dignity from her.)

'Consider me the Divorce Fairy,' she smiled, hiding the concern she felt.

'Ah. Well, you're a very good fairy. But everything's going to be fine.' Caitlin sounded very sure. About as sure as Myra was that things would get worse for her friend before they got better.

'It's going to be fine,' repeated Caitlin, giving Myra a look. 'Say something!'

I hope so, thought Myra. But I don't think so.

'You could be right,' she said noncommitally, getting back into her shopping stride, and spying a boutique she'd always wanted to use as an excuse to abuse her credit card. 'Now, if you don't mind, come and watch me buy something ridiculously expensive that I don't need!'

SIXTEEN

'Are you *sure* you don't want us to come with you?' Sarah pleaded, twiddling with her rings, looking as anxious as a new-age cherub who meditates can look. She watched Caitlin swipe some more red, red lipstick over her full, full lips. How can, Sarah wondered, someone make putting lipstick on look like she was pulling out an AK-47? 'Are you *sure* you're okay?' she added, unable to resist.

Madeleine, who was counting how many times Sarah had asked if Caitlin was okay (five times in twenty minutes) was busy repressing her own desire to stalk her daughter and was about to settle on pure, maternal determination. My daughter, she thought, is not going to go through this alone. Even if she wants to.

Both were lolling on Caitlin's former marriage bed, watching Caitlin savagely get ready to have her first-ever legal briefing outside of her job. Her swift, harsh movements gave everything away, though she *said* was fine. Fine, fine, fine, she insisted, more brittle each time she had to say it. With every *fine*, Sarah's feeling of foreboding grew stronger and stronger. She was on the verge of giving up and shutting up. She knew Madeleine hadn't given up yet. She could just feel another question coming on. It was hovering in the air between them, tense, just waiting to land.

She was right. Madeleine was far less easily put off. Before Caitlin had even finished glossing her lips her mother rallied and launched another protection offensive.

'We could come along and just ... hold your hand, so that you know you're supported through this,' she wheedled. Loudly.

Caitlin gave her a brief glare, then started pulling her carefully tousled ponytail out. Hair exploding around her pale face, she accentuated the mad-lady effect by picking up a tube of product and viciously squeezing its contents into her hands. She rubbed her hands together and started poking the product into her hair. 'This is just all wrong,' she muttered into the mirror, shoving her hair this way and that while she pointedly ignored her mother. Again.

Sarah actually shook her head in disbelief. (And she *never* did things like that.)

When the ponytail had gone up she'd thought Caitlin had finally stopped messing with her hair and was about to maybe talk to them. About being frightened, pissed off, nervous and angry. But she was *fine*, apparently. Except that the dead giveaway that Caitlin was really, truly upset was her hating her hair. She'd twist it, poke it, prod it, smooth it, blast, spray and scrunch product into it. To make it wrong. But this went beyond even the normal Caitlin vs. her hair face-off. Even Sarah, who'd witnessed twenty years of this very power struggle, had never seen her fighting so hard to control her curls.

Sarah opened her mouth. Just one last time wouldn't hurt. 'We could —'

'No,' snapped Caitlin, scrunching moisturiser through her thick curls. Everyone breathed a sigh of relief. At last, her hair was obeying. It was perfect, glossy, smooth and shiny. Both Sarah and Madeleine took a deep breath, but Caitlin got there first.

'And *no* for the next time you ask! And — no, no — not a word! I'll be fine. I hardly know why I'm going,' she said, flustered. 'Oh. That's right. It's just to shut Myra up! I didn't realise both of you would want to come along and watch me waste my time and money. You've both moved in. Now you don't want to let me go anywhere … it's like I'm on suicide watch.'

Both women flinched.

'It's a joke!' Caitlin exploded.

'If you're so fine, why are you so … angry?' demanded Madeleine.

'Because it's annoying being treated like you're … you're *broken*. There's nothing the matter with me. Nothing *wrong* with me. Look — arms, legs, head, all still on. Lots of people have it way worse than me. You're usually out helping them, and now *I've* turned into one of your walking-wounded projects. It's … it's just that I'm all *right*!'

Madeleine and Sarah both kept very, very quiet. The word 'protesting' and the phrase 'too much' did not even get close to being mentioned.

'And anyway, why the scrutiny? It's just an appointment. Is my life really that much more interesting than anyone else's?' Caitlin was feeling good now. Anger gave her the impression of power. Unleashing it felt immensely better than the endless tears she'd been shedding in private, the depression that kept threatening to creep over her and have her retreat under the doona for the rest of this lifetime.

'Why don't you … watch *Date Squad* or something?' she said. 'It probably needs the ratings.' While she ranted, her hair began to slowly unfurl from the product-rigid smoothness and twist into kinks again. (That's Caitlin's hair. It gets knocked down, then it gets up again.)

Unlike her mood at that moment, which was plummeting. Why isn't anyone backing me up? she thought. She caught a glimpse of her hair unfurling, and swore at her reflection.

'Your hair is beautiful,' snapped Madeleine, unable to help herself. 'Stop telling us how fine you are and leave it alone. It wants to be free!'

'You don't think she might have a point?' interrupted Sarah tentatively, sitting up, and stuffing a pillow behind her back.

'The ratings *are* down.' Caitlin just stopped herself from adding *ha ha ha*. 'Kevin rang me today and wants to have a clandestine meeting.'

Both Sarah and Madeleine looked bewildered.

'We weren't talking about your *work*, darling,' explained Madeleine, once she'd untangled the crossed wires. 'We were talking about your *life*.'

'Oh. You mean *Myra* might have a point?'

Sarah nodded, and braced herself for the blast.

'She does have a point,' admitted Caitlin. 'It's just not relevant to me. It's all going to be *fine*.'

'I'm glad you've turned yourself down slightly,' stated Madeleine. Loudly.

'*What?* Have you heard yourself recently?'

'Yes, but I am naturally loud. You are not. You are angry. You've been yelling at us for about half an hour.'

Caitlin swung around and faced her mother and the best friend she shared her with. She stuck her hands on her hips. Her stilettoed feet drilled into the carpet as she took a tipsy step toward them. They both shrank back into the duvet.

'For some reason you all think Max is going to try and steal everything from me. I know him. I married him. I lived with him for years. I know it looks like he's an irredeemable single-celled life form, but he's not *entirely* evil.' She gathered her notebook and her laptop, and took one last look at herself in the mirror. 'Anyway. Nothing's happened yet. I don't know why you're all so worried. It's making me nervous,' she mumbled, fiddling round for something in her bag.

'You think he's going to just … leave it be?' asked her mother wonderingly, managing to infer that that was very, very doubtful.

'Mum, after what he's done, he wouldn't even *think* about taking anything from us. He just … wouldn't.' She looked blankly around, her bag having failed to provide.

'Your keys are over there,' Madeleine pointed out in reply, waving a hand at the side table.

'Oh. Thanks,' said Caitlin. Her green eyes narrowed. 'And don't go thinking that's significant, either of you,' she warned. 'It's not some kind of sign, that I can't find my keys. It doesn't mean my home is lost, or that I'm not wanting to face up to things, or that I'm feeling insecure.' Her hands shook as she spoke, and she jammed them back into her bag to hide them.

Sarah and Madeleine had both seen her hands quivering, and both of them said nothing. In fact, they said nothing so loudly and clearly that their every thought was completely obvious.

'Okay. Well, thanks for … thanks for worrying,' Caitlin repeated, tying her hair back. Again. 'But everything's going to be fine,' she insisted. Again.

She left them both looking concernedly at each other in her room, and headed off to Sean's bedroom, where both daughters were gazing rapturously at the beautiful young stick insects starring in this week's episode of *Date Squad*. Caitlin took one look at the worship on Molly's face and snapped. 'Molly, I don't love you watching this at all. Nor you, Sean. Look at them!' she exclaimed, waving her hands at the telegenic teenagers on screen. 'They're all sticks with heads! Who have they got *on*? What happened to the real people?'

'It's *okay*, Mum,' Sean interjected, her voice so completely reasonable and so obviously inflected to soothe Molly that Caitlin realised how verging-on-a-nervous-breakdown her own voice was sounding. And how hollow saying the word 'okay' or the word 'fine' had become. 'I'm explaining everything to her,' Sean continued, in tones that suggested her mum might want to consider being a grown-up for a minute. 'I'm pointing out that they're all bulimic and that —'

'Sean, you can watch it,' Caitlin interrupted, taking charge. 'But Molly — you have an appointment with Sarah and your gran in the kitchen. Now.'

Molly scrambled up and rubbed her eyes. 'This *sucks*. I couldn't watch *The OC* in case Marissa overdosed. You said I could watch it later. Then it finished! *Now* I can't watch *Date Squad*, even though I told everyone at school to watch it because it's your show,' she objected.

'Bye, honey.' Caitlin feigned cool, controlled parenting, but inside she was horrified. Molly said 'sucks'! She never said 'sucks'!

'But, Mum!'

And she never, ever protested. She rallied, giving another strong-parent-with-boundaries impersonation.

'Look, it's just for now, honey. This storyline … it's all wrong,' she said, realising she was being pulled in. Both by the show and her kids.

'It's true, Mum. It's weird,' pointed out Sean. 'They've changed the set, and Kennedy's —'

'Kennedy?' Caitlin said. She flinched. There was that defensive note again.

'Kennedy was actually *on* it —'

'What? Kennedy's got air-time?' she demanded, incredulous. Right on cue, the screen flashed to a scene of Kennedy advising two young people on what looked like …

'What is she pointing at?' asked Caitlin, her wide mouth an oval of disbelief.

'It's a shag chart, isn't it? Sex positions and stuff?' Sean provided.

'Sexual positions!' Caitlin exploded. 'That bitch! What is she *doing* to my show? She's turning it into ... some kind of sleazy ... festival for horny —'

'But, Mum!' cried Molly, slamming her hands over her ears. Caitlin remembered with a shock that she was still in the room. 'Kennedy is our friend!'

'Okay. As I can't be trusted to control myself, I really need you out of here,' said Caitlin to her youngest, gently pushing her toward the door. 'Now. Go.' First my husband, then my show, now she's your friend, she thought. Out-bloody-rageous.

When Molly had slow-motioned her way out, Sean gave Caitlin one of her meaningful looks. 'Don't worry, Mum. *I* don't think she's our friend. *I'm* not telling Molly that. She just wants us all to be happy. That's from Dad. No one's to blame and we all love each other and we're still a family. But I know Dad fucked up.'

Her bitterness wasn't at all thrilling. No triumph at all. Caitlin found it profoundly depressing. 'I'm sorry,' she said, trying not to stare at the screen, where Kennedy was now nodding as a date expert walked the couple through their kissing and fondling paces. 'Don't worry,' she said, smoothing back some hair from Sean's face. It fell straight back across her wide, black-lashed and oh-so-clear green eyes. She is so beautiful, Caitlin thought. She's so young. Just because Molly's the baby doesn't mean Sean isn't feeling this too, she reminded herself. 'You're great, I'm proud of you, you're an amazing daughter and a fabulous big sister, and I love you.' She bent down and grazed her daughter's cheek with her lips. Not too soppy, she reminded herself. 'See you soon.'

'Where are *you* going?' Sean raised perfectly arched brows.

'Just out.'

Sean snorted, feeling the delicious thrill of a teenager about to point out an adult's inconsistency. 'You'd never let me get away with that.'

'Nope. You're right,' grinned Cait. 'Gotta go.'

As the credits of *Date Squad* rolled on screen Sean sat and wondered if her mother was going on a date. 'As long as it's not with Dad,' she thought darkly, turning her mind back to chords, soundtracks, what a bitch Asia at school was and how Summer got her hair to slink in inky waves halfway down her back. Blonde straight hair, Sean thought moodily, is so over.

Meanwhile, Caitlin kissed everyone in the kitchen, where Madeleine and Sarah had cornered Molly.

'Love you,' she said, opening the front door and looking behind her with a worried face. 'I'll see you all later.' She blew a kiss, and refused to look at their faces, all concern and disbelief that she was fine, again.

When she arrived at the shopping complex, it looked weird — colder, shabbier and far more alien than the day she'd sailed through with Myra. Without the shoppers, it was hollow. A place without a purpose. It's all empty and full of echoes, Caitlin thought. Like my life, she added, for a masochistic touch. Ghost town. Looks good, feels awful. And Kennedy's bloody touched my show! she raged, walking toward the office that had looked so reassuring the other day. Her heels clicked and echoed through the cavernous halls of the shopping centre. She swallowed, squared her shoulders and entered.

A different receptionist greeted her at the lawyers' stainless steel offices, initiating Caitlin's first attack of nerves. Her stomach surged as she obediently followed an ancient crone, grizzled, disapproving and sour, through a grey labyrinth. She may have been ancient, but her tiny legs moved at lightning speed. Caitlin felt like a kid being marched off to the headmistress's office, who knew she was about to get into big, big trouble. And she didn't miss the unsubtle once-over the ancient one gave her as she pointed at a room that Caitlin could only assume she was meant to enter.

'Here, Caitlin,' said a very blonde woman, looking like a pencil-skirted heroine from a Hitchcock film.

'My lawyer, I presume,' smiled Caitlin, stepping forward.

'I'm Amanda Savage,' replied the woman, her eyes cold and blue and hard.

Oooh, frostbite, Caitlin thought. Her smile faded, and she shivered to herself as she sat down at the desk. She looked around. While the reception area had been glamorous, the office's peeling paint and flickering fluorescents were hardly inspiring.

'Now,' Frostbite said in cool tones, shuffling papers importantly and glancing at her watch. 'Let's go through things. You're going into mediation?'

'Not really …'

Frostbite gave her The Look. (A look that she'd spent months perfecting to hurry clients up when they threatened being vague, emotional or anything less than businesslike. Counselling was for therapists. She was about money, and the time it took to make it. So her look said, I am an Impatient Bitch. Waste My Time and I Will Hurt You.) 'I'm very expensive, Caitlin,' she said, with a frigid little smile. 'I don't want to waste your time, or your money.'

'Okaa-ay,' Caitlin said, wondering if this was a joke. Apparently not. She hated how wishy-washy she sounded. But it wasn't as though you trained for this sort of situation. She pulled herself up straight and gave Frostbite a smile. 'I'm here just as a precaution, really,' she started, sounding jaunty. 'I think my husband's unlikely to actually want anything from me. But just to know where I stand I thought I'd … have a talk with someone like you.' A professional bitch, thought Caitlin as a smirk tweaked the side of Frosty's mouth. Easy, Caitlin. Maybe her collagen injections are playing up.

'Then you're here because …?'

The fake question mark in the lawyer's voice was very, very irritating. Just because she's seen 3 000 divorces doesn't mean she knows what *my* husband's like, thought Caitlin. (And yes, she thought it defensively.) 'I just want to know … where I stand. In case. I suppose.'

'You have to get legal advice before you enter the mediation process, in order to really get a grip on what's happening, or what's likely to happen, with any kind of settlement. So it's good that you're here. Well done.' Thank God I've got that warm fuzzy part over with, she thought. Now let's get on with the rough stuff.

Amanda Savage liked delivering bad news. Ever since her childhood with a mother who'd wept noisily *every single day* over the husband who'd left, she'd been determined to snap everyone else out of their misery and wake them up to the bitter truth.

That no one gave a damn.

'Let's get the picture painted,' she suggested, anticipating some shocks ahead for Caitlin Cooper. Sucker, she thought. Here comes your reality check. 'So. You're married?'

How did she manage to imply that I was lucky to even score a husband, wondered Caitlin? And was that really necessary to ask? Divorce kind of implies marriage, doesn't it? 'Yes. Well, no. I'm separated.'

'How many years?' On autopilot now. Nearly at the good bit, she thought.

'Were we married? Sixteen years.' She thought a moment, checking her memory. A painful blur of memories ran through her head. Ouch. 'Yes,' she winced. 'Sixteen.'

'Children?'

'Yes,' she started, feeling a warm rush and brightening. 'Two. Six and fourteen. They're beautiful, and so funny, and complete pains sometimes of course, but they're handling it really —'

'Assets?' snapped Amanda Savage, interrupting this gibbering reverie. Honestly. As if I care.

'Yes. House. Um, some super.' Caitlin looked down at her lap, feeling like she'd made some huge blunder, unsure of what it was.

'Stock?'

'Er, no.'

'Do you work?'

Caitlin bristled. She felt her face arrange itself into an expression that said outrage, and couldn't be bothered trying to hide it. Who doesn't? she thought. Other than Max. 'Yes, I do. Though that's changed a little because of the separation ... let me explain.'

Amanda Savage really didn't care about the details, but listened anyway. Then she asked for more details about what she did for a living, exactly how much she earned, and so on ... Tick, tick, tick went the pen in the boxes on Amanda Savage's white forms, and her face got tighter and leaner and less approving. Not that it had been exactly warm to start with, but with every notch the pen racked up, the temperature in the room went down.

'You've been married for how long, again?' Amanda didn't need to ask this. She just felt like needling Caitlin. *Asking this one again always got them*, she thought happily.

'I've already — okay. Sixteen years —'

'And the family home is owned outright. So. It's very straightforward,' Amanda Savage said happily. 'In fact, it's so straightforward I'm not sure what you're here for.'

'Can you indulge me then, and just tell me?' Caitlin said, eyes narrowing a little. She didn't mind someone pointing out she didn't know something. What she didn't like was someone being nasty about it.

'That's fifty per cent,' said Amanda Savage, with that slight touch of glee that indicates that someone has just a trace of the sadist about them.

Caitlin said nothing. She felt nothing. If she'd experienced shock on a regular enough basis, she would have recognised its anaesthetic impact. But as she and shock were still relative strangers, she had thought she'd feel something when she heard this.

But no. Nothing. Which made it all the more easy to snuggle back into her denial doona. It was all like an interesting social experiment happening to another person. She detached a little further, wondering what ludicrous statement frostbitten and melodramatic Amanda Savage would make next.

'I guess you'd be aiming to keep out of the courts? And if not, you should. The courts will see what's on paper and give him half.'

She looked at the details she'd scrawled down, nodded to herself, then tapped her Biro on the notepad.

'Best result, you walk away with the house, but you'll have to pay him out to keep it.'

'What? But he walked out …' It's all a theory, Caitlin soothed herself. He's not going to do that.

'There's no *fault*,' said Frostbite disapprovingly. 'It's a role reversal of the walk-away wife. It's about the division of assets. No fault.'

'Why? Why don't we look at how the assets came to be? I mean, he didn't bloody contribute. This is my inheritance! *My* assets!'

'That's *not* how the courts will see it.' Being Superwoman doesn't pay — plus, it wastes the pretty, Amanda thought smugly, comparing her own perfect skin with the dark smudges of grief underscoring Caitlin's eyes.

'But we're not even going to court. And he wouldn't do that.'

'Do what?' Amanda Savage was getting very frustrated now. Did they think their feelings counted? 'Go for what he's entitled to? Do what wives have been doing to men since —'

'But it's my Nan's house,' Caitlin explained carefully, convinced that there was something that Amanda Savage just wasn't getting, and if she could only make it clear to her that there were human beings involved here, she'd suddenly twig to the real point. Like, the ethical and moral part of her story.

'She owns it? Well, then you could put it into trust, and —'

'No — she's dead!' blurted Caitlin, feeling like she was struggling with something that should have been easy. Amanda took a short, sharp breath and looked at Caitlin sceptically.

'I guess it just seems to me … well, how can he claim on something my grandmother gave me? It doesn't seem ethical, or fair, or moral.'

'It's all common property. He can go for fifty per cent of the assets. It doesn't matter if your grandparents wanted you to have it. He'll see it as losing his home too.'

'But she wanted to take care of me. She gave it to me well before I met him …' she choked back some rusty nails that seemed to have lodged in her throat, knowing that what she was about to say would not be viewed as in any way important.

'Sorry, doesn't matter,' replied Amanda Savage, shuffling some more papers to mask her annoyance. She needn't have bothered. It was completely clear how little she thought of *that* argument.

'But I earned most of the income!'

'Really?' Ms Savage replied coolly. More fool you, she thought. What is wrong with these women? she wondered, before reminding herself that she was way too sexy and clever to ever be caught supporting a man. 'I wouldn't say that too loudly, actually. Is he going for support?'

'What? No! Why do you say that?'

'Because he can. Consider it alimony. Keeping his standard of living up. That kind of thing. The kind of thing wives used to do. Before all the wives started working harder than their husbands.'

Caitlin felt outraged, confused and ready to up-end the table full of this smug frosted-blonde's papers right on top of her perfect head. Then she wanted to introduce her fist to Amanda Savage's jaw. Then she'd like to take a full-page ad out in the *Sydney Morning Herald* warning women of what was about to happen to them. And none of that mattered. Not a bit. She took a look at Amanda Savage's impatient face. She thinks I'm stupid, she realised.

She thought about it. Would Max really do that?

No, she calmed herself, scurrying back to her comfort zone. (The land of denial.)

'Oh, he just wouldn't,' she said. She'd been saying that a lot lately.

'Look, it's sexist to assume that a dependent spouse wouldn't want to be maintained if the marriage dissolved. And, tacitly, you've agreed to support him all these years.'

'Look, I just said he just wouldn't do that.'

The lawyer raised one very fine, very plucked and very arched brow even higher up her forehead. 'Caitlin, if you go to court, here's what you are looking at. Fifty per cent of the property.'

Caitlin could have sworn someone had just kicked her in the stomach.

'Some kind of maintenance for at least the next five years,' continued Amanda. 'Maybe the rest of his life. And of course dual custody — shared parenting responsibility.'

'That's not happening,' Caitlin managed to get out of a throat that felt like it was shrinking.

Amanda ignored her. 'But here's the other option. We keep you out of court. You pay him out the value of fifty per cent of the property. You keep your super. He keeps his.'

Caitlin resisted snorting. A derisive snort would have been so satisfying, but slightly pathetic.

'What's the house worth?' Amanda's voice broke into her reverie.

'About, I don't know. It's got to be about ...' she remembered all those mornings she and Max had laid in bed with the papers, poring over the real estate section, reading housing prices out loud, wondering at how Nan's cottage with all its falling-down ceilings and wobbling floorboards and squatting termites could be worth so much money. She had felt so completely secure — she'd never dreamed anyone could take it from her. Least of all the man she shared it with. 'Um, it's worth about ... one million. I know it sounds a lot.'

'It does. And I know that's what it costs to live in Sydney. But you're going to have to pay him out. About ...' she did some figures, jabbing a scary, pointy nail at a calculator. 'Well, truly, it hardly takes a calculator,' she tittered. 'About 500 000. Dollars. But I bet we can avoid maintenance. And you might get to keep your super.'

'How can this be a division of assets that only I provide? They're *my* assets,' Caitlin pointed out, red-faced and clinging to the idea that there was no way something this unfair could happen. Sure, impregnate my colleague, she thought. But steal my house? No way.

'His material assets *are* less tangible,' conceded Amanda Savage. 'But as you say, he worked as an actor, and was paid well ... then he did care for the children — that's classified as unpaid labour.'

The idea of Max's life being described as labour, especially the unpaid sort, made Caitlin smile, just a little bit. Unfortunately, Amanda Savage saw this smile as a breakthrough. The woman's beginning to see sense. Toughen up, she thought. 'I could introduce you to a lot of bitter men who've felt the same way over the years. But, Caitlin,' she said, softening a little. This woman, she thought, obviously isn't stupid. So why is it that she doesn't have a clue?

'Caitlin, look, it's completely clear that you always had more to lose.' She didn't voice the rest of the sentence.

'And it's legal for anyone to go for this much?'

'After eighteen months of cohabiting, yes.'

'How does something that took my grandparents their whole life to pay off, and me sixteen years to fix up, possibly make it fair that in eighteen months anyone can …'

'It's not *fair*. It's the *law*,' Amanda replied scathingly, losing patience.

'Well, I don't have $500 000. And he won't be going for it anyway.'

'You have the house. You might have to sell it if he does. You can start again.'

'Where will we live?'

'You buy another place.' God, she thought. Where did she think she'd live? In a divorced-women's shelter?

Fuck that, thought Caitlin. He's not getting my Nan's house. No way.

(Later, Caitlin would entertain dinner parties and horrify good lawyers by recounting the advice afforded her by her shopping-centre solicitor.)

Caitlin walked out to the street, numb, hair askew, through the empty shopping centre with its gleaming mosaic tiles and cold, cold heart, and stuck her hand out for a cab. She was hardly aware of what she was doing when she climbed into the car that opened its door for her. Her mother and Sarah looked guilty, relieved and full of love. 'We've been driving round for ages hoping to spot you,' explained Sarah, after Caitlin had been hugged beyond being able to breathe. 'We just couldn't let you … well, hear the bad news on your own.'

'Now. Shall we go get a drink?' asked Madeleine, navigating through the rain that had started to come down.

'He can force me to sell …' said Caitlin morosely. 'But surely he won't.' She started to cry. 'Sarah. He can take the house. Or at least half of it. He can. She said. The bitch. And he can apply for maintenance. And dual custody. He can …'

'We won't let it happen, darling,' assured Madeleine, flint in her voice.

'How?' she wailed.

Cait mopped frantically at the salt water coursing down her cheeks, made a note to exclusively wear waterproof mascara in future and made a date with Kelly Clarkson and her room to have an enormous howl at the injustice of it all.

The cottage wasn't amazing real estate. It was falling down, despite the renovations. It was shabby. There was no space and the kids were bursting out of their rooms.

But it had her office, and the frangipani where she'd played when she was a kid. It was where her Nan had held her and tickled her, where the kids were growing up and where she'd loved her soon-to-be-former husband.

I'll be fucked by Catherine the Great's donkey before he takes my memories too.

'Cait … you should know something,' said Madeleine, running a verging-on-red light. 'He dropped around tonight.'

Cait replied with a disgusted snort. 'What did he want — pocket money?'

'With some papers. It looks like they're from Relationships Are Important.'

'We think they might be mediation papers. Or something. You know. Legal-ish stuff,' added Sarah.

'You *think*? What did you do — telepathy?'

They glanced at each other, sheepish. 'We opened them,' blurted Madeleine in a voluminous gust. 'You have an appointment at mediation next week.

'He wants to talk about the settlement.'

SEVENTEEN

CAITLIN'S MOTHER WOKE her up the next morning, *ergo* you didn't have to be psychic to know something was up. Firstly, Madeleine *never* woke up before anyone else. Sleep was a right and a privilege she fully immersed herself in. Besides, nobody ever *wanted* to wake her up, as it gave everyone else in the house some much-needed quiet while she was sleeping.

And when she did greet the day, she certainly never went around waking other people up with a gentle tap on their shoulder. Usually, they were propelled from whatever they were doing with the very first word she spoke, so loud was her voice.

The second reason it was completely clear that something was up was that Caitlin was surrounded. Through foggy red-ringed eyes she could just make out Sean and Sarah's faces, looming into view, like a group gathered for some kind of soft-focus first-thing-in-the-morning intervention. *And* Madeleine was gently patting her shoulder — unheard of. Bewildered, and slightly intrigued, Caitlin slowly sat up in bed, her masses of hair a cloud of red around her, her face a mixture of outrage (*My* bedroom!) and worry (What the HELL has happened?). For a confusing moment she thought Max must have died, everyone was so gentle and loving. Then she remembered they weren't together any more. And then she remembered that if Max had somehow gone from the planet, Madeleine would have thrown a party, regardless of the time of day. (Consciousness comes in stages, first thing in the morning.)

Madeleine's concerned face didn't stay that way long. 'What,' she asked, staring at her daughter like she'd grown another head, her brow furrowing (No Botox for her!), 'are you wearing? It's like something from a museum!'

In fact, Caitlin was wearing an ancient white cotton creation that could only be described as a nightgown. A nightgown she'd dug up from the very gloomy back of the wardrobe. It had been her grandmother's, and even though she knew she was hovering dangerously close to a Miss Havisham moment, she found it comforting, in a black-and-white-film kind of way. (And why shouldn't she be enjoying her moment of Victorian tragedy? White cotton nightgowns play a large part in evoking doomed heroine chic.)

'It's a nightgown. God, most mothers would appreciate their daughters wearing something a bit ...'

'Antique,' Sarah ventured.

'Is that nightwear — or a nightmare?' quipped Sean.

Caitlin giggled reluctantly, simultaneously annoyed at the barb and proud of her daughter's wit — even if she did sound like a twenty-nine-year-old New Yorker.

'I'm sure I've seen it before,' Madeleine said slowly, but not softly, all the while staring pointedly at Caitlin's nightie. 'It looks familiar,' she said, reaching out one hand.

Caitlin responded by pulling the sheets right up high around her neck, making her look even more like a victimised heroine in a silent film.

'Aren't we doing the surprise any more?' Molly's small face appeared round the door, where she'd been hiding, looking disappointed. Madeleine's face flushed with guilt, and Sean took the hint. 'Surprise!' she chirruped, beaming. What was in it for her? Caitlin thought, mother-suspicion on full alert. Why would she be so happy first thing in the morning? She's a teenager! Caitlin turned this scrutiny onto her mother, who had replaced disapproving staring with a completely unconvincing happy, beaming smile.

'First, bring on the breakfast!' announced Madeleine. Molly, who'd been hovering expectantly at the door, wobbled in, holding a steaming bowl on a tray so carefully it was shaking with her nervous energy.

'Dear Mum,' she announced intensely, forehead crinkling as she struggled to remember the speech she'd written last night with her Nan and Sarah in the kitchen.

'Today we celebrate you staying in bed until ten.'

Caitlin sat up further and crossed her arms across her lacy chest, a smile edging its way to the corners of her mouth. What was this all about? No school, probably.

'We will not allow you to leave the bed. There is to be no work today, no taking calls from Kevin, and no developing brilliant ideas.'

'Just for one day,' added Sean, wanting her mother to know she supported her work as well as her taking some time out.

'Are you guys planning on getting a day off, too?' Caitlin asked, pushing her hair off her face and cocking her head to one side.

'No!' proclaimed Molly, bursting with righteousness. 'We will go to school, and you will stay at home.'

'Are you kidding? I've got a —'

'CAITLIN! STAY WHERE YOU ARE!' bellowed her mother, diving for her daughter, who was making get-out-of-bed moves.

'What if I need to go to the toilet?' protested Caitlin.

'Oh dur, Mum,' replied Sean, wondering how her mother the TV executive could be so clueless sometimes. 'Of course you can do that. But if you need anything else, like food or a book or a magazine or chocolates or your favourite CD changed —'

'Not Kelly Clarkson, though,' ordered Molly, heading out of the room on another mission to the kitchen. 'She's banned,' she flung over her little shoulder.

'— you have to ring this bell,' finished Sean.

'Um, everyone …' Caitlin paused, frowning. 'I'm not sick or anything — you get that, right? You know I'm okay, and there's really just so much to do that —'

'Caitlin. This is pleasure, not a punishment. Do you know how many women would love to lie about in bed till ten?' Madeleine pointed out.

'Fine. I'll do that. Then I've got a battle to plan — remember?'

'Oh, but it doesn't stop there. You see, today is a special day. No heading off to work!'

'I don't go to work any more, remember,' muttered Caitlin, fully embracing her inner adolescent, complete with a grudge. 'Technically every day's a special day!' she said, feeling sorry for herself.

'This is an order. Shhh, here comes Molly. She's excited about this!'

Molly entered again, put a steaming cup of coffee for her mother on the bedside table, unfurled a piece of paper and cleared her throat. 'We want you to know that we think you're the greatest mum ever. That even when you cry all day, you're still funny. That even when you feel all alone, you still make us feel loved.'

Sean gestured to her guitar. 'Ditto. And I've written a song for you,' she said, shifting the instrument onto her lap.

'What? Sean, are you serious?' Part of her felt startled. Sean's songwriting girl-band dreams were serious, she knew that, but this, she thought, is when you realise you're living with an artist — when your life starts to get worked into songs.

'Yes,' she said calmly, with one of those sweet smiles that made Caitlin's heart burst its borders. How was it that her teenager was so together and completely lacking the kind of self-consciousness Caitlin was still struggling with? 'Grannie and I have been planning it for days. And I wrote it with Luke. He's been sort of ... well, he's been really cool about the whole thing with you and Dad. Anyway, this is the song I wrote with Luke, for you ...'

Sean's fair hair fell forward, covering her face, and her hands delicately strummed a minor chord. She looked up and that faraway gaze came over her face, all angles and lashes, all creamy skin and lips. She has a really distinctive sound, Caitlin thought. 'It's not just that I think she's really good, is it?' she whispered to Sarah, who was tearing up.

'Oh no,' her best friend answered, squeezing her hand.

'She's amazing. She's only fourteen. It's sort of daunting. What to do with it?' she wondered aloud.

'You don't have to do anything, honey.'

'That's right,' chipped in Madeleine. 'Just let her find her way.'

'Whatever that means,' Caitlin whispered. 'She's been writing a lot lately. And who's Luke?'

Sean had a strong jaw, tilted green eyes and a splash of freckles across her nose. For all that she was a teenager, she didn't ever come to Caitlin with the usual stuff. Boys. Skin eruptions. Boys. Which is why Caitlin was so shocked to hear about a boy called Luke.

'Thank you, darling,' she said to Sean. 'You're amazing. We should ... we should record something. You should, I mean.'

'Really? Because I have about three songs.'

'Well, get ten together, and it's a deal. Studio time ...'

'I'll start writing with Luke now! I have so many ideas, and I can get together with him this week and we can —' Sean's face radiated a very unteenager-like enthusiasm. Caitlin hated to interrupt, but she had to get her back on track before she ran away with the next guy with a guitar who came along ...

'No, honey. You need to get ready for school.' Sean grinned, nodded, picked up her guitar and wandered off vaguely in the direction of the outside world, pretty head already teeming with chords and lyrics.

'Look, I appreciate this,' Caitlin said softly to her mother. 'And that was great. But I don't think lying about in my nightie — which you all hate, don't deny it,' she said, interrupting her mother, who was about to launch into an explanation. 'I know you do! — I don't think that lying round for too much longer is going to be such a great impression to give the girls. They'll think it's okay to have a day off.' In their nighties, she thought, suppressing a grin.

'Oooh, Caitlin, the world will collapse if *you* stay in bed!' mocked Sarah, fanning herself melodramatically. 'How will the world get along without *you*?'

Caitlin felt a surge of annoyance. 'It's not *the* world, Sarah. It's *my* world. *My* world *does* rely on me.'

Sarah looked confused. 'Oh. You're right.'

Madeleine, seeing Sarah completely losing her authority, looked like she was about to jump in. So Caitlin beat her to it. She was adding just a dash of concern, Caitlin noticed, as she got ready to interrupt her mother before she'd even begun. Why is she coming over all worried? Caitlin thought. I'm fine, she thought. 'I'm fine,' she repeated out loud.

'Déja Vu and Irony Alert!' Sarah spluttered, waving her hands around in frustration. 'Remember yesterday? You "I'm fined" us all the way to a mini-breakdown. You could barely walk by the time we got you home! And *now* you insist you're okay again. Woah!' she continued, taking the volume up to near-Madeleine levels. Caitlin winced. 'You're so stubborn. You just can't admit that this is hard on you.' She shut up, and started shaking her head sadly.

'I'm not going to wail because you want me to,' replied Caitlin, not missing a nano-beat. 'Or stay in bed for a week because you'll think I'll be fine after that. It *is* hard. But what can I do?' Bugger, she thought. I asked a question. Now I'm for it.

'You have to learn, Caitlin my darling, that it's at these times that we need to take care of ourselves.' (Caitlin tried really hard to catch herself before she crossed her arms and rolled her eyes.) 'And if *you* insist on modelling to the girls that what they must do is forge ahead and fall apart quietly, wearing Victorian nightgowns and thinking it's pretty to be broken on the inside, *I'll* insist that they see it's all right for you to come first. Besides, they're loving it.'

Caitlin's eyes filled with tears. Damn, she thought. I can see her point.

Madeleine smiled, rather like the Mother Superior does in *The Sound of Music* when Maria is all confused and she breaks into *Climb Ev'ry Mountain*. Thankfully, though, her mother didn't sing.

'In fact, it'll do them much more good to see their mother indulging herself and resting and allowing her pain to register and then pass, until she looks pretty and well and maybe even smiles again!'

It wasn't so much that her mother had waved a magic wand, but by the time she'd been drizzled with healing oils and had bells rung over her and had her scalp massaged with smooth stones and her toenails painted silvery white by a delicate Japanese girl, Caitlin did feel a whole lot closer to the goddess she was proclaimed to be by the girls when they saw her much later that day. Her mother had been busy putting fresh flowers in vases, Sarah had sprayed the rooms with a combination of water and essential oils and, on the way to school, they'd coached the children not to complain about going to their father's that weekend. And everything felt soothing.

'Mum, this is all beautiful. And I feel amazing,' she conceded, giving her a hug, feeling like she could move right through her mother's marshmallowy body, it was so soft and receptive. 'But I feel like I'm not paying attention to what I need to do. I need to plan for this meeting with Max next week. And what I'm going to say to Kevin. And I need to get this show ready to be pitched. And I need to see an accountant … and I —'

'First,' her mother interrupted, 'you've done what you needed to do with … Max, wasn't it?' She paused, a surprised expression shimmying across her face. 'You know, I truly am erasing him from my memory. It's wonderful how we can do that!' (Caitlin waited for her mother to get back on track. One, two, three … she counted in her head.) 'Anyway, darling, you know what you're up against. And you know we're here for you. I think … I think you might have to suck that one up somewhat.'

'What do you mean?' Caitlin was pretty sure she knew what was coming, but needed to hear it out loud. Just like they do in the movies.

'I think he might have a case on paper. As far as the house is concerned, anyway. Which is why you needed a pamper day. Battle goddesses didn't just storm about yelling at the troops. They bathed in milk and had slave boys rubbing them down.'

Caitlin hung her head, tickling the top of her mouth with her tongue to stop herself from beginning to cry. Stupid rose quartz facial, she thought. Stupid healing love energy just makes me cry!

She kept tickling the roof of her mouth, faster and faster. Work, damn it, she thought furiously. Bloody hell! She'd been telling her talent that trick for years. Besides, her eyes really needed the rest — and they were slathered with million-dollar product. What a waste to cry it all away.

'Don't ever try to stop crying, darling,' said Madeleine. Oh, shut up. 'Honestly, if you girls knew how pretty you look after a cry ...'

'Yes,' Sarah put in helpfully. 'Crying makes you pretty.'

'Well, then I must be bloody gorgeous,' Caitlin replied, half laughing.

'Well, you just cry without the scrunching up your face stuff, darling. Like this,' she said, demonstrating, her face immobile, but her eyes welling up gently. 'Then you just let them spill over!'

Sarah nodded, blonde curls toppling into her eyes.

'And don't rub your eyes. They'll go puffy. You can't blub, you've got to do it the old-fashioned way — you know, what they used to call weeping. No good wearing Victorian nightgowns and crying like you're Maria

Callas. Anyway. No need to get puffy eyelids over that ... man. Really. You won't be losing this house. I can't let that happen. My mother planted that garden,' she said with a vague gesture outside. 'You're not selling it unless you want to sell it.'

'Right. I need to get to work, Mum. I've got a meeting with Kevin about this new show — and *Date Squad*.'

'Oh, he just obviously needs help with *Date Squad*,' she said dismissively. 'You have to spoon-feed him the ideas ... otherwise he'll think he's got the ideas and he might not need you. So stick to the *Date Squad* issue. He's probably got unhappy staff and Kennedy throwing her weight around, annoying everyone by being so bossy and right about everything.'

(Her mother must have been listening in on her conversations, Caitlin figured. She'd got yet even more messages from resentful staff during her facial. She hadn't got back to them yet, but they were persistent enough for her to know something like mutiny or even anarchy was on its way.)

'She's probably complaining — *incessantly* — about people not taking her seriously, giving what's-his-face, you know, your ex-type person, hell, and she's probably not having sex with him any more! I'm sure *her* days of booking Brazilians when she was supposed to be working for you are well and truly over!'

Caitlin opened her mouth to wonder aloud at whether her mother had been spying on her, but another thought barged in and took first place in the mind-queue. 'Mum — you know about Brazilians?'

'Well, we don't just lie around waiting to die once we move out of Sydney, darling. Anyway, I hope you didn't get a Brazilian today. Now people are growing their hair back. Nice boys *like* a full muff, darling.'

Caitlin stared at her mother and crossed her arms. 'How do you know this, Mum?'

'For a start, when we were doing all that stuff you're so against us having done in the seventies, at least we actually knew what real people looked like. Hairy! Now all these young boys have grown up with ridiculous online porn, featuring women who are bald! No mystery at all! And those ridiculous bleached bottom holes. Honestly, I worry for Sean and Molly. And what their silly prospective boyfriends will expect their bits to look like. Though this Luke boy sounds nice. I'm sure he won't want Sean to have a —'

'Mum!' Caitlin looked revolted. But secretly, she wanted to know more.

'Anyway. Don't get me started on how we're all supposed to have pretty anuses and be proficient pole dancers.'

'Mum!'

'Yes, all right. Now. Kevin, I swear to you, will want help with *Date Squad* and your suggestions for free. Just make sure you invoice him for them. And mediation's next week. To really prepare, I have a little surprise planned for us all this weekend.'

'Mum, I don't need another surprise! And, anyway, what about Dad?'

Her mother looked shocked. 'Well, *that* was random, darling. What about him?'

'Well, when are you going home? You know — to your Chosen One? The Love of Your Life? The Twin Flame … who you cheated on,' she added, sounding like the mean girl she was feeling like.

'Don't be like that. It's hardly cheating when it's an open marriage.'

'God, I hope Dad's my actual father.'

'Of course he is, Caitlin! I waited till I was pregnant with you till we —'

Caitlin interrupted quickly, desperate to spare herself more gruesome details of her parents' Mr-and-Mrs-Freelove days. 'Look, Mum. Seriously. You can't just worry about me and neglect your … soul twin.' Or whatever he is, she thought.

'Soul mate, darling,' Madeleine protested.

'Twin flame,' Sarah corrected.

'Whatever, Sarah. Mum, Dad must be missing you so badly.' Clever, she congratulated herself. That will send her home.

'Well, of course, as I am him,' her mother replied placidly.

Caitlin held back a snort. Her mother hadn't displayed any of the classic signs of missing someone. Her mother must have read her mind.

'Missing someone isn't all sobbing into your nightie and pouting, Cait,' Madeleine said in the manner of an ancient sage. 'It's … well, I'm here. He's there. We've hardly spent any time apart for years and, to be quite honest, this time out from him has been very good for me. I do miss him. But I needed a break.' That last comment was made in the manner of a post-feminist spiritual woman craving her me-time.

Oh no, Caitlin thought, feeling doomed. She's not going home next week! Maybe … maybe never!

She regrouped instantly, plotting as she went. She had to approach this one carefully. 'Isn't he your chosen life partner?'

'Well, yes, he is, darling. But even chosen life partners can get on your wick a bit!'

Time for a different tactic, Caitlin thought. Use soft, caring, soulful voice for this one.

'It's not Dad's fault Max dumped me, Mum. It's not revenge against all husbands.'

'Oh, that won't work. I'm here. Just try and get rid of me.'

'Ooh, I think I hear the children,' Sarah yelped, springing off the bed and dashing for the door.

'Isn't that my line?' Caitlin smiled at her mother. 'Well, you know. She loves them.'

'Nope …' Sarah said, reappearing. 'But they'll be home any minute,' she said sort of to herself, looking like she was about to rush off and bake cookies.

'Now, what about your home and hearth? Have you moved in forever or something too?'

'Well,' Sarah began carefully, obviously uncomfortable. Uh-oh. She can't look at me, thought Caitlin. (Sarah always gave great eye-contact, except for when she had something she would rather hide. Being so honest, hiding things was not her strength.)

'I've been meaning to talk to you about that …'

'Well, what about your home ... you know, your life?' Caitlin said lightly, hoping she wasn't about to hear something dramatic. She gestured awkwardly to her mother and her best friend. 'You can't both dump everything and move in here ... what about all those boys out there dying to go out with you, Sarah?'

'Well, I've been meaning to tell you something,' Sarah said.

Tell me what, thought Caitlin, tightening up, and staying quiet.

Sarah looked up, and stopped holding her breath.

'I've met someone.'

What Sarah hadn't been telling Caitlin was that she'd fallen in love. And she was terrified. She felt that while divorce was the noughties equivalent of the little black dress of the eighties or the conical bra of the nineties (only a whole lot more expensive, difficult to wear, and uncomfortable), falling in love was just plain daggy. Falling in love with ... well, let's just say it was complicated.

'I've been wanting to tell you for ages,' Sarah explained later, snuggled up in Caitlin's bed. They were spooning, and occasionally having a cry. Only this time it was Sarah crying, and Caitlin patting her, and fending off her own resentment. She was feeling betrayed. And that, she knew, wasn't in the code of friendship.

'Why didn't you tell me?' Caitlin asked gently.

Sarah sighed, bosoms heaving dramatically. 'I didn't want to. I didn't know how. It wasn't the right time.

You were in crisis. When all your stuff happened, it was a perfect …'

'Excuse?' Caitlin prompted.

Sarah nodded, lower lip trembling. 'To not mention anything. I know that sounds awful, but it was like some kind of preordained moment. The best reason to get away. Gently. You know, sort of like a smokescreen, I s'pose, if I'm honest. I got to look like a good friend, instead of … of …'

'Oh, come on. You *are* a good friend,' comforted Caitlin. 'You're a good person. Always have been, right from that first moment I met you at school.'

'Remember how we met?'

'You saved me from getting my head flushed down the toilet by Mary McKenzie.'

'She was horrible,' said Sarah, screwing up her pretty little nose.

'See. You were always my saviour,' said Caitlin. 'You're good.'

'No, I'm not,' she said, curling in on herself. Caitlin couldn't help feeling that it was nice not to be the one hurting openly, for a change. It made her sad that her friend, her best friend, had been feeling all this, and keeping it so very much to herself.

'It simply isn't fair,' boomed Madeleine, who had been overseeing Sean's songwriting workshop in the lounge room with her friend Luke, and Molly's profile-building on MySpace. She wandered in from the hallway, sat down at Caitlin's dressing table and started absentmindedly playing with some make-up brushes, puffing away at her face, gazing at herself lovingly. 'I'd love to leave my husband too and join you all,' she announced, sounding like she was missing out on something wonderful. 'But I can't,' she added, dropping her head and placing a brush down with such tender regret that Caitlin felt like bursting into laughter — or applause.

'Why not?' asked Caitlin cheekily. 'Isn't it part of your weird open trade agreement?'

'Because I love him!' Madeleine said, as if it was the most obvious thing in the world.

Caitlin wasn't going to get to laugh at her mum with Sarah, who now had fresh tears spilling out of her electric blue eyes. 'I love the person I'm with!' she sniffled, as Caitlin stared at her. 'I ran away. I couldn't handle it,' Sarah continued, wiping her eyes.

'Are you all crazy? Why aren't you with him? And why aren't you with Dad? It's as though you've got divorce envy,' Caitlin spluttered. 'It's not a skirt, or a kind of car, or like taking up ... Pilates. You've got a perfectly good relationship already, I suppose,' she huffed to Sarah.

'It's complicated, Cait.'

'You just said you did. Have you slept with him?'

'No. I haven't had sex with a guy for ... ages. And ages. And ages,' said Sarah, sneaking a telling look at Cait, who remained oblivious.

'Neither have I,' piped up Madeleine. 'Not since ladies didn't have the vote. Not since —'

'George Michael was straight?' Cait quipped.

'Exactly. So. Don't hate me for not telling you,' Sarah begged. She stopped short of pouting, but came so close that Caitlin felt she'd wounded a kitten.

'You're spiritual,' Caitlin rallied. 'You're supposed to let me hate you so I can —'

Sarah jumped in, looking distraught. 'But I'm in *love*,' she announced. She sat back, like the breath had been taken right out of her.

Oh. Big. Moral. Dilemma, Caitlin thought, willing her mouth to stay shut, at least till the electric surge of adrenaline she could feel spilling and churning its way through her stomach had settled. She took a deep, deep breath and rubbed her hand through her hair. Her eyes were wide, and she leaned forward. 'Why didn't you say something?' was all she could manage.

'I *couldn't* tell you.'

Protesting, thought Caitlin. Obviously. Justifying, she added.

'Look at how you're reacting!' Sarah went on.

Now that, thought Caitlin, was completely unfair. She'd not even leaped over and called her a skank and started beating her up, Jerry Springer-style. Which she was entitled to, she thought huffily. 'It's official,' Caitlin replied, feeling dark but speaking lightly. 'I hate you! Think how distracting this news could have been.' And she realised once the brittle words had flown out that she did, in fact, hate her a little. Though she knew that would pass.

'No, you don't,' Madeleine leaped in, interrupting her scientific exploration of every one of Caitlin's cosmetic pots. She had red lips and was carefully daubing glittery gloss on top of them. (It's a wonder she could speak at all.)

'I am sick of people not telling me things.'

'Like who?' Sarah said, looking hurt.

'Like *you*! Like Max. Like Kennedy. Like Mum. Like —'

'Oh, don't be silly. It's different from Max and Kennedy. They're cheaters!'

'Wow. I hope it's different. But the principle is the same. Besides, I never said Sarah was a cheater, Mum,' she said, with the unspoken words *like you* hanging heavily in the air. 'Feeling guilty? Cheaters *cheat*.' She wasn't relinquishing the moral high ground that easily. It was her home, she'd found her place and she was staying there. There was no room for shades of grey. You were either faithful or a cheater, she told herself.

'Oh, Cait. You can't hate me. It's not good for you.' Caitlin smothered a snort, and watched Sarah take a deep breath in and give herself a hug. 'I've fallen in love.' Her eyes were so wide and blue, her face so angelic, Caitlin could almost forget how completely irritated she was. So angry.

I hate them all, she thought, her feelings ugly even to herself. But she's my best friend, she thought right back, panicked. I can't hate her. Cait's brain pinged an alarm. 'I'm getting my very first migraine,' she complained, holding her head and grimacing.

'Anyway, can I stay a while? A while longer, I mean?' Sarah corrected herself, flushing.

'What about your lov-ah — why not be with him?'

Sarah flushed. 'I wish it was that simple. I need to have somewhere ... transitional. You know, for it to work out in the long run.'

'*It* being a *who*, right?'

'Er, yes. And I love it here. And I still want to sort your clothes into chakra-colours so you can dress —'

Caitlin interrupted her with a groan. 'Stop it! Come here,' she said, pulling her close and giving her a squeeze. 'I can't even not talk to you for five minutes, you're so adorable. I just can't hate you. So of course you can stay, as long as you like, you, you ... holder-outerer ...'

They laughed, while Madeleine, relieved, resumed her make-up foraging. 'You'll like that one, Mum,' Caitlin said, fighting to keep the hint of desperation out of her voice, 'to your left.' Anything to keep her away from the La Mer. 'And don't think you've heard the last about being a cheater, either,' she said, giving her mother a particularly severe frown.

'Oh, get over yourself,' Madeleine muttered, feeling vaguely like she'd been caught out at something she should feel guilty about. And Madeleine never did guilt.

'So, who's the guy?' asked Caitlin, shaking off the mood and deciding to enter into the spirit. It was weird, she thought. It was faintly exciting. No wonder other people were so keen to talk about her life. She was desperate to hear all the details of Sarah's new love. And part of that was because she cared. But a lot of it was just sheer curiosity. 'Lucky bastard,' she added, looking at her friend. 'Look at you! He must think he's hit the jack—'

'Stop!'

'Stop what? Oh, come on. You have to share. Stop doing this withholding thing. It's not funny.'

'No — I mean, you're making assumptions.'

'About what? Your lov-ah. I know,' she crowed. 'It's that cowboy shaman guy you were telling me about. The one who knows about physics or something.'

'He's spiritual, not a scientist. And no, it's not him. You're assuming you know who it is and you don't.'

'That's right. And that's why I asked. So tell me who your new man is, and stop being such a freak.'

'I knew it! I knew you'd think I was weird.'

'What is *wrong* with you?'

'There's no new man, Caitlin.'

'Oh. Oh no,' she said, eyes widening. 'It's not some *ghost* or something, is it?'

'Don't joke about it Caitlin,' warned Madeleine. 'One friend of mine said she could orgasm with an invisible lover — turned out it was her childhood sweetheart.'

'Was she with her husband while this was happening?'

'Yes! They —'

'No, it's not a ghost,' Sarah interupted in a monotone. She flopped back on the bed, one arm flung over her eyes to shield herself from the onslaught.

Caitlin, however, was on a roll. Picking on someone else's love life was giving her a gleeful taste of fun. She was enjoying herself, even if it was at Sarah's expense. 'Wait ... not some — what are they? — an Ascended Master or something? You've not got some weird dream lover twin flame fifth dimensional toyboy have you?'

Sarah narrowed her eyes. 'How come you can talk my talk all of a sudden?'

'I've been researching my new show, remember?'

Sarah hesitated. So Caitlin knew it had to be good.

'Hmmm. I knew it. It's something weird. He's a — hang on, hang on — let me just tune in ... he's a Trekkie or something, isn't he?'

'No,' said Sarah, looking faintly annoyed. 'You have so far to go before you can even pretend to be psychic, Caitlin.'

'Okay, shock me. Footie player. *Australian Idol* contestant. The homeless guy you gave my cashmere blanket to. No, no, I've got it! It's a *prisoner* you're visiting, and he didn't mean to kill his wife, she just didn't understand him, and you've got this *connection* and —'

'Shut *up*, Caitlin,' said Sarah, sitting up straight, hair awry. 'The new *man's* a *woman*. And she's no space creature either!' she spat, before gathering herself up and hurling herself out the door.

'No!' gasped Madeleine, a compact clattering to the dressing-table top. (Cait's mother was utterly sick with post-marriage relationship envy.) 'No!' she repeated, shaking her head like there was something she'd like to shake out of it. 'All the things I'm too old to do. You don't know how lucky you are,' she said, staring resentfully at Caitlin.

'I'm not doing it,' Caitlin protested.

'YOU DON'T KNOW HOW LUCKY YOU ARE,' Madeleine bellowed through the door. 'You have so much you can do! Everyone would just think I was just an ... an old lezzo if I tried that. Not someone gorgeous and sexy and ...'

Sarah stormed back in. She'd only been hovering outside the door, trying desperately to hear what everyone was saying about her, as well as trying to locate a paper bag to breathe into.

Caitlin and Madeleine looked at each other, a strange combination of the alarmed and the excited whizzing between them. '*Lucky*? If you *tried that*?!' Sarah roared with an upward inflection, her face pink with outrage. 'It's not like that!' she said, defiant, her pretty face deepening to a kind of rose shade. 'Everyone thinks it's just some kinky experiment, some kind of premature female mid-life crisis!'

Well, isn't it? Caitlin thought.

'Well, isn't it?' Madeleine demanded. 'I mean, it does sound quite *sexy*, Sarah, you must admit. And what's wrong with me being envious?'

Madeleine was, Caitlin saw, wildly jealous. Finally, for the first time, there was some evidence that there was actually an age difference between her best friend and her mother. She couldn't repress a slightly spiteful shiver travelling down her spine at *that* epiphany.

Sarah shook her head and buried her face in her hands.

Caitlin could *feel* her frustration leaking out. 'So who's "everyone"? You said "everyone" thinks you're experimenting! Who knows if I don't?' she said. 'You are still my best friend, are you not?' she demanded, feeling like her anchor had just been pulled and she'd been cast adrift.

'That's what *she* thought too. I told her I was in love with her, and she said she wasn't some experiment.'

Caitlin stifled a splutter of laughter.

'It's not funny, Caitlin. I'm in love! And she thinks I'm just after — after …'

'Sex?' Caitlin concluded for her, unable to watch her struggling. She didn't know what else to say. It did sound pervy. But her best friend was hurting, and obviously offended that no one was taking her grand romance at all seriously. Least of all the woman she claimed to be in love with.

But before she could say all that, and offer love and support and tell her she'd be there for her, the question she really wanted to ask just flew out of her mouth.

'Is she dykey?'

Silence.

'Sorry. I didn't mean to ask that. I meant to be all supportive.'

'Oh, shut up, Caitlin,' snapped Madeleine. 'Is she, Sarah?'

Sarah rolled her eyes, then smiled.

'Very. She's so butch,' she sighed.

'Well, if you can fall in love with a dyke, I can wear my nana's nightie.'

And to that declaration of nightwear independence, Madeleine had nothing to say at all.

EIGHTEEN

'The Wild Women's weekend,' explained Sarah, 'is all about us getting back in touch with who we really are ... with our intuition, with our*selves*.'

'Sounds suspiciously like group masturbation to me,' Myra flung over her shoulder, grinning. She did that because she was driving, windows were open, and Madeleine had been put in the back seat. Despite gusts of wind, the cranked-up Led Zeppelin soundtrack and four other people talking, Madeleine was *still* the loudest thing in the car.

'Will there be naked bits?' asked Nadia, looking concerned, casting a worried glance toward her crotch. (It wasn't a moral issue, you understand. It had just been some time since her last wax.)

'Quite possibly,' said Sarah, brow wrinkling, trying to remember the program details.

'Definitely naked bits,' Myra declared. 'Bound to be with all these free-spirit types.'

'Well, *you'll* be all right, then,' Caitlin said to Sarah. 'It'll be lesbianville, won't it?'

Everyone shrank a little, like grannies pulling

cardigans tighter against a cold wind. There was still some residual tension between Sarah and Caitlin. Correction. There was an undeclared war going on. And when they spoke to each other, it literally got *chilly.*

'Can you wind the windows up?' asked Myra, feeling the temperature drop. 'It's freezing in here.'

(See?)

'No, although some people will be gay,' corrected Sarah, sighing and winding the window up. Strangely, it didn't seem to affect the temperature.

'Won't that be distracting? For *you,* I mean. After all, all those naked ladies — you might fancy someone else!'

'Oh, shut up, Caitlin. Stop being bitchy,' Madeleine snapped.

I'm entitled, Mum, Caitlin thought right back, but changed tack. She was not in a good mood. (They'd made her change out of the nightie and into day clothes, robbing her of the right to sulk in style, she felt.) 'You know, I'm not sure why I'm in a car with my mother and my friends and we're going to some women's thingy that feels very seventies retro. Shouldn't I be out planning my twenty-first-century life?'

'This *is* your life,' said Sarah quietly. But oh-so-firmly.

'Noooo!' said Caitlin, mock-wailing, clapping her hands audibly to her face. 'It can't be true!'

'And you asked me to plan this. Remember?'

'No. I have decided I have selective amnesia,' Caitlin grumped, enjoying how much she could get away with now she was officially the friend everyone had to feel sorry for. She knew it wouldn't last forever — but for now, she was determined to milk it.

(I never said she was perfect.)

'Well. Note the camera in your bag, Caitlin. This is going to be *amazing* for you,' said Sarah. 'We're going to get the most *fantastic* footage of people and fire and interviews and great readings and quotes. Kevin will be *blown away*.'

'Kevin never gets blown away,' Caitlin sulked. 'And I'm beginning to think my brain's gone pear-shaped. He's going to be a hard one to crack with this sort of airy-fairy stuff.'

'Oh, rubbish. He's a fool if he can't see what a viewer-magnet this show will be,' Sarah said, hurt.

'And you shouldn't be worrying about it. Note also the fact that on your list of things to do now is have some fun,' said Nadia, sweetly and completely sincerely. 'I can tell it's going to be amazing.'

Caitlin scowled, simultaneously pondering if she needed to point out how overused the word *amazing* was, silently composing a scathing assessment of fun and her relationship with it, *and* polishing up a closing point about how her definition of fun didn't have anything to do with anything called a women's retreat. But she didn't get a chance, because Myra got there first.

'Note finally that you're beginning to sound cranky. Are you getting your period?' Myra butted in, smirking.

'You're going to go back with so many ideas … More than you bargained for, probably,' Sarah said, nodding in that meaningful-nod kind of way. 'It'll be amazing …'

Caitlin knew that when people nod very meaningfully and say the word *amazing* over and over again, but aren't very clear, they usually like you to start asking questions. Or get curious. In short, they're usually trying to talk something up.

But she wasn't going to fall for that, she told herself, reaching for a muffin. Mmmm, chocolate.

One of Madeleine's famous boxes was being passed around the car — this one came complete with food for five women on an adventure. She'd given it to Caitlin that morning, as a deal-breaker. Caitlin had wavered about coming on the weekend. She made out it was all about leaving home and having work to do and needing space, but really everyone knew it was that she couldn't bear to leave the kids. And even Caitlin knew that, while she rattled on and on about responsibilities, it was giving the kids over to Max that was making her weak at the knees. So she'd resisted leaving for the weekend for a while, before remembering that resistance was futile when it came to the combined force that was Madeleine and Sarah. Throw Nadia and Myra into the mix, and there really hadn't been a choice.

Capitulation hadn't meant that calling Max and making the arrangements hadn't made her feel absolutely sick. It *had*. And she *knew* beyond a doubt that one day, one day she'd be used to Sean and Molly going to spend time with Max — and probably seeing Kennedy and her baby bump. But this time was a complete initiation into a new kind of pain. She felt a deep and instinctual, almost savage resentment and surging jealousy at the thought of her children being anywhere near a person who'd so obviously laid waste to her life, and to theirs. And the idea of Molly befriending the person who'd taken her father away from them, and Sean having to swallow her fury just to coexist seemed eminently unfair. Even though Max insisted that Kennedy would be nowhere to be seen, she really had, for a moment, thought that she just wouldn't be able to stomach it. Wasn't a big enough person to handle it. Couldn't stand it. Wouldn't hear of it and wouldn't see it happening, either. Every single sense was in rebellion at the idea of handing over the most precious part of her life to the person she considered most poisonous to her wellbeing.

On the other hand, she knew that with a twenty-first-century divorce, it was quite normal to encourage your six-year-old to spend time with the woman who'd broken up her family and who was carrying her future half-sibling. But that didn't make it any less painful — or strange — that she was having to behave in ways that her instincts fought so hard against. This Wild Women's Weekend couldn't be any weirder than *that*, Caitlin thought, putting on sunglasses to hide the fact she was tearing up. At the very least, she'd be working. And when she was working, Caitlin got distracted. That would be a relief.

She settled back behind the shelter of her sunglasses, accepted the muffin her mother passed her and toyed with the protective amulet Madeleine had insisted she wear on the journey. She secretly loved it. So did Sean, who'd held it up to the light the night before, as Caitlin had read the card that accompanied it. 'Rose quartz for love,' she said, as Sean fingered the milky pink stone.

'What's this black stone, Mum?' she'd asked.

'I like it,' Molly said in her squeaky voice. 'It's shiny and deep.'

'I like it too,' Caitlin had said, pulling Molly closer and nuzzling her. When will she be too old for this? she wondered. Not for a while, she thought. Please let me still have this for a while.

'That's black onyx, for protection,' explained Sarah, leaning over and handling it gently.

'Wow. Can I have it?' Sean said, going to loop it over her shoulders. 'School sucks.'

'No, um, hang on. I think I need that right now,' Caitlin said, reaching out and taking it back firmly. Why does school suck? she thought. Or was that teen-code for *life* sucks? 'You can wear it another time, honey. When you go into the studio — for luck.'

'Here. Let's put it on,' cooed Molly, taking it gently from Caitlin and lacing it through her mother's curly hair, draping the black stone onto her forehead. 'You look pretty!'

Caitlin felt the stone dangle between her brows and actually felt her sight grow thin, her head grow light. She instantly wanted to lie down and sleep.

'Mum?' Molly inquired. 'You look funny.'

'Oooh. Let's take it off,' she said. 'I just had a headspin!'

'That's black onyx,' explained Madeleine earnestly. 'It's extremely strong.'

The rest of the box her mother had handed over as a pre-weekend treat had held her favourite white wine, fruity and green, fresh and bittersweet, along with some herbs. For tea again, Caitlin had learned with relief, remembering her mother's dalliance with Rastafarianism.

'Why have you got a notebook, Caitlin?' her mother asked as she packed.

'To take notes.'

'Why have you got a tape recorder?'

'Because.'

'What about that camera?'

'Well, you know I have an idea for this new TV show, right? And there'll be a lot of ... material on this weekend.'

Back in the car, Caitlin was mentally going through what it was she needed.

Sarah said the sexy witch they'd seen in the magazine was a star attraction at the weekend, plus Caitlin would get to meet a woman who was a medium and someone else who talked to animals, or crystals or something. She could shoot preliminary interviews with them all, get them together for a group session and get some spooky stuff, too, for atmosphere.

'You said the moon would be full, didn't you?' she asked Sarah.

'Of course it's a full moon,' Sarah said. 'In Libra,' she added, as if everyone knew that Libran moons were significant.

'What's a Libran moon look like?' Caitlin, only half joking.

'Good. It'll look good,' Sarah had smiled, too kind to point out that it would look very much like the other full moons Caitlin had seen — if she had seen any, Sarah thought. Most people who worked too hard never saw the moon. Or a sunrise. Or a sunset ... or a rainbow, she added, beginning to warm to her subject.

'As long as it doesn't look too horror-movie,' Caitlin said, interrupting Sarah's whimsical train of thought. She had such a clear vision of how this show was meant to look, sound and, more than anything, how it was meant to make people feel. The idea taking shape in Caitlin's head had everything to do with *Better Homes and Gardens* ... only if the better homes and gardens in question were haunted. Her plan was to shoot and interview these people over the weekend, and firstly assess whether any of them were at all sane.

Next, add haunting music, some nice cutaways of the moon rising over a circle of women and footage of people who were experiencing hauntings — Sarah had lined them up for her, and she'd shoot them next week — and she had a preview tape, or 'the pitch', to show Kevin.

Well, hopefully she'd have a pitch to show Kevin. Hopefully the women she was planning to interview would be reasonably sane, and brilliantly psychic, and utterly likable. It also wouldn't hurt a bit that at least one of them was beautiful, she thought. But she didn't want them *too* sane. Because if they were dull, that's exactly how the show would be. She wanted characters. Big ones, yes, but very homey. People like me and you, she thought, only without the ridiculous drama, and adorably down to earth. Perhaps someone who would be endearingly strict with people who were attracting ghosts and so on, she thought with a little smile. Bring it on.

Anything to distract from the looming mediation meeting of next week. Which was the real reason they were all heading off, she was sure. There was no way she'd make it through this weekend without some sort of strategy meeting being landed on her. Myra, she knew, would be into it — Madeleine and Sarah right behind her. She might, she wondered, just have to hang with Nadia all weekend. At least that way, Nadia being so sweet, she could avoid being bossed.

The crowd squeezed into the Honda, which was heading uphill at a very steep angle, had fallen silent, including Madeleine (who must have been dozing, because that's the only time she was ever truly quiet). The farmed hills they'd been driving through for what seemed like hours and hours had finally given way to thickly forested mountains. At Sarah's prompting, Myra took an abrupt detour that veered off the side of the tarred road, plunging them into darkness. The sun was still up, but here the trees touched each other across the road and there was barely any sunlight reaching the women.

'That way,' said Sarah, pointing to her right. Through the forest they drove, along a road lit up by fairylights.

'This is it,' said Sarah, leaning forward and directing Myra. 'Just up ahead.'

Small cabins were lined up neatly along the foot of a rolling green hill, mist gathering round the valley, with a small building jutting out of the mist's centre, and a long hall just visible to the right. In the distance was a circle of trees on the incline of the hill. Maybe Moreton Bay figs, thought Caitlin, squinting to make them out through the twilight and the mist. In the middle of the circle was a small stone house. It looked very intriguing, a fairytale house … the witch's house … she thought. Maybe a good place to shoot!

Along the valley glinted a free-flowing creek, and the air smelled fresh and sweet.

'Wow. I haven't been out of the city. Ever,' said Myra, taking her feet off the pedals to stretch her long legs. She didn't mind driving, but sitting drove her crazy.

'Not for lifetimes,' said Sarah, gazing about her.

'It's so lovely,' agreed Nadia.

(These weren't fake oohs and ahhs. We have with us here four city girls who you may think are going to shrink and scream at bush and lizard and bee and leaping green frogs, but they got their genes from people who'd lived on the land for a long time, far longer than these girls and their mothers had been squishing their feet into heels that hurt in a city made of concrete. Nadia's family had been farmers in Yugoslavia. Myra's feudal Irish foreparents had made it through the potato famine by foraging. Sarah's had learned how to weave and work with sheep and land, and Caitlin's … again, part of her blood wanted this. Two thousand years of country DNA couldn't be wiped out by one lifetime in the city.)

Myra swung the car into a turning area, and parked roughly where about twenty other cars (with higher than the usual proportion of Kombis and *Magick Happens* stickers) were haphazardly lined up in a gravelled area complete with falling-down shed. Several kangaroos hopped lazily out of the way as the women climbed out and retrieved their bags. The last rays of afternoon light filtered through trees taller than the buildings they were used to being surrounded by. Butterflies flip-flop-flew near the heavy fruit of a huge fig tree.

It was really beautiful, everyone knew, even if Nadia did wince at the fig pulp that was squishing into her sandals with every step. They didn't have to say so. Still, they felt slightly bewildered, and so were pleased when a very purposeful person came looming toward them.

She was huge and gorgeous, and wearing a purple dress that cascaded out in full sleeves flowing from her wrists, and long layers swishing about her ankles. Not a piece of flesh below her neck was showing, yet everything about her was sensual and luscious. She was a big woman. A distinct waist separated her gravity-defying breasts from her heavy hips. She had no shoes on, and her feet were covered in dirt and fig. Her toenails were painted cherry red, peeping out like tiny strawberries from under the swirls of purple fabric.

'Hi, I am Cassandra. Welcome,' she sang out, arms flung wide, before moving in and taking each of them into her curves, hugging them all like distant and rich members of a family at an intergalactic reunion. Caitlin stepped back to watch. Usually Nadia would have hated being hugged by any woman dressed in purple, and Myra would have asked if she was an extra on a medieval kids' show. But today they were all taking any hugs they could get ... besides, this woman was glorious.

Sarah allowed herself to be completely enveloped in the most amazing hug she'd ever experienced, and pulled away dizzy. 'Wow — you could sell those,' she said, blinking a few times.

'Woah,' said Myra dizzily, emerging from Cassandra's purple curves, and sitting down to steady herself. 'You know, I can't think of anything sarcastic to say.'

Cassandra turned to Nadia and prepared to hit her with the hug.

Caitlin's trigger finger was itching — she needed to shoot this woman immediately.

'This is the one I told you about,' Sarah whispered, nudging her. 'She's amazing. Very psychic. Everyone cries.' Immediately intrigued by the thought of sobbing viewers, Caitlin looked a little more closely at the medieval vision in purple.

'Oh! Cassandra? I'm Caitlin,' she said, smiling, when she realised she'd been caught staring. 'Do you mind if —' she asked, gesturing to her camera.

'No. Your beautiful friend here explained that you're putting something together. Go ahead,' she smiled warmly.

Caitlin turned the camera on and shot Nadia disappearing into the universe of Cassandra's hug. She caught the tears shining on Nadia's lashes afterwards, and the slightly stunned look on her face. She also caught Madeleine's impatience at being last to be hugged.

That was the most genuine embrace I've seen from a stranger — or any adult — for a long time, thought Caitlin, smiling to herself. She was exactly the kind of woman she never saw at the television station. Exactly the kind of woman who Kevin would never hire.

Everyone at the station had degrees of gorgeousness — even the girls in the canteen were hot. Everyone was eye candy. 'Keep them like your work,' he'd said once to Caitlin. 'Tight and bright.'

She glanced at Nadia, whose eyes were a little wider than usual. Purple Lady might be a wardrobe stylist's nightmare, but her eyes were twinkling and her whole being radiated laughter.

'Good! So that means you're Madeleine, you're Nadia and you're ... Myra, right? You all have the Artemis cabin — she's been waiting for you.'

Who? wondered Caitlin, being literal. Artemis? The cabin?

'Thank you for that,' said Caitlin. 'Can I get a few minutes of your time after we've settled in a bit?' She felt something land in her hair, and gently brushed aside a butterfly, looking even more like a deer in the headlights than she usually did.

'Oooh, look — you're ready to awaken the Goddess. That's a lovely one!' said Purple Lady, watching the butterfly fly drunkenly away. 'Twenty minutes — sunset at the creek — just follow the track. You'll get some lovely shots there.'

'Easy,' said Caitlin, wondering why she suddenly wanted a hug, too. She stepped forward, ready to be embraced, but Sarah intercepted her, linking arms with Cassandra and propelling her away from Caitlin, who felt vaguely disappointed.

'Oooh, the Artemis cabin. You know, she's my favourite new goddess,' cooed Sarah, walking arm in arm with Cassandra the Purple One.

'Well, there you go — the Universe works again,' said Cassandra happily.

Madeleine trotted happily behind, passing out muffins to strangers, and Caitlin wondered if she was the only person who had her head on straight. Then she noticed Nadia staggering about in her heels, and realised her definition of normal came from a very weird place indeed.

'Madeleine's in heaven, and will probably be gay before the weekend's out, everyone's going to talk about pixies and I'll be the bitch in the corner throwing things,' she said to Myra out of the corner of her mouth.

'Oh, God.'

'Goddess.'

'Oh, Goddess. *And* they'll probably get naked.'

Cassandra turned and gave her a look. It wasn't disapproving, but it was the kind of look that made her aware that she'd seen right through the sarcasm defence shield she'd put up around herself.

'Here's your cabin, friends. Tonight we're having a feast, followed by dancing and singing. And a ritual.'

'Probably fire twirling?' Sarah suggested, glancing at Caitlin mischievously.

(Caitlin had told Sarah she'd kill someone if there was fire twirling.)

'Looks like I'll have to kill me someone,' Caitlin drawled.

Sarah pretended to look horrified, blurting 'cancel clear delete', while Nadia and Myra burst through the door, closely followed by Madeleine, wielding her box of muffins to stop the flyscreen banging into her.

Cassandra just rumbled with laughter and commenced her grand, swaying journey down the path back to the hall. 'I'll see you by the creek, Caitlin, in fifteen minutes,' she called out in reminder.

Caitlin wondered exactly where she meant.

'Follow the trail,' she said, before Caitlin could ask the question.

Artemis was a small wooden cabin, seventies rustic. It had been built in a hurry but it was going the distance, even in the forest, which kept entering it. Insects lived in its corners, goannas under its floorboards and the occasional possum would nest in its roof. Artemis was pretty: one large room in the front had a balcony overlooking a green-grey field dotted with eucalypts and more kangaroos lazing in the late afternoon sun, their long shadows playing over the field. A small lounge room ran off that, complete with a fireplace, and two smaller rooms were to the left and right of a tiny hall leading to the front door. A wooden figure of a woman with a strong nose, a bow and arrow and a crescent moon behind her declared this to be the house of the Virgin Huntress.

'Does that mean we're all going to be single after we leave?' asked Myra, folding her arms and looking at Artemis suspiciously.

'Virgin? Oh, I hope not,' said Madeleine, shuddering.

Everything was wood, and there were plants tucked into corners. Showering practically required a machete.

'Artemis was a Spartan, right?' said Myra, peering through the forested bathroom. 'So that's why there's no sunken bath?'

'Well, she was a Greek goddess,' Sarah corrected. 'She lived in the forest. But she had nymphs helping her do all the mundane stuff,' she added. 'Probably scrubbing her back with olive oil and sea salt down in a sacred pond, or something.'

Caitlin put her arm around her. 'Why was she a virgin?' she asked. She actually knew, but wanted to give Sarah something to tell her. She was getting fed up with her own hostility.

'Well, virgin didn't mean you never had sex. Virgin meant, well, you chose who you had sex with. And she was a huntress because she hunted anyone who hurt the forest. It was her home, and she protected it, along with the nymphs.'

'Who were sex-starved lipstick lesbians,' said Myra from her room.

They both grinned.

Underneath their actual conversation went another, far more real dialogue. They were thinking it, but no one was saying it. And if they were going to, it would have read something like this:

Caitlin: I know you're hating me right now.

Sarah: (Hurt wounded look.)

Caitlin: I can't blame you.

Sarah. (Still wounded.)

Caitlin: Right. I'm just settling into this idea of you having secrets from me ... and a girlfriend. It's just going to take a few days.

Sarah: (Smiling, less wounded, still hurt.)

'So. What happens first?' interrupted Myra, laughing and shaking her head at Caitlin and Sarah.

'Apart from you bonding with everyone, Sarah, and Caitlin committing murder?'

'We play Houses of the Holy and unpack,' said Madeleine from the comfort of her double bed, where she was munching corn chips.

'Can't we just start drinking the wine?'

'No. This is a healing and transformative journey,' said Sarah, a little like she was the head of a women's correctional institution. 'I won't be having alcohol. It lowers my vibration,' she said, voice heavy with significance. 'In fact, none of us should drink at all.'

'Damn,' muttered Myra, thinking of the five bottles of wine she'd stashed under the rug in the car boot.

'Oh, I love our cabin,' cried Madeleine, who was now snuggling under the covers of the only double bed. 'It's so atmospheric and romantic. Oh, I hope it's haunted! Sarah, can you tell?'

'No,' Sarah replied. She went to the fridge and began putting away their provisions. Tofu. Spinach. Something that looked like tofu. Soy milk.

No coffee, Myra thought, at the exact same time Caitlin noticed, way too late, that the only kind of tea that had travelled with them was green.

'Roman could if she was here,' said Sarah. 'But I wasn't allowed to bring her,' she said meaningfully.

'Are you talking about me? I never said don't bring her. I would have been ... well, interested,' protested Caitlin.

'In a sadistic kind of way,' added Myra.

Caitlin gave her a look. (Looks were cheap that day.)

'It would have been torture for them both. Going through all the little moments of newborn love in front of us hungry jackals ...' Caitlin shivered. 'Ergh. I'd have loved to watch, but because I do love Sarah, I'm glad she didn't put herself through it.'

There was a pause. Something Sarah had said suddenly lit up in Caitlin's brain.

'Wait! You're going out with one of your freaky-deaky people? You didn't tell me that!' she exclaimed, offended in her turn. Incredible as it seems, Sarah had still revealed next to nothing about her new lover, charismatically called Roman. Every new piece of information was gold.

'She's a medium. And don't be rude, Caitlin. She's my love.'

'Oh, no!'

'Really? How wonderful! I'm sure she could get lots of work up at my place. There're so many hauntings as a result of the convicts ... lots of activity,' said Madeleine. 'You and Roman must come up and take a look around.' They were seriously bonding. Again.

'I don't think she clears ... sometimes it's earth spirits.'

'Of course. You can't be sending off the *nature* spirits ... some ghost "busters" have no idea at all,' said Madeleine airily, in the manner of an expert. (Her usual manner on all subjects, in fact.)

(Nadia, in case you're wondering, was in the room with Myra, twirling a scarf through her long black hair. She was standing in front of the full-length mirror in an improvised neo-hippy boho outfit. Stylists never sleep. She was even thinking about wearing purple.)

'I'm going for a walk. I'm going to have a chat to Cassandra.'

'It's starting to rain … take an umbrella,' ordered Madeleine.

'Nah, I like the rain,' Caitlin replied, grabbing her camera bag and heading for the door.

'Take an umbrella! You can't walk around in that.'

'Mum,' said Caitlin, walking out the front door, 'I've cried harder than this for days.'

She walked off into the gentle rain. It was absolutely beautiful, she thought, breathing in the scent of … bush at sunset, she guessed, wincing at how hokey she felt even admitting she loved this. There were butterflies dancing in between deeply golden shafts of light, taking shelter from the falling rain in the tall tall trees. The laid-back kangaroos, who if they'd been teenage boys would have looked suspiciously like they had just pulled a bong, didn't bother moving, and just lay there, letting the rain fall on them.

'I like your style,' Caitlin said to them, shooting some footage of a few of them, and making sure she got the butterflies. Women, she knew, loved butterflies. Now, to find Cassandra.

She followed a track, and found herself winding down a path with soft leaves underfoot, muffling her footsteps. She could hear voices through the forest, and running water, and kept her footsteps quiet and got her camera ready.

Oooh, she thought. This is great. I'm sneaking around getting surprise footage … it's like a wildlife documentary.

She sat down by the water, which was rolling over rounded smoothed stones. The banks were covered in ferns and fallen greenery and wood, and sheltered by overhanging branches heavy with huge leaves, so her seat was dry and warm. The light was fading, but there was still enough left for her to get some great images, she thought, especially with the way it was filtering through the trees. Dramatic and golden, it was magic time. She hoisted the camera onto her shoulder, and wondered where Cassandra was.

It was warm, so with her spare hand she took off her shoes to dangle her feet in the water. Idly she clicked the camera on and shot her feet being washed by the creek ... and she didn't hear the footsteps behind her.

'Hey there,' said an American accent. Deep. Resonant. Husky.

Said *a man*.

She turned to see a tall guy in worn jeans and, horror, no shirt. And a hat. One of those bushman's hats, she noticed. What's a half-naked man doing looming out of the bushes, she thought. She gave him a quick once-over, which she thought she'd done subtly. But from the way his eyebrows raised, she realised she'd been busted.

It wasn't like he wasn't, well, asking for it, she thought huffily. He's wandering around with no clothes on. And he has a nice body. Not young-man beautiful. But grown-up-man, lean and muscled.

His torso was still tight and hard and brown, but had lost that smoothness of youth. He had longish hair, blond and sunstreaked, falling heavily in layers to his shoulders, and piercing blue eyes. Her first thought, to her great shame, was simultaneously lustful and critical.

I bet he's taken.

Followed closely by:

Or balding.

And finally chased down with:

Does he have a mullet?

How old? she thought, squinting into the sun. He crouched down, and took off his Akubra.

Oh, she thought, exhaling and relieved. He has hair. Plenty of it. But he does have a slight mullet.

She wasn't sure how she felt about that.

She backed off a little.

'Um. Hello,' she said. 'Don't come any closer. I'm armed,' she said, only half joking, gesturing to her camera.

'I see. You're here on the retreat, yeah?'

'Yeah. And you're …?'

'Oh. This is my property.'

'Yours? Wow. It's beautiful.'

'It is that,' he agreed. 'I usually make myself scarce. I'm not always here anyway — get here as much as I can.'

'That's a shame,' said Caitlin, wondering why anyone would ever want to be anywhere else. 'What takes you away?'

'I do a lot of teaching. I'm an organic farmer — do a bit of talking here and there.'

'Really?'

'Yes, but I should leave you to it. Though Cassandra said something about meeting her down here.'

She smiled. 'Oh, did she?'

'So … you're doing a documentary?'

'Sort of. My mother and friends … they brought me here for the —'

'Experience?'

'And I've kind of turned it into work,' she admitted, smiling at him. 'Yeah. That's it,' she said, nodding.

'Well, you have a good time. I'll be going.' He nodded, stepping back. For a moment she'd thought he was going to drawl *Maaam*, but he didn't. He touched his head with his hand, like a cowboy tipping his hat, and walked away. 'Have a wonderful time. Take care. Tell Cassandra I said hi.'

'Tell her *who* said hi?' she replied quietly as he walked away, before picking up her camera and shooting him, long and lean, limping a little she noticed, straight shoulders and long back. Cowboy, she thought. Walking off into the sunset. Nice shot. Nice moment. Nice guy.

Shame about the mullet. Sort of.

And from out of the bushes, quieter than a woman that size has any right to be, stepped Cassandra.

'Wow. You're very …'

'I'm quiet in the bush. Ah, I see you met our shaman. The cowboy.'

'Oh, that's him. Sarah told me about him. That's such a coincidence,' she said, feeling a tingle down her spine.

'There are no coincidences, Caitlin. None at all. You two were clearly supposed to meet.'

Caitlin felt a rush of excitement, but couldn't help protesting. 'Oh, no.'

'Oh, yes,' Cassandra said, in a tone so definite that Caitlin couldn't bring herself to protest. In fact, she felt thrilled.

Calm down, Caitlin, she told herself. She *set up* the meeting — she sent us both down here! Of course she knows. Next minute you'll be seeing fairies. Just get back in control and do your job.

'Hmmn. An unusual man. Very masculine. Very gentle.' When Caitlin didn't respond, Cassandra looked her straight in the eye. 'Some women,' she said, 'find him very attractive.'

Some women must like mullets, she thought, before she stopped. He is attractive, she thought. Why can't I admit it? It's not like I'm not single. Even though I'm married. Anyway, Cassandra said nothing further, so Caitlin got back to work.

'Let's get some of wonderful you out to the world,' suggested Caitlin, swinging the camera up.

Cassandra pointed out two trees nearby. 'Let's go there. The sun will come right through those trees at the moment of sunset — we might even get the green flash.'

Whatever that is, Caitlin thought, but said nothing. She wasn't getting caught up in spooky-speak until the camera was on. 'Sounds good to me,' she agreed.

Half an hour later, Caitlin's shoulder ached from balancing the camera, but she had some amazing stuff. The light had been beautiful. She'd shot Cassandra down by the creek where the water had turned pink, as well as between the trees with golden-red light pouring through. It had only taken twenty minutes, but the big woman's laughter and warmth and her incredible compassion would just come through on screen, she knew it. She had no fear of cameras — you could see it in her eyes. Some people's eyes went all fearful, or had no energy. Cassandra was warm and loving and passionate and funny. She'd told her some wonderful stuff. About her life, about what she did when she healed — Caitlin could just see this woman on television. She'd already pointed out enough to create a first episode, a character sketch. She decided to wind down with a few details.

'What would you describe as your speciality?'

'My speciality is energy,' Cassandra said cryptically.

'That sounds really vague and general. Can you explain more?'

'You might want to turn off the camera before I do.'

'No, I'm fine,' she said, wondering what on earth the woman was on about.

'Okay. You, for example. You have an enormous amount of pain around your heart. I can see it. Dark patches. Pain. Wounds. And there's something to do with a man who has never done this,' she said, gesturing grandly at herself and then to the camera. 'Not as much as he'd like, anyway.'

She's obviously talked to Sarah, Caitlin reasoned from behind the lens. I know who she reminds me of: she's like Mum. Only not annoying. And Mum would never wear purple crushed velvet.

'Anyway. You okay? Yes? Then let me tell you a few things that are going to happen. Firstly, the little one is going to be fine. Neither of them is actually going to want to spend much time with your ex. They love him, but they don't trust him, and it's too confusing for them. Stand up for that. And the other little one is having a tough time — she is about to have her first relationship — and she's so very full of hate for her father that this could compromise that experience. She's going to write music with this boy — he's called Luke …'

Caitlin stared.

'And you get frightened in crowds. You have what people call panic attacks. Mild, I know. But they frighten you. I can give you an exercise to help with them …'

'Hang on. Stop.'

Cassandra looked up, her gaze still slightly otherworld-y. Her hair drifted around her, and the dying light made her look like some ancient oracle.

'I'm just going to turn this off.'

While she was 'feasting', Caitlin found herself mulling over Cassandra's words, and looking at her on the other side of the hall they were all gathered in. Fairylights twinkled and, happily for Caitlin, omnivores ruled at the barbecue. Wine was being splashed into ceramic mugs, and life stories were being swapped. The women had entered as a group, but now everyone had spread out. Sarah was laughing and chatting with some women who all looked just like her; Nadia was being given a back massage by two women who looked like elves; and Myra was comforting someone who'd just started crying. Madeleine was cooking, and bellowing something about lining up for herbal sausages on her *right*-hand side, not her left. She'd been flirting with every woman who looked vaguely interested in women, so Caitlin supposed she should be grateful her mother was back to handling sausages.

Cassandra smiled at Caitlin across the room, and she smiled back, thinking, her camera still sitting next to her.

Had anyone spoken about her? She couldn't help wondering. Cassandra had assured her no one had, but Caitlin knew Sarah. And her mother. Besides, she rationalised, they were reasonably easy guesses. Anyone with a lifespan of more than seven years would have had a heartache or two.

But how did she know about the panic attacks? a voice inside her protested. And Sean? And Luke? And Molly?

Anyway, she concluded, mulling it over. I'll never know. But she knew that it hadn't just been *what* that witch had said. It was *how* she'd said it. So kindly. With so much understanding.

'Okay, everyone,' Cassandra called out after clapping her hands. Everyone fell quiet quickly, respectfully, but good humour and bonhomie still hovered expectantly in the air. 'Moon's coming up in … Anyone here still wear a watch?' Everyone giggled.

'Why is that funny?' Caitlin asked.

'Only muggles believe in linear time,' replied a nearby woman with spiky hair.

'Oh.'

'Okay, moon's up in … fifteen minutes. The ritual area's over there, and Rachel is going to be performing a beautiful welcoming ritual.'

This is amazing, thought Caitlin, reaching for her camera. No one seems at all embarrassed by these words. Ritual. Moon. Muggle.

'How's it going?' Sarah said, squeezing up next to her. 'Did Cassandra blow your mind?'

Caitlin didn't know what to say. She didn't want to admit just how affected she felt — but she couldn't lie, either. 'Yep. I have to say, I'm impressed.'

Sarah rolled her eyes. 'Just admit it, Caitlin. She's great at what she does. And she'll be great for the show. All that emotion!'

Caitlin looked directly at her best friend, who, to her knowledge, and despite having hidden her new girlfriend from her, had never, in all the years she'd known her, lied to her. 'Sarah, you didn't brief her beforehand, did you? I know you want to say you didn't, and I want to believe her too, but I really, really need to know the truth. Did you? Did Mum?'

'Nope. Not at all. That's not what we do. She's got loads of integrity — that's why I thought she'd be brilliant.'

'I don't know. Maybe she's just ...' Caitlin stopped, knowing she was fumbling for the right words.

'Telepathic? Nope. It's slightly different. Wait till you see Rachel, though. She's spiritual eye candy. Kevin,' she added in a meaningful undertone, as the friends stood and joined the crowds heading outside, 'will *love* her. Isn't the fact that you're affected what's going to make this interesting to watch? To see people opening up to something they used to dismiss?'

Caitlin knew she had a point, but had no time to take it further. Everyone was moving out toward the paddock and, though the tall trees hid the moon, its light was shining brightly between the leaves, flattening colours and changing shapes, shifting shadows and making the smoke from the candles twist eerily.

How long is it since I've done anything like this? she thought, remembering vaguely being with Max, drinking, under the moon, making wishes together. Ages ago.

I wish for you to love me forever

I wish for you to remember how much I do love you

I want to have a baby

I want to be a massive star

Twinkle twinkle … so it's no good wishing on the moon then, is it?

She came back. Everyone was closer together, forming a kind of circle over the uneven ground. It was very quiet; everyone was talking in hushed voices, and the music from the hall had completely disappeared. Caitlin could hear the sound of the breeze moving through the eucalyptus leaves, and the occasional night-bird call. Someone reached out, and before she knew it, Caitlin was part of the circle of women.

She'd carried her camera out, and now stepped back, letting the thirty or so women move in. She wondered how invasive it would be to shoot from inside the circle, and stayed on the outer edge for the moment. The circle was huge to her, and she could hardly keep track of her friends, or her mother.

From one side of the circle a tall blonde woman dressed in white raised her arms high in the air.

Everyone followed suit.

Caitlin's camera went on.

'I, who have been called Artemis, Hecate and Diana,' began the woman, and the other women's voices repeated the lines after her.

And what the heck is this? thought Caitlin. The part of her that was feeling self-conscious was suddenly far less powerful than the part of her that was feeling excited and, somehow, a little high. What was in my chop? she wondered, as the ritual began to unfold.

She caught a group of kangaroos, moving closer, and some night-birds in trees, who appeared to be watching.

Sneaking quietly around the other side, she found a ledge to perch on, and zoomed in.

Rachel Moore was a beautiful woman, Caitlin realised. She was stunning. She was tall and lean; her arms were toned and white and long. She could easily have been an actor or a soap star — or backstage at a fashion show — but to Caitlin's good fortune, this stunning woman was a working witch. Her hair was perfect — long and flowing, pale blonde. Her face was beautiful, with a broad, high forehead and wide-open brown eyes. She had a soft, hypnotic voice.

Ker-ching, thought Caitlin. It's coming together. Cassandra: the mumsy one. Rachel: the sexpot. This really could work, she thought, adrenaline running through her veins.

She filmed the rest of the ritual, which didn't seem to consist of a lot — there was some chanting, some dancing about, some anointing the earth with fire and water and air, represented by some giant feathers.

Bet she's the shaman's girlfriend, she thought. Bet they have some sexy, weird, spiritual thing going on. They look right for each other.

(She would have wondered, if she'd had time to notice, why she felt a bit disappointed at that thought.)

She moved into the circle and turned, whirling the camera to get movement and effects. She crept back out and shot the group with arms raised, invoking someone or other.

And at one point, the moon came shining out from behind the owl-filled trees, and all the women began to howl.

Oh, this is fantastic, Caitlin thought, feeling slightly dizzy, almost drunk on the images she'd seen and captured. She was tempted to throw back her head and howl at the moon herself.

(But she didn't.)

It was the looks on the faces of all the women who'd witnessed the moon ceremony that made it so very special. After it was over there were tears and smiles, and everyone turned and hugged. They really were happier. Even the women crying were looking joyful. It was like every participant had just remembered the happiest moment of her life, simultaneously.

Nadia had lost her self-consciousness, and was showing someone how to tie a scarf, she noticed through the camera, and Sarah was hugging someone. Which wasn't unusual. But still.

She walked over to the woman in the centre, feeling a little starstruck.

'Rachel,' she said, putting out her hand. She held back on the usual business-meeting thrust. Rachel smiled warmly and took her hand. 'Goddess bless,' she said gently. Caitlin stared at her. Was she for real?

'I'm Caitlin. You are a very beautiful woman. And that was just amazing. Thanks for letting me get so into it. I hope I didn't distract you too much.'

'Oh, I hardly noticed. I tend to go into a light trance. It's hard to know what's happening in the real world when I'm out there,' the witch said with a light gesture that seemed to take in everything.

Caitlin was speechless. She began to get tingles. The urge to whip out a contract and sign her immediately stormed through her.

If she's the real deal, I have to work with her.

She might have been getting a divorce from her husband. She might have left her job under less-than-ideal circumstances. But her instincts were still brilliant. And every single cell of every single instinct told her she was onto something big.

NINETEEN

Caitlin's first day back in Sydney after the Wild Women's Weekend was heralded by a summons to an emergency secret casting meeting with Kevin.

Caitlin sighed, and looked at the editing suite she'd set up in her office. 'I was wanting to get to work on the pitch,' she said, knowing she'd already lost the battle, but feeling up for the fight anyway. She was coming in. She could feel Kevin's order dragging her toward the station, like small metal filings to a massive magnet. Didn't mean she couldn't have some fun resisting.

'But you can't let *her* know I've got you in on this,' he hissed at her via his mobile from underneath his desk, where he was being watched by an alarmed Linda. 'She doesn't know it's happening. I've sent her to budget school for a week. But she keeps popping in to tell me things.'

Linda shook her head-full of newly frosted blonde foils disapprovingly. If only he'd learn not to employ these young women full of … hormones, she thought. (She was grumpy due to the influence of her own diminishing hormones.)

'I won't be telling her, Kevin,' said Caitlin. 'But you know someone will.'

'She can't know!' he said, desperation tingeing his voice. 'She's gone completely mad. And because she's up the duff with *your* husband's baby, HR can't touch her. It must be the hormones.'

'Kevin, pull your head in,' she said tightly. Up the duff? she thought. He was so nineteen-fifties it scared her at times. Anyway, was it her fault Kennedy was running amok? You've taken her off the leash, she thought, but didn't say. '*You're* the boss,' she pointed out to him. 'Take charge.'

'Boss? There's been a coup, Caitlin. HR rules these days. Apparently they signed away all my rights in some … maternity leave debacle. I can't even fire her till she gets her leave out of the way.' He started spluttering, causing Linda's heart to thump alarmingly. If anything happens to that man, she thought, keeping the watch of the hopelessly-in-love, Kennedy is dead.

'Right,' said Caitlin. She was concentrating on Kevin, but momentarily distracted by the footage of the cowboy shaman walking away into the sunset. It was such a gorgeous shot; she wanted to use it somehow in the pitch, but she just couldn't figure out how. And why hadn't he called her? she thought. What else was that 'accidental' meeting at the creek about?

She paused, and got her mind back to the business at hand. Saving Kevin from Kennedy. 'Kevin, I realise she's a problem. But what do you actually want me to do?'

'I want you to come in, of course,' he said loudly, before panicking and hushing himself.

'Now? Can't,' she said sweetly, rewinding the footage and watching the cowboy walk into the sunset again. 'I'm really flat-out getting my pitch ready for you. Remember?'

'Pitch,' he mused, buying time. 'The pitch,' he added vaguely, deliberately goading her.

'For the new show,' Caitlin said impatiently. 'Which you will want to see.' She felt herself growing annoyed. Honestly. Be a Good Girl, Caitlin, she thought. Save the day. Be the hero. And if she didn't play, he might refuse to view the pitch. Which he'd already given his word to do.

But when had making a promise stopped Kevin from breaking one? she reminded herself. He'd just develop one of his memory problems.

'What? Forget your pitch. I need you here today,' he demanded. 'We've got big problems with casting *Date Squad*.'

'Obviously. I saw who was on last week.' She'd been astonished to see that what had previously been her good-hearted show was now featuring (along with lollypop nymphettes and Kennedy the Kama Sutra Consultant) two people who should have been kept off television screens for the good of the nation — and for their own benefit, too. Single twins with tattoos, bad teeth and un-ironic mullets had had a very unpleasant onscreen fight over the right way to use a soup spoon — viewers were horrified, the police were now chasing them cross-country and the show's etiquette expert remained traumatised. A rival station's news reporters had followed up on the disaster, airing a story about one twin's unsavoury dealings. They had both reportedly gone on the run, and were currently holed up in the pub of a small Victorian town, with the added disaster of their hostages (the girls assigned to them by *Date Squad*, no less) having done a runner. Gus and Carol had kept her on top of the story, which had been breaking all weekend.

'Does she think it's Jerry Springer?' he wailed, forgetting he didn't want anyone to hear him.

'Everyone here hated it, too,' she said, honestly agreeing with Kevin. 'The kids — my *mum* even hated them. And she doesn't hate anyone.' (Except Max, she thought, correcting herself.) 'Sarah said they had bad energy. They should have been on *Most Wanted*. How'd you let that one past you?'

'You were away,' he said resentfully. 'She said she thought it would be good for viewers to watch a car crash.'

'You know, Kevin, showing viewers a car crash with bloody bodies hanging out the side on a highway works in a world that doesn't have to feel anxious all the time. We're living the car crash. Every day. Inundated with it. The news. Current affairs. Evil stuff, Kevin. Awful, tragic horrible things. Viewers need a comfort zone, especially with a show that's borderline voyeurism. They don't want to feel creepy about love, Kevin. That's their last hope.'

He snorted.

'So it didn't have a happy ending for me. But why should I ruin it for everyone else? We were so careful to make it about love. We gave it a warm heart, so the audience wouldn't fall out of love with it, feel turned off, and *switch* off.' She had to physically stop herself from stamping her foot at this stage. What wasn't he getting?

'You've said yourself that car-crash TV can work.'

'Well, of course it can work,' said Caitlin, heat and defiance in her voice. 'It's about *context*. It works in daytime or very late night slots, or on the right station, or with the right message behind it. But *Date Squad* was set up to be feel-good and family. Now you've gone and confused people. And personally I don't want to be involved in anything that contributes to people feeling down.'

'Very erudite, Caitlin,' he said, sarcastically applauding, then bumping his head on the desk above. Linda snuck another look around the doorframe, but all she could see was Kevin's large posterior, backing out from under the mahogany. His assistant sighed. Did it really need to be so undignified?

'Look,' Caitlin reasoned down the phone. 'Kennedy is a brilliant organiser, but she's not a great communicator.'

'I say she's just gone and fucked up our ratings. And you said you'd work with me behind the scenes. I'm calling you on that. Come in. *Now.*'

'Well, if you put it that way,' grinned Caitlin. She hung up and winked at the image of the cowboy on the screen. 'I'll see *you* later,' she said, reluctantly clicking on the shut-down command. She felt the ache of withdrawal as she headed off to find something to wear to the office. 'Silly,' she said to herself, shrugging off her Nan's nightie, which she'd just spent the night in after rescuing it from the bin for the third time. 'It's not like he even really said anything. And now you have a crush!' She shook her head and focussed on business.

The beauty, she thought, as she dressed in jeans and silk shirt, of working from home on my own projects in my own office, is that there's no pulling on nylon tights or worrying about hair. So if Kevin wants me in, it's going to have to be as I am. She threaded an embroidered belt around the slim waist of her jeans, slicked on some lipgloss, gave her lashes a coat of mascara and put something in her hair, but that was it. She completed the outfit with a pair of pink flats. Mary-Janes to the office? Well, they're better than the thongs I'd rather be wearing, she thought.

'This is who I am now,' she said to her reflection in the mirror, not noticing that she looked ten years younger than the last time Kevin had seen her. 'Take it or leave it, Kevin.'

Caitlin felt a surge of power. She wasn't particularly worried about *Date Squad*. She knew she could pull it together very quickly. After ten years in television, this was familiar territory. She got on the phone and within forty minutes she had casting alerts on high-rating radio stations. By the time she got in to Channel Five, there would be a hundred-metre line-up of *Date Squad* hopefuls slowly making its way past security.

Twenty minutes and a fast drive in the yellow VW later, Caitlin was walking with Kevin down the corridor to a spare studio, a long way from her old office. He was slinking along, trying to merge with the walls, which was hard because they were plastered with shots of the network stars, and he was a very large man. It didn't seem to stop him trying though.

'She's going to find out, so just take a deep breath and deal with it,' she counselled him. Back to their old banter. It felt easy, and familiar, and the level of irritation was just enough for her to find the thrill of a challenge in the situation, stupidly ludicrous as it seemed to her sensible side.

'You shouldn't have resigned,' he said darkly, giving her an accusing look. 'Traitor,' he said under his breath.

'How do you know they won't be ugly?' he demanded, clambering through the small back door of the studio floor to avoid being seen.

'That's what we're here to discover. This was actually done and finished with months ago — you left it to me. I had lists of great talent.' He had the grace to look slightly abashed. 'She probably threw them out, right? Rescheduled? Threw production into chaos?'

He shrugged. 'It's not surprising; that's what usually happens when the leader walks.'

'I was pushed, Kevin. You *know* it was an untenable situation. In fact, you *knew*.' She stopped in her tracks, forcing Kevin to pull up.

'You wanted to see, didn't you?' she said, stepping back, looking him straight in the eye and wagging a finger at him. (She hated it when she did that, but she couldn't be bothered stopping herself. She was too inspired by the sudden epiphany.) 'You wanted to see just what would happen if I wasn't here!' She paused and screwed up her still-Botox-free brow, puzzling it out. 'Oh! You didn't know if I was all that valuable to you any more.' She stepped forward and stood right in front of him. 'You didn't, did you?'

'I wanted you to come in today, didn't I?' he said, eyes sliding away from hers and taking a step backward. The people standing over near the production office Caitlin was to borrow worked even harder to pretend they weren't listening.

'Oh, Kevin,' she admonished, shaking her curls. 'You silly bastard!'

'Look, can we get on with this?' he snapped impatiently. 'There's a crew over there, and here,' he pointed out, waving his arm about, 'look, here's a desk, and ... and people and bits of paper and money and the whole thing.' His volume was escalating. If he'd had enough hair, she would have expected him to pull it out. While it was alarming, slightly, to see him so agitated, part of seeing him so desperate for her help was undeniably satisfying.

'Just ... do whatever it is that you do, and we'll talk later,' he said soothingly.

'Fine. But I do want to show you this program I'm getting together. Come on, Kevin, we have a deal. Besides, when have I been wrong?'

'You haven't. Smart-arse,' he acknowledged, resentfully.

'Anyway, I've got footage of the talent I originally cast here,' she said, patting her green-shopping bag, her current briefcase. (Her old one had been given to her by Max, and she was damned if she was carrying that around with her. Mind you, patting green fabric didn't seem to have quite the same impact as tapping very expensive leather.) 'Plus production schedules, contacts, locations and scripts. It all just needs to be reactivated. You'll need to send me an assistant, too.'

'Can't Linda do it?'

Caitlin had no patience for his 'how much will this cost me?' routine. She knew it far too well. '*And* I need someone from the show up here now. Could I have Gus and Carol? Stop stalling,' she said, as the colour drained from his red face. 'Kennedy will find out, and she'll freak, but you have a ratings crisis on, right?'

She'd rung Oztam that morning, so she knew she was right. The promise of early shows had slid, leaving the station looking fragile. With the twins from hell, it was a double catastrophe. 'Did advertisers call after that show?' she asked innocently.

'Call? They're threatening to pull,' he admitted.

'So we'll get them back. Just please send me Gus and Carol — they know this show inside out. Honestly, Kevin. You should have known how difficult she was going to be,' she muttered to herself.

'Well, I'd never had to deal with her before. And I thought *you* were difficult. You did all the dirty work, remember?' he reminded her petulantly.

'I can't believe you're pissed off at *me* for leaving! For refusing to work with someone who you're now too terrified to work with. Goose? Gander? Now you know why,' she said, shaking her head, and just resisting the urge to go back to shaking a finger at him, too.

'Just sort this out. It's your show. And you can't work for anyone else for a while, either,' he said smugly. 'That's our agreement.'

'It's only our agreement *if* you let me make this new show. I *will* make it,' she muttered, looking around at the boys on the floor wheeling cameras into position.

'Is that the sound of my balls being twisted, Caitlin?' Kevin asked, looking green. Must be thinking about the words *contract*, *witness* and *signing*, she thought.

'I think it's the sound of one ball twisting, Kevin. Kennedy's got you by the other one.'

He glowered, but his snort told her he knew she'd got that right.

'Agree to take this program on.'

'I can't even look at anything for at least a month,' he began, hands held up in protest before him, backing away from her slowly as though she was very, very scary.

'Then I haven't got time for this,' she replied, heading in the opposite direction, which led to the main hall. Through the main building. Where everyone was bound to see her.

'Caitlin, this isn't like you,' Kevin protested, stopping her in her tracks. 'You've never let me down.'

She swung right round and faced him, feeling fury building. 'Kevin, *I'm* not like me. Here's the deal. I start this, you take my show. Take it or leave it.'

'I *look* at your show,' he counteroffered, folding his arms over his belly.

Reluctantly, she knew she wouldn't get any more from him, not right now. He couldn't realistically commit to something sight unseen.

'Well, I know you won't want anyone else getting it. Not with this station's production in such a mess,' she counterbaited, seeing a props guy she knew out of the corner of her eye tidying up wiring.

'Hey, Ryan,' she called out, waving.

'Hey, Caitlin,' he grinned, genuinely pleased to see her, and even more pleased to be singled out for acknowledgment. By name.

'Are you back?' he asked. 'I sure hope so. Things have been …' he tapered off when he realised the station boss was also listening to him.

(She didn't answer the question. Kevin needed to be kept hanging. And she was glad Ryan had let slip something was wrong.)

'Wow. Hi, sir,' he said, surprised to see the legendary CEO in front of him and thrusting out his huge hand. Making contact with executives was not something floor staff ever really experienced.

'Hello, son,' he said, grumpy, taking the gangly boy's hand, and finding himself enjoying the boy's obvious bedazzlement.

'You should get out on the floor more, you know, do the ordinary-bloke-meeting-with-everyone thing,' she said once the deed was done and she was ushering Kevin out. This is my floor now, she thought smugly. See ya! 'It'd go down very well, and make you feel fantastic.'

'Why don't I do some charity work while I'm at it?' he grumped. 'Who do you think you are, giving me all this advice?'

'Apparently, I'm a very highly paid station consultant,' she smirked.

He grinned back, despite himself. He'd always enjoyed these stoushes with Caitlin.

'Now, if you'll excuse me, I've got some of your work to do for you.'

Hours later, Caitlin was dizzy. Linda had joined them and proved useful, if oddly snippy. Gus and Carol were almost hysterically relieved to have her back. Caitlin had seen hundreds of people, had okayed scripts and had a stack of other briefs to take home and look at. She snapped open her phone and called Kevin upstairs. 'I've just signed twenty-five possibles for the show — guys that is. Thirteen women. Some are gorgeous, some are just lovely on the inside and some are overcoming some great life challenges ... they're all compelling. Plus I've rebooked the people we'd already okayed.'

'Who Kennedy ditched,' mouthed Carol. Linda gave them a glance, not saying anything. Gus felt a warm surge of happiness run through his veins. Sucked in, Kennedy, Caitlin thought. That's for telling me my ideas were cheesy.

'Have they got teeth?' Kevin snapped from his desk, which he was now sitting behind. He was still wrestling with relief that the show would soon be back on track, as well as smarting from being, well, outsmarted. He'd spent some of the day marching round the corridors shaking hands and indulging in *hello*s, as well as being particularly hard on a couple of interstate executives to reassert his feelings of power, lost in the battle with Caitlin. Back in his comfort zone, he could admit to himself that her advice to meet and greet the common folk — the staff — did in fact work. Smile, shake, move on, she'd said. Don't talk too much, you don't want to be like that guy on *The Office*, he thought. But saying hello does make a difference — and the *things* you see! he thought, thinking of the three office affairs, the web-surfing and the novel-writing he suspected he'd uncovered before lunch. He brought his attention back to Caitlin's phone call. Unlike lots of his staff, she seemed to actually be doing her job.

'They're aged between twenty-two and forty-six and they're good-looking and healthy and they have clean records. Some of them even have personality. We'll get down to about ten from there. But there's someone I really want you to see.' She looked over the headshots on her desk. 'I'll show him to you next week, okay?'

'Tell me. He's hot, young, and all the girls will want to fuck him,' he chuckled. 'All the boys will, too, if it's in Sydney.'

She sighed. 'Actually, you're sort of right. It *is* this gorgeous man. He's sixty-eight.' She flinched, waiting for the objection.

'What? You want to put *old* people on television?!' With a vast degree of effort, he reined in his temper and took a very deep breath. 'That,' he said in a falsetto, 'is what *radio's* for.'

'He's not *old*, Kevin. Old these days is like,' she waved her hands around, 'um, a hundred and four. And women are having children at sixty, so —'

'Urgh. Never say that again,' he protested, blanching.

'Anyway,' said Caitlin, suppressing a giggle. She'd forgotten how much fun she had, baiting Kevin. 'He sorts of looks like a handsome dad or grandpa, but he is looking for love.'

'We don't do seniors on *my* station.'

'Well, we should. And no one says "seniors" any more, Kevin. That's *outré*. Anyway, you should see him. He doesn't look old, Kevin. He's only a couple of years older than you, and you could hardly be described as a senior.' She winked at Gus, who winked back. Linda saw it too, but decided she'd let that one slip by.

'Anyway.' She waited patiently for the coughing to pass. Most of Kevin's coughs were fake, merely theatrical methods of stalling for time, or making you feel bad. She didn't buy it for a moment.

'And there are a lot of single women out there watching this show with their kids. Big advertiser dollars in this. Don't forget the baby boomers — they're important.' I should know, she thought. I live with one of them.

'And he's very eligible,' she continued, on a roll now. 'I think we could turn him into something. A special.'

'If he's so fabulous, why does he need *Date Squad*?' asked Kevin, still stalling.

'He's been busy running his incredibly successful sports company, and now he's on the verge of retirement and he wants to spend his life in love with a wonderful woman who he can take round the world and indulge in anti-ageing treatments with,' she said. She paused, waiting for Kevin's shouting to begin. She was beginning to have a very good time indeed. He was obviously doing some deep breathing, so she plunged ahead.

'He's great, too. Cheeky. Funny. Lots of sparkle in his eyes. Why don't we give him a bit of a freshen-up, and the experts can put him through his paces. But I think what we'll find is he can tell them a thing or two.' She smiled goodbye to Linda, who gave her a less-frosty-than-usual stare — perhaps, Caitlin suspected, because she'd seen the aristocratically named Edwin Cadenhead too. Cait had noticed her response. She fancied him. And with Linda on her side, Kevin had no chance at all.

Gus finished packing too, and came and gave her a kiss on the cheek. 'Bye, beautiful,' he whispered. 'See you next week.'

She smiled goodbye, and gave his hand a squeeze, never missing a beat of the conversation with Kevin. 'Anyway. I think we're back on track. I've met with the girls and they're shooting next week, so you know you're going to have two eps in production.'

'Oh, God,' he groaned. 'Kennedy will know.'

'Well, that's not going to be my problem. Show comes first,' snapped Caitlin, shifting a box's weight onto one hip and getting ready to wind up. 'So I pick a crew, and a production team, and it's best they work out of my place. There's no other way. And don't forget this meeting on Wednesday. You'll have two new hit shows next season,' she grinned. He would be going red, she thought delightedly to herself. I always know I'm on the right track when Kevin goes red.

'You'll be too busy doing your real job to even get that pitch together,' he bellowed, before she flipped her phone shut. She saw a stack of papers she hadn't collected, put her box down on the desk and looked around for another shopping bag. Finding one, she started stacking shots, briefs and photos swiftly into it.

Out of the corner of her eye she noticed someone hovering, and she froze for a moment, narrowing slanted green eyes to make out who it was under the glare of the lights, before relaxing as she recognised the young man moving forward purposefully. Ah, the professional snowboarder, the Canadian guy, she thought, remembering him from throughout the day. Funny, good-looking. Very smart, and very sweet. What are you doing here? she thought, moving forward and picking up the box, swinging the shopping bag over her shoulder, ready to move.

She looked at him directly, one eyebrow raised. She noticed his hair (wavy brown, streaked with blond), his skin (that golden tan you usually see on models) and large brown eyes (flecked with gold and ringed with black lashes). The height, the span of the chest and the nipped-in waist didn't get missed either.

'Green, right?'

He nodded, looking eager. 'Green Monroe.'

'Look, um, Green Monroe, I'm leaving — I need to get out of here,' she said. 'Yoga class. My friend runs the centre and is leading the class, so I can't be late.'

'Wow,' he said admiringly. 'Yoga. I knew you were cool.'

Caitlin didn't feel the need to tell him it would be her very first time — reinforced with Cassandra's recommendation, Sarah's persistence had finally paid off. 'So, can I help you with anything, Green?'

'Look, I just wanted to say how much I enjoyed meeting you today, and talking to you,' he said in his soft accent and deep voice, falling into step beside her.

Why am I surrounded by men with this accent? she thought, flashing back to the cowboy shaman's American twang at the impromptu meeting at the creek. Why hadn't he called? she wondered testily, but only for a moment. Now this boy, this Green Monroe, had the same accent. Kind of. Only he was a man, too, she corrected herself, remembering he was nearly thirty.

'Oh,' she replied, smiling briefly, and waiting for him to go. 'Thanks,' she said, hinting that the conference was over.

'I really liked meeting you,' he repeated, taking the box from her. 'Let me help you with this.'

'Ohhhh,' she said, getting it.

Caitlin was used to flattery and helpful hopefuls. TV producers get it all the time. This kind of spontaneous meeting was priceless face-time, could be an aspiring starlet's one chance to make a lasting impression, and compliments were usually the starting point for a you-really-need-to-see-my-showreel conversation. One that Caitlin wasn't willing to have. She wanted to get yoga over with, chat to Madeleine, call the girls then get stuck into editing her show. She gave him a look that said she knew what was going on. What most young actors, men and women, just didn't understand was that without camera charisma, they were never going to get on air. This guy had made it to her short list. He'd been informed. No more time needed.

But there he was, still standing there, looking at her … *admiringly*. Maybe Green Monroe wants to be a producer, she thought. Shame. Waste of a great body. Bad Caitlin, very bad, she admonished herself. First pondering cowboys with mullets, now looking lustfully at young men improbably named Green. *What's up with that?* she wondered. *I thought I was dead. And now I'm feeling things. And not just pain and hatred.*

'No need to schmooze me, Green,' she said with a grin, red hair falling into her eyes. She pushed it back, and turned away distractedly. 'You're in. You're on the list.'

'About that,' he said, stepping forward. She felt him move closer, and turned back. He was grinning, and even though she was alone with him, she felt safe. He gave her a challenging look, and she put one hand on her hip, returning it. Caitlin wondered ever-so-briefly whether she should call security, but then dismissed the thought. He was okay, she thought, but he was definitely flirting.

'I might not want to be on the list,' he said teasingly. 'I might want something else more.'

'Well,' she said decidedly. 'I don't want you off it. You were great. It pays well, too,' she added, wondering what his turn-on was. Fame? Exposure? Approval? Money? 'What exactly is the problem?'

'I think,' he said, stepping closer and smiling, 'it's going to be a conflict of interest for you.'

She raised her eyebrows. 'How so?'

'Because you're coming out with me this Saturday night.'

TWENTY

'Oh God,' chortled Myra hours later when Caitlin was filling her in from the speakerphone in her *Freak Squad* production home office. On the wall was a framed picture of her Nan looking glamorous and screen starlet-y and another of her holding a five-year-old Caitlin's hand, looking every inch the wholesome Nana. Despite being in the throes of decorating and lacking a watercooler, the production office was already experiencing some seismic nine-to-five-style gossip.

'Being asked *out*. By a *younger man*. That's just *sensational*,' Myra crowed.

'A younger man called Green Monroe. He's a snowboarder,' said Caitlin, gloating slightly.

'I bet I'd cry if he took off his shirt,' said Myra, sounding teary. 'He sounds so hot.'

'Yep,' sighed Caitlin. 'He sure is. And Green Monroe was great for my ego in so many ways. He must have waited for ages to ask me — we saw him at noon, and there he was at six. It was a fabulous moment. One I'll flashback to on my deathbed,' she added.

'Oooh. Perish the thought,' giggled Myra. 'Anyway. You're now my role model. You're doing yoga. Your potential sex life is much healthier than mine. You started meditating … I just keep drinking, eating, working out and not-meeting men who think it's heavy and needy to suggest actually meeting in person.'

'Online dating, huh?' Caitlin was relaxed, unwinding after the class, which had been harder than she'd expected, and more fun than she'd imagined.

'It sucks. Weeks of flirting and text messages, not to mention a lot of really dirty, cheap and filthy sexual innuendo.'

Caitlin snorted. 'Tell me more!'

'But then,' continued Myra, without missing a beat.

Here we go, Caitlin thought, reminding herself to sound surprised when the big moment came.

'When it comes to actually meeting, they shrink. Like frightened turtles!'

Caitlin laughed, then did the thing all dutiful friends do. 'Why?' she asked in outraged (and *surprised*) tones. 'It just doesn't make sense.'

Liar, she told herself. It so does. No way am I telling my friend where she's going wrong with men. Not when my husband's been shagging my assistant — probably still is. Maybe Kennedy's really, really ill with morning sickness and can't stand him anywhere near her. Maybe —

'Maybe it's this bizarre new concept of having explicit, in fact adult-themed, no, *X-rated* flirtations and having your ego stroked online. No actual contact — a whole lot less mess to clear up when it goes pear-shaped,' Myra was continuing.

'That's sad,' Caitlin said, reminding herself to never, ever join an online dating service. No matter how tough things got, she promised herself, unconsciously wrapping her white nightie tighter around her.

'It's *frustrating*, that's what it most definitely is,' snapped Myra. 'The only benefit I can possibly see at this close range is that all the sad fucks involved, including myself, can keep their completely unrealistic self-image intact.'

'Hmmm. Maybe there's another reason,' Caitlin pondered, imagining a world full of men without erections. It was not a cheery thought, she realised.

'No, I truly think the internet dating thing gives us all kid-in-candy-store syndrome. There are just so many profiles to choose from, no one wants to limit themselves by settling,' she said, an edge in her voice. Someone who wasn't a close friend would hear a woman laughing at herself. Caitlin could hear the slight breaks that meant it was upsetting her. Not that Myra would admit it. And not that Caitlin would mention it.

'It's like an endless stream of drinks, or 24-hour-a-day sport on cable — for only sixteen dollars a month — and it's really hard. I'm competing against single girls in their twenties who don't even *need* the microdermabrasion and the eyelash-bloody-transplants they're getting. Not to mention the breast things.' She sighed. 'Young men are so silly. Sorry, Caitlin. You're about to go out with one.' Caitlin flashbacked to Edwin Cadenhead, a snapshot of his handsome face suddenly lighting up her mind. Hmmn, she thought. I wasn't going to suggest it, but now you mention it ...

'I wasn't going to suggest this,' she said carefully. 'But now you mention it, you're right, young men can be silly. There's this amazing guy who came in today to audition. I just thought he was incredible and … well. I won't put him on … not if you're interested.'

'I don't know,' Myra replied. 'Maybe I wouldn't have to meet him. Maybe we could just send e-mails and text messages and he can send money.'

'Oh. A traditional relationship, then,' teased Caitlin, the corners of her mouth curling up.

'I need to just … meet someone.'

'Who's unavailable?' Harsh but fair, Caitlin told herself.

'Yeah!' she said, cynical. 'That's my mantra. If there's no chase — no competition … ' she trailed off. 'I know. I'm my own worst enemy.' She followed that up with an expectant pause.

Caitlin was momentarily distracted from providing the obligatory friendship reassurance. She was too busy stifling a giggle at Myra's melodramatic yet absolutely sincere self-chastisement. 'Oh, you're not that bad,' she choked out finally. 'Bad. But not unbearable. And don't worry about knocking back Edwin …'

'Edwin?'

'The man I've seen for the show. He's going to be inundated with women wanting to go out with him.' A comment designed to pique Myra's interest.

'Oh, you didn't mention he might be taken,' Myra quipped. '*Now* I'm feeling something …'

'It is weird, though, isn't it, that these guys go online but don't want to actually meet?' Caitlin said, cautious.

'Maybe I should go and see Cassandra? She's good, isn't she?' Myra wondered.

'Amazing. But we have more of a professional thing,' Caitlin lied smoothly. She refused to give away just how fascinating she was finding the esoteric world she'd encountered. 'I talked some more with her yesterday before we left — I'm working on the pilot script tomorrow.'

'What are you calling it, then?'

'Oh, *Freak Squad* for now,' Caitlin replied, smiling.

'No!'

'Shamefully, yes. I really have to get a better name,' she commented, half to herself. 'Oh, Myra. It's incredible. Well it will be, when I have a moment to put it all together. I can see it, in my head, and I have all the shots planned and the style, very romantic, beautifully shot, like a feature film, only factual. We can't waste the full moon and the sunset — I've got a storyboard and everything.'

'So you're nearly done then,' Myra commented, blithe about the mechanics of production as all people outside the industry were.

'Well, then I'll need to shoot more footage, with a crew, and after I've done that I will need to choose the shots and edit it and then find music and edit *that*, then get a voice-over and then grab a presenter from somewhere and … and thank God no one is here for a few days.'

'Are the girls at Max's?'

'They are. We're trying a one-week-on, one-week-off scenario this time. See if that settles them more. I miss the girls awfully, and the other weird thing is that I feel I *have* to say that. Like if I don't, I'm some kind of awful mother. But it's a given that I love them. And being without them for a few days makes me feel sort of … insecure. Like they'll like him more than me.'

Myra guffawed. 'Not likely.'

'But that shouldn't be a good thing. And at exactly the same time, while I should hate that they're at Max's — and I do — I also *don't*. I'm relieved I can have a few days to go through everything in this room and sort out this pitch and … just have a breathing space.'

'Change,' sighed Myra. 'We all hate it.'

'It sucks. And it doesn't. I'm going to have some weird times getting used to this part-time-mother thing. Not to mention the part-time-mother-*guilt* thing.'

'You're never really part-time, okay? Like, maybe it's a part-time *hands-on* mother thing.'

Caitlin thought. 'Yeea-ssss. I guess so. I definitely full-time-mother in my head — but some of that is love, some is worry, and some is even sheer self-interest. If I don't think about them, I feel guilty. So I think about them. It's not just about love.'

'Jeez, Caitlin,' spluttered Myra, frustrated. 'Most of it's about love. But it can't be all-perfect. You're only human.'

'But it's interesting — why is it different? It's not like I used to think about them all the time when I was at work. I think it's because I left them behind myself, before, and now I feel like they've been taken away from me.'

'Want some company? Or have you already got the boy stashed in the back room somewhere?'

Caitlin laughed, shaking her head. 'No! It's actually a relief that everyone's out or away. I can sort of keep this date thing a secret. And get on with the show. So to speak,' she smiled at the pun. 'I keep smiling, Myra.' She touched her jawline gingerly. 'My face hurts a bit.'

'You get that when you're doing yoga. And meditating. And, er … about keeping Green Monroe secret …'

'And, er … yes?' she said, mocking Myra's embarrassed tone lightly.

Myra said nothing. Very significantly.

'Oh. That's my cue to say "What's the big gap in the conversation about, Myra?"'

Silence. A guilty one.

'Now it's your cue to tell me,' Caitlin prodded, knowing what was coming.

'Well,' Myra admitted, 'I texted Nadia already. *And* Sarah.'

'Ohhhh. So who's told my mum?'

(Madeleine would have needed to be told. She had left abruptly after receiving a call from the local outpatient unit saying Allan had suffered an accident while playing tennis, and was concussed and asking for her. Reluctantly, she'd headed home — but not before demanding that she be kept in the loop about Max and *Freak Squad*.)

'The neo-lesbian did. She said you can't be mean and leave her out of the fun.'

'I suppose I can't,' Caitlin said regretfully, wondering why she didn't feel very annoyed. Too busy, she supposed. Too glowing, thought a relieved Myra, who was wondering the same thing.

'Now look. I've got mediation Thursday night. I've got one night to recover, and then I've got this date on Saturday. So you need to take me shopping. With Nadia,' she said, feeling a little sizzle work its way up her spine.

I'm excited. By a date, she thought to herself, stretching luxuriously. Who knew?

'You don't *need* to go shopping. You've got *plenty* of clothes,' Myra scoffed.

'Are you my *mother*? Besides, yes, while I've plenty to wear there's nothing I actually want to put anywhere near my skin. Everything I have has been out with Max before. May even have his DNA on it,' she gave a little shudder. 'I feel like doing a ceremonial burning of everything. If I wasn't so busy I'd be scrubbing down the walls. I keep ... feeling his fingerprints everywhere.'

'Oh,' Myra nodded, understanding creeping in. She wouldn't want any of her ex-husband's DNA near her. She'd practically scrubbed herself with a wire brush to get any remnants of his touch off her skin. 'Hmm,' she pondered, wincing at the memory of that scrubbing. 'Should we have a witches' pyre of your wedding dress?'

'I don't know. Maybe. It's tempting. Do you think it might traumatise the children to see me cackling round a bonfire burning the dress I married their father in?'

Irreverence, and a date, and contemplating burning her wedding dress, Myra noted with satisfaction.

'I think you're right about one thing,' Myra replied, looking over at her own wilted wardrobe of single-career-woman clothes. 'We should all go shopping.'

'First,' said Sarah, throwing a dress at Caitlin, 'try this on.'

'Then this,' said Nadia, shaking another dress from the other side of the boutique and flicking back loads of jet-black hair. 'And this. And then this. Don't argue — it costs me a lot of favours to have this place stay open just for you on a Wednesday night!'

Caitlin shot them both a dirty look, struggling under the pile of starlet frocks she was carrying to the change room, and clutched the last three Nadia had flung over. How come they get to tell me what I should wear? she thought grumpily.

(Truth be told, she loved this. The bad temper that kept surfacing was really about her pre-mediation nerves. And it was a whole lot safer to give these girls the occasional glare than to even go near the possibility of what might happen when she met up with Max.

She kept fantasising, even though she knew it was unlikely to happen, that he'd back off and leave her be. Just walk out and make no claim on the house. Be happy with Kennedy — if that's a possibility, she thought wryly — and be happy he could still see the kids. Get a job, work for his new family. Never, ever cross her path again.

But that wasn't Max's style, she knew. She kept hearing hopeful stories of men who did that, who would never take anything from their wives and kids. But he was, she could tell, from the brief phone calls and texts, upset. Stressed. And desperate.)

God, I just didn't marry very smart, she thought. I was in love. I didn't think we'd be breaking up. And I didn't think ... well. I didn't think, she concluded, feeling deflated.

She pulled on one dress. Strappy, short and bright, with red leggings to match, she felt ridiculous. Like a liar in a dress that said *I'm seventeen and happy.*

'I can't wear this,' she said, sticking her head out of the change room. 'I'm not seventeen and happy. I'm nearly forty, and I'm not miserable — not right now — but I'm terrified.'

'How can you be terrified? You're going on a date.'

'I'm terrified *because* I'm going on a date, silly! Take my pre-date jitters from before I was married, now multiply that and —'

'Shhh. Have some champagne,' replied Nadia, passing her a piccolo, its rim encrusted with icing sugar. 'You're just talking yourself into being scared.' She came in and had a look. 'Oh, Sarah, that dress is so wrong on her. You're banned from making suggestions now. Even trying on a bad dress can break a woman's confidence,' Nadia explained to them. 'It's my job to protect you from that,' she continued, earnest and sweet.

'But that dress is hot! And red is for courage. And —'

'Sarah, you stick to the spiritual stuff. Caitlin, next dress, please.'

'I don't know,' Caitlin replied doubtfully, pulling the happy-seventeen dress off and putting it on a hanger, and eyeing the others suspiciously, a bit like she thought they might bite. 'They're ... they're beautiful. But they're clothes someone *under* forty would be wearing,' she said critically, touching one pastel yellow dress regretfully.

'Please! You're still under forty … and besides, who cares?' Nadia called out from behind a stainless-steel rack bending under the weight of not-yet-in-the-shops designer dresses.

'Remember what happened to Elle Macpherson when she wore that short white dress?' Caitlin said ominously from the enormous cubicle. 'She got run out of town! It's like being mutton's a crime!'

'Yes, but we're not asking you to step out in a falling-down strapless mini-dress in front of eight hundred guests and a swarm of paparazzi.'

'And she's Elle Mac-bloody-pherson! And there are no sleeves here. I want sleeves,' moaned Caitlin, flicking through the garments for something that would cover her arms.

'No. No sleeves. It's a dinner date, and your arms are still very good. They're toned. Here. Hold them up,' Nadia ordered, flinging wide the cubicle curtains. Caitlin rebelled, finding this humiliating, but obeyed, wincing as she imagined flesh falling earthwards. 'See,' said Nadia. 'Not a sag. Not a swing. You can do it,' she said. 'No sleeves.'

'Besides, that dumb rule about sleeves over thirty went out with having to cut your hair short when you turn forty. Didn't it?' Myra asked, scrunching her face up.

'Of course it did,' Nadia said soothingly. 'They're old rules. For the old world. This is the new world, and you are all gorgeous woman. However, we do try to look our best,' she added, giving the dress that had been rejected a disapproving look. The dress, if it had been a human, would have been hurt.

'You're like a dress coach,' Caitlin commented, knowing that Nadia was usually paid thousands of dollars to do what she was doing right now for her. Although the stylist had been fibbing about her arms. Her upper arms were way softer than they'd been in her twenties. And they did have some give. But maybe I don't need to be so paranoid, she thought. It's a body. And it's still quite a nice one.

Parroting Caitlin's gesture, Sarah and Myra held their arms up to a mirror. 'You can get stuffed. I'm doing sleeves,' Myra told Nadia, who opened her mouth to protest. 'You can't *make* me go sleeveless. At least till we get me back to a gym.'

Nadia nodded. 'If you like. I mean, we'll all have the arm thing happening sooner or later.'

'It's loss of oestrogen that does it,' Sarah said, all informative. 'Yoga helps. You can tell.'

'Still,' Nadia added. 'Age happens to all of us. It's nothing to be ashamed of, or to feel bad about.'

They all glared at Nadia.

'What?' she asked, confused by the sudden wave of death-ray looks.

'Nadia, you're thirty-five!' Myra spat. 'We're all … nearly forty.'

'Yoga,' muttered Sarah randomly. (She was hoping to take the heat off Nadia, make Myra feel better about her sleeves issue and make Caitlin loosen up a bit. All at once.)

'So, it's all thanks to the diminishing-hormone thing,' Myra said, looking at herself and taking another slurp out of the straw she had plunged down the neck of her baby champagne bottle. 'I bet your lov-ah loves your yoga buns, Sarah,' she continued, taking a breath and inhaling some more champagne. 'No one's even seen my bum since … well, never mind,' she concluded, coming up for air and pushing the thought of the internet date with the foot fetishest right to the very dusty back corner of her mind to which all bad dates were banished.

Nadia was in her element, marching about, gently tugging clothes off racks, flinging them down on couches and teaming them with other items. Part of the beauty of being a stylist, *and* being one who was almost famous, meant she could call up designers and they'd rush their unreleased works of art to her favourite boutique. Meaning everything the girls had gathered to try on was cutting edge, stylish as fuck and had never been worn. 'Not even Lindsay Lohan has had her hands on these,' Nadia muttered triumphantly to herself.

'I don't want to wear anything she's had on,' Myra objected.

Sarah patted her shoulder. 'Look, she may seem crazy and out of control and spoilt, but it's just that she's demonstrating her Indigo traits.'

'Stop patting me, Sarah,' said Myra. 'It makes my arm wobble.'

Sarah patted Myra again, and Myra scowled and moved away.

'Oh no. Not this Indigo thing again,' Caitlin said. 'They're kids. It's just another label.'

'It's not. And you're going to have to come to grips with it — it'll come up on the program all the time.'

Nadia just smiled and let the banter wash over her as she mechanically sorted and chose shades, shapes, cuts and textures, matching them with her friend's colouring, size, height and personality.

Caitlin stopped looking through the clothes Nadia had selected for her and luxuriated in her private shopping experience. 'Do you know how great it is not to worry about someone seeing my underpants?' she remarked.

'What?'

'Well, if I go shopping normally, I have to be really careful about my outfit,' she said, flashing back to a time when she'd shopped with Kennedy, and she'd given her underwear a disdainful look. Now she knew why.

'Wow, we're pushing forty,' said Myra, who was trying on a pair of very high, very red, very shiny pin-up-girl patent leather peep-toe pumps. 'We're amazing, aren't we?' she said, turning to check out her behind in the mirror. 'I have a nice arse,' she said. 'Wow. Hello! How are you? Haven't seen you for ages.'

'She's been strapped in suits and squashed up against a chair while you write e-mails to losers,' Nadia teased. 'Oops. Was that a bit too edgy?' she asked, big brown eyes full of apology.

'Nope,' replied Myra. 'We're both forty and fabulous,' she said, speaking on behalf of her backside, whose peachy roundness was looking excellent. 'We can take it.'

'Good. I'm still learning about teasing,' admitted Nadia, frowning.

'What? I thought fashion would be full of it,' Sarah said.

'Oh, it is,' relied Nadia earnestly. 'But it's also full of gay men. And you get into this weird world where you think everyone's a gay man on the inside, and can handle being called a bitch. I mean, I can handle it. When a man, a gay man, calls me a bitch. Because it's like admiration. But then someone called me a bitch at that wild weekend thing and I wanted to cry.'

'Who called you a bitch?' demanded Sarah, sounding like she was going to hunt down the offender and take them to pieces. 'That's psychic attack!'

'Isn't it just an attack?' Myra asked. 'Or am I missing something?'

Nadia and Sarah went on, ignoring the muggle questions.

'Well, to be fair they only sort of implied I was a bitch,' explained Nadia. 'They didn't actually say it. But I knew they were thinking it.'

Sarah nodded. 'You're probably right. You're very empathic, Nadia. You need clear boundaries. And people with good energy.'

Nadia nodded back. (Myra felt annoyed at all the new-age agreeing going on. Caitlin couldn't see, being busy in the change room.)

'But banter can be confusing. And doing it with friends is even worse. I used to only tease people at work. I'm trying to branch out and banter with my friends, rather than just being really, really nice all the time,' Nadia said, completely unselfconsciously.

'I need to learn to do that before I'm forty. Everyone over thirty-five has wit. I just have charm,' Sarah lamented. 'And I want to be fabulous like you all are!'

'And you are,' Nadia went on. 'Forty for my mum was, like, a full-time dress rehearsal for her funeral.' (Everyone freeze-framed for a moment. None of them had ever heard Nadia say anything remotely unpleasant about anyone.) 'Marinated in bitterness,' shrugged Nadia in explanation, and everyone breathed out and continued to rummage. 'So pissed off over Dad's … floozies, her weight, her pain. But *you*!' she said, turning and gazing critically at Caitlin. 'On with that sundress. Now. You're fresh, vibrant, gorgeous *and* —'

'You're about to be fucking someone,' finished Myra flatly, flopping back on a chaise. 'Do you know how long it is since I had sex?' she asked, sighing heavily.

'Two years, three months and fourteen days,' replied Sarah, Nadia and Caitlin simultaneously, suppressing grins.

'Yes, you do all know!' she crowed, kicking her high heels in the air. 'And it's a long time, isn't it?'

Everyone stifled giggles, but she continued. Seriously, this time.

'So how is it fair that *you* have sex first?' she demanded of Caitlin. 'That *you* get taken date-shopping first? Why? Why?!'

'You don't *know* I'm about to have sex,' Caitlin soothed.

'Not yet,' interjected Sarah. 'But you will be within … hmmmn,' she narrowed her china-doll blue eyes and stared intensely at Caitlin, tapping a ballet shoe in concentration. 'Yep. I give it ten days,' she said, with a little nod.

'How can you tell?' asked Myra, a determined set to her chin. 'And if you can tell, tell me when *I'll* be having some!'

'Oh, it's an intuitive thing. Well, there are some definite pointers.' (Sarah didn't like demystifying her secrets.) 'Caitlin's just got that look,' she said sweetly.

'What look? A horny look? But *I'm* horny!' Myra objected loudly.

'Not exactly,' Sarah replied, all patient and kind with the nonbeliever. 'Women who are about to have sexy affairs have a certain vibe — their skin is dewy,' she instructed. Everyone moved closer. 'They look ever so slightly ready to, well, sweat. See?' she explained, moving over to Caitlin, who was backed into a corner in the change room in her knickers. 'She's got that pre-sex gleam.'

'All over!' Myra affirmed, taking in Caitlin's underwear.

Nadia came over and looked at her too. 'She's right. Check.'

'Such women have only good hair days and they lose weight just before they have to get naked.'

'Checkmate,' Myra quipped. 'Hey, maybe she's just ovulating. Don't we hook up easiest when we're ovulating?'

'Why haven't you, then?' Sarah asked innocently, before popping her hand over her mouth. 'Oh — you're not — are you?'

'I'm still ovulating, if that's what you're implying,' Myra snapped. 'Sorry,' she said, reining herself in. 'I'm premenstrual. Thank God.'

Everyone laughed, easing the tension in the room. No one wanted to admit that the promise of being peri-menopausal was way worse than being premenstrual.

'This theory of yours is great, Sarah,' Nadia said. 'You should have her on *Date Squad* as the relationship person,' she advised Caitlin, who was relaxing a little now everyone had stepped back from her cubicle.

'I'm not working on that show any more,' she replied automatically, sticking her head outside the change room to deliver her announcement before popping it back in again.

Nadia stuck her head inside the change room, where Caitlin was now sheltering like a snail in a shell. 'You know, that colour looks incredible with your skin and your hair.' She tilted her shiny black head to one side, giving her a critical look. 'I know who you remind me of,' she declared, smiling. 'You look like a Varga girl.'

'Like a what?' Myra asked. 'A *Viagra* girl?'

'No, not a Viagra girl. A *Varga* girl.'

'A Varga girl was an illustrated form of pin-up that reached cult status in the sixties. Pin-up girls were huge. Like Linda Darnell.'

Blank looks all round.

'Okay, like Jessica Rabbit, then.'

Even blanker.

Nadia shook her head. 'That's it. You can't live … in the *dark* like this. I went to your weekend thing,' she said in a wounded little voice to Sarah. 'I said I'd start yoga. You have to come to my world soon.'

'Okaaaay,' said Caitlin slowly. 'Back to Pin-up Girls 101, please, oh passionate one.'

'Anyway. Pin-up Girls 101. Okay, they usually had fair, lush hair — often strawberry blonde or red. They nearly always had curls, and they always had curves. They were cheeky-looking and sexy, but it all felt very innocent. Very peekaboo. Not like strippers now, who all look like they could run a four-minute mile. Like sex is athletics. They were all their own fair skin and curves and wobbles; they were sweet and innocent.'

'Did they wear aprons and do the ironing?' Myra asked sarcastically.

'Actually, Brigitte Bardot does exactly that in a film, wearing a gingham bra just like the one you're holding — it became a cult look.'

'Hmph,' said Myra, who wanted to say she found it all disturbingly old-fashioned and disempowering. But she didn't. And she didn't put the bra back, either.

Meanwhile, back in the change room, doing her best to forget about being compared to unfit apron-wearing soft-bodied pin-up girls, Caitlin had pulled the yellow dress on. It floated about her for a second before falling gently, sliding over hips, snug around waist, gathered in soft folds over bust, making her look, well, *gorgeous*. But is it still sort of … mutton? she wondered.

Nope. The mirror was a harsh critic, and it was giving her rave reviews. She looked beautiful; her arms were long and rounded and her shoulders looked delicate under the straps. The pale, pale yellow made her skin look creamy and her hair a lush golden red with sparks. With the dash of scarlet lipstick she'd applied in the car she was as close to breathtaking as she'd ever been.

'Oh. You look … delicious,' breathed Nadia, whipping back the curtain with a flourish. Everyone else took a breath in too, right on cue.

'You're all whipped cream! Yum,' said Myra.

'You're so pretty! I want you bad,' giggled Sarah. 'Joking,' she said, putting her hands up toward them in protest when they all turned and stared. (Caitlin's was a particularly dark look.) 'It's all right for *you* to make my-new-lesbian-friend jokes, but not quite enough time has gone by for *me* to make them, I see,' she said, mock-offended.

'*He's* going to want you so bad,' said Myra, returning to the subject at hand and shaking her head. 'Oh. You're going to have sex!' she said dramatically, blinking back tears, and turning away like a mother at a virgin's bloody sheets.

Caitlin sat down on the little velvet chair in the room and crossed her legs neatly at the ankle, making her look even more deliciously fifties. She thrust her chin into her hands, then glared at her friends, who'd all invaded the dressing room.

'No, I'm not,' she declared, forthright and steady.

(Stunned silence, punctuated only by the sharp hiss of Myra's outraged in-breath.)

'That's right,' Cait said, folding her arms so tightly she was beginning to resemble a human pretzel. 'I'm not going to go out with that … that boy.'

Cue protests.

'And I'm certainly *not* going to take my clothes off with him.'

'Why not?' Nadia said, perplexed and vaguely annoyed at the idea of ingratitude for her Stylist's Magic. 'You look wonderful!'

'Hang on. It's not about how she looks,' Sarah interjected. 'Aren't you ready?' she asked softly, coming over all sensitive.

'Ready? No! There's no need to be ready. You just have to dress up. It can just be dinner,' Nadia protested.

'Yes, just dinner,' echoed Sarah, catching on. 'You don't have to —'

'It cannot be *just dinner*,' Myra stepped in, proud face flushing, fists curled up. 'No! She *has* to have sex,' Myra continued firmly. 'How can you do this to me? If I can't get sex, you have to have it for me! You *have* to — you have the *look*! Sarah can't be wrong!'

Caitlin led the way back out of the change room, steadying Myra with a hand on her shoulder. 'Look. It's just … it feels very strange. I haven't been with anyone for a long time. And I hadn't really had many, you know, sexual encounters,' she finished delicately as they all found places to perch in the boutique.

'Fucks!' Myra exploded. 'They're fucks!'

'As I said, I didn't have that much experience — or very wide experience — before Max, anyway,' finished Caitlin, eyeing Myra carefully, and patting her shoulder to comfort her.

'Don't even say his name. It makes me shudder,' said Sarah.

'Why? This makes no sense at all. If you haven't had much experience, why not get some now?' asked Myra, who was clearly not getting it at all.

'It's just, well, *because*, really,' Caitlin finished lamely. (Myra snorted.) 'Look, it's simple. He's twenty-nine years old, and I'm *so* not. And he's a professional snowboarder from Canada who obviously wants to just have —'

'Sex,' everyone finished for her.

'And the problem with that is?' Myra demanded, wiping her eyes, standing up and moving over to the change room, shrugging off her business jacket, and peeling off her pencil skirt and tights. 'He's hot. Snowboarder. Yum. You're giving me his number.'

'I don't think it works like that,' Caitlin replied, feeling backed into a corner again.

'Why not?' Myra said, tugging a skin-tight red and black dress down over her hips.

'Because he's not Pass the Parcel!' Caitlin said, realising she was feeling possessive.

Myra ignored her. 'I'll get me into this stripper thing and I'll get his number and we'll have hot gratuitous going-nowhere-serious sex and — *oh no*!' she interrupted herself in heart-rending tones, looking at her reflection with total dismay. 'No way! I look like a has-been Betty Burlesque heading off to the old folks' home strip-a-thon. No *way*. No wonder I can't have go-nowhere sex!'

'And you know what?' said Caitlin softly, ignoring Myra. (She'd calm down in a minute, she knew.) 'Honestly. I sort of thought that man from the weekend would get in contact. I have a little bit of a … thing … for him.' She gave Sarah a look.

Sarah nodded. 'I thought you might have. Cassandra made it sound like … well, I thought he would have called you.'

Nadia (being empathic) looked sad. She understood crushes better than most. Working with impossibly handsome tactile gay men had a lot of drawbacks.

'In fact,' Sarah went on thoughtfully, 'I would have bet that's who you had the look for. It started around that time,' she added to herself.

Caitlin didn't say anything.

'Maybe he'll write you a letter,' Nadia said. 'You know, maybe he's old-fashioned.'

'Who writes letters?' scoffed Myra, sitting down in her underwear next to Nadia, who was pondering what to put her in next given the red dress had been such a self-esteem disaster. 'Serial killers and kidnappers and … and old people, that's who,' she sulked.

'Not any more they don't, they probably send text messages. Anyway. Caitlin, you've got other things to get on with, like these,' said Nadia.

Caitlin backed away from the small, ruby-red piece of fabric and its edging of fragile white lace. She winced ever so slightly.

'That's not a dress, is it?' Sarah inquired dubiously.

'Of course not,' exclaimed Nadia. 'You silly-billies!'

'Oooh, big attempt at an insult,' Myra added childishly, still inconsolable after her dress disaster.

'It's matching underwear!' Nadia said patiently, unperturbed at Myra's netball bitchiness — it was very close to fashion bitchery. 'Look. Here's the bra,' holding up two half circles, 'and here are the pants,' holding up tiny little shorts-like knickers. When everyone still looked confused, she lost patience. 'Girls! I'm so disappointed you don't know your boudoir wear. Or your fashion!'

'Oh!' Sarah exclaimed, relieved that it wasn't a dress. 'Well. They are beautiful,' she said by way of conciliation.

'Wow, you're relentless,' Caitlin said to Nadia. 'You've only just got me in this number.'

'And tell me you don't feel and look great,' Nadia came right back at her.

'And now you want me in these,' Caitlin finished smoothly, raising one golden eyebrow.

'Why not?' challenged Nadia, free hand on one slender be-denimmed hip.

'Because,' Caitlin said, scrunching up her face. 'They're knickers! With frills on them.'

'Who's going to know?'

'Oh, come on! Nobody wears knickers like this unless they want someone to see them. I still can't believe I said yes to this date,' she groaned, shaking her head in self-admonishment. 'He's so young. It's just irresponsible. What will Sean and Molly think? They'll be home tomorrow and —'

'They'll think that if they ever have a partner who fucks up like yours did, they can get on with things and meet handsome younger men,' parried Nadia.

'Well. I suppose. But they're home on Saturday night. I'll have to find a babysitter.'

'Like that's hard,' said Myra, voice dripping with sarcasm. 'There's, oooh, Sarah, and er, me, and Nadia and by then your mum will be back. Big crisis there!'

Caitlin knew she was running out of objections. 'Well, then there's the fact that I can't very well have sex with someone at the house when my kids are there, having just got home from their dad's. That's very … I don't know. It just feels wrong.'

'Who said you have to have sex at home?' said Sarah.

'Yeah, just think of the opportunities,' Myra said eagerly. 'Backs of cars, alleys — this is your opportunity to re-enact all those sleazy movie scenes you would never have bothered with if you were still married. And which I'll never get to do!'

'And he's up for *Date Squad*. Office rule number one: never date the talent.'

'Oh. But you said he's pulled out of the program. And you said just a while back that it wasn't your show any more. And you're not exactly employed by the station, either. So you're just … hedging. Like a nervous pony,' said Myra.

'Maybe you'll get married,' Nadia mused, all dreamy.

'What?' Sarah said.

'Where did that come from? Are you serious?' Myra inquired, incredulous.

She shook her head vigorously, after which lots of sleek black hair fell perfectly back into place. 'No. Just imagining wedding frocks.' She snapped herself out of the stylish meringue-free fantasy world she'd just been in. 'Look, Myra's right. You're just stalling. Go in. Try these on.'

Caitlin, grateful to get away from the drama, slipped into the dressing room and stripped off the yellow sundress, whose price tag she'd been avoiding looking at. She stood and looked at herself in the mirror, in her own seen-better-days underwear. She ran her eyes over her body, trying to be objective about her own flesh. It wasn't as hard as you'd imagine — she was used to assessing people's physicality. She just hadn't tuned her eye on her own for a while.

Long thighs, a vein beginning to fragment, just like a star or a river system, faint and blue under her pale skin. Her stomach was flat, but didn't have the firmness of the others'. They'd never had babies. She looked at her breasts. They were large and heavy and round, and still beautiful, she thought, moving her eyes up to the skin under her throat, which had softened slightly. From the neck down, she could see traces of sun damage, milkiness spotted intermittently with the occasional freckle or raised capillary, trying desperately to protect her skin from more sun damage. She smiled at herself, and turned to her side and smiled again. Her teeth were white and her skin was beautiful. Her eyes were still good. She gave herself a nod, said 'you'll do' and pulled the small panties over her own shabbier, slightly grey ones. (They'd looked all right till she'd seen the contrast.) She looked, well, *imperfect*, but soft and lovely.

Nadia stuck herself inside, and Myra darted behind her.

'Wow.'

'I'm trying to imagine what a twenty-nine-year-old snowboarder would make of this,' Caitlin said. 'But in a way I don't care.'

'I can't understand why this wouldn't be beautiful, — for anyone,' said Myra seriously. 'I'm so proud of you!'

'But for a guy who's twenty-nine?' Caitlin repeated. She paused, hearing her phone go off. Sarah tossed it in through the open curtains. Cait caught it, glanced at the number and felt her mood plummet.

It was Max.

She flipped it open.

'Hello,' she said. She could not bear to say *how are you*. She couldn't bear the small courtesies right now.

'Hi — we're set for tomorrow night for mediation, right?' he asked, voice friendly like he was talking about something very casual and normal, she realised, frowning. She shook her head, trying to get the small electric pulses shocking and sparking inside her scalp to ease off. The dissonance between now and the past — the very recent past — was so peculiar, like the rush of taking off but still being on the ground. That's exactly the sort of thing they would have said to each other before meeting up for dinner. The contrast, like that between the new red knickers and her old grey underpants, was startling.

'Yeah. I'm okay with it. It has to be done, right?' she said, aiming for a cool, businesslike tone, and hearing a faint wobble in her voice. Damn, she thought, noticing her free hand was shaking slightly.

'I know, I know,' he soothed. He lowered his voice, sounding intimate and close, as he had when they'd talked to each other in bed, so as not to wake the kids. She felt the knife that she'd forgotten was lodged inside her twist sharply. Is he whispering, she wondered, so Kennedy doesn't hear him?

'Look, I just want you to know that I'm sorry. And I

really didn't mean for it to end up this way. We could have gone on. Worked it out somehow.'

She said nothing. She didn't think she could.

'Caitlin. It's very hard to start again. To be so unsettled. Without you.'

She softened a little. So he wasn't having the time of his life, she thought, with a rush of relief. Maybe he's really unhappy. She cheered up ever so slightly.

'Especially at this stage,' he went on awkwardly. 'We're getting older … and for women …'

What is that supposed to mean? she thought. 'This stage?' she repeated, finding her voice. 'What do you mean?' She sat down, feeling a little dizzy. 'What exact stage are you talking about, Max?'

'Look, don't be like that,' he warned. Like what, she wondered. 'Look. I'm just sorry. I want you to know that.'

Fuck you, she thought. You're older than me, but you're saying I'm the one who's — what? — lost her chance at having a life?

'What are you doing right now?' he asked, trying to change the subject.

None of your business, she thought. Then again, why *don't* I tell him? He asked.

'I'm trying on red silk panties. And they look fucking great. See you tomorrow.'

She hung up.

'Oh my God!'

'You were brilliant!'

The girls swarmed around her — she had forgotten they were listening in.

'It's the pants,' Sarah said excitedly. 'Oh my God. They *are* magic. You were transformed.'

'I've seen these pants work before,' agreed Nadia breathlessly. 'They have some kind of effect on women — they make them feel so great, they're practically indestructible.'

'I thought it was your character that gave you that,' Myra asked.

'No. It's your underwear,' Nadia said, serious.

'You have to wear them tomorrow night. Especially after that conversation. Max will sense them.'

'Why do you think they work?' Sarah asked, wondering. 'Oh! Oh! I know. Silk,' she intoned, 'is made from a cocoon. A cocoon is the home of a former silkworm that has turned into a butterfly.'

'Moths, Sarah. They turn into moths,' Caitlin interrupted.

'Pedant,' teased Sarah. 'You know what I mean. It's a brand new you!'

'Are you saying I'm a butterfly or a caterpillar?' Caitlin asked. She felt a little frisson of triumph from getting at Max. He'd always had a weakness for underwear. (And for taking it off her.) And though she knew it was petty, making him hurt just a little made her feel powerful.

'I'm saying that you're emerging,' explained Sarah. 'And the perfect fabric for a woman emerging from a struggle is silk.'

'Then that settles it,' Caitlin said determinedly, picking up a bottle of champagne and drinking deeply from it. She wiped her mouth with the back of her hand

and pointed one by one at the items on the floor of the changing room. 'I'm getting that yellow dress, *and* that red one you tried on, Myra.'

'Oh, thanks. Make me feel like shit,' Myra said. 'Just kidding. Be my guest.'

'And four, no, six pairs of these,' she said, taking another swig from her baby champagne and gesturing vaguely at her underpants.

And she did, much to the joy of the shop owner, who'd been hiding out the back for hours, waiting for them to go. All up, thousands of dollars changed hands before all four women left the building and drove a very tipsy Caitlin home. She was tipsier still when she got there, having insisting on drinking all the way.

'Why are you drinking?' Sarah asked.

'Kids are at Maxsh's,' slurred Caitlin in reply. 'And I keep hearing Max saying I was past it. That will take a while to delete. I'm not past it,' she objected drunkenly to nobody in particular when she got in the front door, leaving Myra and Nadia to take each other home. Sarah, meanwhile, was walking ahead of her, busily removing sharp objects from Caitlin's reach. 'Past being made a fool of,' she followed up, swaying slightly as she made her way to her room, while Sarah helped her put her new underwear away, and chucked out a pair of underpants Max had really loved.

Very nearly past not being over you, she thought, drinking the huge glass of water Sarah thrust under her nose, before passing out in her silk underpants on top of her bed, the Victorian nightie safe and unworn under her pillow.

TWENTY-ONE

Not quite twenty-four hours later, Caitlin, who was walking slightly stiffly due to her new underwear, which she was sure everyone could tell she was wearing, snuck cautiously into the offices of Creating Better Relationships.

Despite its upbeat name, it was very obvious that this place wasn't designed to bring people together. It was dour and gloomy; a faint smell of mould with an undertone of something having gone off wafted occasionally through its corridors. This, thought Caitlin, taking in the scenery with a sweeping glance around the reception, is one of the most depressing places I've ever seen.

On a dull brown chest of drawers stood a cloudy, green-tinged aquarium. Within it swam a listless-looking goldfish (only one, naturally, Caitlin thought wryly, lifting a chestnut eyebrow). Mysterious stains decorated the beige carpet, making Caitlin wonder if murder had once been committed in the rooms, and nobody had ever bothered to clean up properly afterwards. There was only one very worn and threadbare tobacco-yellow couch, which looked like it'd come direct from a garage sale, and several bewildered, shellshocked-looking souls shuffled past it on their ways somewhere and back, desperately avoiding eye contact with each other. It looked a little like a very genteel mental institution from the forties, Cait thought, wondering if Frances Farmer was about to make an appearance. Nope. No one remotely famous or glamorous. Just plenty of crushed members of the walking-wounded tribe, all looking like they'd rather be anywhere than at Creating Better Relationships.

Except for her ex-husband, of course.

She looked straight at him, head held high, unaware that she was the only person in the room who looked at all like she wanted to be there. And like she had a purpose. She felt the hairs on her arms stand up, and a little thrill of electricity ran through her system, starting somewhere at the back of her head and running right down her spine, leaving her whole body feeling awake and alert. Adrenaline, she thought vaguely, feeling its tingle reach her scalp, and half-heartedly lifting her hand to her head. Fight or flight. And she was definitely here to fight, she told herself, pushing back a stray red curl sliding out of its bronze clip, and tucking it behind her ear, green eyes fixed on her soon-to-be-ex-husband.

Meanwhile, Max was happily oblivious to his soon-to-be-former-wife's scrutiny.

He was seated right in the middle of the reception area's ugly couch, and was deep in the pages of *Filmink*, where he was enjoying vastly the tales of the troubled making of Mel Gibson's new religious epic. She watched him laughing out loud once or twice to himself, registering the heartbreaking familiarity of his movements. His mouth stretched wide over white-white teeth, deep lines running from the corners of his eyes to his strong chin, the long lines of a body muscular and graceful in his jeans and suit jacket. He folded one long, lean limb over the other exactly as she'd seen him fold it about a million times before. She shook her head slightly, feeling stunned at just how she could know him so very well, so well she could predict his expressions and the way his body would lean. She knew the colour of his eyelashes and the way the hair sprang up along his arms. She knew all about him. And here they were.

She wished she could wipe out the details of his physical repertoire, be oblivious to how his body moved, or how he looked when he said *I love you*, or how his eyes changed colour when he was angry. She wished she could forget how he'd sworn never to leave her.

She wished she could forget how loved she'd felt. How safe she'd thought she was.

And, she reminded herself, it wasn't as if *he* had actually left *her*. Strictly speaking, she had thrown him out — because he'd made it impossible for her to have him stay. *Bloody* impossible.

She sighed, feeling a heavy weight settle somewhere under her ribs. We will never do this again. Like your wedding day, it's a one-off, she thought desperately, feeling her will slide a little, and depression replace her adrenalised battle surge. How can I be hard enough to do this? I've spent more time loving him than hating him.

She thought of all the times she'd seen him going through the trade magazines like this, at coffee shops, in bed, on the (very nice and definitely not threadbare or tobacco-coloured) couch at home … and that she hadn't thought to see him reading tonight. Maybe he could have been thinking. About what a mess he'd made. Perhaps sitting with his head in his hands, or on his knees, ready to beg her not to go through with this. Or maybe just looking a little sleepless and sad. Regretful didn't seem too much to ask.

She sat down carefully, with great dignity, next to him, turning her body slightly away to let him know it wasn't exactly what she wanted to do. When he still didn't seem to notice, she looked at him again, and gave a little *humph* of disapproval. It was silly, she knew, and childish. But she couldn't help herself. Or, if she'd admitted it to herself, she could. But she just didn't damn well feel like being well behaved any more.

He started slightly when he noticed her next to him, and his eyes shadowed, looking caught out for a moment. She raised her chin and slowly, coldly nodded her head in acknowledgment, but nearly flinched in shock at the change in expression that came over his features. He looked hurt; there was naked longing in his eyes. And she realised she truly had a dirty fight on her hands. With herself.

Just as quickly, his mobile and fluid face shifted and changed once more.

He folded up *Filmink*, shifted his legs again, and the smile that had been playing around his wide mouth completely disappeared.

She looked at him, head slightly tilted, wondering. His eyes slid away from hers, looking down ever so slightly. Somehow that made her furious, and she felt the surge of adrenaline reinforced by a little anger. She felt like a furnace was being lit inside her.

How dare you? she thought, fired up now. I had our children. She was slightly embarrassed to be remembering just how that had come about in such a place. Don't be melodramatic, she told herself, continuing to stare at him. But it was true.

The truth was, he'd betrayed her. In that old-fashioned, cheating-on-her kind of way. All the clichés. With someone younger, who now had a baby on the way.

Even though they'd been happy together.

She licked her lips nervously, feeling like she was being forced to sit side by side with someone she was about to battle in a boxing ring. Or to make quiet chit-chat just before a duel. Swords would be more in keeping, she thought. I'd love to actually hold one right up over his head and bring it down, hard, slicing him in two, bellowing fiercely, like some kind of Amazon on a mission of destruction:

YOU BETRAYED ME.

She shook her head as small stars exploded in her brain. She absently scratched at her temple, resisting the urge to give it a thump. *Woah.* Must be a flashback to some Celtic firebrand ancestor, she thought, steadying herself. Which wasn't going to help right now. She breathed just like she'd been practising since the Wild Women's Weekend. She felt herself calm slightly. Even though she was getting consistent results, it still shocked her, the difference simple breathing techniques and visualisation could make.

Maybe … maybe there was a way to make it bearable. He might behave with honour. If she could just find that part of him again. Or had she just made up the fact that he was a good man? Surely it couldn't have all been an act, she thought urgently. He had to be there, somewhere.

'Max?' she said tentatively, trying to find some kind of connection.

But he refused to meet her eyes, staring steadfastly at the other side of the room, like it housed an answer to her question if only she'd look over there too.

He can't meet my eye. Bastard, she thought, feeling the urge to either lean forward and push him, or rush out and keep running.

But she didn't, and instead fought every instinct she had, and went back to her breathing, feeling the strange rhythm work its magic again.

'Oh, hello. How are the pants going?' he grinned, still managing to look sad.

She had to admire his nerve — flirting with his wife, just before they divorced.

'You'll never know,' she snapped.

'Hmmm. Well. Here we are,' he said.

Before he could go on, and before Caitlin could start her breathing exercise again, a woman bustled out to meet them, her grey and brown and silver hair like a large fuzzy cloud behind her, her angular face harried.

Caitlin felt her temperature drop, and rubbed her arms instinctively, self-protective.

'Sorry I'm late,' the woman with the mad hair said, a broad smile showing off her slightly crooked and very large teeth. Caitlin liked her immediately. 'I've been in *court*,' she said, with heavy dramatic emphasis on the last word, and a roll of her large, round, dark grey eyes. 'Oh! Tina Glass, hello, hello,' she said absently, thrusting a hand in the direction of Max, who had to change positions to grasp her hand. After a brief shake, she then thrust it at Caitlin, who smiled, feeling somehow reassured by this woman's presence.

She glanced at Max, whose face was carefully closed. It's not likely to be fair at all, she thought. More like a filthy bar-room brawl, complete with broken glass and biting, and a whole lot of hair-pulling. She was amused at the image conjured up. 'Urgh,' she said out loud, shaking her red curls, trying to get her mind back on track. Tina met her eyes, and snorted gently with laughter.

'Yes, it is a bit like that,' she agreed. 'Awful offices. At least they don't smell tonight!' Caitlin raised her eyebrows, curious as to how much worse they must normally smell.

Despite her exhaustion, cynicism and obvious air of being well over it many years ago, at least the woman leading her down the corridor wasn't full of it. Caitlin hurried along to keep up.

'Boy, I'm glad we do this instead of heading straight for the courtroom,' Tina commented, breathing out heavily and opening a door which led to another corridor, lined with white plastic chairs, and doors through which a series of small rooms could be seen. Caitlin was beginning to wonder just how much of a rabbit warren this place was. She glanced at Tina, wondering if she knew where she was going. She had heavy rings under her eyes, which were faintly rimmed with red, and slight, wiry energy, making Cait feel her mediator was propelled by sheer nerves. She's not the sort of woman you could imagine relaxing, Caitlin thought. She's on a mission.

'Court is *not* where you want to end up,' Tina repeated, waving her hand around vigorously. Caitlin wondered what had happened in court to make her so relieved they weren't there. 'No matter how difficult this may seem to be,' she said a little too loudly, answering Caitlin's question before she'd had a chance to ask it. She bit back her other questions, and felt slightly less hostile and scared. At least this woman had some … balls. Some honesty. She wouldn't bullshit her, she felt. Not, she thought, that my bullshit detector is anything to be bragging about. Look how accurate it was with Max and Kennedy.

She wondered for a moment how Kennedy was — she'd heard from Gus and Carol that she was sick, like lots of expectant mothers, and pale and bad-tempered. But she wondered how she *felt*. It was a little like losing her husband to the little sister she'd never had. She'd pushed aside most thoughts of how her husband and her assistant interacted — what they did in bed, when they went to the doctor's together, whether they'd tenderly watched their baby's heart beating on the ultrasound screen. She'd tried very hard. But seeing Max meant seeing Kennedy. She could feel her presence — threatening, hostile, faintly alarmed that Max and Caitlin were anywhere near each other. 'You have nothing to worry about,' Caitlin said out loud, as she felt Kennedy's resentment for a moment. 'He's all yours,' she whispered.

Max gave her a look, but she hardly acknowledged it. Tina didn't show any sign of having noticed anything unusual. (She'd heard far worse.)

They got a bit stuck in the corridor as several of the doors opened and a handful of weary-looking couples bottlenecked. They squeezed past each other without acknowledgment — obviously the no-eye-contact rule was enforced, Caitlin noticed. Then she started — a darkly handsome and somewhat familiar someone was leaving another of the poky rooms that were sprinkled along the corridor. He squeezed past her, looking down; she turned and glanced back, and caught him looking at her too. They both looked away, knowing they were part of each other's past, and not wanting to acknowledge where they both were now.

They'd met on holiday with a large group of mutual friends, about twenty years ago, before she and Max started going out. How weird to see someone who'd known her when she was single, just as she was about to become single again.

The last time she'd seen him was at a group dinner table with a whole lot of *sake* going down the throats of the people collected around it — suntanned, with sunbleached hair and the reckless confidence of the very young, they'd been drinking much too much cheap wine and talking, probably incoherently and naively, she thought, about life and what they wanted out of it. They'd been sweet.

And appearing in this scenario right here had never rated a mention, not during that or any of the many other drunken conversations that had taken place in that short haven between exams and the real world. That much she could remember.

She wondered if he'd recognised her, then as he turned to look at her one more time before entering a small conference room, it became clear that he did. Good luck, she thought, sending him a mental wish, turning a little pink and feeling tears prick at the back of her eyes.

It was not that it was embarrassing. It was that it was sad. And somehow, breaking into that sadness with greetings and verbal recognitions that youth's dream had shattered for both of them didn't seem right at all.

'Ah,' said Tina, with a gusty sigh of relief. 'Here we go,' she said, ushering them both into a tiny room.

Inside was a very short, very round man balancing awkwardly on a cheap metal chair. He was pale, bald and childlike. She sat down opposite him and smiled, holding out a hand. 'Caitlin Cooper,' she said, forcing strength into her voice.

Max was still hesitating at the threshold, like he wasn't sure whether he should actually enter or not. 'Erhhh-hmmmmm,' he interrupted, poking his head into the room, which already felt crowded with three people in it. 'Don't we have …' he paused, looking embarrassed. 'Isn't it protocol to have separate sessions to begin with?' he finished.

'You're absolutely right,' said Tina cheerfully, matching his volume. Max winced.

'What we do first is we take each of you aside and have a chat. So that's bye-bye to you,' she smirked, closing the door on Max's startled face and sitting down opposite Caitlin, and next to the man, who had broken out in a sweat. He gave a little cough, and shot a meaningful glance at Tina.

'And hello to you!' she said to him. 'Now, it's been a long day.' She winked at Caitlin, who smiled back. She knew this should all be terribly serious, but she was enjoying Tina's slightly mad approach.

'This lovely gentleman is Charlie Hubbard, my associate. We'll have a little introductory speech from me. Then you'll have some questions. Then you tell me how the fairytale went wrong. Then you can collect yourself outside while we see your husband.' Caitlin's grin faded at the word husband. 'Yep, he still is, for at least another twelve months, *and* until all this is sorted out. Kids and houses tend to put the brakes on divorce. They all need to be dealt with. Anyway. After he talks with us, we'll all talk together. Oh. Hang on. I forgot to give you the drill.'

'Ahem,' Charlie said, giving her a baleful glance.

'Don't worry, Charlie, it'll all be done by the book,' said Tina reassuringly. 'Charlie,' she explained, turning her attention to Caitlin, 'is a stickler for the rules. He's wonderful though,' she said, smiling warmly at her colleague, who shrank back a little in distrust.

'Now. The drill.' She took a deep breath, put on what Caitlin could only imagine was her serious voice, and started.

'We're not here as lawyers,' she said tiredly, 'we're here to help you meeed-eee-ate.' She dragged the word out. 'A lot of people think that what we're doing is getting together to represent you both. We're not. We're trying to get you to come to an arrangement that's legal, and that keeps you out of the courts.'

'What's the terrible fear about the courts?' Caitlin asked.

Tina stared at her briefly, then the shock faded and her toothy grin returned. 'I guess that means you've never been in court. Good for you! They're dreadful places. They're like the anti-Disneyland. They're the unhappiest places on earth.'

Caitlin frowned, feeling like that hardly answered her question, and Tina shrugged in resignation.

'Look, I know it sounds melodramatic. But trust me on this.' She lowered her voice to a dramatic whisper. 'Courts tend to reward men at the moment, and leave women shattered. Sorry, Charlie,' she said to her partner, who was looking a little offended. Or perhaps it was the smell.

'Tina,' he said, in clipped tones. 'Stats would indicate your … theory … does have some weight.'

'It does indeed,' Tina replied warmly, giving him a hearty slap on the back. 'Let me fill you in, Caitlin. Time me, Charlie,' she ordered. He nodded, looking pained. 'Let me know when three minutes is up.' She took a deep breath, and launched herself.

'A lot of women who are like you,' said Tina, waving a hand vaguely in Caitlin's direction, '(and I'm making a guess here, you know), you're successful and you're educated and you're one of those ones newspapers would probably describe as a high-flyer. Cringeworthy term, but there it is. Now, there's a downside to your success. It's called a property settlement. It forces these women — women like you — to pay out huge sums to their less-wealthy ex-husbands. I can tell you that all law firms are reporting an increasing number of cases in which men are earning windfalls through divorce as women like you outperform their husbands in the workplace.'

Caitlin nodded faintly.

'In court today,' Tina continued, her voice becoming husky and dry, 'I represented three women who each earns more than her husband. That's three today. I have seven more I'm representing.' She disappeared under the table and reappeared with a bottle of amber liquid, which she poured into a coffee mug.

'Is that whisky?' Caitlin asked, trying not to wrinkle her nose.

'Yes, it is. Not a very glamorous container, I know, but my voice is going and I need a shot. You?' she offered.

'No. Thanks,' Caitlin smiled.

'Sure? I can dig up another mug.'

Caitlin tried not to start laughing, as Charlie shifted back in his chair and folded his arms firmly across his chest. His whole being resonated distaste.

'Unconventional, I know, Charlie, but you'll be pleased that it gets me through twelve hours of court, then however many hours we're here. It's just a nip.'

Charlie rolled his eyes, and mouthed, 'I'm so sorry,' at Caitlin.

'I saw that, Charlie,' Tina said, humour sparkling in her intelligent grey eyes and sharp features.

'You know you've only ever seen me have the one. Just does the trick,' she said.

'Now,' she went on, getting back to business. It had worked, Caitlin noticed. Her voice was fuller and smoother now. 'If the court sees you as a serious player

— you know, an earner, and capable, and successful — they are going to make you pay money to your spouse. That's a division of assets, and there are many, many boring forms attached to that process. The decision needs to be made, then these forms need to be filled in with pinpoint accuracy, otherwise every single time a lawyer breathes on them, or takes that call to correct one of their innocent — *not* — mistakes on the form, you'll be coughing up more money. Lots and lots of money.' She rolled her eyes, had another slug of the whisky in her coffee mug, and went on.

'And of course, there's the issue of a spousal maintenance order to the husband … and all the boring forms attached to that little rort. Those boring forms will go to a junior partner in a big law firm and they will make lots of little mistakes. When you correct them,' she took a breath, 'well, you'll be paying. And you've always paid, haven't you, Caitlin? That could be the eternal pattern here if we go to court.'

Charlie glared at his partner.

'I know,' she said in reply to his look. 'You're quite right, Charlie, that was most unprofessional, even if it is undeniably true.'

Caitlin stifled another giggle, even though she was feeling very, very angry. This was horrible, but most entertaining.

'Anyway, Caitlin, most women don't imagine they would be liable for spousal maintenance, so it surprises them. Sexist of them of course.'

Caitlin nodded. The lawyer had gone through this with her. 'I can't believe Max would go there, though.'

'Well, you didn't think he'd put his dick in another woman, did you?' said Tina bluntly. There was no nastiness. Just the jaded view of someone who'd seen it all before. 'I know. I'm presuming. But I've seen the signs. So wake up and smell the bitterness. That's one of the deals we had to work out today. Not a very happy lady. Very happy ex. Complete bastard of course.'

Caitlin, once she'd finished shutting her mouth, which had fallen open, realised she knew all this. 'I know. That's why I'm here,' she said, determinedly, feeling a little hopeless. 'I won't give him more than the figure I've come to in my head. It's not fair.'

'A lot of women feel that way,' Tina said, with a wicked-looking grin. 'And a lot of women feel completely confused by this. I mean, the rate of change has been rapid. I've been through my records. Twenty years ago there were no reported cases of men obtaining money from their wives on divorce — now it's getting to be routine.'

'But this is an inheritance,' Caitlin said, feeling her voice begin to crack. 'We were married. I get that. But why should he get *anything* my Nan left me?'

'Charlie?' said Tina, beginning to sound a little tipsy. 'Care to chip in at this point?'

'Sure,' he said, faintly sarcastic. 'We've still got ninety seconds. In a divorce, parties can be required to hand over a portion of any asset — even money that they inherited before meeting their partners,' Charlie declared seriously.

'It's not like I have any money just sitting there, though,' protested Caitlin. 'I'm sorry to interrupt you, but I have to set up a company. I had to leave my job because he was … involved with my closest colleague, and she was protected by a workplace agreement, and is pregnant. And — and I really do *not* want to move, and upset the children any more than they already have been.' She wondered if she was saying too much, or saying it the wrong way, but then realised that she couldn't stop. It was all coming out in a rush now. She careered forward, driven by anger, frustration and the sheer need to stay a person, not be consumed as a statistic. She shook her head vehemently, red hair tumbling forward across her face, cheeks a patchwork of crimson and pink.

'I don't want to fund my soon-to-be-former husband and his new partner — my ex-colleague — and their child; that's entirely unfair. Especially under the very painful circumstances.'

Charlie nodded, feeling his eyes well up with tears. Perhaps, he pondered, now she was alone, he could step in and show her what a real man would —

'It's also morally reprehensible,' said Caitlin, glaring at Charlie. It wasn't personal. He just happened to be there. But nevertheless it made him blink back the tears, square his shoulders and get his mind back on the job.

Tina, meanwhile, was nodding. 'You certainly seem to have the moral high ground. It's a shame the law doesn't recognise it.'

Caitlin drew a sharp breath in, feeling like she'd been slapped.

'It feels like a slap in the face to a lot of women,' said Tina. (She wasn't a mind-reader. She'd seen a lot of women in this situation, remember.) 'They feel doubly cheated.'

Caitlin's white teeth bit into her red lower lip to stop herself from crying out.

'So often it's just rich men you read about having to pay off their wives. Well …'

'It's not like that any more,' said Charlie, looking at her soulfully.

Tina took another sip of her whisky and rubbed her eyes, red-rimmed and strained from too many hours going over documents that seethed with anger and resentment. 'Divorce is about dissatisfaction and unhappiness,' she mused, running her hands through her hair in a gesture of despair. 'Fathers who don't believe they have enough access to children; men who believe they have paid out too much — and wives who believe *they* have paid out too much.' She shook her head, like she was wondering how she'd ended up in the middle of it all.

'Time's up,' said Charlie, glancing at his watch reluctantly.

'Caitlin, enough from me — us,' Tina said with a hand on Charlie's arm, reminding him to sit back in his chair and stop panting. 'Tell us your story.'

Caitlin took a breath, and put her hands firmly where she could see them — she wanted to see just how much they'd shake, or how often they wanted to ball into fists and smash down on the table. She steadied herself, and then opened her folder, which was bursting with all her notes, with the piles of documentation, everything that she needed, including her lawyer's advice and questions Myra had suggested. She knew she had to tell the story again, and not for the last time, but still, she felt a rush of anger at having to reveal her betrayal and humiliation for all to see. She was ashamed.

But she told them, running through the details quickly, trying to separate out her mind, her voice, and the various emotions that filtered through as she described the end of her marriage. She steeled her nerves and detailed, briefly, their lives, talking in a low, firm, calm voice that was hiding a slight edge of hysteria.

Tina took notes. So did Charlie. Tina jotted. Charlie scribbled, then doodled elaborate hearts around his jottings.

'So that's it,' Cait finished, green eyes very wide. 'Is that ... all you need?'

'Okay,' interrupted Tina. 'Did he actually pay for *anything*?'

'Of course,' said Caitlin defensively, making sure she told the truth, even though she wanted to yell out 'fuck all, really'. 'Some things, yes.'

Caitlin was left with the very distinct feeling that she'd made some kind of colossal blunder, but was still completely unsure of what it was. This, she thought, was like shouting underwater and expecting to be heard clearly.

'Time to see your husband.'

Cait got up, straightened her skirt, adjusted her underwear ever so slightly and as subtly as she could, and left the room. Outside was like a different world. If only this could all just stop now, she thought, as Max stood up to go inside.

'Your turn,' she said, not looking at him. Max tip-toed around her, giving her a wide berth. She sat down on a plastic chair, and breathed, willing herself to stay calm, and tried to listen to the conversation taking place inside. Then tried *not* to listen. Then tried *to* listen. Then just got up and walked away.

Moving would have to alleviate the pain. Walking, she could see that other couples had been broken up during this process. Men and women lined the corridor, like a hospital hallway.

She went and got a plastic cup, filled it with water from the cooler in the main reception, and went and found a chair far away so that she could pretend she didn't care what he was saying to Tina and Charlie. She closed her eyes, rubbed them hard, then moved her neck around, loosening up the tight bands of muscle running down either side. She rubbed her head, which was still feeling vaguely buzzy from the intermittent adrenaline surges. She willed herself to stay calm. To stay focussed. To know what her aims were. To know what she could accept, and what she would have to walk away from.

Just like any other meeting, she told herself. It's knowing when to hold 'em and when to fold 'em.

The Kenny Rogers song filtered through her head, and she stifled a giggle. Bloody hell. I'm a little unhinged, she thought, and found her phone in her bag.

Two messages. She flipped it open and rang the message bank.

'It's Sarah,' said Sarah's voice conspiratorially. 'Look, I know you're with Max, and you probably don't want him to know, but that boy, the snowboarder, called about dinner. Just to confirm. He's e-mailing you all the details,' said Sarah, sounding approving.

'Anyway, don't want to take up too much of your time. Hope it's going great — and hey, at least you've got something to look forward to!'

There was another message, from a number she didn't recognise. Time for that later, she thought.

Caitlin snapped the phone shut, then rubbed her temples, feeling exhausted. I'm way too old to go on dates, she thought, feeling like she could instantly sleep. I'm way too old to be starting yoga. I'm way too old to go shopping with girlfriends. She closed her eyes and breathed softly, going back to the meditation technique Cassandra had taught her.

Caitlin breathed deeply, and her pending anxiety attack about her divorce and her hot date surrendered. Meanwhile, Max was stumbling through his side of the story. Tina Glass had wanted to tell him the same story as Caitlin, or at least outline what he might look for in a settlement. It seemed only fair. But there just wasn't a chance. She couldn't get a word in.

Charlie, relieved at not having to time Tina's speech, was wondering how long this couple would take to crack when they finally got together in the same room. People were always impressive separately, he thought, looking at Max dispassionately. Good-looking. Charming. Sincere. Clearly still loved her. Had all the nice-guy mannerisms. Seemed trustworthy. It was sad, he thought to himself. They both seemed like nice, reasonable people.

It was when they got together that it all melted down and got ugly. Very ugly, he thought, with a tingle of anticipation, shifting slightly in his seat and re-focussing his attention on Max.

'What we usually find,' explained Tina, when Max had stopped, 'is that each person becomes a little less ... strident in his or her version of the story once mediation really gets under way. And as there is no fault in Australia, we really won't be going into blame.'

'Blame?' said Max, puzzled.

'Unlike in England, for example,' she explained, watching as his handsome features rearranged into a serious, listening-type face, continuing without a pause, 'Take Paul McCartney and ...' she trailed off, stumped. (Or blurred by whisky.) 'You know,' she said, turning to Charlie. 'What's her name?'

'Heather Mills,' said Charlie, brightening. He was an avid reader of *NW*.

'In England, you can cite blame, emotional damage, cruelty and so forth — that's why you get such ... bitterness, and so many ugly stories coming out. But here we don't do that,' she explained, hands on the table.

'I sometimes wonder whether that's fair,' she said, half under her breath.

'Well, for what it's worth, I think that could be *very* destructive for the children,' Max said.

'Yes. That's what the courts feel too,' she said, smiling right back, just as sincere. 'Anyway. In this case, I understand that the no-fault system could actually work rather to your advantage,' she said with raised eyebrows and a slight smile, wondering just what he'd say to that. She was being deliberately provocative, she knew. She was supposed to be impartial. But she could twist things up just a little. Just to see which way the worm would turn.

He smiled back, confused at the turn the questions were taking, felt himself beginning to slowly spin, like a worm at the end of a fishing line being lowered into very cold water full of hungry fish.

'Well, theoretically, it could,' Max said. Tina narrowed her grey eyes ever-so-slightly.

'Ah,' she said softly, conveying understanding without saying a thing to imply she felt it.

He hesitated, managing to look so wretched even Tina felt a little sorry for him. 'We'll be sharing the children — we always had a very strong partnership, Caitlin and me — and I hope we'll move forward to co-parenting. We should both be able to maintain our current lifestyles and take good care of the children. They come first.'

Tina smiled, nodding. 'Of course,' she said dryly. 'But where are you going with this?' she asked him baldly. 'A fifty per cent division? Is that right?'

'That's right,' he said, crossing his arms, defensive.

'Right. Though you have not matched your wife's earnings at any stage. Is that correct?' asked Tina, running her eye down a page of figures. She looked up, detached.

'That's hardly relevant,' Max smiled back, fighting her cool tone by forcing warmth into his voice.

'That's right,' said Tina reluctantly. 'It is not.'

TWENTY-TWO

Things had broken down when Max had said he'd given her everything he had.

'Hopefully not the STDs you're getting from Kennedy,' Caitlin had shot back, leaving Max looking strangely prim for a man who had fucked his wife's assistant.

Caitlin felt entitled to snipe. She hadn't told Max — indeed, why would she? — but on Sarah's advice, she had gone to see her gynaecologist.

The gynaecologist was a woman (Caitlin had already seen her many a time over the years, for both her pregnancies and for post-pregnancy contraception), for which Caitlin was now very grateful. At this early stage of her newly single life, she wasn't quite ready to have a man seeing what she kept up her skirt.

It had all been very simple, really.

'Hi, Caitlin,' said Dr Donaldson. 'I haven't seen you for a long time. What can I do for you?'

'Um. I need a check-up,' Caitlin said, straightening her skirt.

'Okay. What seems to be up?'

Caitlin just sat there, feeling numb. And she also couldn't seem to say anything, which was strange.

'Caitlin,' Dr Donaldson said. 'I'm doing my professional doctor thing here, and you're just looking very uncomfortable. What is it?'

'I … Max …' she said, feeling tears prick at her eyes, furiously wiping them away with her sleeve before they could fall. 'Oh,' she said, tipping her head back. 'Sorry. Can I have a tissue?'

'Sure,' her doctor said, passing her an entire box. 'What is it?'

'I need … I need an STD check.'

'O-kaaay. For which STD exactly?'

'For everything. Everything that exists,' she replied, sounding a bit mad.

'Okay. That's a lot of tests, Caitlin.'

Caitlin shrugged bitterly.

'Let's see if we can narrow it down. When do you think you were exposed?'

Caitlin looked puzzled.

'Okay. How many partners have you had?'

'One. You know that,' she said, knowing she sounded defensive.

'I know that's how it was, Caitlin, but things seem to have changed,' the doctor explained gently. 'Anyway. One,' she said, making a note on a chart. 'Now, some diseases are asymptomatic,' she said, snapping on some extremely attractive clear gloves, 'but we can test today for HIV, chlamydia, PID … '

'What?' asked Caitlin, head spinning, and feeling a little slow.

'Pelvic inflammatory disease,' explained Dr Donaldson. 'We can also test for herpes; um, let's see. What have I missed?' she asked herself, frowning slightly. 'Ah. Syphilis, gonorrhea and HPV. That should do it,' she said, sounding satisfied.

'HPV? And that is what when it's at home?' asked Caitlin, feeling quite impressed at just how many diseases Max might have given her.

'HPV? *That* is a fancy name for warts. I'll do a swab and get you the results back as soon as I can. Which will be super-fast; the lab is fantastic.'

'Er. Good,' said Caitlin, trying to sound enthused, but failing.

'Oh yeah it's good,' replied Dr Donaldson, nodding her head with vigour. 'Some doctors have terrible labs. Results get mixed up, answers take days, you name it. We're lucky. So,' she said, looking up at Caitlin, who was still trying to look enthused about a good lab. (Her emotions, she noticed, seemed to be on some sort of delay.) 'Let me ask all the questions I have to ask. Don't take them personally. Any partners apart from your husband?'

'No,' said Caitlin, feeling like a fool. Who has one partner? she thought. Even nuns probably have had more partners than me.

'So that leaves either Max or toilet seats as the source for your concern.'

'It's not the toilet seat,' said Caitlin, beginning to smile.

'Ah,' Dr Donaldson said, scribbling a note. So. 'Do you know how many partners your husband's had?'

'Nope,' Caitlin replied, trying for humour, and failing.

'Is he likely to tell you?'

'Nope.'

'Hang in there, Caitlin,' soothed Dr Donaldson. 'One more question then we're done. Has he been to Thailand, Cambodia, Vietnam, Africa or New York lately?'

She grinned. 'Nope.'

'Great. We're doing well. You're holding up great. Now, he must have had at least —'

'At least one other partner,' she said. 'I don't think there are any more …' She trailed off, feeling uncertain. 'No,' she said, rallying. 'He's had just one other partner.'

'Okay. Don't worry. We can let your blood and the swab — sorry, nasty term — do the talking. Let's go,' she said, standing up. 'Knickers off and up here, sweetheart.' She patted the examination table.

Caitlin slid off her pants and carefully folded them, and obediently climbed onto the examination table.

'You know,' Dr Donaldson said conversationally, switching on a bright overhead light and aiming its beam between Caitlin's legs, 'someone comes in for this kind of examination nearly every week now.' She sighed, warming a speculum in her gloved hands. 'It's enough to really put you off.'

And with that, apart from a few technical details and a polite phone call, Caitlin was cleared of any of the communicable diseases that are sometimes the unfortunate result of liaisons of the pleasurable kind.

Not that she needed to tell Max that.

Back in their mediation meeting, Max was looking very offended at Caitlin's STD comment.

'Caitlin,' he huffed disapprovingly. 'That's a bit below the belt.'

'Exactly,' said Caitlin, raising an eyebrow.

Max opened his mouth to speak, but found he had nothing to force out.

'You know I'd never been unfaithful before — not once,' he muttered darkly.

Charlie and Tina both brightened at that.

'That doesn't make it okay!' Cait said, resisting the urge to bang her hand down on the table for emphasis.

'You're saying you had nothing to do with this situation?' Max demanded. 'What about how much you worked? I could only see you if it was convenient for your schedule.'

'I know! But you said it was okay! That you could handle it …' Caitlin said, her voice rising, to the joy of bored counsellors in other rooms.

'I was bloody lonely,' he said, shaking his head. 'And Kennedy liked me.'

'I liked you too!' she said, her voice carrying even further. Even the receptionist was now able to enjoy the show.

'Well, I loved you,' Max said angrily.

Charlie leaned forward, a little gleam in each of his small brown eyes. This was spectacular. And she looks beautiful when she's angry, he thought.

'No you didn't. Couldn't have,' she said.

'Caitlin,' Max said defensively. 'That's not fair. Or true.'

'What's the truth, Max? That you've fucked around, been caught out, and now I have to put up with you *and* her, who is by the way pregnant with your next child, my children's half-sibling. How could I ... what? Be vulgar? Well, how could you put your dick in my assistant? What was that about? My *assistant*, Max.'

She felt like she'd just found out all over again. She hadn't had the pleasure of saying much of this to him before. And what a pleasure it was. The truth was harsh, but sweet, and it didn't hurt to voice it. Instead of pain, she felt fury flying from every pore, felt like her hair was standing on end, like her anger was volcanic and she could throw him across the room without even touching him. That's how powerful the truth made her feel.

It also made her ever-so-slightly psychopathic. Just for a moment. 'You couldn't just find someone else to fuck — you had to find the person you could most fuck me over with.'

The receptionist gasped. This was a good one! She was half tempted to call a friend and put them on speaker.

'She then went on to fuck up my working life, too — which you're well aware of.'

'Caitlin,' he said, just managing to hold his anger in check. 'Nobody meant for you to get so —'

'So *what*?'

'Well, it's not what I think that matters,' he said, sounding very hurt. 'It's the law that matters. And we need to work out a settlement.'

'You son of a bitch,' she raged. 'A fair settlement would be both of you spontaneously combusting. A fair settlement would be both of you traitors going to live on another planet with all the other cheater beings — where you can all eventually fuck each other indiscriminately. A fair settlement would be me and the children never having to see either of you ever again. You've put us through *hell*. And you're smug about having the law on your side?' she roared, leaping to her feet.

'Caitlin!' yelped Max, moving back.

And it was very lucky that Charlie held her as tight as he could (knowing, as he did, it might be his only chance to be that close to her).

Tina made some noises about making another appointment, and looked wistfully at the whisky bottle.

Wow, Cait thought, watching herself from far, far away. This could be a turning point. The one where I actually do something that I pay for, for a long, long time. And she watched as her body slowly relaxed, shook off Charlie a little like a terrier shaking off a flea, straightened herself up, picked up her bag, and walked out. That's that, she thought, slowly coming to herself. I said it. I said it all. Maybe now we have a real place to start from.

Max, sitting shocked in his chair, started apologising. 'I'm *so* sorry,' he said heavily to Tina, who was pouring herself another drink.

'Oh?' she said, looking at him over the mug. 'Why?' (She was interested, you see, in what he'd say.)

'Well, that was awful ...' he trailed off, looking bleak.

Charlie and Tina gave each other their 'we need to debrief' look.

'Right. Well, we've made a start and that's what counts,' Tina said cheerfully, standing and thrusting papers into her briefcase. 'You can pay outside, Max. Please give us a call when you and your wife are ready to set up another appointment.' She gave him a smaller, tighter, fuck-off-right-now kind of smile, and Max stood and took himself off, feeling strangely as though he'd somehow failed to score the point that should have been his. He shut the door behind him.

'It's a living,' Charlie said, humouring Tina, who looked very, very pissed off.

'They'll schedule another meeting. Hopefully,' she said.

Outside, Max recoiled from the bill, then resentfully paid the receptionist the full amount. Over three hundred dollars.

Charlie, who had followed to spy on Max, ran back to the mediation room, laughing.

'What are you finding funny?' Tina snapped.

'She's walked out, and left him to pay,' Charlie snickered.

Tina rolled her eyes. 'Yes, Charlie, it's very dramatic.' She yawned. 'Come on, he will have gone by now. Let's get out of here. We've got respective empty homes where no one's waiting for either of us. There's TV to be watched and take-away to be eaten. We don't want to miss out.'

TWENTY-THREE

AND SO IT STARTED. The real break-up, Caitlin called it. And date or no date, yoga or no yoga, and breathing techniques or … anyway, she was feeling less than hopeful about her prospects. And although her date that coming Saturday night did distract her, a little, she spent most of the day after mediation in a very low place, from which not even the prospect of sex with a younger man could lift her. At best, the thought seemed to provide her with glimpses of a tantalising otherlife. At worst, she just found herself ridiculous.

She'd started outlining her future life options soon after collapsing into bed directly after the meeting. She spent much of the next day refusing to take Kevin's calls, receiving texts from her date, wondering about how her children were and wrapping her grandmother's nightgown tightly around her as she made list after list. Her options didn't come out any differently, no matter how many times she wrote things down.

One. Gain and/or lose ridiculous amount of weight.

Two. Have casual sex with guilty-looking yet smug men. (This one was inspired by Myra.)

Three. Seduce her own husband, win him back from Kennedy, then leave him for her hot snowboarder.

Yuck, she thought, immediately crossing that one off.

There was another option, a cool part of her brain reminded her.

Four. Become even more incredibly successful and fall in love again.

There it was. She decided to do it.

'You see if I don't,' she said out loud to Max, as though he was there in what had been their bedroom.

Which, she was blatantly aware, he wasn't. And the kids weren't there either. Suddenly exhausted, she switched her laptop off, put her phone onto silent, and rolled over to go to sleep.

She could start work on the new show another day. She could call Gus to work, check in with Sarah and look at the yoga studio to shoot part of the show in the next day. Now it was time to be quiet, and still, and a little sad again.

It was all of 8.10 p.m.

Meanwhile, about three hundred kilometres away, a man was writing her a letter. He had taken days over it.

It was a simple letter, telling her about what he'd done that day — cleared some land, put in a pond, checked the vegetable garden and put out some feed for the rainbow lorikeets. He told her what the sun had looked like coming up through the trees that morning, and how he was bringing fallen wood in to dry under a shed he'd built.

What it didn't say was how he kept thinking of her face, when the light from the water had shone up into it, illuminating her eyes and sending her hair a thousand different shades of red. What he didn't say, not yet, was that he had a feeling they'd be seeing more of each other. What he didn't say was that he'd had a dream about her.

What he did mention was that he would be in Sydney before too long, the weekend after next, and he hoped he could take her for dinner. And that he would write again before he arrived, with the details.

He addressed and stamped the letter, silently thanking Cassandra for handing over the address. And then set off to walk to the post box three kilometres away, a sense of fate tracing each firm step in his mind. He wanted to remember this. He could feel change coming. And he thought he knew what form it was coming in.

Meanwhile, back at Max's serviced and yet shambolic apartment, Caitlin's kids were plotting their own revolution. Safe in the haven of their converted bedroom, they had slung clothes over filing cabinets. Max's desk was now the support structure for both Sean's recording equipment and Molly's online empire. The Roboraptor was propped up by the bed. Max's sexy white Apple Mac was adorned with a series of spontaneous Lego sculptures by Molly, who'd also commandeered the laptop for personal use. For two babies, the tiny room was crowded; for two girls, it was a kind of prison cell. The bunk beds their father had bought and half-heartedly installed made them feel like two strange objects filed away in the corner.

(Said father, by the way, was not with his daughters — although, technically, he was with an unborn child.)

While they could have just fallen into a hostage-to-fate mindset, and tried very hard to get along in their new circumstances, they were not made of that stuff. They were freedom fighters planning the first stages of guerrilla warfare designed to get them out of the cramped surroundings and back into their mother's home.

'I can't believe Dad's taken Kennedy to see the new place,' Sean said.

'We could have gone,' Molly said. 'We said no.'

'I need to talk to Mum,' Sean said.

'It's gone to message bank again,' Molly said at 8.11 p.m., holding out the phone to Sean, who was scrunched up on her bunk bed.

'Okay, try her mobile. That's always on.'

'Not tonight,' Molly replied, shaking her head. (Her hair stuck up madly, just like her mother's.) 'Already tried it.'

'Must be having a night in with her very good friend Kelly Clarkson.' They looked at each other, and Sean pulled a face. They knew that the only thing their mother ever turned her mobile off for was Kelly Clarkson and Kleenex. They would have been more concerned if they didn't have such faith in her working it out somehow, and both had their own problems. Despite him buying them copious quantities of useless but tantalising stuff, they had a deep, burning dislike of their father that had almost burned away the tremendous love they had for him. Dad was annoying, distracted and worst of all, disloyal. They kept overhearing him talking on the phone, mostly about their mother, in low, urgent tones.

And so, instead of moping about coping with this strange new world they found themselves unwillingly jammed into, they decided to develop a foolproof escape plan.

But first, like most kids whose mothers sob after 7 p.m., they worried about their mother.

'Is she going to die, do you think? Should we go home and see if she's okay?'

'No, Molly. People don't die of broken hearts.' Sean thought for a second. 'Well, not *quickly*, anyway.'

'It sure sounded like she was dying when we heard her crying last week,' Molly pondered, recalling one night when even Kelly couldn't mask the moans.

'Yep. Everyone feels like that when they get dumped,' Sean said wisely. 'So if we *did* die from broken hearts, most of us would die at about fifteen.'

'Oh. So it just sounds like they're dying.'

'It probably feels like they're dying too. I don't know.'

'Have you ever been in love?'

'Not yet. Thank goodness,' she added softly.

'You know that boy at my school?

'Which one, Molly? There are about two hundred of them.'

'The one I like. Kaelan.'

'No. What's he like? And how far has this gone?'

'He's funny. And very intelligent. And he likes me. At least, I have a suspicion he likes me. He gave me a hug.'

'How could he not like you?'

'But what if we fall in love?'

'That might actually be nice.'

'But …' she whispered, her little face intense. Sean nudged her gently. 'I'm not going to die, am I?'

'No, sweetheart. You're not. Even if you break up.'

'Or he breaks up with me?'

'Nope. No corpse for love. You'll be okay. If we weren't, we'd never make it through Year Nine. Everyone keeps getting their heart broken once they turn fourteen.'

'You don't.'

'I know. I just don't want to.'

'Sean. Did Mum break up with Dad, or did Dad break up with Mum?'

Sean's head whirled. She took a deep breath, and started to answer in vague terms about decisions, and having no choice, and promises, trying to keep it light enough so that Molly didn't ask too much more, but trying, really trying to treat her little sister like the person she was. While Sean had been struggling with suddenly having two houses, and with her fury, sometimes her parents' problems had faded into the background, superseded by the other problems most fourteen-year-olds had. Madeleine had told her often enough that she shouldn't worry about her detachment, that it was part of being resilient. But she worried that perhaps her true reason for not falling apart was that she was missing some vital emotional ingredient. She'd never been in love, and while she thought her dad was pathetic, she just couldn't hate him long-term.

She didn't care about falling in love and all that. Though she did like Luke. He was talented, and funny, and very good-looking. And she found him easy to talk to. But I wouldn't describe the hanging out together as love, she thought, disbelievingly. So maybe, just maybe, something was wrong with her?

Madeleine had been quick to assure her that all the people at school suffered more than anyone ever knew, and that even adults had just been programmed to immediately forget about it once they left. And that just because Sean didn't walk around sobbing didn't mean she hadn't had a traumatic experience, one that would be a major life lesson she would learn plenty from, and be able to channel into her music.

'But *why* can't adults remember how awful school is?' Sean had asked her grandmother.

'We forget because we're fated to stay hopeful, and stay in the system.' Madeleine had gone on to encourage Sean to never, not *ever* get sucked in by the system. Whatever that was, exactly. Sean thought it probably had something to do with school, university, marriage and jobs.

Meanwhile, she was still trapped in Year Nine, the year she had dubbed her own personal hellhole.

Year Nine *was* dreadful for Sean. Her singing career was currently stalled due to being at school, and to being between two homes. Her songs were being written with Luke, but they were all about hating Kennedy. Which meant that, other than the one she'd written for Cait, she had twelve different versions of one great song. She just couldn't get past it at the moment.

She shrugged. 'I just feel like the world's getting smaller and smaller. Like this room.'

'I really don't like this place. At Mum's we have our own rooms. At Mum's we have our stuff. At Mum's ...'

'We should just not be here. I hate Kennedy.'

'Kennedy's not nice. I thought she was, but she's not,' Molly said thoughtfully.

'No,' Sean agreed. 'We liked her, and let her hang out with us, and look what she did. She stole Dad.'

'Can you actually steal people, though? It's not like we own them,' Molly wondered out loud.

'Of course you can steal people. She stole him, and she stole our whole life. Just so she could ... have someone else's dad.'

'They've got to want to be stolen, though?' Molly asked.

They both fell silent. For about a minute.

'Can you think,' asked Sean, 'of one nice thing about Kennedy?'

Both sat in contemplation, Molly's head tilted to one side.

They sat. And thought.

And they sat a bit more.

'Nice clothes,' said Molly definitely. 'She absolutely has nice clothes. Maybe we could try to like her. You know, if she and Dad do get together.' She went on after a small pause, her little face a ball of frustration.

'You want her to come and live with us?' Sean asked, aghast.

Molly didn't know about that. 'Not really. I'm scared of Kennedy making me rub her tummy and talk to the baby, for example. That would be creepy.'

'If she does, I'm going to use all her make-up *and* wear her clothes,' Sean declared hotly. 'And I have to practise the guitar. *Electric* guitar. And I'm going to start bringing boys home. Like, not just Luke.'

'I just had an awful thought.'

'What?'

'Who am I going to talk to about my periods? What if I get my periods *here*?'

'You won't,' Sean comforted, pulling one of Molly's falling-down singlet-straps up over one rounded shoulder.

'What? You can *tell* them when to come?'

'Well, no. But you're six. You won't get your periods for ages. And I'll be here. Or near, anyway.'

'I always thought Mum would be there.'

'She will be,' said Sean.

'Not if I'm here.'

They both turned at the gentle knock on their door. Their father was home. His face, smiling, appeared.

'Come on out to the kitchen, girls. Let's have some family time.' Despite the smile, Max's voice seemed edged with desperation.

'Get stuffed,' Sean murmured, back up on her bunk.

'Sean? Don't think I won't …'

'What? Throw me out? Go right ahead.' She turned over and faced the wall.

Max sighed, and sat down next to Molly.

'Dad?'

He looked down at her, almost comically haggard. Molly thought he looked funny — like he might cry or something.

'Yup?'

'I don't hate you,' she whispered lightly, so Sean wouldn't hear.

And that, Max knew, was the best declaration of love that he could hope for at that moment.

TWENTY-FOUR

THE NEXT DAY, while her daughters were at the beach, Caitlin cut *Freak Squad* (now called *Mystic Chicks*), took calls and held one of her now regular secret meetings on *Date Squad*. (Kennedy remained oblivious to Cait's involvement, preoccupied as she was with her morning sickness, doctors' appointments, the rigours of running the show and doing a course.)

And after all that, she went into the station and spent over two hours pitching the psychic show to Kevin, who was happy to drag himself — and Linda — in on a Saturday morning if it meant a better chance of keeping his association with Caitlin a secret from her usurper. The Big Kahuna, due to his feeling very confident that Caitlin was his girl once again, was being dismissive, rude, insulting and blunt about whether her pitch was, as he called it, a 'ball-tearer'. Only Caitlin wasn't buying into it. She'd already faced the worst in that mediation room, which meant Kevin's rebuffs and snide remarks were met with a cool: 'Well, you get first look. According to our contract. If you're passing ...'

(Caitlin, by the way, was seriously bluffing. She

knew if Kevin passed, she had to create new relationships and risk the politics of moving away from him. It was one very fucked-up relationship, and she craved her independence from him. But she also knew — in fact was hyper-aware of — how many bills she had to pay. Including the ones coming up to cover her ex-husband's lifestyle and her ex-assistant's new role as mistress.)

'I'm not passing. I just … look, if we were to do something like this, we'd come to you. But I don't know. It feels … weird,' he said, brow furrowed tightly. 'I mean … it's all bullshit. We don't do bullshit shows.'

'What? We don't explore and experiment, you mean. I never thought you were the kind to play it so safe, Kevin,' she said, baiting him lightly.

He scowled darkly. 'You know I take risks. I hired you back, didn't I? I'm looking at this, aren't I?' he growled.

'That's fine, Kevin,' said Caitlin, remaining detached. (She'd heard it all before.) 'I guess if it feels weird to you, you might not get it. And she needs to be with people who get her. Now, back to *Date Squad* …' she said, squashing down her resentment.

Because it wasn't as if she didn't know Kevin, or hadn't seen him behave like this before. Anytime a woman with any power had any freedom to go with it, he got ruder and ruder until she either buckled, or bailed. People, and especially ones with breasts, did what they were told in Kevin's world. If he could get them to do what they were told for free, he'd be happier. (He really did resent paying people … it meant he earned so much less. Which is why there were so many people at the station on such low wages. He scared them out of asking for more.

(Most men knew how to work Kevin. They just made sure he knew he was top dog, and they bought him a lot of drinks. Caitlin had *thought* she'd had a different relationship with him. Until he threw her to the HR wolves, of course.)

But in *this* situation, Kevin really wasn't sure what to do. He could feel his twin aphrodisiacs, control and power, slipping out of his meaty grasp. He'd never had to work with a woman he hadn't bought via salary before — the ownership issue was a little cloudy. Caitlin's independence, and the prospect that she could go elsewhere, was very, very irritating. What was her problem? He was taking care of her. Lord knows there were enough invoices crossing his desk. He signed them. Eventually. What more could she want?

But back to the meeting. 'This is bullshit,' he elaborated. 'All this spiritual crap, this love and light, everyone's this-good-to-each-other shit. Don't these people watch the news?' he shot at Linda.

Linda, who was enjoying the pilot, did not answer.

'Kevin, come on. It's good — you know it is,' said Caitlin, trying to snap him out of it with a bit of banter.

'Don't cajole me, Caitlin,' he frowned at her.

'Come on, mate. It'll be great.'

He laughed. He couldn't help himself.

So he sat back and watched it, all the while making gagging noises, rolling his eyes, and claiming loudly that he needed a drink to watch any more.

But he watched it.

And Linda loved it. She watched every moment, asked Cait questions about all the right people, and went slightly pink when the cowboy shaman made his appearance.

'I ... I don't know what to say, Caitlin,' she said. 'I love all this stuff!'

Caitlin felt warm. Linda never liked anything, except for Kevin.

'I hate it. It's shit,' was Kevin's take. 'I'll let you know. I have *Date Squad* to worry about,' he said, narrowing his eyes at her. 'If you get your act together on that one, I might have another look at this,' he said, reaching out to take the DVD.

Cait reached the machine just in time, and smoothly enough to make it look like it wasn't that big a deal that she'd snatched it out from under his big, meaty nose.

'She's the only copy I've got. Need to hold onto her.'

'You're not leaving me one — you're slipping, Caitlin,' he said, point-scoring.

'You know, creative drama would be a great genre for you to explore, Kevin. You've rewritten everything that's happened over the last couple of months. That version suits you. But it's not the truth. I didn't walk out on *Date Squad*. And you know why,' she said, voice edgy with suppressed — barely — anger.

And, just like that, she up and she left. Kevin was shocked. Linda hid a smug smile. She'd been waiting for someone to do something like that for a long, long time. She felt a little seed of respect for Caitlin shoot and burst forth with life deep inside her.

(Besides, Caitlin had won her loyalty in a much more tangible way. She'd set Linda up with the very attractive, very venerable, very charming Edwin Cadenhead. And that relationship was going along swimmingly.)

Driving home, Caitlin was having a sour Kevin moment of her own.

You were my work husband, she thought, feeling dark, thinking of his smiling face at the launch of *Date Squad*, followed by the debacle with Kennedy, followed now by his making fun of her new show — which she knew was good. She knew it. He might hate it, but he knew it was good. Why else did he have Linda sit in?

He'd been her work spouse. They'd been partners. But, she thought, feeling angrier and angrier, *you* weren't faithful either. Max *and* Kevin. You both, she realised, cheated on me with Kennedy. So it might be time to give you both the same message.

Which, for husbands, meant Another Man. For work husbands, it meant Another Work Man. Logically enough.

Pulling up outside the house, Caitlin felt cool and *ready*, and called a producer she knew. Time for a bidding war, she thought, as she set up a time with Larry Allen's assistant to pitch the show. Kevin only respects you if you have power. And if I don't look like I'm in demand, he'll just fuck me over and find this project very unsexy indeed and it'll stay on the blocks in Maybe Land, going cold. And for some stupid reason, I want him to want this. I want him to say he made a mistake. And help me get an offer that's going to help sort out this other mess with my husband and the woman he's temporarily fucking.

Caitlin came in from the car to find Sean and Molly back, with smug faces that she didn't have the time to investigate, but which made her feel a whole lot less running over with Mummy Guilt. She knew she hadn't abandoned her children — but she couldn't help but feel completely bizarre about handing them over to Mr Infidelity. It felt like they were hostages of a situation they'd had no choice in, but Caitlin held onto the belief that they knew they were loved, and they could in fact still make a choice if it came to that.

Which made her all the more determined to go on her date. And have a damn good time.

Caitlin dressed very, very carefully. She slid stockings up her legs, which had been shaved, exfoliated and moisturised. She strapped fishnets to a suspender belt, which fitted smoothly on her belly, which had also been through the pre-date pampering regimen.

'Isn't it amazing how it all just comes back to you?' Sarah cooed, looking at her friend fondly.

'It's not like I dressed down for my husband,' Caitlin pointed out. 'I didn't exactly let myself go.'

'No, but you're going on a first date, and look at you — you're hot.'

Caitlin pulled a slim, red sheath dress over her head, shaking out her curls, tilting her head slightly to get them to fall perfectly.

'Come on, tell me. What are you thinking?' urged Sarah.

Caitlin turned, looking slightly stressed.

'Really? Well, I'm thinking that I am standing in front of my mirror and trying to figure out if fishnets at my age are just … whatever. And I'm also concerned about what sort of message I'm sending with this dress.'

'Why do you care? It makes you look hot. He's hot. Let nature take its course.'

'Have you had sex with your girlfriend yet?' demanded Caitlin.

'No. Can you tell?' Sarah said, frowning.

'Yes. Because you're so desperate for me to have sex. You and Myra, and even Madeleine — you're all desperate for some hot sex stories. Get some of your own.'

'Well, I'm not the one wearing a — a *signal* dress,' Sarah pointed out defensively.

'I don't really care about the signals. I want to send the signals. I just don't want to look all wrong when sending them.'

'You look delicious.'

Cait sighed, confused at Sarah's about-turns.

'I don't look too bad,' she conceded. 'My hair's behaving. That's weird. What does that mean?'

'I know. It wants to have a good time,' laughed Sarah, hugging herself.

Caitlin gave her a fond glance, feeling her stress lift. At least someone was excited about this date, she thought. Why don't I feel excited? she wondered, spraying some perfume behind her knees.

'Why, you dirty thing!' Sarah crowed.

'I always put it there — you told me to never put it on my neck — it makes you photosensitive, remember?' Caitlin said.

'Sure. You just want him to smell your legs!'

'Sarah — that's disgusting.'

'Not really. Are you sure you're not excited?' wheedled Sarah, sounding plaintive.

'No,' said Caitlin, giving her a look.

'Why did I get that look? I'm not forcing you to go.'

Caitlin put lipstick, wallet, perfume and keys into her handbag, and zipped it up. 'I am going so that I can at least have one man between me and my husband. I also said I'd go. Strangely I am still one of those people who does what she says she will do. He's picking me up in ten minutes, probably in a ridiculous car, and we are going to the most expensive restaurant he can afford and ... we'll talk, and he'll figure out what he has to say to get me to ... you know,' she finished, coy.

Sarah shrugged. 'I'll go make us a drink,' she said. 'Meet you in the lounge.'

Cait fiddled with her hair a bit more. There really wasn't anything much else to do — she'd completed her make-up, her face pale, eyebrows arched and drawn in, her lips red and plump, her cheeks rouged, smoky-grey eyeshadow and lashings of black mascara. She gave herself a final glance, and headed out to the lounge, where Sarah was popping ice into two tall glasses.

Sarah handed her a gin and tonic, and took a huge slug of hers. 'If I was going on a date with my girl, I'd be so excited,' she said wistfully.

'Come on, you can tell Mum all about my outfit. And our conversation. All my secrets,' Cait said, cheering her up. Sarah didn't take the bait.

'What's to tell?' she said, fishing.

'I might sleep with him,' she teased. 'You could tell Madeleine that.'

'I don't know. You *had* the look — but it's not there right now. Except … I could have sworn there was someone you were excited about.'

There was, Cait thought, thinking of a man she'd met once, at sunset, by a stream, accidentally on purpose. But I haven't heard from him.

TWENTY-FIVE

'SO, TELL ME ABOUT yourself,' said Green, who was being charming, endearingly eager and generally adorable.

'Um. I'm a television producer — but you know that. And I'm a mother,' she said, testing him.

He practically lit up. 'I love kids,' he enthused.

'Honestly?' Are you for real? she wondered.

'Yeah, I like them. They're cool. So, you're ... separated? Divorced?'

'In the process of divorcing,' she said.

'So, I hit on a married woman,' he said, self-deprecating. And charming. 'Seriously, though. What's it like? The divorce thing?'

'Well. It's weird.'

'How so?' he asked, looking right into her eyes.

'Okay. I thought my life had a full stop. You know? It was all sorted out. A husband. Two kids. Job. A house. And then you realise it's not the end of the story. There's a beginning happening that I hadn't planned on. And that's ... hard. And exciting,' she said, feeling flattered by his attention. Okay, so maybe he just wanted to shag her. But at least, she thought with a frisson of triumph, he wanted to shag her!

He reached over, and took her hand gently. She raised her eyebrows — they weren't even on dessert and there was handholding happening?

'I have to be honest. I was really drawn to you,' he said, looking intense. 'Not sure why.'

She smiled. 'Thank you,' she said, feeling faintly embarrassed, and slightly befuddled. How could he feel drawn to her? She was at least ten years too old for him. He didn't even know her. She corrected herself. She'd felt drawn to someone, she reminded herself. And she'd only spent about ten minutes in *his* company. She smiled, and brought her attention back to Green, whose other hand, the one that wasn't gripping hers urgently, was now stretching out to her face.

'Hey look, you,' he said, smiling gently. 'You've got something in your hair.'

'What?' she laughed softly, feeling flirtatious for the first time since ... since the *Date Squad* party, she remembered, having a sudden flashback.

'Can you get it out?' she asked, forcing the memory away, and sounding slightly provocative, even to herself.

His hand moved deftly into her curls, stroking slightly. She felt warm, faintly aroused and a little bewildered at being touched so intimately by someone who wasn't her husband. She closed her eyes, and enjoyed him stroking — and touching, and rubbing ... and ...

His hand suddenly withdrew. Her eyes snapped open.

He stared at something he was holding between two fingers, then gave her a shocked glance.

'It's moving,' he said, sounding faintly horrified.

'It's what? Here, show me,' she ordered him, feeling panic rise.

'I can't,' he said, sounding panicked himself. 'It jumped,' he gasped.

'Oh my God,' she said, feeling sick.

'There's another one,' he said, looking at her scalp.

She reached her hand to her head and scratched, before realising what she was doing. Her face flared pink, and she stared at him, slightly unsure of what to do in such a situation.

'Have you,' he said carefully, 'got nits, Caitlin?'

Nadia rang first thing Sunday morning.

'How was your date?' she asked, sounding ready to be thrilled. 'Did you get to show him your underwear?' Caitlin tried not to laugh, feeling slightly mean that she was about to deny Nadia the proof of the power of her undies.

'Nadia. I finally found something stronger than the underwear.'

'What?' replied Nadia, baffled.

'Can I put it this way? The only thing more powerful than the pants is lice.'

'*Lice?*'

'I *know*! Can you believe that he didn't want to sleep with me once he pulled a louse from my hair?' Some liquid trickled close to her eye, making her blink.

'So you didn't sleep with him? But you had the look!' Nadia protested.

'I know! I had the look. I had the pants. But I also had … lice! Nadia? I have to call you back. I have nits. I'm doing my hair with treatment stuff now, but then I need to shave my head and boil the sheets. You might want to do the same.'

'No!'

'Well, no,' she giggled. 'But I do need to get on with this. It's running into my eyes and I might go blind,' she said, feeling ridiculously liberated. 'Promise I'll call you back,' she said, replacing the phone and re-wrapping the towel that was threatening to slide off altogether under the weight of wet hair, lice treatment, and presumably, heavyweight lice.

'You won't really shave your head, will you?' Sarah said, looking disapproving.

'When,' said Caitlin, ignoring Sarah's question, 'are you seeing your girlfriend next?'

'I don't know. Tomorrow I thought, at work.'

'Well,' she said, tossing her the tube of noxious-smelling treatment shampoo. 'You might want to run this through your hair first.'

Sarah looked shocked. 'I don't have nits!'

'Oh, nits are very democratic. And I saw you scratching. For sure you've got friends, too,' she grinned. 'Get the kids away from *Video Hits*. We can all have a massive delousing treatment.'

Sarah paled. 'I feel itchy,' she muttered, grabbing the tube of treatment and heading toward the bathroom.

TWENTY-SIX

THE NEXT MEDIATION meeting snapped at the heels of the last, and was just as dreaded, but somehow Caitlin could feel the process closing in, just like her lice treatment had killed off the itch she had mistaken for nerves. At least this time she knew what to expect — and what to do.

The finishing-off of her marriage was definitely in motion, and it was inevitable that she and Max would begin to get somewhere close to an agreement of sorts. They had to. Kennedy, according to Gus and Carol, was growing larger, sicker and snappier by the day, and sometimes Cait found herself shaking her head at Max's ability to create a disaster. Not that it was her problem, exactly. Only the kids had to deal with her.

The next Wednesday, she walked into the same room she'd exploded in a week earlier, running late from another *Mystic Chicks* production meeting. Caitlin, already harried, felt a surge of anger as she glanced at Max. And then felt a little ripple of adrenaline snake its warning down her spine. Something weird was happening. He was shrinking away from her.

She sat down, and had a better look at him. Something was most definitely up.

Max wasn't the kind of man who needed this season's suit to look good. His uniform had always been well-worn jeans, old leather jackets and very cool T-shirts. But he looked different today.

It wasn't just that he was looking like he hadn't slept much since he'd left. It was more like he looked older, and exhausted and … she struggled to put her finger on it.

'Max?' she said, a question mark in her voice. 'Is something wrong?' she asked, sounding puzzled. 'Apart from the obvious,' she grinned, with a nod to Charlie and Tina, who, she noticed, looked as confused as she did.

'I'm all right,' he growled, shifting his body slightly away from her.

'Okay,' Tina stepped in. 'Who would like to speak first?'

Caitlin looked at him. She wasn't worried about who went first. Not today.

'I will,' he said, leaping into the gap.

'The rule is we let the other person talk,' Charlie reminded Cait nervously. Or perhaps that was *excitedly*.

'I'm worried. For the children,' he stressed, aiming his plea at Tina.

'Would you like them to go live with you?' Tina asked baldly.

Caitlin smothered a cry of pain.

'No! I mean, of course I would but I could never do that to Caitlin. They need their mother,' he said. 'And she definitely needs them.'

Tina nodded sympathetically.

Caitlin knew it was time for the plan to kick in. Looking at Max squarely, chin lifted upward, she gave him the benefit of a grade-A killer glare.

'Can I,' she said calmly, 'have five minutes alone with my husband?' Her gaze never wavered from Max's face. 'I think,' she continued, 'if we have a moment, we might be able to reach an agreement.'

Once Charlie and Tina had scurried out to position themselves so they could best hear every word, Caitlin turned to her husband.

'What is it you *want*, Max?' she said softly, genuinely curious.

'It's been very hard —'

'I know,' she said, feeling strangely detached. She cared about him. But she didn't care. She felt ... concern, yes, but detachment, too.

He sighed, and his shoulders slumped.

She waited.

He ran a large hand through his plentiful hair, and looked forlornly at her.

'What is it,' she repeated, 'that you want?'

(Well, he wasn't going to tell her that, was he? He wanted to come back. To his life. To his kids. To his home.

To his *wife*.

But he wasn't handling the script. So he just had to go for the next best thing.)

'It's the kids,' he mumbled. 'I want to make sure I can see them. Fifty–fifty. I've been told ... warned really, by everyone, that you're going to go for full custody. And I can't lose you and lose them too.'

(And that was the moment they both finally knew it was over. The fight. The relationship. And in that moment, a small space appeared where something new could begin.)

'Fifty–fifty … with the kids, you mean? But what about the house?' she said. 'Don't you want me to sell it, give you half?'

'No!' he said, looking horrified. 'That's your nan's house. And I never said that. Who told you I wanted that?'

'Well, who told you I wanted the kids to never see you again?'

'My lawyer. The one I had to see before I came here. Who told you I wanted the house?'

She grinned.

'My lawyer. And a whole lot of other people.'

'Oh. Your mum, no doubt. Can we talk about this properly now then?'

'I think so,' she said.

'Because Kennedy and I … have discussed being together. Once the baby comes. Trying to work it out. I want to introduce her again — slowly — to the kids. I hope we can agree on that, Cait. But I can't lose them.'

'What about money?'

'Kennedy's working. And I'll stay at home once the baby comes … and I'll get something. Things always come up.'

She took a deep breath. 'I know of a great part being cast. I can help you get it.'

'What's the catch?' he said unhappily. 'I move to

another city?' He shook his gorgeous head. 'I won't do that.'

'Of course you wouldn't. Why would you? But what if it was a short-term role on a long-playing soap? Shooting locally? But of course you'll have to think about it,' she said, getting up to leave.

'There's a catch, isn't there, Cait?' he said suspiciously.

'Of course there is,' she said, beginning to smile. 'We have to learn how to all get along together. It'll be bloody hard, but I think … I *think* we just might be able to do it.'

Later that evening, Cait was dressed like she'd stepped out of a movie set some time in the nineteen-forties … Rita Hayworth hair and red, red lips, a slick of eyeliner and her pale skin highlighted by the candles glowing in the bar. She was having a great deal of trouble fitting most of her plush behind into a chair, and some of that trouble was due to alcohol.

'So, what's the catch?' Sarah asked, about to throttle Caitlin if she didn't spill.

'It's in Melbourne?' Nadia said hopefully.

'Melbourne. Oh. Genius. So he —'

'Nope. Not that I wasn't tempted.' She resisted the urge to punch the air triumphantly. Just. 'It's local. And yes, it's a favour. From a producer. Who wants *Mystic Chicks*.'

Nadia looked puzzled. 'Why would he want it *that* badly?'

Caitlin smirked happily. 'Because there was another producer who wanted it. And the other producer who wanted it started a bidding war. And so …'

'Oh, *wow*.' She took a big sip of her drink. 'So was the other producer Kevin?'

'Kevin,' Caitlin said, shaking her head at how wonderfully it had all worked out, '*passed*. He has another option for my next show. That's if he gets over his pride. That's if *Mystic Chicks* is a hit.'

'I'm psychic. It will be,' declared Sarah.

They started laughing together.

'So *Mystic Chicks* is going to be made!' Sarah said joyously. 'I knew it would but — now I *know* it is!'

'It is,' Caitlin smiled, reaching over and hugging her friend fiercely. 'And I couldn't have done it — at all — without you. I'm so relieved. It's saved my life, Sarah. *You've* saved my life.'

'I know,' Sarah said. 'But I'll make you pay. You're going to shoot so much of it at the yoga studio that it's going to be worth it in new customers.'

'Hey, you two — is getting cheated on, dumped and the girl version of cuckolded meant to be this much fun?' asked Nadia.

'It is right now,' Cait smiled, her eyes sparkling. 'Where is everyone, anyway?'

'Myra's texting some man. Madeleine's parking. They'll both be here in a second,' Sarah explained.

Right on cue, the two bundled in, charged up to the bar, issued instructions to an amused-looking bartender, then charged over to join their friends.

'You look happy,' remarked Madeleine, hugging her daughter tightly — *before* she got to Sarah, which was a first. 'What's happened?'

'Have your couple-friends dropped you? Have you

just realised you'll be stuck with people like us for life?'
Myra demanded, grinning.

'Why would couple-friends drop you?' Nadia asked
innocently.

'Why? Look at her!' cried Myra, looking outraged.
'She's hot. She's single. And she represents everything they
don't want to happen to their marriages. A single roving
woman is bait. And they can either hold you close or act
like you want to be alone. You're too good-looking to let
get close, so my money's on the second option.'

'Maybe they *are* frightened of how hot you are. You
might excite their sex-starved husbands,' Nadia mused.
(She could relate. She was so stunningly beautiful that
most men became incoherent in her presence. Which
meant most of their wives became incandescent with
worry whenever she was near their partners.)

'Maybe they're just fucking bitches,' Myra declared
hotly, 'who are selfish and don't give a fuck how you
feel.'

'Yeah!' the foursome shouted.

'So. The decree,' Myra demanded, once the cheering
had subsided. They huddled closer, and formed a
protective ring around Cait, who felt like they were kids
in a playground about to start a very important game of
Chinese Whispers.

'Hang on,' barked Madeleine. 'Turn that music
down — come on, she's about to tell us something
excruciatingly important!'

Obediently, the bartender — all too-tight shirt,
artfully messy hair and lazy turquoise eyes — turned the
music down.

'I'm *so* going to fuck him later,' Nadia stated baldly, smirking. 'Oh, sorry, Myra. Unless you want to?'

'No, it's cool, Nadia,' said Myra impatiently. She didn't care about the bartender. She'd already lined up an internet date for later that week. And Nadia had taken her underwear-shopping. And she had already treated herself for lice. So this time, nothing was going to go wrong — not that she was about to jinx it by talking about it. Besides, she was mad keen to hear what had happened with Cait's mediation.

'Sarah?'

'No! I'm taken.'

'Oh, that's right,' said Nadia cheekily. 'You're having your lesbian moment. What about you, Cait?'

'Me? What does he look like?' She glanced over. 'Yum! No, I'm kidding — no thanks!'

Sarah was relieved. The letter she had in her pocket was burning a hole through it. She hadn't wanted to give it to Cait till she'd told her the mediation story — and now she was surrounded, it didn't seem like the right moment. She patted her hip gently, reassuring herself it was still there. It can wait a little longer, she thought to herself. It's not going anywhere.

'All right,' snapped Myra. 'Enough fighting over fucking the bartender. Now tell!'

'Okay,' Caitlin said, taking a deep breath and looking around her circle of friends. Oh, and her mother.

'Well, you know we said he wanted half of everything?'

Everyone knew, but in solidarity, everyone exploded.

'That's your nan's house. She left that to you.'

'Yeah, and he's lived in it for sixteen years. For free!'

'BASTARD!'

'First *bastard*,' sang out Nadia sweetly. 'Stop! Stop the story.'

On cue, the bartender appeared at the table with a tray laden with shot glasses. A round of vodkas was lined up.

'Down!' Myra ordered. No one would have dared disobey her.

'What are you …' said Caitlin, blearily shaking her head. 'Oh my. Is that going to happen every time someone says —'

'Don't say it. If it's said, the boys have orders to deliver another round within seconds.'

'Every time?' Caitlin asked faintly.

'Yeah. Every time we hear of some serious bastardy on the part of the bastard, we have to drink to his passing.'

'Why doesn't he just *die*! The b—'

'Shush! We have to pace ourselves. Did you drink beforehand, Myra? You know that's against the rules.'

'I couldn't help it.'

'But this is Cait's moment,' Nadia said.

Cait smiled, gave Nadia a hug, then settled back in. It was like telling a fairytale, with herself as Cinderella. And instead of ugly stepsisters, she had beautiful angel-friends.

'Well, it's been really shocking. You know, husband fucking assistant, assistant pregnant, kids moving out half the time, mother and friends moving in — buying new knickers, getting lice ... husband being unfaithful. Hang on. I already mentioned that!'

'Oh, God!' Nadia said melodramatically. 'I should have told you.'

'Told me what?'

'Told you about him!'

'Him who? Max? What do you mean?'

'You didn't fuck him?' Myra asked, clearly ready to strike.

'No!' protested Nadia. 'But he flirted, and I never told you, and if I had ...' she breathed in, dropping her head into her hands and tugging at her perfectly styled rain-straight black hair. 'If I had you might have stopped this thing with Kennedy ...'

Caitlin smiled. 'Sweetheart, he flirted with everyone. He flirted with me. He always will. He's a flirt.'

'Look, stop stalling. What happened?' Madeleine demanded, bristling at the affection in Caitlin's voice.

'Max gets shared custody of the girls. Fifty–fifty.'

'How can you do that? Doesn't it make you sick?' protested Madeleine.

'Mum. He's their dad. I don't want to stay angry, even if you want me to.'

'How can he do that? He should just walk away and —'

'And do you still have to give him some money?' asked Myra eagerly.

'We've worked that out too. And that was *not* what he wanted. Everyone got it wrong. The lawyers all assumed he'd want half of everything. And he could. But he doesn't. He wants half of the time with the kids.

And I'm going to make sure the money thing's all right for everyone anyway.'

'Why do you have to give him anything?' grumbled Madeleine.

'You know,' Sarah said in an authoritative tone, 'women didn't always get a payout from a divorce.'

'Tell me about it,' said Myra.

'Well, no, I mean way back. I mean, it would be even worse in Ireland, around 1540, for example. You would have given him everything and set out to beg, until you could marry again. At least things are civilised now.'

'It's not civilised,' parried Madeleine. 'I have girlfriends who have done very well out of marrying. And divorcing. And marrying again. The husbands were the ones who complained about *civilised*. Not wives!'

'Times have changed, Mum,' explained Cait wisely. 'We changed. We earn money. We support our kids. And when marriages go under, we can't just sit back, file our nails and wait for the alimony to come in. We have to learn to get along with each other, and sometimes it even means we have to learn to get along with the new people in our partners' lives. Like Kennedy. That's my biggest challenge,' she admitted.

'God. Why are you like this?' Madeleine groaned. 'Why don't you *fight*?'

'Because I don't have the will to fight a battle that will only hurt everyone, Mum,' snapped Caitlin, running out of patience. 'He made a mistake — and we'll never get back together. Now he's working on dealing with this situation with Kennedy, and how they're going to parent, and how he can have a relationship with his kids. And he deserves one. He's not evil. He was just stupid!'

'What?'

'No! He's a *bas*—' shouted Myra, face aflame with passion, hand smashing down on the table.

'Oh, no. Here comes the vodka. Things are *different* now. If things had stayed the same, Myra wouldn't be internet dating, I wouldn't be able to pass Green Monroe's number on to Nadia, and Sarah wouldn't be about to settle down with her perfect woman.'

'How did you know?!' gasped Sarah.

'Oh, come on. Look at you. How could she hold out?' she said, giving her best friend a hug.

'So it's a good thing that things have changed, yes? Let's drink to that.'

They took a moment, held their glasses high, and let loose a volley of '*Bastards*' (so loud that they didn't have to ask for quieter music), before the scalding fire of vodka burned its way down their throats.

'Weirdest thing is,' Caitlin continued, blinking back tears. (The vodka, you understand.) 'He rang me afterward, all happy. And we talked about when each of us will have the kids. And soon,' she took a deep breath, 'I'm going to sit down and talk with Kennedy.'

Myra narrowed her eyes. 'You sound delusional.'

'We'll see,' said Cait. 'I don't really think there's much of an alternative to getting along.'

'He thinks you don't hate him,' Madeleine muttered.

'Maybe *he* just wants to be able to get along, too,'

suggested Sarah hopefully, feeling she might be about to be showered with empty vodka glasses.

Myra glared ferociously.

Madeleine's breath was sucked in like she'd been slapped.

Nadia looked confused.

'What's with your faces? Would it be so bad for us to get along?' Caitlin asked.

'What?' Myra asked, aghast.

Caitlin said nothing.

'You … you do *hate* him, don't you?' her mother asked, imploringly. 'You have to, after all he's done.'

'You know, everyone hates him. The kids hate him, my friends hate him — even Nadia the Angel hates him,' Caitlin pointed out.

'I do — even if he is very attractive,' put in Nadia. (Myra slapped her arm.) 'Ow!'

Caitlin just smiled. 'He is attractive. God, tonight, even while I was doing my best to clear him out of my life, I could still see what he's got. I really miss what I thought we had,' she said, a little sadly.

'You hate him then!' Madeleine crowed, triumphant.

'Mum, clearly you just *love* hating him. It gives you a thrill just thinking about how much you hate him. *Dad* really hates him. And you're both so thrilled now you can talk about it. So with everyone hating him so much for me,' she said, taking a breath, 'it's kind of taken the sting out of it.'

'Oh my God,' breathed Sarah, awestruck. 'You've reached enlightenment.'

'What?'

'The opposite of love isn't hate. It's detachment.'

'Oh. Well, detachment sounds bloody boring.'

'It means reattachment elsewhere.'

'Hmmm.'

'Maybe this might help,' said Sarah, shoving an envelope under her nose.

'What's that and why are you shoving it under my nose?' Caitlin said suspiciously.

'I haven't read it, if that's what you mean.'

'But you've psychically spied on it, haven't you?'

'Yes. It's from the cowboy-man.'

'The cow— oh.' She flushed red, and snatched it away. 'Why didn't you give it to me earlier?' she demanded, trying to keep her voice steady.

'I thought I'd try and give it to you alone.'

'Oh my God. Is that a letter from the guy from the Wild Women's Weekend?'

'At last,' Myra breathed rapturously. True Love!

Without a single skerrick of sarcasm, irony or doubt between them, they all turned to look at Caitlin. She looked back at them, wondering what on earth she was supposed to do. It was, after all, just a letter.

Wasn't it?

'Well,' said Madeleine imperiously. 'Aren't you going to open it?'

www.ingramcontent.com/pod-product-compliance
Lightning Source LLC
Chambersburg PA
CBHW050111120726
47904CB00004B/1310